Brooklyn Girl: Growing Up Norwegian in New York City

Jan Carol Simonsen

Dedication

For Erin and Christian

Table of Contents

Foreword

This is a story of acculturation and coming of age. The characters are fictional, but the places and the historical events are real. It's a tale of a girl born into a large immigrant family in a pocket of ethnic culture in New York City. Pre-conceived beliefs and rigid ideologies define family life, with sometimes harsh, albeit well-intentioned, parenting. The protagonist and her close friends and cousins, most of whom are second generation Norwegians, learn their families' histories, embrace American customs, and ultimately discern who they are as individuals. Any similarities to actual persons are purely coincidental.

Legend: Norwegian dialog
Text and English dialog

Cover by Joan L. Tolliver, a Tallahassee artist

Cast of significant characters

Protagonist's Nuclear Family*

Adolph Torgersen
Cornella (nee Gabrealsen)
    Ingrid Liv
    Solveig Andrea

Maternal Grandparents
Andrea & Gabreal Gabrealsen

Offspring
    Arne (m. Torhild)
    Augusta (m. Magne Saudeland)
        Arnt
        Ole
        Annalise
            Gretl (Greta)
    Hedvig (m. Werner Wolff)
        Werner (m. Agatha)
            Liv
            June
            Johnny
        Wilhelm (m. Nina)
            Margit
            Karen
        Gudrun, (Goody) (m. William Johnson)
        Dagmar, (DeDe) (m. Richie Leaky)
        Magnhild (Maggy) (m. Paul Bensen)
            Lars

Johann Torvald (m. Hulda)

- Sven
- Vigdis
  - Johann Torvald

Anton

Jakob (m. Bergitta)

- Sigurd
- Stanley
- Salve

Magda

Borghild

Leif (m. Ragna)

- Karl
- Johann
- Harold
- Liv

Clara (m. Olav Hansen)

- Bente
- Tor Asbjørn
- Alice
- Sonya

Cornella (m. Adolph Torgersen)*

- Ingrid
- Solveig

Sverre (m. Reidun); (m. Gerd)

Aslaug

Paternal Grandparents

Alma & Gustav Torgersen

Adolph (m. Cornella)*

Ingrid

Solveig

Signe (m. Bendix Strandberg)

Arvind

Odd

Marit (m. Karl Swensen)

Erick

Key friends factoring in story:

Hannah

Henning

Josefina (Joey)

Martin

Otto

Reidar

Sven

Tony

Torhild (Tory)

Chapter One

Origins

I was born in Brooklyn, but my earliest memories are really of Norway. After I came into the world at the Deaconess Lutheran Medical Center, my parents brought me home to their flat on 79th Street, just off 7th Avenue, and my sister, Ingrid, who was five, met me for the first time. I do remember quite a bit from our years in that flat, but those memories are mostly from after we had lived in Norway for a little more than a year and then returned to Brooklyn. My parents were immigrants from southern Norway, which, despite the country's current great wealth, was then very poor. Yet there was a self-confidence, a hubris, that permeated the Norwegian community in Brooklyn, and immigrants were eager to show the prosperity gained in the new land. So it was that many young immigrants who had established themselves in this borough of New York and had become part of the thriving Norwegian-American community made a pilgrimage back to the old country.

My parents had left behind their parents and many siblings when they came to America, so we had many relatives in Norway, mostly in the south. When I was two, in the early spring of 1948, our family of four made the pilgrimage to the old country.

As young as I was, I remember snippets of that adventure. We traveled aboard the *Stavangerfjord*, a ship in the Norwegian American Line fleet, which set sail from a New York westside pier and arrived nine days later in Bergen, on Norway's west coast, before moving on to Stavanger, then Kristiansand, and finally Oslo. My recollections on board were mostly of the rocking of the boat and the smell of vomit; so many on board were seasick, the result of turbulent seas in the North Atlantic. They tell me small children rarely get seasick. That must have been so in my case, but I'm not so sure about my seven-year-old sister or my mother, who mostly lay in her berth moaning.

What I do remember is some heated yelling from my mother, which frightened me. I learned much later that she had accused a ship's cabin attendant of having stolen a brooch from our cabin. Some start to our Norwegian adventure: she accused a fellow countryman of theft! In time, my sister told me our mother subsequently found the brooch, which had slipped from a cabinet top as the ship pitched in the sea. Did she apologize? I wonder.

For this homecoming trip, my father had taken a leave of absence from his job, bought a light blue 1949 Ford and had it shipped on the boat with us, with the intent to sell it in Norway before we returned to America. Thus it was that our small family was set to make a debut in Norway, replete with an American car in which to drive around the country.

We debarked in Oslo and spent a few days in a flat off Karl Johans Gate with my mother's eldest brother, my Onkel Arne, and his wife, Torhild. They were a no-nonsense, efficient couple who were childless but had a Pekinese dog—a fluffy thing they called Per that claimed most of my attention. Onkel Arne, a big man, walked with a limp, so the thump-thump of his step as he walked on the flat's wooden floors was somewhat scary, but it didn't scare Per, and I found that reassuring. In time I would learn that his limp had been caused by polio, which he had suffered in his younger years. I gravitated more to Tante Torhild, a large and formidable woman but kind nevertheless, who made wonderful little pastries that she allowed me and my sister, Ingrid, to devour.

When that visit was over, we drove south to Spangereid and the farm in Jorstad where my mother, the eleventh of twelve children, had been born. In my adult years I learned that it was Jorganstad, not Jorstad, but such was the dialect of the area that the name was truncated, making the place virtually impossible to find on a map. Mama's parents, my Bestemor and Bestefar, Andrea and Gabreal Gabrealsen, lived there on a small farm without indoor plumbing or central heat. Bestefar Gabreal, retired after many years of work as a carpenter, tended just to the farm, and Andrea worked alongside him.

An early memory of Jorstad is of Bestefar Gabreal sitting at the table in the dining room drinking coffee and offering me a sugar cube dipped in the pungent brew as I clung to his knee. For some reason, his heavy mustache and smiling eyes attracted me to him, and I knew him to be kindly. Of my grandmother Andrea I remember less, except that she was proficient in the kitchen and well in charge of the household. She would have had to have been since she raised so many children in this five-room farmhouse, tucked into the base of a cliff. Of the twelve children she bore, one every few years since her marriage in 1898, ten survived to adulthood. A son called Anton died in infancy, and a daughter Borghild of the Spanish flu in 1918. But it would be some time before I got to know my aunts and uncles and their offspring. I would learn their stories as I grew adept at listening.

To be sure, some still lived in Norway. I had gotten to know Onkel Arne and Tante Torhild in the flat in Oslo where we had been. Mama's elder sister Augusta and her family lived in Grimstad, but truth be told, I had no recollection of them from this first visit to Norway.

Years before Ingrid, whom I called Ingy, and I experienced life at Jorstad, many of Mama's siblings and their families had made it to

New York. But that year, our grandmother bustled about, delighted that we were there, and she could get to know the young Norwegian-Americans who were her grandchildren. It was fascinating for us as well. At Jorstad, water came through a hand pump from a well in back of the house. Chickens clucked in the yard behind the house, and we spread seed for them to peck at. One time I saw our grandmother grab a chicken and cut its head off; it ran around then dropped. It was dinner.

Bestefar led two cows from the barn each morning so they could graze in the field by the road. Then at dusk he'd bring them in to milk. He gave me a short, blue Maxwell House coffee tin and let me pull the udders of one cow, and to my amazement, milk squirted out! The cows lived in the barn, but the outhouse was there, too, a fifty-yard walk from the house. But as a two-year old, I had a tisse-potte (potty), and I suspect the adults used such devices, probably what we would call chamber pots, during the night as well.

The time we were at Jorstad must have been fun for my grandparents, because their house was now mostly quiet, since their grown children were gone. Mama and her mother would talk about Mama's siblings and what fun they had had as children. How could so many children live in the small farmhouse? The house had but two bedrooms upstairs and none down. When I was older and puzzled about the very same thing, Mama told me that she and her brothers and sisters would sleep, nestled like spoons, as many to a bed as could fit. Of course, there was good sense in that as well, since there was no central heat, and they kept each other warm. And by the time the youngest child arrived, some of the older ones had already left the homestead.

When we were there, it was just a few years after the war had ended, but of course I was too young to appreciate the legacy of the Nazi occupation. That would come later, told by family members who had lived through those times. What I do remember vividly is Tante Golovna, my grandmother's sister, who lived across the road and grew strawberries. Røde rosiner (red raisins) I called the small fruits, and she shared them, sweet, succulent, and warm from the summer sun, with me. I remember being scolded for crossing the narrow dirt road and walking to her house by myself, but the lure of the berries and other treats she would dole out was irresistible. She grew produce during the short summer months, and every week a man would come in a horse-drawn wagon to pick up her bounty and take it to market. That's how she survived I later learned, for she was a widow, having lost her husband when the Nazis shot him for aiding the resistance during the war.

We have pictures that show us in Norway, some from behind my grandparents' home, some from hagen (the garden), the front yard with the white picket fence. It was there in June, months into our visit, that the family celebrated my third birthday with a spread of sandwiches and cake. When I look at the black-and-white photos now, I think back on the people who were so much a part of our lives, when Norway was still poor and people struggled to survive. Mye god mat (lots of good food) was a measurement of status, and thus a common expression in describing social gatherings. A chubby child was sunt og godt mate" (healthy and well fed). Those expressions remained a solid part of the insular Brooklyn community in which I grew up, but they were founded in the old sod of Norway.

While we lived on Jorstad that time early in my life, we visited with Papa's family too. We spent some time just outside Lyngdal on the farm where my father's mother, my other Bestemor or Farmor (father's mother), still lived. Alma was a grim, no-nonsense woman who lived alone, "making do" with what little she had in a small hamlet called Hundingsland. There, Alma lived piously, reading her *Bible* and rarely smiling, so it was that I feared her a bit. But it was at Hundingsland where I first met my father's sisters, my Tante Signe and Tante Marit. Both were thin and elegant with admirable bearing. Signe's husband, Onkel Bendix, was a big man with a hearty laugh, and he doted on their sons, Arvind and Odd. Tante Marit, Papa's youngest sister, had married Karl and their union had produced Erik.

How I loved these cousins, Arvind and Erik being my sister's age, but Odd exactly my age, having been born in 1946 like me. Odd was mine immediately—just as tall as I and happy as well. Thus, during the war, Bestmor Alma had both daughters, two sons-in-law, and three grandsons living nearby. But her only son, my father, Adolph, had fled to America before the occupation and there, in Brooklyn, had married my mother, Cornella, paving the way for my sister's and my debut into the world.

Why was Bestemor Alma so grim? I later learned that she had been wooed long distance by my Grandfather Gustav. In 1913, as a young man, Gustav had left Lista, the windy peninsula where he and Alma had grown up, to follow the call to preach God's word. His calling took him to New York where he ministered to the Norwegian community. But he never forgot Alma, and eventually wrote to ask for her hand. When she agreed to marry him, Gustav brought her to America. They were in Brooklyn for six years, and she bore her three children, 13 months apart, in a flat on Henry Street.

Indeed, my father, the oldest, actually started to go to school in Brooklyn before my grandfather heard and answered the call to return to Norway and minister to his countrymen. I imagine now how it must have been for Alma to make that transition. She had probably become used to living in a city with paved streets and shops she could walk to pushing her baby buggy with Marit, the youngest, nestled inside, and her son and other daughter trotting alongside. Their earliest years were spent on the streets of Brooklyn, and when they returned to Norway, Adolph was six,

Signe five, and Marit almost four.

On the return to Norway, Gustav determined to live in Hundingsland, a short buggy ride from Austad and Lyngdal, crossroads in southern Norway. With its rocky craggy ground rising to a ridge overlooking Grønsfjord (green fjord), Hundingsland was named for the Viking King Hunding. In fact, Hunding's remains are actually buried on the family land, and his grave is now a national historic site, albeit a mostly untended one. You would miss it if you didn't know it was there in the hills behind the house and barn. But I digress.

When Gustav and his young family first returned to Norway, he purchased a house in Kvass, then had it disassembled and moved to the land he had bought in Hundingsland. Back then two other families resided in that hamlet, each owning a plot of land that they farmed. My father over time told me that winters were hard, made even more so because my grandfather, a traveling evangelist who worked for the state church in Norway, would travel to distant towns staying with host families from the churches on his itinerary. Back in Hundingsland, Alma tended to the farm, as did the three children, each of whom had designated chores. One of my father's was to start the fire in the downstairs fireplace before his mother and sisters got up and dressed. The family continued to subsist, and my father even recalls that they were better off than most during the depression that swept through the country in between the two great wars.

Then tragedy struck, and my grandfather Gustav died from a ruptured appendix when he was just 46, leaving Alma and her, by then, three teenaged children to fend for themselves. That event ended my father's schooling, and he took a job on a fishing boat where he nurtured dreams of coming to America. He had Amerika feber (America fever) big time. He corresponded with his uncle Torleif, his father's brother in St. Albans, Queens, and Torleif agreed to sponsor him. So off he went to America, where the streets were paved with gold and opportunity awaited.

Ironically, while my father was growing up near Lyngdal, Jorstad, the place my mother spent her formative years, was just a half hour's row across Grønsfjord, (green fjord), but during those years, my parents never met. It was only when both got to Brooklyn that fate intervened. The First Evangelical Free Church, like many other churches in this borough of New York, was a haven for southern Norwegians who had learned in Norway that the state church was less than godly, and that church and state should be separate—hence the word "free."

My mother got to Brooklyn because she had had the same America fever, and it had fueled her quest to immigrate. She left her parents and her childhood home and set sail on the *Oslofjord,* which took her to New York. Here she was reunited with her sisters Magda and Clara and her brother Leif. This was in 1938, when grumblings of the coming war were surfacing, but for these Norwegians, new to America, it must have been a marvelous adventure, full of hope and promise.

Mama's sisters Magda and Clara attended the First Evangelical Free Church on 66th Street, a large and stately brick edifice, and my mother soon joined them. The church was a bit further from the heart of Brooklyn's Norwegian community, whose main thoroughfare was 8th Avenue in the 50s, commonly known as Lapskaus Boulevard, named for the popular Norwegian stew that was a mainstay of the diet.

The 66th Street church had originated on President Street in 1897, but soon relocated to 4th Avenue and 15th Street, where it became known as the 15th Street church. Subsequently as it grew, an annex opened on 8th Avenue and 52nd Street. That church soon grew independent and called itself The Second Evangelical Free Church.

Then, in 1928, the First Evangelical Free Church was constructed at 649 66th Street facing Leif Erickson Park. Thus, the multiple relocations of the church reflected the migratory patterns of Norwegian immigrants, who first settled in Manhattan in the 1800s, then downtown Brooklyn, followed by Sunset Park, and finally Bay Ridge.

The 66th Street church must have appealed to my father, Adolph, as well, and he joined his cousins Erling and Abraham who had immigrated earlier and were in the church's String Band. Now when I look at the photos of the 66th Street String Band, I see how young they all were—mostly in their twenties and smiling at the sheer fun of making music in God's house together. My father played the violin and mandolin, and both Erling and Abraham had strong voices. There were several guitar players, and my mother was one of them. So that's how they met.

Fellowship together as Norwegian Christians was what it was all about. While not at church, friends and family took day trips. Coney Island was a favorite spot in the warmer months, and Bear Mountain with its famed ski jump lured them in the winter. Going to Coney Island was by car or subway, the Sea Beach Express, which took beachgoers to within a block or two of the boardwalk.

In 1939, when there were 63,000 Norwegians living in New York—the largest concentration of Norwegians in a city outside of Norway—Crown Prince Olav and Crown Princess Martha arrived on the *Oslofjord* to officiate at the World's Fair in Flushing, Queens, like Brooklyn, a borough of New York City. It must have been quite the event, with officiates in native bunad (traditional dress.) At the same time, the *Christian Radich*, the beautiful sailing ship docked at the 69th pier in Brooklyn, adding to the festivities the Norwegian community enjoyed. When the Crown Prince and Princess were honored at an open-air meeting at Leif Ericson Park, right across from 66th Street church, 15,000 people, more or less, attended to get a glimpse of the royal couple.

There was always lots to do. Most destinations were reachable by public and local transportation, but other venues demanded a car; there was no other way to get there. But the young men all seemed to have cars and were eager to take weekend drives out of the city. You have to wonder how they determined having a car was important. This was New York City, after all, and public transportation—street cars, trolleys, buses, and trains—ran regular routes, and you could get anywhere in the city for a nickel fare. But driving your own car brought with it a sense of importance, of status, that was virtually non-existent in the old country.

A car was part of the American Dream, a measure of success, and to achieve that dream required regular employment. For young Norwegians in Brooklyn in the late 30s, there was no lack of work. Men were either on the harbor, working on tugboats and barges, or in the building trade as carpenters or carpet layers. My father, Adolph, found work as a deckhand on a Humble Oil and Refining Company barge pumping oil to ships berthed in the harbor, while his cousins Erling and Abraham were snekkere (carpenters).

The women in like order did not have difficulty finding employment. Some worked in shops like Norwegian bakeries or Norske varer (Norwegian goods), waitressed in restaurants like The Atlantic, or were domestics, working for wealthier families living in Bay Ridge, many along Shore Road, which sits overlooking the mouth to New York Harbor and faces Staten Island. Two domestic employment agencies, Magda Sandes Teslekontor and Atlantic, posted positions and found suitable matches for families seeking domestic help. That's what my mother, Cornella, did—she worked for two families, one on Fort Hamilton Parkway, another on Ridge Boulevard, a stately street with stately homes.

Once established as a domestic, Cornella set about learning English. There were English classes offered at night in many schools, and she availed herself of the ones taught at Bay Ridge High School; then she set about teaching herself the fundamentals of becoming a United States citizen and eventually passed her citizenship test. My father did exactly the same and was soon proficient in English as well as a brand-new citizen. They were Americans now for sure, as were my mother's siblings now living in Brooklyn or on Staten Island.

The size of the Gabrealsen clan changed dramatically while

Cornella, Magda, Clara, and Leif were busy acculturating. In April of 1940, the *Bergensfjord* arrived in New York Harbor, and on board was Mama's older sister Hedvig with her husband, Werner, and their five offspring. Also on board was Mama's brother Johann Torvald, his wife Hulda, and their two children. If that wasn't enough, Mama's brother Jakob, his wife, Bergitta, and their three offspring were also on board. It was a family exodus from the old country, save for Mama's siblings Arne and Augusta, who remained to live in the homeland through the war.

The remaining sibling, Sverre, was at sea with the Norwegian Merchant Marine. He, the youngest of the Gabrealsens, had gone to sea at 14 on the *Sørlandet*, a tall, beautiful craft without auxiliary power and one of Norway's school ships that prepared boys to become men of the sea. So, it was with glee that the family greeted him as well when his ship made port in New York, and they were happy when they learned that the ship could not return to Norway because of the occupation. Thus Sverre too was in the U.S.

Mama had known her nieces and nephews well before she left Norway. Indeed, some were almost as old as she. Now they were mostly all together in Brooklyn—17 more family members added to the size of the clan. Mama now had more siblings in America than in Norway!

Tante Hedvig's husband, Werner, a congenial man, quickly found work as a carpenter and settled his family on 57th Street, just off Lapskaus Boulevard. The family began attending the 59th Street church, which was the Norwegian Evangelical Lutheran Church in the heart of the ethnic neighborhood and within an easy walk from the four-family house where they lived. Mama's brothers Jakob and Johann Gabrealsen settled with their families on Staten Island, and these men also found work easily through the Norwegian network as tugboat men on the harbor.

My father had no immediate family in Brooklyn, but he did have his two cousins, Erling and Abraham. He must have been attracted to Mama's fun-loving family though and being a part of the familial network must have held some appeal. He told me years later that as those around him married, including his two cousins, the pressure to join ranks became acute.

Pressure was probably more so for the young women who were terrified of "not getting a man" and becoming an "old maid." Thus, it was not surprising that Cornella, after keeping company with Adolph for a time, proposed, and he simply said, well, okay. And they planned their nuptials.

They married in early 1941 in the First Evangelical Free Church and were a handsome couple. Cornella wore a white gown, my father a dark suit, and Mama's sister Clara and her husband, Olav, were the attendants. The only photo I have of their wedding was taken at the Hamilton House, the restaurant where they had a small dinner after the ceremony. After that it was home to a cramped apartment in Sunset Park, the area that was home to so many young immigrants.

My father years later told me that Cornella wanted two things: not to work and not to have children for a few years. Well, she got the first, because she didn't get the second. She got pregnant right away. It may have been fortuitous, though, since many men from 66th Street church were recruited and had to serve the war effort. Papa's cousins, Erling and Abraham, put on uniforms and became soldiers. But Adolph had a different plan. He went to the recruiting office once he got his notice and showed them his pregnant wife and Merchant Marine license along with proof of employment fueling war ships in New York harbor. He never went to war. This history I learned slowly over time by listening to the adults in the family reminisce.

At the Deaconess Lutheran Medical Center, Ingrid entered the world in September of 1941, a beautiful blue-eyed baby. I imagine the three-room apartment soon became crowded, but they managed with a crib in their bedroom for a few years, saving their pennies for a bigger place. The two-family house on 79th Street was the outcome, and that's where I came home to after I was born at the same Lutheran Medical Center in June of 1946.

Chapter Two

Spit Shine

Mama and Papa spoke Norwegian at home, although Ingrid, at nine, spoke English fairly well after years of American schooling, despite missing most of 2nd grade when we were in Norway, and she had to do lessons from the books PS 127 had provided. Mama and Papa had both gone to night school to learn the language almost as soon as they arrived on U. S. soil. I was struggling to understand them when they weren't speaking Sørlands språk (a southern dialect of Norwegian) and lapsed into English. Mostly Mama and Papa would speak to us in Norwegian, and my sister, whom I called Ingy, would answer in English and I in Norwegian. Talk about a linguistic challenge for a four-year old!

"The ice man is here, the ice man is here," said my sister in English one day as she peered over the railing of the porch in the front of our second story flat.

"Good," said Mama, "we are almost out." Then she went out on the porch and looked down at the driver in the horse-drawn wagon and said, "Hei."

"Do you need more ice?" he asked. "Ya," Mama replied. "Come up; I'll get the door." She went downstairs and let him in, and he carried a big, clear block of ice suspended between the two prongs of a metal tong. Up the stairs he came, dripping all the way into the kitchen. He plopped the ice in the sink and released the tong, then opened the door to the wooden icebox with its metal tray where the ice was to sit. He held the block up and tried to slide it in, but it wouldn't go. Back to the sink it went, and he pulled out a long, sharp pick and chopped away. He repeated the motion a few times until the ice could slide into its spot. Takk (thank you), said Mama as she paid him and sent him on his way.

Watching the street from the porch was a favorite pastime, especially for me since I wasn't old enough to go out and play by myself. I would peer through the railing and watch the passersby, the cars, and the occasional horse-drawn wagons. A favorite of Mama's was the vegetable man, who would come up the street shouting "fresh vegetables, fresh vegetables," and my sister would tell Mama the vegetable man was "down there." Then Mama would say, "Tell him to wait. I'm coming down." And down she went, and after a while came back with fresh produce which would show up in our dinner.

It wasn't just vegetables that she wanted, however. Being a farm girl, she knew the benefit of horse manure as a plant fertilizer. After the vegetable man had moved on to another street, she'd peer over the porch rail to see if the horse had left anything behind. And when he did, she'd give my sister the dustpan and tell her to retrieve it. This never made Ingy happy, but she did it, because displeasing Mama had consequences. So, what Ingy did was to find fault with me. "Dummy," she said to me under her breath as she went down the stairs. It was a chain reaction that occurred whenever Ingy was made to do something she didn't want to.

While I liked to play on the open porch, listening to the sounds of the street below, what I liked even more was going out with Mama while Ingy was in school. Those adventures might be a trip to Lunde's bakery on 5th Avenue and 80th Street, a long walk for a four-year old, since we had to cross first 7th Avenue, then Fort Hamilton Parkway, and after that 6th Avenue before we got to the shops on 5th. It was a good walk nevertheless, because the bakery ladies would always find a cookie for me. Mama talked to them in English, which I didn't fully understand. She would typically buy white mountain bread, and sometimes Swedish Limpa and kringle. Papa liked almond kringle, but Ingy and I liked raspberry. If Papa was at work, Mama would buy raspberry. Home we would go with our still-warm bread in a paper sack and kringle in a white box tied up with red and white string. I had learned the word "cookie" from these trips and could say it quite well.

Sometimes a trip outside was quick—to the candy store on 7th Avenue to get *The Daily News, Brooklyn Eagle*, or *Nordisk Tidende* newspapers or to the grocery store to get some milk. Always Mama could talk in that language that all the people in the shops spoke. I began to catch on just by listening. Then I began to speak the language that was different from the one I spoke at home. When the greengrocer sliced me a piece of bologna, I said it was "nudely," and that made him laugh. Nydelig means "very nice" in Norwegian, but when I tried to put an English pronunciation on the word, "nudely" was what came out.

The English-Norwegian mix seemed quite normal to me after a while, and I began to speak a little of both without discerning the difference. When an acquaintance of Mama asked what color I liked best, I said "Blue is min faiebrett," meaning "favorite." That made the Norwegians around me hysterical, since faiebrett means dustpan. I wasn't shy evidently and didn't lack for trying new words in either language. But it made me angry when people laughed at me, and I would stomp my foot. "You are angry today," Mama would say and chuckled to herself.

When the weather was nice, Mama would bring me and my little red tricycle outside so I could ride on the sidewalk, and she would sit on the stoop watching. "Solveig!" she would holler if I ventured too close to the street. "Don't you dare!" If I put as much as a toe over the curb after that warning, I knew what was next. "Do that again, and you'll get a spanking." Sometimes she meant it, and I got a spanking, but other times it was just a threat. The result was that I never knew what was coming, but I feared her wrath, even when I was four, and I knew she was mighty strong.

One time I got a spanking that I still remember to this day. We had walked to McKinley Park on 75th Street where we met my mother's friend Ragnhild and her two sons. Audun was in a carriage, but Jervod was my age, and we played in the sandbox quite nicely until he sprayed sand on me. I told him to stop it, but he didn't. He did it again and again, cleverly when the mothers weren't watching. I couldn't help myself: I bit him. It was justifiable, I thought, but Mama didn't, and Ragnhild was very angry. Consequences followed as soon as we got home.

Mama and Papa must have remembered childrearing practices from the old country. And surely what they heard in church reinforced what they practiced. "Spare the rod and spoil the child" might have been their mantra. Nevertheless, we were kept in line, my sister and I, although it seemed she didn't get in trouble nearly as much as I did.

But how I loved Ingy! I would wait for her to come home from school each day just after three. On nice days I would be on the porch waiting to spot her walking up the street from PS 127. "Here comes Ingy!" I would shout as she climbed the steps to our door.

When Mama let her in, Ingy would come bounding up the stairs. She would then sit at the kitchen table, having a snack and starting her homework. I was content simply to sit and wait for her to talk to me. "Get me an eraser, Dummy," she would order, and I was happy to comply. I didn't mind so much that she would say mean things, but it was a while before I realized she never did when Mama could hear. Nevertheless, I marveled at her books and how she could write. And I wished I could go to school.

I also waited repeatedly for Papa to come home from working—jobben (the job) was what he called it. "When is he coming?" and "Why does he have to go away?" I would ask. I missed him when he was gone. Like so many Norwegian men, he was a seaman working in the harbor and surrounding waterways. Papa had switched jobs from Mobil to Esso, which is what Exxon was called back then. A deckhand on a barge that fueled ships brought in by the tugs, he would be gone for four days, working and sleeping on the barge, home for one, gone again another four days, and then home for seven. How I hated when he would pack his little bag and go to the harbor, but I was so happy when he came home. So were Ingy and Mama. With Papa home, everything was good.

When he was home, he drove us to Sunday School in the big brick church that stood overlooking Leif Erickson Park on 66th Street. I had started to go as soon as I turned four, hearing *Bible* stories and memorizing verses in English. While my Sunday School classmates were all Norwegian, and that's what we mostly spoke with each other, our teachers spoke to us in English. It was surely language immersion learning. It was great fun hearing the stories about people like Moses and Jonah and coloring pictures in our little workbooks. After Sunday School, we had a little time before church services started and would play tag or tell jokes. Who could make the most people laugh was the goal. "Solveig, behave yourself!" Mama would admonish as my class spilled out onto the street, laughing and giggling, to where the parents waited for us. I did my best, but it wasn't easy.

After Sunday School it was time for church, and I went to the Norwegian service in the upstairs auditorium with my parents, while Ingy at nine could attend the English service in the downstairs auditorium with our cousin Bente, who was ten. While we mostly spoke Norwegian at home, church talk in the Norwegian department was different, and I understood barely a word. The pastor would drone on and on, and I had a hard time not fidgeting. Papa would give me a pinch on my thigh if I squirmed too much, and I have to admit I hated that place, with its brown wooden seats and the inevitable pinch. Mama must have understood how tough it was to be me in church, so she would often ferret out a pencil and some paper, and I could kneel on the floor and draw pictures on the sloping seat. It wasn't easy.

I was always relieved when church was over. I knew the pastor—

or presten—had delivered a strong message that must have rung true to the adults, since so many nodded in agreement, or simply said "Ya" or "Takk Gud" (Yes and thank God) in hushed voices. At times the pastor raised his voice and pounded the pulpit with his fist. I hadn't really understood a word, but it was mighty scary to be there.

How I wished I could attend the English-speaking service—anything but that droning I had to endure in the upstairs sanctuary. The church had started an English department long before I was born, hiring an English-speaking pastor who was an Evangelical Free Church man when it became apparent that the offspring of the Norwegian parents spoke more English than Norwegian, the byproduct of American education. "When you are older," Mama would always say, as I clamored to join my sister and cousin downstairs for the English-speaking service.

Ingy carried her *Bible* to Sunday School and church piously and with an air of importance. She had had it since she was seven, and I knew that I would get one also in a few years. One day at home I had picked up her King James tome and saw it had words I couldn't yet read but the text was in red as well as black. "How come it's in different colors?" I asked.

"The words in red are the exact words of Jesus," she told me, speaking slowly in English. "The black writing is the word of God." "But who wrote it?" I asked, not sure how what she said could possibly be so.

"Men wrote it, but God told them what to write" she said, a little irritated, as she often was when I would challenge what she told me. That God could write in English was marvelous, I thought to myself.

After church we would meet Ingy on the sidewalk outside the church, and then Papa would drive us home for dinner—middags they called it. Most times Mama or Papa would start the dinner before we left for church and let it roast in the oven, so it was ready and emitting tempting aromas when we arrived back home. But truth be told, we liked some dinners better than others. Roast chicken with mashed potatoes was good, but kjøtt suppe (beef soup) was definitely not. Neither Ingy nor I liked that. Nevertheless, we had to eat what was put before us because it represented God's bounty. Before we ate, we always said grace:

I Jesu navn gar vi til bords,
A spise or drikke pa dit ord
Deg Gud til aere, oss til gavn
Sa far vi mat i Jesu navn. Amen

(In Jesus' name, we go to the table,
Eat and drink by Your word
To God the honor, to us the gain
We accept our food in Jesus' name. Amen)

This was the first Norwegian prayer we learned and learn it well we did. But in hindsight, I realize that it was the only Norwegian prayer we ever knew. After grace, we would eat heartily, because whether we liked it or not, we had to eat what God provided.

Sunday afternoons usually meant an after-dinner nap, but there would be no exertion, no work activity, on the Lord's day. On the seventh day God rested, and so must we. Why was Sunday the day of rest, I often wondered, since it was the first day of the week, not the last? This was a mystery. And how come Papa could be on the boat when it was Sunday if God didn't want anyone to work on his day? Another mystery for sure.

If we were lucky, however, and the weather was nice on a Sunday afternoon, we might get back in the car after middags and take a ride. A favorite venue was Shore Road, where you could walk along the sidewalk and sit on the park benches overlooking the harbor with Staten Island across the water. You could see the big green Brooklyn Ferry passing back and forth between Brooklyn and the island.

Even better was when we'd head out to St. Albans where Papa's Onkel Torleif and Tante Borghild lived. The way to get there was on the Belt Parkway that started at Fort Hamilton and ran along the water's edge. Ingy and I would sit in the back seat, each looking out a window as the car sped along at 35 miles per hour, the posted speed limit. "What are those funny buildings," I asked one time as I spotted some round roofed buildings of what looked like shiny metal.

"Quonset huts," Papa said, explaining that after the war there weren't enough houses for people to live in, so those structures provided temporary housing when the soldiers came home and started families. There had been a war, and American soldiers had evidently fought and then come home. There were such fascinating things to learn, and I never ceased to ask questions.

"Oh, shut up," said Ingy, who would easily tire of my constant queries. But I soon shut up all by myself, after I announced I was going to throw up. Papa found a place to pull over and Mama led me to an inconspicuous place along the road, and I hurled what was in my stomach. Then Mama cleaned my face so that I would look decent for Tante and Onkel in St. Albans. The cleanup was what she often did when I had a dirty face: she spat into a handkerchief and wiped my face until it shone to her liking. I didn't always throw up when I had ridden in the car. How far we drove and how much I looked at what we passed determined how nauseated I would become, and the spit shine was a strong incentive for fighting back the nausea.

While St. Albans required some driving time, going to other venues didn't make me carsick. Coney Island, for example, wasn't that far at all. Sometimes we'd drive out to the beach, and Mama would spread a blanket on the sand, close to the water's edge. Then Ingy and I could take off our clothes, which we had on over our bathing suits, and venture into the water. On one of those outings, I was standing knee deep in the foamy surf when a giant wave knocked me over, and I tumbled and tumbled under the water, seeing the swirling sand as I bumped around hitting the sandy bottom. Then suddenly a strong arm reached mine and pulled me to safety. The arm belonged to a big, dark-haired man who had been walking in the surf and saw me go under. He picked me up as the water I had swallowed spilled out of my mouth like a faucet. Mama came running—"How did she away from our blanket?" she asked, but then switched to English and thanked the man, because I was clearly okay. Miraculously, I continued to love the water.

Another road trip, a popular one, was to Sheepshead Bay. Mama and Papa knew that there was fresh seafood to be had from the fishing boats. We would go in late afternoon, when the sun was glistening on the water and the fishing boats approached the dock. We would walk along Emmons Avenue and watch as deck hands leapt from the boat bows and secured their crafts. On these outings, Papa always had a bucket, which he lowered over the edge of a low dock and filled half full of sea water. "It will stay really fresh this way," he explained. Soon he had negotiated some fish, some crabs, and a few lobsters from the fishermen on the wharf. He put these treasures from the sea in the bucket, which then went in the backseat on the floor of the car. Ingy was the guardian of the bucket; she had to make sure it didn't tip over, so she'd sit with her ankles pressed to either side of the bucket while holding the wire handle in her hands.

One time after such an outing, Mama determined that I was just too cranky and needed a nap, so she put me to bed in my room. "I want to help cook the crabs and lobster," I declared, stomping my foot. Mama put me in my crib anyway. I must have needed that nap, since I nodded off almost immediately. When I awoke, I was groggy, but as my eyes adjusted to the late-afternoon light, I felt a weight on my chest and looked toward it. What I saw was horrific: there was a red beast on my chest, with long feelers and menacing claws. I couldn't move for fear it would. Then I tried to scream, but I couldn't get enough air in to make a noise. I was alone in the bedroom.

Finally, I gasped in enough air and let out a piercing scream, and then I heard wild laughter coming from the kitchen. I screamed and screamed, and the more I did, the more Mama and Ingy laughed as they came into the bedroom to watch me in my terror. Mama laughed so hard, she had to wipe tears from her eyes. Those weren't the same kind of tears I was producing.

Finally, Papa strode into the room, took one look at the scene, moved the lobster to the foot of my crib and picked me up. By now

I had the hiccups and was sobbing as he held me and berated my mother. "How could you be so mean?" he asked.

Mama just looked at Ingy and said, "You have to admit, though, it was funny," and they laughed some more as co-conspirators.

I remember that incident distinctly, and I can still recall the terror I felt. Bed should have been a secure place for a little girl, but quite often it wasn't. I didn't like being in bed when Mama and Papa weren't home. The First Evangelical Free Church had lots of meetings— always on Sunday morning and Sunday evening, and sometimes on Sunday afternoon. These we all went to regularly. But the church also had business meetings on Wednesday nights, and my parents would often go to those as well. Leaving a four-year-old and nine-year-old to fend for themselves was never on the agenda, so my mother called her sister Hedwig and asked if Magnhild, our much older cousin who insisted we call her Maggy, could babysit.

So Maggy would come, but you know, she was just a little scary. Sweet and respectful to my parents, she was bossy and full of pronouncements as soon as they left. She'd say things like "Just be glad you're Norwegian and Protestant. It would have been awful to have been born Catholic. Catholics do awful things to Protestants." She never exactly said what it was that they did, but I understood enough to realize that Catholics were to be feared.

What would we do if a Catholic came to the door when Mama and Papa were gone? Could Maggy protect us? We were easily scared, and Maggy knew it. She would threaten to leave the house if we didn't do exactly what she said.

One time she walked down the stairs, opened the door to the street and stood against the backdrop of the night's darkness. "See, I'm really going because you are such bad girls," she announced to the two of us, who were peering down the stairs at her. She came back in though, and sat in the living room reading a book, while we put ourselves to bed in the bedroom we shared. We surely feared being left alone, but we feared Maggy just as much. I was pretty sure I could hear a man's deep voice at times talking to Maggy, but I was never certain.

Sometimes, when it was dark, and I was in my crib and Ingy in her bed, I would come awake and know that there was something bad in the room. I could sense a presence, maybe even see a dark shadow standing by Ingy's bed. I lay as still as I could, trying not to breathe or make a sound, hoping the shadow would not come and do whatever it was it did. Rigidly I lay there, aware that Ingy was awake and lying just as still, until the door to the hall opened, and we were alone in our little room. Our terror was almost palpable. This was not a one-time experience, but we never talked about it afterwards. It became our secret. I always welcomed the morning after "the presence" had appeared, and when I awakened, I wondered if the malice I sensed was the product of a dream or a reality. But there would be long stretches where there was no bad presence in the bedroom, and life was good.

But sometimes I would wake up with free-floating anxiety. Sometimes it would come over me—for no apparent reason that I understood, and my chest would become tight, and I could barely breathe. I couldn't get enough air out to allow more air in. When my mother would witness my struggle, she calmly said it was simply fear of falling that caused it. When I was nine months old, I fell down a flight of stairs and screamed for a bit, but was otherwise unhurt except, as I now know, for the trauma. But emotional trauma didn't count back then.

When I was older, I heard my mother explain that my sister, Ingrid, had left the expandable child gate unlatched upon her return from first grade at PS 127 just down the street from where we lived. The child gate had been at the top of the stairs leading to our flat. It's interesting, I know, that my sister, who was only six at the time, caught the blame for the whole thing. I still wonder, however, if that falling was at the root of the anxiety that would take over at the slightest trigger or if it was something else, something dark and sinister that occurred in our bedroom. I would never know for sure.

Some days were better than others. They had "events." Mama often had friends who would come to visit. To amuse me on sunny days when she was expecting women friends to share kringle, coffee, and gossip, Mama would bring a big wash basin, which she filled with water, and some old plastic cups to the porch overlooking the street and let me play, pouring water from cup to cup. That was a treat, and if I were lucky, I'd have a cup full just as Ingy was coming home. Over the railing the water would go, and Ingy would look up as the water came down, sometimes a direct hit, other times a near miss. Ingy would yell, "You little brat" or some other epithet.

When Ingy complained, Mama would say, "There, there. It's only a little water and it's a hot day. You'll dry in no time." And to her visitors, she'd exclaim, "Girls will be girls," whatever that meant. Water mischief was a good thing; being clean was next to Godliness, and cleanliness was a constant topic among Mama's friends and sisters. Indeed, I would often hear Mama and a guest assessing the housekeeping skills of someone not present.

Often after Mama had had a visitor, she would later recount the conversation with Papa. I would hear her tell Papa things like "Agatha said Esther came to Dugg Draaben wearing lipstick! Can you imagine?" (Dugg Draaben, meaning dew drop, was the church women's group.) "She wore lipstick to church!" she repeated, aghast. The very idea appalled them, so I was pretty sure putting anything on your face must be a sin. I had even heard Papa quote from the book of *Leviticus* in the *Bible* that confirmed how mad God got if you tried to improve upon what you had been born with.

Yet I had a Norwegian friend my own age, a freckle-faced, red-haired girl, who lived a few houses from us; her name was Mary Anne. Mama let me play on the sidewalk with Mary Anne as long as she could watch from the upstairs porch or the stoop. Mary Anne spoke English as well as Ingy did—and at least I could understand most of it, but sometimes I got it wrong. She never corrected me or laughed at me, though. She also had a pretty mother, who had rosy lips and strawberry blond hair. I wished my mother could be like Mary Anne's mother — not short and round but slim and pretty and full of fun. Mary Anne's mother always had the radio on with peppy music, and sometimes she would do a little dance for us, keeping step with the music, and she would take our hands and lead us in some steps pushing us back and then pulling us forward. "It's the cha cha," she would say, or "the lindy."

One day Mary Anne's mother showed us her makeup and let us try some on. Wow! I had red lips, and that made me smile, although I bet God wasn't smiling much at what we had done. Neither was Papa when I arrived home and got a swat on my behind and was told to "Go wash your face!" But at least Mama didn't step in with her handkerchief to do the job.

I still got to play with Mary Anne, though, but we never put her mother's makeup on again. Mary Anne's mother still liked me just fine, and she was good to us. When the Good Humor man came peddling up the street pushing the ice cream box and ringing his bell, Mary Anne's mother would come out and buy us ice cream.

She gave him coins which he put into a metal case strapped to his belt, and he made change by pressing levers that released coins with a "ca-ching." I loved ice cream, but we didn't have it much at home since it didn't keep all that well in the ice box. So, it was we came to revere the bicycling ice cream man in his crisp white uniform.

Soon another family moved into a house on 79th Street, and we met Gina, who was five and had started school. In the afternoons when we'd play on the sidewalk, Gina was full of stories about everywhere she'd been. The family had been to Washington, D.C., our nation's capital, and even Italy, where her grandparents lived. Gina had long black eyelashes and dark hair and wore beautiful barrettes. I thought she was the prettiest girl I had ever seen.

I didn't go into her house much, though. The few times I was invited in and went with Mama's permission, I was surrounded by unusual smells. Once I smelled smoke and asked, "What's on fire?"

"Nothing," said Gina. "My mother smokes, that's all." Imagine a woman with a cigarette! Surely that must be a terrible sin, since my parents often spoke disparagingly about those they knew who smoked.

"What's that?" I asked Gina another time, as I detected an unusual aroma.

"My mother's making gravy with meatballs," she responded. "Come, look." And she lifted the lid off the big pot on the stove, and we peered in.

"That's not gravy," I said. "Gravy is brown, not red."

"No, it isn't. It's always from tomatoes," said Gina. I guessed she just didn't know any better.

What really startled me, however, was the cross hanging in the living room of their flat. We had a cross at home and at church. It was to signify that Jesus, who had been put to death on the cross, had risen, and so the cross was empty. But it wasn't in Gina's house—it had a dead body on it. It was just gruesome. When I spilled this news at home, Mama simply clucked at little and said, "They are Katolikker" (Catholics).

"But I know they go to church," I said. "What are Katolikkers?"

"They go to a church that believes different things than we do. They are not saved," Mama said. "It's a pity they are so ignorant."

"But Gina is so nice," I said. How could she not be saved?

"You can be plenty nice, even if you're not saved," said Mama, "but don't listen to them if they talk to you about their church. If they do, you just start singing *What a Friend We Have in Jesus*, and remember, that's the truth."

I was fascinated, though, by Gina and the different way her family was. I had never had a friend with a name like Gina, and I could say it pretty easily. But Gina couldn't say "Solveig," so she just called me "Sue," which I liked. How I yearned for an American name like Mary Anne! On fair weather days, when we would be outside making pictures on the sidewalk with colored chalk or playing hopscotch, Mama would stand by the railing and holler for me to come home. "Solveig, Solveig," she'd holler from the porch, stressing the last syllable so it sounded like "SoolVEY." Gina thought it was hysterical.

It was right around this time that I became aware that not everyone I knew was Norwegian or even born again. Surely it was best to be Norwegian, I thought, and I knew who the Norwegians were. We were the ones who were going to heaven because we always went to church and prayed over our food. The Norwegians most special to me were my cousins. Mama's sister Clara and sister-in-law Ragna had lots of blond, blue-eyed children who were close in age to me and Ingy. We saw them a lot, and maybe Mama liked Clara and Ragna best as well.

We saw Tante Hedvig, too, but not as often. She had grown-up children; two sons lived on Long Island I knew, since Tante

Hedwig spoke of them and her grandchildren often. A middle child, Dagmar, had an apartment in Manhattan, and we rarely heard about her. But Gudrun and Magnhild, the ones we called "Goody" and "Maggy," still lived with Tante Hedwig and her husband, Werner, on 57th Street in a four-family house. We saw them often enough, but we saw Maggy more frequently because she babysat for us.

Tante Clara and Onkel Olav had four children, and the family lived on 67th Street, between 7th and 8th Avenues, across from a park, and just 12 blocks from 79th Street. They could walk to our house easily, since these were the Avenue blocks, shorter in length than the numbered streets like the ones we walked when we went to 5th Avenue.

Tante Ragna, however, was farther away; she and her family lived on Staten Island, but they would often come to visit in Onkel Leif's old Buick. When they did, Onkel Leif would give us each a dime and we'd march down to the candy store on 7th Avenue and have ice cream cones or sometimes candy. If I planned it out carefully, I could stretch that dime so that I had a pocketful of penny candy that I selected through the glass over the candy case. I really liked the candy cigarettes—they made me feel so grown up, like Gina's mother, but I'd better not let Papa see me pretending to smoke! It was safe to buy the "dots" that stuck to a strip of white paper, and

I could pull them off and tell my cousins to "take a pill." With our cousins we had great fun—they were more like siblings to me, and I knew they felt the same.

Every so often, in our flat or Tante Clara's, Mama and Tante would get together to sort our outgrown clothes and shoes, many to be sent home, home being Norway. There were many shirts and pants and pinafores, which we just kept outgrowing. What we couldn't fit into anymore or pass on to smaller cousins got folded neatly and placed in cardboard boxes to ship to Norway, where we heard so often that people were quite poor. Evidently my mother and aunts had lots of cousins who had lots of children on the other side of the Atlantic. How they kept track of who was who was a wonder. We were told often enough how good we had it in America. This message seemed to reiterate whenever it was time to sort and ship clothes. It was good, I guess, when Tante Clara came and I got her daughter Bente's best church dress, which didn't fit Ingy, and was too big for Bente's little sisters, Alice and Sonja, who would most likely take possession of it when I outgrew it. Visits like this came with a bonus.

But I think my favorite visitor was Onkel Sverre, who was single and often stayed with Tante Hedvig and her husband. He was like a sixth child to Hedvig, since her sons were grown and gone, and he was single and about the same age as they. He wasn't there all that often since his job kept him away a lot. I had often heard my parents and my aunts and uncles talk about him with pride.

The whole family loved Sverre, the youngest of the band of Jorstad siblings; but it wasn't just love, it was pride as well. I had heard how Sverre had sailed off to sea at the tender age of 14 on the tall training ship *Sørlandet*, the one that had no auxiliary power and relied solely on the crew to hoist the sails and navigate. By the time Sverre had reached adulthood, he had joined the Norwegian Merchant Marine. Then when the war broke out, he was stranded in New York. It couldn't have been a difficult transition to become an American Merchant Marine, and that's what happened.

We all loved him because he was always in such good humor, and he was funny. Hedvig laughingly told her sisters how she asked him to go to the grocer and get a loaf of bread on a Tuesday morning. He said, "Sure," and grabbed his jacket. He came back on Friday, somewhat disheveled and a little unsteady, but he had the bread! Yes, they always had good Sverre stories to share.

When he would come to visit us, he would hoist me up in his big, strong arms—and he was a strapping, ruddy-faced man! He would swing me around until I squealed. He called me "gulle" (goldy) and told me I was his favorite. He had to know he was my favorite, too. When he kissed me, I smelled a sweet scent that none of the other uncles had. That made him special, too. Mama would tell her brother, "That's enough. Put her down. And you have had enough too." Mama could wear quite a scowl if she wanted to.

In late October, we had other visitors. On a Monday morning when Papa was not "på jobben" (on the job), he and Mama were more excited than usual, and Mama was hustling in the kitchen, making sure she had enough food for smørbrod (open faced sandwiches), and of course kringle and coffee. She sent Ingy to the grocery store for cream for the coffee. Then Papa left in the car. He and Onkel Olav each drove a car to New York, to the pier where the *Stavangerfjord* had just docked, and collected seven people debarking from the ship. When they arrived at our flat on 79th Street. Papa said, "Thank you so much" to his brother-in-law Olav, who replied, "nothing to thank for" and went home to his family on 67th Street, since the visitors were not even related to him at all, just to Papa and us.

But what visitors they were! We were excited to see Papa's sisters, Signe and Marit, their husbands, and their sons when they came up the stairs and into our flat. Were they in America to stay? I found out later that my father had spoken with his sisters when we were in Norway and told them what he had learned. The 14th Amendment to the US constitution said, "All persons born or naturalized in the United States, and subject to the jurisdiction thereof, are citizens of the United States and of the State wherein they reside."

That meant my father had already been a citizen when he took the citizenship test. He hadn't needed to pass any test to be an American. The clincher was that his sisters were, too, since they had also been born on Henry Street in downtown Brooklyn, before their father moved the family back to Norway. That gained knowledge was what led them to the momentous decision to move to the United States.

But back then, all I understood was that Odd was in my house! And so were Arvind and Erick. I started jumping up and down and clapping my hands, but Ingy was surprisingly shy and so was Erick, who hung back behind his mother. Arvind was full of fun though— laughing and joking with us. I took Odd by the hand and brought him into the bedroom I shared with Ingy and showed him my toys. "Dolls," he sniffed. "Don't you have any cars?"

"I have blocks," I responded, and we set about building a tower.

However, Arvind and Erick, who had quickly gotten past his bout of shyness, started to wrestle and soon were pretty raucous. Then we heard a thumping sound from the floor. Thump, thump, thump, it went. "It's coming from downstairs," laughed Arvind, who promptly grabbed the container of blocks and thumped right back. A short while later, the flat became unbearably hot.

Papa then went downstairs to the landlord and explained that we had three boys upstairs, and to please forgive the noise. "We will be more quiet."

"Oh," said the landlord. "When we heard the pounding on the floor, we thought you wanted more heat."

The adults opened a few windows until the flat cooled down, and then Mama laid out a spread of smørbrod and coffee, with milk for us children. At the table we first said grace— *I Jesu Navn*—then learned why they had come to America. They were here because they wanted to be in the land of opportunity.

It was crowded in the flat that night. Odd slept in my bedroom on Ingy's mattress on the floor, and she slept on the bedspring, bolstered by a padding of blankets. The grownup guests slept on borrowed bedding and army cots, and Arvind and Erick slept on the sofa and sofa cushions in the living room. What an array of bodies!

The next day, after breakfast and lots of coffee for the grownups, a car caravan set out for New Jersey, with Papa driving our car, and Onkel Olav his, since he had again volunteered to help Papa and his sisters. West Orange, New Jersey, was where the newly arrived Norwegians were to live with relatives of our two uncles. Tante Signe and Onkel Bendix went to his sister's house with their two boys where they would stay until they found a flat of their own. Tante Marit, Onkel Karl, and Erick went to live at his brother's house until they could do the same. All was good.

Chapter Three

Ferrytales

We loved to visit the cousins, and most times we could just walk since they lived in Bay Ridge or Sunset Park. But when we went to the cousins on Staten Island, it was a day trip for us. Sometimes Tante Clara and her children would meet us on the corner of 69th Street and 8th Avenue, and we'd wait for the streetcar to take us to the ferry that sailed from Brooklyn to the island.

We inhaled the salty aroma of the sea as we watched the big green ferry approach and dock, bouncing from side to side against the wooden pilings. Then the deckhands secured the ferry, released the chain and made sure the metal plates were in place for the cars to drive off. Next a deckhand unhooked the chains so the foot passengers could debark.

As soon as a deckhand signaled us to board, we stepped onto the main deck and scampered up the stairs to the upper level. Below us, cars passed from shore to ship, clanking over the metal plates. From the upper deck, we could watch the activity on the harbor while we waited to get underway. Soon the deckhands hooked the chain across the back of the boat, signaling that the ferry had boarded as many cars as it could, and we set sail. As often as not, we could look back at the shore and see the queue of cars that didn't make it aboard and would wait for the next boat. Such patience.

As foot travelers, we loved approaching St. George, Staten Island, for the boat would bounce off the big wooden pilings, making us lurch as we lost our balance and sought something to hold onto. Once the ferry docked, we debarked via the passenger walkway, while cars drove off one by one beside us. After that it was a short walk to the bus stop on Bay Street and the bus that would take us up the hill on Victory Boulevard. This was a real bus, not a streetcar, and it wasn't hooked up to overhead wires—quite modern. Once we were aboard and seated, the bus driver would close the door and we'd start out. One time my cousin Tor Asbjørn asked the driver how he closed the door. It was a metal bar that he pulled, like an accordion, and the door shut. "Don't talk to the driver while the bus is in motion," the driver retorted.

"Tormann, sit still and be quiet," Tante Clara said, a little embarrassed. But my cousin was impressed by the authority of the driver, and he told me that when he got out of school, he was going to drive a bus!

One lovely spring Saturday, we got off the bus on Slosson Avenue and walked to Tante Ragna's house, which sat on a pretty street by Clove Lake Park. How happy we were to see more cousins, for Tante Ragna had four children: three boys. Karl, Johann, and Harold, and Liv, a girl a year younger than I. Tante Ragna had lunch waiting for us, and we washed our hands and sat down at the kitchen table, saying *I Jesu Navn* before digging into a veritable feast of Gjetost (goat cheese) on homemade bread accompanied by tall glasses of saft, which was really grape juice diluted with water. Tor Asbjørn called gjetost "brown soap cheese," and forever thereafter, that's what it would be to us. But lunch was always good at Tante Ragna's, especially when followed by homemade berliner kranz, her signature cookies. Satiated, we said our "Takk for maten" (Thanks for the food) and raced to play in the park, with Ingy, and Bente admonished to "keep an eye on" the younger kids.

Off to the park we went to play, usually hide-and-go-seek, our favorite. Sometimes Ragna's boys would bring toy guns, a no-no in our household, but just fine in theirs, and we'd play cowboys and Indians, although I never liked it when Harold would point a gun at me and say, "Bang, bang, you're dead."

"I am not," I would reply, indignant that being dead would mean I could no longer play. We died many times, but we always resurrected.

Tante Clara's son, Tor Asbjørn, and Tante Ragna's boys were good friends, more like brothers than cousins. But that's how I felt about these cousins too—so many of them, more like siblings than anything else. Time always passed quickly when we were on Staten Island, and the day wore on much too fast. By late afternoon, it was time to reverse our trip, and we set out for Brooklyn, which wasn't nearly as much fun as getting to Staten Island, for we were dirty and tired. I was always grateful not to get Mama's special spit shine, but then we were going home, so it didn't matter much how we looked. We had traveled a lot that day, but evidently the journey had been most memorable for my cousin Tor Asbjørn.

The very next time we walked to Tante Clara's house, Tor Asbjørn was waiting for us. All the portable chairs in the house—from the kitchen, the dining room, and bedrooms— were lined up in two neat rows. In front of the left row stood a single chair, and behind it a long piece of tape was affixed to the rug. "Line up and wait for the bus," he said. And of course we did that. We pretended to board the bus and deposit fares in the cardboard box on the floor, while he sat on the forward chair. I had another idea, however, and said, "I have a transfer" and proceeded to hand him a piece of paper. He examined the paper, "Just to make sure it's valid," he said. "Take your seats, or stand behind the line," he said officiously as he motioned to close the imaginary door. Then, you guessed it, he said, "Don't talk to the driver while the bus is in motion." And he made a rumbling engine noise while we sat down and wondered where the "bus" would take us.

For most of our real outings in Brooklyn, public transportation was good—we could take a streetcar or bus and get almost anywhere we wanted. But when Papa was home, we drove. He always had a clean and shiny car and would spend hours in the small backyard cleaning and polishing. He kept the car in the garage behind our flat, which he rented from the landlord, who didn't drive. Then in 1951, when I was five, Papa bought a brand-new Chevrolet, a black Powerglide. We were proud when he took us to our 66th Street church and we'd step out of that car—it was a statement. I knew Papa was proud, too, especially when he could tell the men outside the church how he bargained for a good price and got extras thrown in. "Why," he said, "I made them throw in a visor mirror, something they would have charged me for." There was no doubt that Papa was a man with a head for doing business. He gave a tire a good kick and said, "Chevy makes a solid car."

It wasn't long before Mama decided she needed to learn to drive. I had heard her talking to Papa about how she could get us to church when he was on the boat, and she was making a pretty convincing argument. After that Papa took her out in the Chevy for a little driving lesson while Ingy was in school and I was playing at Mary Anne's down the street. That was probably a bad idea, because Mama came home with "the look" and started stomping heavy-footed into the kitchen. That action was followed by clanking and banging noises. We knew to keep out of that room!

"Women! They should never drive," Papa muttered, as much to himself as to her. "We all know about women drivers, and you just confirmed that." Well, Mama wasn't done, not by a long shot. Pretty soon she signed up for real driving lessons with a complete stranger. And guess what? When she was finished, she got her license on the first try, much to Papa's amazement. When she put her mind to something, she got what she wanted.

So now when Papa was on the boats, we could drive where Mama wanted to go. That's not to say we still didn't walk to 5th Avenue or 86th Street to shop, or even all the way to 8th Avenue where we could get Norske varer (Norwegian goods). But having a car meant we were liberated, to say nothing of the status we attained because we had a mother who could drive.

On Sundays when Papa was working, we would take the car to church without Papa at the wheel, and Mama would pull up to the curb on Leif Erickson Park. The car had little feelers on the hubcaps that made a scratchy noise, signaling that she was close to the curb and could parallel park neatly. Once parked, we'd get out and she'd lock it up before we crossed the street to the First Evangelical Free Church. "Look at her," I heard a woman say once.

"Look at her. She thinks she's so special." It was a puzzle. Mama never seemed special, just ordinary to me. But that day she was wearing her stone martens over her coat—replete with heads, tails, and even glass eyes. Yup, real fur! But still, when she stepped out of the car, she had to know people outside church would stop talking to each other and look at us.

One time when we were getting ready for church and Papa was on the boats, Mama backed the car out of the garage, then got out to close the garage door as was expected by the landlord. As she pulled the garage doors shut and latched them, the car started to roll backwards with Ingy and me in it. Mama ran for the car—she had left the driver's door wide open and the car in neutral on the driveway that inclined somewhat—but she was too late. Back it rolled into the corner of the brick house, and off came the driver's door. How was she going to explain that to Papa, who would be home in a day or two? I never knew the outcome, but the car got fixed, and Mama and Papa still seemed to like each other okay, and things were harmonious in our five-room flat.

One piece of furniture seemed to dominate our flat. It was a big wooden radio in the living room, as tall as I, with mysterious knobs and a line that moved from side to side in a little window. Mama would turn the dials, and music or sometimes just talk would emit from it while she cleaned and straightened—something she was extra good at.

With the radio on, I was learning new words in English every day. "What's an 'ol' kit bag?'" or "Where is 'blueberry hill?'" I asked when music streamed forth. But talk coming from the radio puzzled me, too. "What's a commie?" "What's a red?" "How can a curtain be 'iron'?" I queried. So many words to learn, but what did they mean?

Learn words I surely did. I had books as well, and Mama would read to me and point to the words and voice them, stressing the first letter. My favorite was *The Billy Goats Gruff*, a Golden book. When she got to the part about the trolls under the bridge, I would squeal with feigned fright as she held my arm out like a bridge and walked her fingers along it like a billy goat. Then suddenly up popped the troll!

Since I was five, I knew enough English and the written word to read a little of the Golden books by myself, or maybe I just pretended to, since I knew the stories so well. The result was that I knew I was ready for school. I would lobby to go to school as Ingy did. "Ikke mas" Mama said repeatedly. (Don't pest.) But she did go to PS 127 and sign me up for kindergarten to start in the fall. I would attend from 8:30 to noon, three and one-half hours. I was sure once I started I was going to love it.

I didn't. When I got to my classroom on the first day, Mrs. Timberlake, the teacher, asked me what I would like to be called since she said the other children would not be able to say my name. The truth was, she couldn't say "Solveig" either and when she tried it sounded like "soul-ve-hig." She tried again, and what came out sounded more like "Saulwig." The attempts made some of the children giggle.

"I have a friend who calls me 'Sue,'" I whispered. It was funny, though, that she decided Jens could keep his given name, which she pronounced as "Jenz," even though the rest of us knew his name sounded like "Yenss," and sometimes we'd giggle at that.

"We will call you 'Sue,' too," pronounced Mrs. Timberlake. I didn't like that much, but she was as old as God and just as tough. "Silence! There will be no disruption in my classroom," she said. "You will speak only when spoken to." That was pretty hard for me, since here I was surrounded by boys and girls the same age as I, and I wanted to know them and be friends. How could that happen if we couldn't talk to each other?

After the first day, I decided I wasn't going to do it again. I had had enough. "I don't want to go back," I told Mama.

"Well, you really don't have a choice. You are signed up, and you wanted to go, so now you have to." Thus, I continued to go but didn't much like it. We would have a mid-morning milk break, which I hated—come to think of it, I still don't like milk. But the milk we had then came in little cardboard boxes lined with wax, and it was lukewarm, not cold, because it had come to the school early in the morning and had sat there without refrigeration until our mid-morning break. But we all had to drink it, even though little bits of wax would sometimes break away from the container and wind up in our mouths. Whose idea was the milk break, anyway?

Sometimes Mrs. Timberlake would tell us to fold our arms on the desks and put our heads down and take a little nap. I would tilt my head so that one eye was just above my elbow, and I could look at my classmates. One little boy sat next to me and did the same. We had a staring contest, and what usually resulted was fits of laughter. That didn't sit so well with the teacher, and I often wound up sitting on the tall stool in the back of the classroom.

One time I decided to put some crayon on my face—make-up, I thought, just like Mary Anne's mother wore. When I did that, I went home with a note pinned to my chest that said, "Sue misbehaved today." Sometimes I would wear home notes that said, "Sue is a chatterbox" or "Sue is disruptive."

And then Mama would put me in my crib for the rest of the day. "You just stay there, until you learn to behave yourself," said Mama. Behaving—whatever that meant—was a challenge. I never thought to remove the notes, however, and even now I wonder why not.

About kindergarten I do remember, however, that it was fun to march around the classroom in time to the lively music Mrs. Timberlake played on the upright piano that stood at the side of the room, just under the windows. It was good to get up from the desk and move, which we did for various reasons, always in a controlled and orderly way. Several times a week we'd line up double file and walk behind Mrs. Timberlake to the gym, where we would march in large circles as she kept time by clapping her hands.

But I think the best times were when the PA system emitted a warning sound, and we would get out of our seats to prepare for an air raid, "just in case we're attacked by the Koreans," Mrs. Timberlake said. This was when America was at war in Korea, and we feared the yellow menace, whatever that was. Taking cover was an adventure: we all stood up, then folded ourselves under our desks and put our arms over our heads.

After months of regularly taking cover under our desks, someone must have realized that the glass windows could break, thus presenting a whole new danger. From then on when the PA warning erupted, we'd get our coats and jackets from the hooks in the back of the room and file into the hall next to our classroom, as students from other classes did the same. "Take cover," we were told, and we sat down and put our outerwear over our heads and huddled, anticipating the planes that were to zoom in over our school and blow us to smithereens, but they never did.

As my first year of school drew to a close, Mama and Papa began to talk about what we would do during the summer months. Previous summers had taken us to the Catskills, near the Ashokan reservoir, where we stayed in a wooden cabin for a number of weeks. This year, however, we were excited because we were going to Rawlings, Pennsylvania, for a whole six weeks. Papa and Mama had rented a cabin and promised us lots of fun swimming in the Lackawaxan River and playing games with some of our cousins and other Norwegian kids. The anticipation was delicious since Tante Clara, Onkel Olav, and their four children were going, too. Onkel Leif and Tante Ragna had also promised to come with their four children, at least for a week.

Finally, the last day of school came, and we were ready to set off. Being in kindergarten, I got home before Ingy, who had to stay in school until 3. I helped Mama and Papa pack the Chevy till it could hold no more. Then as soon as Ingy came home from school, we set out for the wide-open country, unsure what awaited us but excited nevertheless.

I sat in the back as we motored along the Gowanus Expressway and into the Brooklyn Battery Tunnel where we saw men walking on an elevated platform that ran next to the car lanes, monitoring traffic and breathing in what the cars emitted. Then it was up the west side of Manhattan to the Lincoln Tunnel approach, which on a Friday afternoon was backed up. "What's that smell?" I asked.

"It's the slaughterhouse. It's where the city gets its meat," said Papa.

Then Mama said, "Why do you have to ask so many questions?" Why indeed?

That wasn't the only place that had a foul smell. By the time we got to Secaucus, on Route 3 in New Jersey, we were regaled with the pungent odor of the pig farms. Now what was left in my little stomach was wanting out, and I said, "I'm going to be carsick." Mama handed me an empty Maxwell House coffee can, and up it came.

"Eww," said Ingy. "That's disgusting." But I felt much better.

Finally, I closed my eyes and nodded off. When I woke up, we were in Pennsylvania, zipping by the Zane Grey Inn and the bar called Jungle Jim's, two erstwhile landmarks in this part of the state. "Uff," said Mama as we passed the bar. "There goes Sverre. He's full again." Sverre was the uncle we were always so happy to see. For me it was good to hear that Sverre was in Rawlings because we loved him so much.

Sverre was a seaman too, like Papa. Sverre was a cut above, however. He carried the prestige of having learned to sail aboard the *Sørlandet*, the Norwegian school ship, and that history gave him credentials. After he left the Merchant Marine, he worked on the New York harbor for a pilot's association that brought larger vessels to their dockings, since captains of larger ships had to relinquish the helm to a pilot once a ship was in the bay. His story was impressive, and the family's pride in him increased continually despite his errant ways.

Sverre had planned to come to Pennsylvania when he had time off from work. The rest of us, my Tante Clara, my four cousins, and Mama and Ingy and I, would stay in the country for more than half of the glorious summer! And the best part was, there was no way to get to church because we didn't have a car when Papa was working.

When Papa was in Pennsylvania, however, we did go to church, a small Lutheran Brethren facility, where services were in English. I have to admit, I liked that better than the Norwegian department at the 66th Street church, where I couldn't fathom what the pastor was saying. But truth be told, services at this country church were still boring, and I was always relieved when a service was finished.

Sunday afternoons were nice, though. We didn't go swimming in the Lackawaxan River, because it was a day of rest, but we could put on our play clothes—to save the good church dresses from getting dirty. Our cabins had wooden picnic tables, and Tante Clara and Mama would make a picnic lunch, no small enterprise, despite the fact that our side-by-side cabins actually had small electric refrigerators, which of course we all still called ice boxes.

On Sunday our middags was not a dinner like it was in Brooklyn; it was Limpa smørbrod of sliced egg topped with sardines, or ham and swiss cheese, artfully constructed with the ham rolled up and pulled through the holes in the cheese. Sometimes Tante Clara would make her special salad of macaroni and mayonnaise, lots of globby white mayo tossed with mushy, overcooked pasta. It was so American, Mama remarked. She also made a favorite of mine—made more possible because of refrigeration—a jello mold of three layers in different colors with fruit suspended within each layer. This was also called "salad," but to us it was more like dessert.

After our lunch we would go to the open field behind our cabins and play croquet with an old set Onkel Olav had once found discarded by a trash bin on a street in Brooklyn. It worked just fine, except that one mallet was missing, so while we each had a different colored wooden ball, two of us had to share a mallet. And one of the hoops was fashioned from a wire coat hanger and was squarer than the others. If you hit someone else's ball, you could put your foot on your own and give it a real whack to send the opponent's ball flying, with the opponent raging "No fair"!

What was the best of those days and nights in Pennsylvania was being with the cousins, all six of us residing side-by-side in two identical cabins. After supper and before bed, we played Go Fish or Old Maid, the two card games we were allowed. I learned from cousin Bente, the oldest of us, that cards with symbols like paw prints, hearts, pointy black shovels, and diamonds were ones gamblers used and thus very sinful, right up there with using the Lord's name in vain or, heaven forbid, drinking alcohol.

One event especially stands out from that time. It was late morning as we watched an old black Ford with big white wall tires come rumbling down the dirt road, wondering who could possibly be coming our way. It was my most special cousin Odd with his brother, Arvind, his mother, Signe, and father, Bendix. They had brought Erick along too, all the way from West Orange, New Jersey. They spilled out of the car in the warm summer sun, laughing and hugging us all. "How wonderful to see you," Papa exclaimed. "What a nice surprise." These relatives had come to spend the day, unannounced, since we had no telephones to convey information. Surprise visits were always welcome, especially when they were by people dear to us.

The early August day was clear and bright, with billowy clouds floating overhead. We swam in the river with the adults sitting on the rocks watching us, lost in animated conversation. Then we went to the cabin, where Mama somehow dished up a meal of lapskaus (stew), followed by cake Tante Signe had purchased in New Jersey. What a feast we had. After supper, it began to get dark—the days were shorter as the summer drew to a close. We loved the time between daylight and darkness—dusk was the best time for hide-and-go-seek.

I was silently counting to 10 with my head and hands resting on the trunk of a tree while the others scattered. It was quiet, but I could hear the grownups talking in hushed tones, so that made me want to listen in, and even though the conversation was not for children, it was fascinating, for it was of another time and place. I soon found Ingy and Odd and silently motioned for them to follow me to the side of the porch, where we sat down and listened. The others soon realized no one was looking for them, so they ventured out from their hiding places and ducked down to sit beside us.

"Was it so bad in Norway during the war?" Papa asked Onkel Bendix.

"Karl and I had a radio in the barn, and we would listen to messages transmitted unlawfully," said Onkel Bendix. "We knew it was dangerous, especially since there was a collaborator right down the road, a real Quisling follower. One day two Nazi soldiers came to our farm, just to 'pay a visit' to the locals, they said. There had been reports of radio activity in the area, and they were designated to check each farmstead. I could see Karl was nervous, but then, he had that way about him normally. But the soldiers were two young men, nice and cordial, who introduced themselves as Jon and Hans and shook our hands. We had no choice but to let them in. But to tell you the truth, if it hadn't been for the German uniforms, they could have been Norwegians.

"They looked around the house, checking each room carefully, opening closet doors and moving clothing aside. They were very polite, doing their duty for the fatherland. Then they went to the barn, where we had lots of hay. The soldier called Hans picked up a pitchfork and started jabbing at the hay. Karl and I stood quietly and watched, knowing that if they found the radio, which was in there pretty deep, we would soon die. But they didn't find it, and they apologized for the disruption and thanked us for letting them in.

"Right before they left, the soldier called Jon, who had been mostly quiet the whole time, turned to me and said: 'Your name is Strandberg, isn't it? Are you any relation to Nils Strandberg over in Kvinesdal?'

"I hesitated, then said, 'He is my cousin, the son of my father's brother.'

"'I was stationed over there for a while and got to know Nils quite well. He has been invaluable in helping us establish order in the region. There is talk of making him the mayor when the war is over. He will certainly get a commendation, at any rate. You know he wears the uniform of the Reich and is very proud,' the soldier called Jon said.

"'Oh, oh,' I stammered, saying, 'I know that he has been a great asset,' quickly grasping the idea that perhaps my cousin, the traitor, the one we were all so ashamed of, might be the reason the search of our barn wasn't more thorough. I had the right name."

There was a weighted pause, and then Mama said, "My goodness. That must have been a terrifying experience and dangerous. You were lucky that time."

"You know, my cousin Nils wasn't so lucky. He had to escape to Sweden before the war was over, but it's a good thing he made it."

"What do you mean?" asked Papa. "We thought he was in tight with the Germans. Was he one that would have been executed with the other traitors after the war? Is that why he fled?"

"No, no," said Onkel Bendix. "We were all fooled by him. Even his mother. What she endured was amazing. She believed Nils was a traitor, and the shame was horrible."

"What do you mean 'fooled'?" asked Papa.

"Nils wasn't a traitor at all, even though that's what we all thought. He was working the whole time for the British and had a radio in his house. The Germans would have staff meetings in his very house, and they didn't suspect a thing. Nils was feeding them false information about the Norwegians and giving the British information to help drive the Germans from the land. But after a while, he began to sense a change. They were acting more suspicious, and he fled, making his way by night, sleeping in the fields and eating next to nothing, until he reached Sweden."

Sitting beside the porch, we cousins looked at each other, while the parents' conversation drifted to other topics. "Did you know about the radio in the hay?" Ingy whispered to Arvind.

"No. And we were told to always be polite to the soldiers and to mind our own business."

"But your father must have been in the resistance," said Bente to Arvind.

"Not that I know of, and that they had a radio is news to me," said Arvind. "But I knew there was a bad war going on, and Norway had tried to resist the invasion, but couldn't stand up to the German force. And what I remember most about being there during the war was that we had less food, and really no candy, unless we got it from the soldiers who seemed to have lots of it. We more or less liked those guys just fine."

We were in awe that these cousins had lived through an actual war. Moreover, listening to Arvind astounded me for his English had become so good in such a short time. Then the grownups came out and told the boys that it was time to go back to West

Orange and home. And, of course, it was time for the rest of us to go to bed so we could have another glorious day tomorrow.

Summer days followed one after the other, but by mid-August nights were chilly, and we had to wear sweaters if we were outdoors even though we were lean and brown from the sun. Ingy had always had golden curls, but now they were even lighter. How pretty she is, I thought. And then I would look at myself and pray for golden curls like hers, but God didn't see fit to answer affirmatively. My thin, pale brown hair hung limply, and Mama kept my bangs trimmed straight across my brow.

Right before we left Rawlings for Brooklyn, Mama and Tante Clara gave us all six of us haircuts while we sat at the picnic tables beside the cabins. "You must look good when we go back home," said Mama. And I knew in a few weeks I would be back at PS 127 in the 1st grade, and Ingy would be one of the big kids in school—a 6th grader. Was I looking forward to it? I honestly don't know. I remembered I hadn't liked kindergarten, but this was going to be the real deal, so I had a little bit of excitement tossed in the mix.

Brooklyn was still hot when we came back. Seventy-ninth Street steamed after a rain, and there was a permeating, earthy smell that we hadn't had in the country. Since I had grown some, Mama now let me out to play by myself, only checking once in a while from the porch overlooking the street. I happily greeted Mary

Anne and Gina once more after our long absence, and we were glad to see each other. Mary Anne and Gina seemed to share some secrets that I didn't, and I was uneasy. But then Mary Anne and Gina had spent the summer in the city, and I hadn't.

"I went swimming in a big river that flowed very fast," I boasted.

"So what," said Gina. "I have my own pool—all mine in my backyard."

"Sure," said Mary Anne, "we've had so much fun all summer."

"I'll ask my mother to fill it up, and we can go in it today. It's pretty hot," said Gina. "Go get your bathing suit," she said to me.

I rushed home to ask Mama if I could go in the pool. But Mama said, "No."

"Why not?" I whined. "It's just Mary Anne, Gina, and me."

"You don't know about polio," said Mama. "It's a bad sickness. It can kill you or cripple you for life. And you can catch it from being in pools."

So, dejectedly I made my way to Gina's back yard and announced that my mother wouldn't let me. "That's so mean," said Gina.

Gina's mother, who had just finished filling the pool, said, "Hush, Gina. Sue's mother has her reasons. She's not mean." And then I sat down and watched as Mary Anne and Gina splashed in the pool.

But my two friends had done more than play in the pool that summer. They had become experts at jumping rope—better than we had all been before the summer. I turned the rope with Mary Anne, and Gina jumped in. Her rhythm was impressive. When it was my turn, I tripped and went down on my knees. Mary Anne and Gina burst into fits of laughter.

That's when Mary Anne's mother stepped out of the front door to their flat and stood on the stoop. "I have two much longer pieces of clothesline, and I know something you can do that's more fun." That's when she taught us to do double-dutch. With two lines swung by two of us, the third would time it just right and leap into the center, moving from one foot to the other as the ropes passed each other and slapped the ground. It was fun to be back home.

Pretty soon Mama called from the porch: "Solveig, come in now for supper. It's school tomorrow." I did, and after supper, Mama put bobby pins in my hair so I would look good when I started first grade. Then it was time for bed. I still slept in the crib. How could

I be sleeping in a crib when I was not a baby? When I complained that Mary Anne and Gina had real beds, Mama simply said, "You still fit, so that's where you'll stay until you can't anymore." And that's the way it was on 79th street between 7th and 10th Avenues where we lived. But I was determined that things should change.

Chapter Four

Collect Call

In Brooklyn, we had a party line, not a private line, but we did have a telephone, when many others didn't. The signal that was meant for our household was one ring, one ring, a pause, and another ring. Sometimes the little black box that was on the server in the dining room would emit a rapid four rings, and Mama would pick it up but not say a word. It was quite a peculiar thing to witness. She would just stand there with the receiver held to her ear with her left hand, and her right hand on her hip.

"Who is it?" I would ask. And Mama would put her right index finger to her lips, but alas, it was often too late, because the parties on the phone had heard me. And Mama would say into the phone, "Oh, I'm so sorry. I thought it was my ring." But later I would hear her talking on the phone to Tante Clara about the Bensens and their troubles. "Why, he drinks so much, he can't make it home. Can you imagine? Poor Gunnel was on the phone with her sister the other day and was complaining about what to do." That's how I knew there was trouble in other households, and Mama seemed to know all about the woes of other folks.

When Papa came home, he would often berate Mama because of the phone bill. "Do you have to talk so much? Why, it's 10 cents every time you call Clara, Hedwig, or Ragna. Can't you go a day without talking on the phone?" I wanted to add that she also listened without talking quite a bit, but I knew better than to add to the fray. What I did know was that Papa really thought a lot about money, and how he could save every penny. It was no surprise that he got really angry one day when Mama picked up the phone and said, "Ya, I'll accept the charges." Then she talked for a while in clear Norwegian, animated by the conversation with whoever was on the other end. When she hung up the receiver, she turned to Papa, who was standing with his arms akimbo and scowling. "It was my nephew Ole, calling from Idlewild. He just arrived from Norway and is on his way. He said he didn't have any money, only travelers' checks, and he really wanted to talk to me."

"He should have gotten money before he called," snarled Papa. But Mama was happy, while Ingy and I were perplexed. Who was Ole? Mama explained that Ole was her nephew, the son of her older sister Augusta and her husband, Magne Saudeland. Ole was all grown up, much older than Ingy and me or Clara and Ragna's children, Mama explained. He had just gotten out of the

Norwegian army and was planning to stay in America, working for Onkel Johann on Staten Island.

Mama quickly started fussing in the kitchen, telling Ingy and me to set the table in the dining room while she made smorbrød. Then she filled the aluminum coffee pot with water and measured a half-cup of Maxwell House coffee to be thrown into the pot as soon as Ole arrived at our doorstep.

We waited eagerly for this grown-up cousin to reach our flat, and after what seemed like an interminable period, the doorbell rang. Mama rushed down the stairs and threw open the door as a big, blond man took her in his arms and hugged her until we were sure she had no breath left.

"Come up, come up," Mama said, flushed with excitement. "I have made us some lunch." Ole shook hands with Papa and said, "It's good to see you again Onkel Adolph." Evidently we had been to see the Saudeland family when we were in Norway, but of it I had no recollection. But we wouldn't have met Ole anyway, since he had been in the Norwegian army, stationed in Berlin, Germany, when we were in the old country.

But here was our strapping cousin, happy to be in America, and happy to be with the Tante of whom he had good childhood memories, for it was my mother, just a teenager, who was his babysitter when her older sister Augusta, Ole's mother, would visit Jorstad with her husband and children. Imagine that. This cousin, who was many years my senior, had grown up in Norway, just like Mama and Papa had. And he had been a soldier, too.

"How is your mother"? Mama asked. "And what of your father and brother?"

"Papa and Arnt are just fine," said Ole. "I have a sister, too, you know," Ole said pointedly.

"Ya, well," said Mama as she wiped her hands on her apron.

"What was it like in Berlin when the Allied forces were there?" Papa asked, changing the subject.

"It was terrible, so much damage from the bombing. You have to wonder if it was all necessary," Ole responded. "There I was, with other Norwegian boys, stationed in the homeland of those German boys who had been stationed in Norway when I was young. Life sure is funny. It was an ironic reversal, but I felt sorry for the German people, because life was hard for them. They had suffered so much."

"But the Norwegians had also suffered at German hands. Don't forget that," said Mama.

"It's true," said Ole, slowly, "they rationed food and petrol and the people had to do without, but the soldiers really didn't have a choice about what they had to do. Most of the soldiers were nice to us, often giving us German chocolate and smiling at us."

"So as a boy, you weren't afraid?" queried Papa.

"No, not so much. There was one time, however, that I was plenty scared. I had just been confirmed in the State Church, and Papa gave me a motor bike. Imagine! I was thirteen and had my own transportation. I was so proud. But Papa cautioned me about riding on the main roads, because petrol was scarce, and it would make us suspect with the Germans if we were using it frivolously."

"Well, how did you get the petrol for that bike?" asked Papa.

"My father, he knew the driver of the bus that went through our village and was able to buy a kilo of petrol from him from time to time," answered Ole.

"My goodness," said Mama. "That was risky for the driver!"

"Yes," replied Ole, slowly. "But there was so much of that sort of thing, and often the Germans, depending on who they were, looked the other way. But on the day I was out on my motor bike, I was feeling pretty good and was anxious to show the boys I knew what I had, so I set out on the main road, keeping an eye out for German vehicles. I was on the that road, about a mile from home, when I got to an intersection, and there, sitting in a truck smoking, were two German soldiers and an officer I hadn't seen before.

"'Halt,' said a soldier, and I did of course. They had guns on their backs, but they didn't raise them at me. Still, I was scared—but really not so much of them as of my own father, who would be furious!

"The soldiers put my bike in the back of the truck, made me get in, and asked for directions to my house. When we got there, Papa was out in the field, but Mama was home. She blanched when she saw me and the Germans.

"'We are taking your boy into custody, but we want to question his father, too,' said the officer.

"'No, wait,' said Mama. 'Let's be reasonable. I churned fresh butter this morning, and I will let you have it, if you let my Ole go. I promise, he will not ride his motor bike.' She bargained with them, and she was successful, but not until she had added some coffee to the ransom. Then they left. That's when I began to be really afraid, because I knew Papa, and Papa had a temper. He was plenty mad when he got back to the house—butter and coffee given to the Germans! A beating I still remember followed, and the bike stayed in the barn."

"The Germans seemed reasonable then," said Papa. "Bargaining and exchange of goods is the way of men, especially when times are tough."

"Everything wasn't about bargaining," said Ole. "The Germans pretty much took what they wanted. Why, my father's mother, my Oldemor, had her house taken over by the Germans because it was right near the water on Lista. It became a headquarters for the Germans, who put up barbed wire and dug bunkers all to position their guns to protect the shoreline.

"My grandmother cried to us one time, telling us that she had just fed seven young German boys who then boarded a ship and set out on the Skagerak, the body of water between the coast of Norway and the northernmost peninsula of Denmark, a strategic access to the Baltic," Ole explained for Ingy's and my benefit. "When she heard the bombs, she knew the ship had been hit and the boys lost. They were just sixteen and seventeen years old. So young to be sent to war and to die! But that was near the war's end, after Germany had lost so many men on land and sea.

"I was just a kid myself, so it was hard for me to imagine that boys my age could die so young," Ole added.

"Your Oldemor must have been very special to take in those soldiers and feed them the way she did," said Ingy.

"She was like so many old folks during the war. They didn't understand the war, and they didn't understand why Germany had invaded Norway. We could easily have been allies," said Ole. "In fact, Norway almost did side with Germany."

"What! That can't be true!" Papa was heated now. "The Nazis were pure evil."

"Still, there was talk about such a union. It seemed a real possibility after a German ship was damaged, and the captain asked for safe harbor in Jøssund fjord, which the Norwegians granted. Those arrogant British just followed them right in and sank the ship! But then the Germans invaded Norway, so that was the end of that talk," said Ole.

"Imagine that," said Papa. "Things might have gone quite differently if the Germans hadn't actually invaded," he added, his voice rising more like a question than a statement.

For me and Ingy, the talk was about a time and place in which we had had no part, but it was fascinating just the same. "This is America," said Papa. "It's inconceivable to think that one nation could invade another," he stated matter-of-factly. "It would never happen here." He paused, then said again, "It could never happen here," with emphasis on the "never."

"You have bad stuff here, too," said Ole. "You have the organized crime—the mafia. And they do some ugly things."

"Oh, not so much," said Papa, dismissing Ole's comments.

"Now, wait," said Ole. "I heard people at the airport talking about the murder of some guy named Arnold Schuster, and I asked them what it was all about. "

"How could you do that? Would they understand Norwegian?" asked Mama.

"Oh, my English is good enough. Don't forget I was stationed in Germany, and we worked with the American military. The Berlin airlift was underway—in fact that continued for a number of years since the German citizens needed rations for survival. They suffered after the war as much as during. Anyway, one of the Americans at the airport today told me a story about a terrible murder committed by a Frederick Tenute—they call him 'the angel,' but he is short and ugly, with black hair and a dark complexion. He just killed an ordinary guy named Schuster outright. So yes, bad things happen here, just like they do everywhere."

"Oh yes," said Papa. "I know about that murder. It was in the papers. Evidently Schuster recognized Willie Sutton, the bank robber, told the authorities, and that led to Sutton's capture."

"Was Tenuto a friend of Sutton's—maybe a bank robber, too?" Ingy asked.

"No, but Tenuto is a member of organized crime, and his mafia boss told him to kill Schuster, because he hated a snitch," explained Papa in English, now that he knew Ole understood both languages.

"Funny word, 'snitch'" replied Ole in his accented English.

“What’s a snitch?'” Ingy asked.

Papa said, “It’s a tattletale.” And I thought, Ingy’s a snitch. It was a good word to know.

Ole said, “Organized crime is a recognized problem here, then,” switching back to Norwegian.

"No, not so much," said Papa. "We have the normal mix of people, and most are good. This is a God-fearing land. We are really so blessed. Here God comes first. America was built on godliness, and God will always protect this land."

I experienced a surge of love for America, proud to be an American, born in the land of the free and the brave, in the words of *God Bless America*, which we sometimes would sing at assemblies at school. It felt pretty good to be an American, and we were happy to know that so many Norwegians, friends and family, had come to this great land. It seemed a little odd, still, that whenever our extended family talked about Norway, they still called it “home.” But there were still so many puzzles, and I couldn’t begin to put them all together.

It wasn't too long after that visit first visit from Ole that people began wearing red, white, and blue "I Like Ike" messages on buttons and hat bands, and patriotism swelled. "Let's clean house with Ike and Dick," the radio in the living room blared. It played the song "They Like Ike," composed by Irving Berlin. And this message repeated: "Get in step with Ike. You like Ike, I like Ike, everybody likes Ike – for president! Hang out the banners, beat the drums, we'll take Ike to Washington."

Papa opined that he hoped Ike would get elected. He said that, in church, the pastor had declared from the pulpit that "Good Christians must vote for Ike" because the country needs change. There was the ever-present threat of communism, and the country had apparently been infiltrated with communists. Why they could even be your next-door neighbors! It was pretty scary to think about, so we got on the I-like-Ike bandwagon, because we knew he could clean the house that was America.

"A people that values its privileges above its principles soon loses both," were words from Eisenhower, emitting from the radio. I wasn't sure what "privileges" and "principles" actually meant, but it sounded good. Ike's campaign was a crusade for freedom, and the Norwegians we knew were adamant about seeing Eisenhower in the White House, that is, except for my cousin Bente and my sister, Ingy, who often declared they preferred Adlai Stevenson.

"He's a Democrat and therefore for the people," Ingy explained smugly. "And what does a general know about running a country?" she queried, just for the record.

Mama and Tante Clara didn't have much to say about being a Democrat. It was pretty much understood that being a Democrat meant you were liberal, and if you were liberal, you weren't that far from being a communist. People were talking about the "cold war" with communism and how it was heating up. How could that be? A war could be "cold"? More mysteries. And we were still at war with Korea, which Eisenhower promised to end.

One day Tante Magda, who was Mama's older sister, the one we didn't see too much because Mama and Papa didn't encourage her to come to the house, showed up. "Uff," I had once heard Mama say, "She has different men, and they go to bars. Even worse, they go the Sons of Norway, where everyone sees them drinking. She rarely comes to church anymore." To me, Magda was a lot like Onkel Sverre—fun to be with, someone who would talk to you and listen even if you were just a girl. She was good in my book. But the race for president had a funny way of uniting people. My parents softened a little to Magda when she showed up at our house wearing "I Like Ike" sunglasses and carrying *Life* magazine, an extravagant purchase at 20 cents an issue.

"Look at these pictures," she said animatedly, opening the tabloid to the centerfold. "They're of Eisenhower liberating the camps. Can you imagine how horrible it was? This is exactly why this country must have this man as president. He won't stand for any abuse to humanity." Magda sounded pretty convincing to me, and of course Mama and Papa were already in agreement.

Ingy piped up with "Stevenson is the better candidate because he's a Democrat." It had become her mantra, and she kept at it despite being surrounded by Republicans and me, who didn't get the whole thing.

Magda looked directly at Ingy for a long time, then said pointedly in clear English, "Well, Eisenhower really didn't belong to either party, but when he was pressured to run for president, he had to choose, and he chose the Republicans. That pretty much tells me he's not really a party man." Magda was so reasonable, so rational. And Ingy said nothing in response.

But while that exchange was occurring, I had snagged the copy of *Life* magazine, which had been lying face down on the coffee table, showing a doctor with a stethoscope treating a patient—and at the same time smoking a cigarette! "Nine out of 10 doctors smoke Camels," it said.

That was interesting to be sure, since I knew smoking was a sin, so nine out of 10 doctors were sinners. But what I really wanted to see were the pictures of the camps Magda had talked about. There they were in the centerfold: General Eisenhower and his soldiers standing by stacks of dead human bodies, so emaciated they didn't look like they had ever breathed. But they must have. How could other people let something like that happen? It was unfathomable. While I was pondering this evil—something I never dreamt could happen to God's people—Mama saw what I was doing and snatched the magazine from me.

"That's not something for you to look at," she said. I said nothing because I was speechless, a rare condition for me overall. But I had seen it, and then I knew great evil was possible.

A short time later after the November election that year, *The New York Daily News* ran a front-page headline declaring "Ike Wins!" We were on the right track as a nation. Eisenhower would take office in 1953, three months after the election, the first Republican to hold office in many years. America had been blessed by God yet again.

It was around then that my teacher at PS 127 announced there would be a change in our *Pledge of Allegiance,* which we were required to say every morning at school, as we held our right hands across our chests and recited dutifully. "It's now 'one nation, under God,'" she told us, and that just affirmed what we already knew and what we had learned from our parents and at church. The "right" candidate had taken office, and the nation was on a godly track.

Ingy and I faithfully went to Sunday School, and after that to church, although the "faithfulness" wasn't emanating from me, but from my parents' dedication to showing up in church. Sunday School was okay. My teacher was a housewife with children of her own, and she told us *Bible* stories and let us color pictures of the story in our workbooks.

It was very important that we go to Sunday School. The reward for a first year of perfect attendance was a Sunday School pin. Subsequent years of perfect attendance would bring a new bar to hang below the pin. Some of the older kids in Sunday School had many bars dangling from their pins, which they wore proudly. I envied them their histories. I, too, would one day have a long, dangly pin of my own, I vowed. To have other Norwegians acknowledge the faithful devotion to church attendance that such a pin attested to was really important to my parents as well.

It was so important that when I got chicken pox my mother stood me up, put a coat over my pajamas and led me to the car where Ingy was already sitting in the passenger seat. Mama let me lie down on the back seat while she drove to 66th Street and marched me into my Sunday School classroom as Ingy headed to hers. "She's here," Mama said. "Make sure you mark her present." Then she hustled me back to the car, back to our flat, and back to bed.

When I was well, I didn't mind Sunday School, but I can't say I loved it, because Sunday School was followed by church in the upstairs sanctuary. Mostly I continued to not understand the Norwegian the pastor spoke, but sometimes we would have a guest preacher from Norway, the area where my parents were from. That Norwegian I could understand just fine, but there was one time I really wished I hadn't understood, because the preacher had a stentorian voice that bellowed at us about something he called the rapture. "Two will be in the field," he said, "and one will be taken, and one will be left. You do not know on what day your Lord is coming"—this was from the book of *Matthew* in *The New Testament*. Scary stuff indeed. What if I wasn't taken when the Lord came?

"Those who are left are condemned to hell fire and brimstone. Why, to burn in Hell is the ultimate finish for non-believers." You can bet I was determined to believe. But it was so puzzling. I knew Gina was Catholic; worse, she wasn't even Norwegian. Would she burn? And what about Mary Anne? Did she really believe, or did she just go to the Norwegian church on 4th Avenue because she had to, as I had to go to 66th Street? It didn't seem fair on so many levels.

When we got home from church after the rapture sermon, dinner was waiting. Mama had put a chicken in the oven before she and Papa left for church; its rich aroma made my mouth water, and I realized I was hungry. "It will be a few more minutes," Mama said. "I have to boil the potatoes and vegetables." It seemed a long wait, but when we finally sat down to middags, we said *I Jesu Navn* all the way to amen, and we could eat. It was so good. But I wasn't totally distracted by the succulent chicken and wanted to know about the disturbing message I had heard at church. I asked my parents about the rapture. What did it mean?

"It means that Christians who are 'born again' will be taken to heaven, and non-believers will remain on earth. And on earth, after the second coming, there will be wars and rumors of wars, and people who are left will suffer," Papa explained. Then he turned toward Mama and said, "Gunnar believes we are living in the latter days, and that he is not going to die, because the rapture is nearly upon us." Gunnar was a deacon at 66th Street church, so maybe he knew something other people didn't. I felt a little dread creeping through me. I really didn't want to go to heaven, at least not yet, but if all the people I loved went to heaven, what would it be like on earth? Would it be all-out war?

"I saw the pictures of Eisenhower when he ended the war in Germany, those in the *Life* magazine that Tante Magda had," I said. "And there's a war in Korea," I added, even though I wasn't sure exactly where Korea was, and even though we were surely prepared for an attack by the Koreans at PS 127. "Could the Lord have already come, and we missed it?" I asked fearfully. "There's no need to be afraid. The Lord has not come yet. No one knows when he will come," said Papa reassuringly. "What's most important is that we are ready. We live in the world, but we are not of the world," he explained. This was so much to grasp.

It seemed to me that when the radio station blared *Radio Free Europe,* the threat of a war was real. Evidently there was an iron curtain somewhere across the ocean, and we should be very afraid of what was going on behind it. I had heard "iron curtain" before, but I wasn't any clearer about what it was. But try as I might, I just couldn't imagine—it must be so heavy. And how big was it? But I knew one thing: I had better get myself ready to be taken to heaven.

So that night I straightened my area of the room I shared with Ingy. And right after I got into my pajamas and brushed my teeth, I went to Papa and asked, "Will you forgive me my sins?"

"Of course," he replied, as he patted my head and kissed my cheek and off to bed I went—or I should say, I climbed into the crib, feeling light and pure. My feet could touch the footboard, so I slept on my side, with my knees drawn up to my chest, with my thumb in my mouth until morning.

As the weeks after the rapture sermon rolled by, I became less afraid. Brooklyn was a good place to be—especially if you were Norwegian. One day after church, Mama, Papa, and I stood outside waiting for Ingy to come up from the auditorium in the basement as the English service ended. Tante Clara and Onkel Olav saw us and came to chat; they were waiting for Bente, too. "What a wonderful place heaven will be," said Tante Clara.

"It will be full of Norwegians," said Mama in response. "Just like home," she added, and I knew she was talking about Norway, not 79th Street.

The Norwegian community in Brooklyn was strong—we had stores that sold Norske Varer (Norwegian goods), and in many of those establishments, Norwegian was the language they spoke. But the strongest bonds were forged in churches like 66th Street. There were lots of Norwegian churches—all Protestant, and most with congregations that hailed from southern Norway—so we were all enmeshed in the same culture.

As the Sunday School year drew to a close, we were eager to see who had earned another bar on the Sunday School pin. This was also the year when I would get my very own *King James Bible*. We also looked forward to the Sunday School parade, which brought so many of the Norwegian churches together on Flag Day in June. Each year the parade made its way along 4th Avenue, which the city had nicely closed off to vehicular traffic.

Much planning preceded this annual event. A committee determined the colors that would represent each church, and then families bought crepe paper in the designated colors. One year our color was light blue and white. I had an oversized tricycle and set about making it the most beautiful vehicle to grace the parade. Through the spokes on the three wheels, I wound strips of crepe paper which Mama had carefully crimped for me. On the handlebars I wound alternating blue and while bands and made streamers that hung from the handlebars. It was something to behold!

Ingy, being older, had volunteered to carry one end of the Sunday School banner that announced "First Norwegian Evangelical Free Church" at the head of our contingent of walkers, some pushing baby carriages spruced up in blue and white, still others, like me, on tricycles or bicycles also adorned with the signature colors. It was a journey, but after it was over, there was always a bonus as we arrived at a host church for an ice cream feast. That year it was at our church, and we had ice cream in neatly folded cups from Karl Droge, the ice cream place on the corner of 66th and 6th Avenue. We ate the ice cream with little wooden paddles that were supposed to be spoons. We were content and confident that our own Sunday School had had the best display.

A few days after the parade, when I was close to finishing the second grade, we had a surprise. "We have bought a house," Papa said, "and we will be moving in August."

"But I like it here," I said, determined not to leave 79th Street. "Mary Anne and Gina are here. How far away is it? Why do we have to move?"

"It's just three blocks away, on 80th Street between 10th and 11th Avenue. It's a nice neighborhood," said Papa.

"And you will have your own room," Mama added, "and we will buy you a new bed."

Well, that was something, I suppose. I wouldn't have to share a room with Ingy, who, if truth be told, wasn't always that nice to me. Squirt and Dummy were her pet names for me. It might be good to have my own space where I could shut the door and keep Ingy out. And that very night, Mama and Papa went to a business meeting at the church, and Maggy came to babysit. After we went to bed, I felt a dreaded presence in our shared bedroom. I lay as still as I could, pretending to be asleep, but terrified that my breathing was too loud and that it was giving me away. I was awake in the crib, with my feet against the foot board.

I woke up in the morning at dawn, still scared, but thinking it might be nice to have my own room. That's when Ingy said, "I will like it when I don't have to share a room with you," as if she knew I was thinking vile thoughts about her, which I really wasn't. "I want to choose which room is mine," she added.

"Ingrid, you can have the back bedroom, and Solveig will have the middle room, next to our bedroom on the second floor," said Mama to Ingy over breakfast. Okay, so I didn't have a choice, but it would still be my own space. That was a consolation, even though I was apprehensive about moving away from Mary Anne and Gina. When I voiced my sadness, Mama said, "It's not far to 79th Street. You can still go there to play, as long as I can take you across 10th Avenue." I was puzzled by the lack of an 8th and 9th Avenue here. Seventh Avenue was the next avenue down from 10th. So I posed a question.

To this Mama explained that 8th Avenue angled off 7th just after McKinley Park, and that's the way we walked when we went to Tante Clara's. Ninth Avenue didn't start until it intersected with Bay Ridge Avenue, just below Fort Hamilton Parkway. This was surprising news to me. Had we ever even been on 9th Avenue?

There was more news coming. We would have to leave PS 127, too, although for Ingy that wasn't an issue, since she was graduating from 6th grade anyway. PS 201 was to be our new school. I would start my next year of grade school there, while Ingy would go into the 7th grade. Mama went to the school and registered us to start in September, right after Labor Day. And then we moved.

Chapter Five

Big Events

The new house was big compared to our flat on 79th Street. It looked even bigger from the street, since it was attached to another house on its left. We had a front door and a back door and a driveway that we shared with the homeowners to the right. There was a little backyard, big enough to sit outside and have a picnic, which we did frequently that summer after we moved. A rosebush teaming with bright red blossoms graced the very back of the yard, next to the garage, and it was a beautiful backdrop to our little feasts on the ground. We would make little smørbrod and a pitcher of iced tea and carry our meal from the kitchen at the back of the house. And even though we were outside, we still held hands and said *I Jesu Navn.* I remember the air was crisp and clear on late summer days while we were getting to know our new abode.

Getting used to a new house was an adventure, and I had my own room at last. Before we actually moved, we had gone to the wallpaper and paint store and Mama let us look at the pretty wallpapers in big, bound books. There were so many of them! But I finally decided on a pale green paper with vines and birds intertwined. "I will call my best helper—my brother-in-law," said Papa, and we knew he meant Onkel Olav, who was always willing and eager to help. Onkel Olav and Papa soon hung the wallpaper in my bedroom, the one off the hallway between Mama and Papa's bedroom, which was at the front of the house, and Ingy's, which was at the rear, right next to the single bathroom. I admit I thought the room at the back of the house was nicer, but I didn't have a say in the matter. Besides, I was the youngest, so Mama said I had to be close to her and Papa. But nevertheless, it was my own space at last.

Best of all, I didn't have to sleep in the crib anymore. On 79th Street my feet had been on the footboard, and my head touching the headboard, unless I rolled up on my side, a habit I had adopted. In fact, let me say, I had adapted to the circumstance, liking to lie on my side just in case the evil presence appeared. I had become good at pretending to be asleep so that I could escape whatever it was that would descend irregularly on that room in the dark. But that was behind us now. Whatever that presence had been, surely it couldn't find us on 80th Street.

My bed had a Hollywood headboard in quilted pink plastic with pleated edging. Mama had bought me a pretty pink chenille bedspread and shown me how to roll the pillow and tuck the bedspread around it as I made the bed, a daily expectation. I arranged my dolls and bears along the headboard so that they would greet me whenever I came into my room. My bed was on the far wall, so I could see the doorway to the hall, just in case.

I had heard Mama and Papa talking late one night in their bedroom, shortly after we had moved. "Do you have to spend so much?" Papa said, his voice higher than usual.

"Things cost," said Mama. "Ingrid and Solveig need their own space, and besides, I bought those bedspreads and towels at Lynns. For a good price," she added.

"Hmmph," muttered Papa.

That conversation must have triggered what followed the next day. He sat me, Ingy, and Mama at the kitchen table and started in. "You have no idea what things cost."

"You" he pointed at Mama, "you can answer the phone but can make no more than two calls per week, and you cannot speak for a long time. How long does it take, after all, to deliver a message?"

Then, to all of us he said, "You must turn off the lights every time you leave your rooms. If you can see where you're walking, you don't need lights. And as for water—you don't need to shower or bathe every day." Here he was talking directly to Ingy who had begun to take frequent showers. And then to all three of us he said, "And if you do have a bath, don't fill the tub all the way up. And here's the most important thing: you use a lot of toilet paper. From now on, I want you to use less: three sheets for the front, six for the back." Okay, I knew he had sisters, so he had to understand something about female physiology, and of course (I had seen him), males just shook it.

Me, I was embarrassed, and I looked at my hands in my lap. What a thing for Papa to talk about. I did try to comply, however, for I always wanted to please him. So, evidently, did our cousins.

Tante Clara, Bente, Tor Asbjørn, Alice, and Sonya were frequent visitors since they could walk from their flat to our house in less than half an hour. We'd love when they came, sometimes all of them, sometimes just Tante Clara and Alice and Sonya, the two youngest, who were close to me in age. Shortly after Papa's lecture, I took the girls aside, in my room, and explained Papa's rule about the toilet paper. Alice's mouth gaped, and Sonya said, almost inaudibly, "Okay." It wasn't long before Sonya excused herself and went to the bathroom. She came back into my room and told me and Alice, quite proudly, "I did number two. And I didn't use ANY toilet paper!" I didn't know what to say, so I said nothing, trying to process what Sonya had told me.

It happened that day that Tante Magda was also visiting, and she sat with Tante Clara and Mama at the kitchen table, and as Sonya bounded down the stairs towards them, she announced: "I pooped and didn't use any toilet paper at all!" Tante Clara's eyes widened, and Tante Magda put her hand to her mouth to stifle a laugh. It didn't work. Pretty soon Magda was laughing uncontrollably. Poor Sonya, though, turned beet red, as Tante Clara pulled her over and whispered for her to go back upstairs and wipe herself.

Mama called us to come downstairs a short while later, and no one mentioned Sonya's shame. Tante Clara had brought potets kage, her culinary specialty and our favorite treat when spread with butter and sprinkled with sugar. We ate our fill of these tortilla-like, potato-based Norwegian staples rolled up. Mama admonished us not to be grisunge (little pigs), but Tante Clara just laughed and said, "Let them eat as much as they want. Potatoes don't cost much and see how they love them. Better they should eat these than junk."

One day, right after we had moved in, Tante Ragna, Mama's brother Leif's wife, traveled by Staten Island ferry to Brooklyn to visit, with Harold and Liv in tow, explaining that Karl and Johann were spending the week at the Pouch Boy Scout camp, so it was an "easy" week for her. There was a palpable excitement when they stepped into the house, since Mama was the youngest of the sisters, and now she actually owned real estate in America. Mama welcomed them proudly, set coffee on to perk, and sliced the Hazelnut Bar Cake that had come from the Dugan's bakery truck that regularly made rounds in our new neighborhood.

At the kitchen table, we said *I Jesu Navn* and devoured our slices of cake with glasses of saft. After our snack, Mama and Tante Ragna took a second cup of coffee into the living room and sat down to discuss matters, or should I say, church people, notably the women, who were members of disparate Norwegian congregations throughout Brooklyn and even Staten Island. How many churches were there after all? It seemed like thousands!

While the sisters-in-law kept up an animated conversation, we cousins were allowed to explore the neighborhood, with Ingy admonished to keep an eye on us, the three younger kids. I had not, until then, been allowed to venture beyond the corner of our street. That day, we went to the corner and turned right onto 11th Avenue, which intersected with our street. What grand houses stood on one side, neatly manicured, some with high steps and fenced-in front yards.

On the other side, where we walked stood a church, Saint Phillip's

Episcopal, with grounds grandly taking up the length of the city block. But on the next corner, just past the church, there was something even grander: a mansion with a big concrete wall and wrought iron gates in front of a driveway leading up to the house's big double doors. We gaped at the opulence, awestruck by what was in front of us. The grounds were manicured and garden-like. "Who could possibly live in such a place?" I asked.

"It has more than one family living in it," said Ingy authoritatively, giving me the disapproving look I had come to expect when I asked a dumb question.

We took it all in and once back home reported what we had seen. "That's nice," said Tante Ragna, "but that kind of church is just like Catholic, so that's not a place you want to be near."

"Yes, stay away, from that church," Mama said, then adding, "and that house, too," leaving us bewildered. We decided to retreat to my room to read comic books, and as we made our way upstairs, I heard Mama say, "That big house they talked about belongs to Anthony Anastasia, brother of Albert. God help us, what kind of neighborhood have we moved into." Anthony who? I thought. And what a strange name. Was "Anthony" like the Norwegian "Anton"? And that last name—it didn't end in "sen," "berg," "land," or "stad." There was so much to know about this new place where we lived.

In my room Harold complained that *Little Lulu*, the only comic book I was allowed to read, was stupid, so we parked ourselves on the floor and played Parcheesi until Tante Ragna called out that it was time to head back to Staten Island. "We'll walk to 69th Street and take the bus to the ferry," she said, and off they went.

Our first few weeks in our new house on 80th street between 10th and 11th Avenues were pleasant enough. I made friends with Neil, who lived next door. "Italian Catholics," said Mama of them with derision, but she didn't stop me from being friends with Neil. Our collective jobs were to keep the sidewalk in front of our adjoined houses cleanly swept. "Hey, "I said one day, as Neil swept debris from the sidewalk in front of his house to the sidewalk by mine, "I just swept that."

"Well, I don't want it," he said. So, with a deep sigh, I set about sweeping it back to his side, an act that infuriated him. He took up his broom and swept the debris right back again. I, of course, was equally infuriated, and we escalated to name calling—"Katolikker," I said.

"Boxhead," he said, staring me down.

When I told Mama what Neil had called me, she laughed and explained that "boxhead" is another name for "squarehead." "That's what they call us here." My fight with Neil that day was not the last, but we remained friends anyway.

Labor Day was approaching quickly, and we got together with Tante Clara for the great clothing exchange—who could fit into what and was it appropriate for school? What we got as hand-me-downs was supplemented by careful shopping trips—mostly to Lerner's on 5th Avenue or to May's in downtown Brooklyn, which we got to by taking the 4th Avenue subway—the RR train. It was never Abraham and Straus or Martin's, although Mama got many of her clothes there. "You grow so quickly, it's not worth spending so much money on your clothes," she explained when I asked why we couldn't just look in those stores.

As a result, the cheaper stores were mostly where we got our clothes. I remember those shopping forays, usually on Monday afternoons because Monday was the big bargain day, and we would come back with a big white bag that said "Every Day's a Sale Day at May's" in bold red letters. Getting a good buy was a good thing; that's one thing I knew for sure. That we were frugal was extremely important to Papa.

When we didn't find clothes that met Mama's strict criteria, we traveled to The City, which is what we called Manhattan, to shop at the big May's or S. Klein. For this outing we usually took the Sea Beach Express to 14th Street. This train had caned seats, and if the seats were torn, you could get a good scrape. But what an awesome thing The City was! The park across from the stores was bustling with people sitting on benches, reading newspapers, or eating hot dogs from the Sabrett's vendor. As intriguing as The

City was, it was always good to come back home to our own private house on 80th Street.

Labor Day that year before we started at our new school was a special treat. Papa was off from the boats, and we packed up the car and rode all the way to Coney Island, where we were to meet Papa's friend Ingvald and his wife, Dagmar, and their three boys, Ole-Jakob, Stein, and Nils. "Make sure you say, 'Mr. Samuelsen and Mrs. Samuelsen' if they speak to you," said Mama. "Be polite but say nothing unless they talk to you first."

We got to the beach early in the afternoon and met the Samuelsens by Bay 8th Street, then went together to the water's edge where we got to know the Samuelsen boys. Ole-Jakob was just a little older than Ingy, and I could tell she liked him immediately. Stein and Nils were twins a year younger than I; they had their own language, part Norwegian, part English, and part made up and known only to them. I was fascinated.

We body surfed in the waves that rolled us up to shore, and then Mama and Mrs. Samuelsen called us to the blankets they had spread on the sand for a picnic supper of gjetost sandwiches, the cheese we called brown soap, and saft in paper cups.

Soon it was time to leave, and we said our goodbyes, piled into the Chevy, and headed back to our part of Brooklyn. I chatted about how we had made new friends, and I was sure Ingy would marry Ole-Jakob someday. "That's ridiculous," Ingy scoffed, but I could tell she was pleased.

After Ingy bathed, I did so as well to rid myself of sand that had found its way into every fold and crevice on my body, and Mama put Noxema on my red and tender skin. Then it was off to bed. The next day was going to be a big one: our first day at PS 201.

Mama made "havregrøt" (oatmeal) for breakfast, even though it was still quite warm outside. "You need a good breakfast so you can stay alert and pay attention." Then, "Listen carefully to what your teacher says. I'll be waiting to hear all about it when you come home."

"Aren't you going to walk with us to school?" I asked.

"Ingrid knows the way," Mama explained, then added, "Hold hands when you cross the streets."

"Great," Ingy muttered to herself, but I knew Mama had heard her.

Off we went, Ingy marching ahead, and me trailing behind until we got to the curb and had to cross an avenue. Then Ingy took my hand, releasing it with force as soon as we were on the sidewalk on the other side. In this manner we made our way to the big brick building that was PS 201. Right about then I felt my chest constrict and I couldn't breathe. I couldn't get air out so I could get air in. "Wait," I said to Ingy. "I can't go in."

"You have to," Ingy said taking both of my hands in hers, being kind. "Mama enrolled you, and they are expecting you in your classroom."

Slowly I made my way up the stairs to the big door, and right there was a woman who smiled at me and asked if I was a new student and who my teacher was. I responded "yes" and "Mrs. Smith." Then the woman checked a list, noting that I was on the premises, and gave one of several older students a card with my name on it and told her to take me to my room.

"I'm Rebecca," the girl said. "Come with me," and she took me by the hand, and we made our way to my classroom. That wasn't so bad, I thought, until we were through the door and into the room and Rebecca, reading my name on the card she held, announced, "This is Saul vagg Toor grr seen." I felt my face get hot and then that breathing thing started again as some of the students snickered.

"They called me 'Sue' at my old school," I mumbled.

"Welcome, Sue," said the teacher. "I'm Mrs. Smith, and we're going to have a good time this year. Your seat is right there in the fourth row, two down." I gratefully took my seat, and the day progressed.

Ingy waited for me outside the main entrance after the dismissal bell rang, and we made our way home. "This school is going to be really easy, after PS 127," Ingy said. "I already had some of the math we're going to do here."

Well, good for you, I thought. I was still apprehensive. PS 201 seemed so far from home and the neighborhood so foreign. But I got used to it, and after a while it didn't seem too bad. Besides, there were other things going on that were quite good.

Sunday School was starting up again, and I had another year to work on a bar for my perfect attendance pin. And there was a Sunday School picnic to kick of the new year. That would surely be fun.

When Papa came home from the boats one day, he announced, "I have some good news. I have been talking to Ingvald Samuelsen about 66th Street church. You know he still thinks there's no heaven, only Valhalla. It's so frustrating, but I told him how good the church was for the family, and that we are mostly all Norwegians, and not only that, but Norwegians from the south of Norway just like him. I told him in no uncertain terms, however, that church was not a 'social club' but a place of worship and going would be good for his boys and his wife, Dagmar."

Wow, I thought, my new friends Stein and Nils might be in my Sunday School class. Wouldn't that be something? And sure enough, the very next Sunday there they were, but they were in a different class, the one Sonya was in, since they were younger by a year. But there was sad news, too. When we got home from church and were getting ready to have middags, I heard Papa talking to Mama about Gunnar.

"It's so sad that he's gone. They said it was a heart attack and very sudden," Papa said. Wait. Wasn't that the same Gunnar who was a deacon at church, the one who said he wasn't going to die, and that he would live to the second coming? I guessed Papa was right: no one knows.

The weeks passed, and I went to Sunday School and then the Norwegian department church services at 66th Street every week. At PS 201, I developed a routine and walked home the same way every day, usually following Ingy ten steps behind, as she pretended I didn't exist. After all, she was almost a teenager, and I was just a kid. I got it. We always walked down the driveway when we got to our house on 80th Street. The back door was the one we used, to save on the carpet in the living room which came right up to the front door.

Then one day when I came home from school, trailing Ingy by a good five minutes, I heard Mama and Tante Hedwig deep in discussion. When I let myself in, they were at the kitchen table, their hair in tight rollers with paper in each—and what was that stink? I had smelled it before. It wasn't pleasant. "What are you doing?" I asked.

"I am getting a Toni, Solveig. To curl my hair," said Mama. "We want to look good, because we have a very special event coming up."

Tante Hedwig always addressed me and the other kids in the family in English, unlike her sisters, who mostly spoke to us in Norwegian or a mix of English and Norwegian. She seemed proud that, as the older sister and the last to come to America, she had mastered this language. "Well, I am getting a Lilt because I am more particulate," she said. "Lilt is better." Tante Hedwig always used such big words, I thought. Why didn't she speak to us like Mama and Tante Clara did in Norwegian? I, like Ingy and my cousins, mostly answered either language in English anyway.

"Why are you getting permanents?" I wanted to know. "It stinks."

Mama said, "Don't be fresh." Then, "Bestmor is coming to Brooklyn."

"Wow," I said, trying to picture the Grandmother I sort of

remembered from when I was three. "Is Bestefar coming, too?" I knew they still lived on Jorstad, for my mother talked with her sisters about Mor and Far (mother and father) often.

"No," said Mama, and paused, taking a deep breath. "It's very sad. Our father has died. It was a few months ago, but I didn't want to tell you because I didn't want you to feel bad. That's why our mother is coming alone." That's a good reason to bring her here, I thought. I would have a real grandmother, one I would be able to talk about at school, just like the other kids did.

Soon Andrea Gabrealsen was to arrive in New York via the Norwegian-American line. The family coordinated preparations to make the matriarch's first taste of America as impressive as could be. Tante Clara and Onkel Olav were to go to New York to pick her up, and with Papa on the boats, Mama, Ingy, and I would be with our cousins at Tante Clara's flat on 67th Street to await our grandmother's arrival. Tante Hedwig, Onkel Werner, Magnhild, and maybe Gudrun would be there too, they said. Good, I thought. As young as I was, I was fascinated by Onkel Werner, who was by far the best-looking man in the family.

On the eventful day, we got ready for the big event. Mama made us each take a bath, then clipped my fingernails. I hated that, because she always cut them so close that my fingertips bled and would hurt for a day or two. Ingy never had her nails cut. She did that all by herself with her teeth. Her fingertips weren't so good-looking either. Then we got dressed in our Sunday clothes and Mary Jane shoes for me, flats without straps for Ingy, the ones Mama had polished so they looked like patent leather. We looked ready for church, but it was Monday, so it was a little strange.

I was awed as I watched Mama, with her recently curled hair, put on her veiled hat and one of her best dresses and high-heeled red shoes, strappy and open, showing a lot of her feet. She turned her back to us and asked, "Are the seams on my stockings straight?"

"Yup," we replied. Then we put on our coats—it was already cold in early October—and Mama draped her stone martens over her shoulders. We certainly weren't going to walk to Tante Clara's, not with Mama in those shoes! And sure enough, Mama backed the Chevy out of the garage and Ingy and I got in, Ingy in the front passenger seat, and me in the back, squarely in the middle so I could see through the car's windshield.

Mama drove to 67th Street, but there wasn't a parking spot to be found. She circled the block several times looking to park as close to Tante Clara's as possible. Then we waited, double parked, for 15 minutes, until a man got in a car and pulled away. Into the spot went the Powerglide, with the feelers scraping the curb. Then we got out and walked half a block to Tante Clara and Onkel Olav's flat. It had started to rain, and Mama fussed, holding her purse over her head and urging us to hurry up.

Our cousin Bente greeted us at the door, and we could see she was upset. "Mama and Papa left an hour ago for New York and the ship," she said. "Mama is going to be furious when she sees what Tor Asbjørn has done."

"What has he done?" asked Mama, aghast.

"He has torn up his Christening certificate, and Mama and Papa will blame me for not stopping him. But I couldn't," Bente wailed.

Mama went right to Tor Asbjørn's room, and we followed, still in our coats. There he was sitting on the floor in tears of rage. I had never seen him cry, and I never expected him to act like a girl.

"Tormann—what are you doing?" Mama said, clearly worried that her sister might hold her accountable. "That's your Christening certificate!" Next to Tor Asbjørn lay an empty frame surrounded by bits of torn paper, a large piece still in his hand.

Tor Asbjørn gave the last piece a violent rip and said, "My friend Eddie was here and saw it and called me 'Tor Ass Burn,'" he said. Ingy giggled while Bente told Mama, "I tried to stop him, but you know how strong and stubborn he can be!"

Mama then said to Tor Asbjørn, "Just stop. You don't have to use your middle name. Just go by 'Tor.'"

"That's a stupid name, too. Why couldn't I be 'Robert' or 'Charley'?" Tor Asbjørn said as he stormed from the room and headed toward the front door. Where would he go? Surely not outside, for it was raining pretty hard by then.

"You are a Norwegian boy. It's fitting that you have a name that tells where you came from," Mama called after him. "And now I have to make supper to feed all of us and my mother, so don't go outside."

It wasn't long after that Tante Hedwig, Onkel Werner, and their two youngest daughters, the ones we called Goody and Maggy, showed up at the door. Maggy had her boyfriend, Axel, in tow, her hand firmly on his arm as she led him into the living room. Tante Hedwig, taking off her damp coat, said, "Rainy weather is hard on the sciences." Then she pulled a hankie from her purse and blew her nose with gusto. Goody rolled her eyes.

We were actually surprised to see Goody, since she rarely came to visit, and we hadn't been expecting her to be here. Like Maggy, she still lived with her parents on 57th Street, but was standoffish—you could tell she was finer than we were. "A snob," Mama often said of her, and sometimes "condescending." Fifty-Seventh Street was also where Onkel Sverre stayed when he wasn't working. He must have been gone that day, because if he weren't he would surely have been at Tante Clara's to welcome his mother.

Maggy said, "You all know Axel, don't you?" I thought to myself, as I usually did when in his presence, he gives me the creeps.

Axel said self-assuredly, "Good day everyone," and then proceeded to give the girls, especially Ingy and Bente, hardy hugs. "You are so beautiful," he said to them.

Onkel Werner asked Mama what was going on with Tor Asbjørn, who was still sniffling and red eyed. She told him in no uncertain terms, adding that she hoped the church could make a duplicate of the certificate. Onkel Werner had a good laugh directed at Tor Asbjørn, then said, "You know I used to hate my name, too. My parents said 'Werner' very nicely, since my mother was English by birth, and pronouncing things correctly was important to her. By the way, that's why I can speak English pretty well, too. Because of my mother's insistence, people we knew in Germany could say my name correctly, once you told them how, beginning with a w, not a v. But most people who didn't know us well pronounced my name 'Verner,' just like they do in Norway and you do here."

"Wait," I said. "What were you doing in Germany?"

"I grew up there, in Berlin. My mother met my father, who is

German, in London, while he was there on business; they married, and then they moved to Germany, where I was born. My parents had a nice apartment in the city," said Onkel Werner, "and they both spoke English and German to me, so I grew up bilingual."

"Wait," said Bente. "I thought you were Norwegian. You speak it just like the family does. How in the world did you meet Tante Hedwig?"

"After the First World War, there was a depression, and things were not going so well in Germany. There was a Juggenbund, an official Nazi party group that so many young people were joining. My parents didn't want me to be in the Hitler Youth, so they encouraged me to do other things. I came to Norway for the first time with a German youth group to hike in the Norwegian mountains."

What was he saying? Mama had told me Tante Hedwig and Onkel Werner had come to America from Norway. I hadn't known Onkel Werner was German, that he had grown up in Berlin. I had heard a little about Berlin from our cousin Ole, who had been in the Norwegian army and stationed there for a while. Berlin was a big city. Wasn't living in a big city much better than living in southern Norway? It was a puzzle.

Hesitatingly, I asked, "Did you stay in Norway, then?"

“Well,” he said, “I met Hedwig on one of those hiking trips, and as they say, ‘the rest is history.’ Of course, I went home to Germany, and when I had finished school, I came back to Norway. For Hedwig,” he added.

What we young cousins learned that day was that we didn’t call him “Werner” with a “w,” which was obviously his real name. We all said “Onkel Verner” when we talked to our handsome uncle, the one who always had something clever and amusing to say to us. He made us feel like we were almost adults. He made us happy. Pretty soon Onkel Werner had Tor Asbjørn laughing like conspirators at the silly names Americans gave their kids.

“Yeah, what about Elizabeth?” said my cousin. “Sounds like ‘lizard breath.’”

"How about Miranda? I did some work for a woman named Miranda, and her kids called her veranda—that's a porch," said Onkel Werner.

“That’s nothing,” said Tor Asbjørn. “Eddie’s sister is Veronica, but we both call her ‘Moronica,’ or ‘Harmonica.’” Tor Asbjørn had recovered from his fit of pique, evidenced by his laughter. He loved Onkel Werner as much as we did, that was obvious. “And there’s a boy in my class named ‘Bruce,’ and I told him one day his real name is ‘soda,’ ‘cause that’s what we call soda in Norwegian, ‘brus,’” he said.

Ingy joined in with, "We have a cousin in New Jersey whose name is Odd," and she pronounced it in correct Norwegian, which sounded like 'Uhdd.' "I bet they call him "odd" or "strange" at school."

"Yes," said Onkel Werner, "names can be puzzling. There's even a movie star, John Wayne, whose real name is 'Marion.' I'll bet pretty soon people will be making up names for their kids, instead of using perfectly good names we all know."

Just then Bente piped up with "Some of the kids called me 'Bent Girl' in school, so I said to call me 'Benny,' and now they do.

"Wait," chimed in Tor Asbjørn, "we have a girl named Beirit in our class. Some of the boys call her 'bare it.'"

With that, Mama said sharply, "That's enough name calling. It's not nice."

With that Mama and Tante Hedwig proceeded to the kitchen to finish cooking the kjøtt suppe (beef soup) that Clara had started before setting out to fetch her mother. It was simmering on the stove, and Ingy and Bente set the kitchen table, which had been extended to its full length and augmented with a card table so we could all dine together. Alice, Sonya, and I played paper dolls in their bedroom as we waited for the big event. The excitement was palpable. Maggy sat on the sofa, leaning on Axel, who, I should say, didn't seem that interested in her. Nope, he seemed more fascinated by Ingy and Bente.

And then the door opened, and they were here.

The old woman took everything in as they came through the door. After Onkel Olav had taken her coat and said in that Sørlands dialect we all spoke, "See, here are your American grandchildren." She came up to each of us and held us each in turn by the shoulders to have a good, close look. I think I saw tears in her eyes. I certainly smelled a strong musty odor emanating from her corpulent being. While she held me, she said, "You have certainly grown since I saw you last."

While she said this, I heard Mama whisper to her sister, in English, so their mother wouldn't understand, "Did you point out my car?"

"No," Clara hissed back. "It was raining too hard. Besides, we couldn't see where you were parked, and Olav got busy with the luggage." I could see Mama was disappointed. After all, she was the only one of our grandmother's daughters who could actually drive. Her lips were pursed together in a thin, straight line.

Bestemor then hugged my mother and Tante Hedwig, in a kind of a-frame way—not too close with the body parts. Then she took Onkel Werner's hand. "It's good to see you are living well in America, Werner," she said to him, and smiled warmly. "It's better for you to be far away from Europe." We knew then that she thought he was something, too! It was clear as well that she knew he was different from the rest of us.

When it was time to eat, Tor Asbjørn whispered to me, "I'm not eating any shit soup." Sure, kjøtt was the Norwegian name for meat, but it sounded like "shit" in English. Okay, I thought, maybe I wouldn't either.

When we sat down to eat, we said *I Jesu Navn*, which I could tell Bestemor really liked. Then we passed the food—boiled beef, carrots, and potatoes in a broth with islands of fat floating on top.

"Look at the pearls floating on top," said Tante Clara proudly in her best Norwegian. "What a fine meal." We all knew Clara to be 'the cook' in the family. In Norway, she had gone to cooking school. As a result, the expectation was always that meals on 67th Street would be superb.

"It's a prefect Norwegian meal, a real feets," pronounced Tante Hedvig in her unique English. This, I'm sure, was to let her mother know how well she had mastered the language of the land they now lived in, even though her mother understood not a word. But Tor Asbjørn and I refused to eat. And seeing that we would not eat, Alice and Sonya refused too.

"Well, you can just sit there, all four of you, until you decide to eat what we put in your bowl," said Onkel Olav in English. But there wasn't much rancor in his voice; it was more like amusement.

Sit there we did, talking and laughing at the table until it was time to go. We never did eat the soup, which had become cold and the "pearls" floating on top had congealed into solid fat. What our grandmother thought of all this, we didn't know. What we did know, because the grownups had talked about it during our meal, was that our grandmother would spend her time living with her various children. As it turned out in time, she liked living with Hedwig and Werner the best, but that flat on 57th Street had to have been mighty crowded.

Chapter Six

The World Comes In

We were going to Tante Hedwig and Onkel Werner's house late one Saturday afternoon for an event we had anticipated eagerly. Onkel Werner had bought a Dumont television, and we would be able to watch it. I was no stranger to TV since some of my friends had television sets, and if I visited with them after school, I got to watch *The Mickey Mouse Club.* But this was big—no one in the family had owned a TV until now.

We had frequently asked Papa why we couldn't have one, and he said, "It will bring the world into the house, and we don't want that." What this told me was that that was the position of authority from our church. Since Tante Hedwig, Onkel Werner, and their daughters all attended the 59th Street church, Ingy said it must be okay for that congregation to own TVs. Personally, I thought money might have something to do with it.

When we got to Tante Hedwig's, the TV was already on. It was housed in a wooden cabinet and had a 12-inch screen, and our cousins from 67th Street were already sitting on the floor in front of it, hardly glancing our way as we came in. We plopped ourselves on the rug and crowded in as close as we could, enraptured by the screen before us.

We were many in the flat that day. Tante Hedwig and Onkel Werner's three daughters were all there. Goody and Maggy we knew well because they lived with their parents, but Dagmar was a rare sight. I had often heard Tante speak of her—she was a career woman driven to succeed in business. That she lived in The City was awesome enough, but she also worked at Gimbels on 34th Street, right next to Macy's, two stores too expensive for us to frequent.

Having a rare Saturday off, she had traveled on the Sea Beach Express to the 8th Avenue station and walked from there to her parents' place in really high heels and a tight gray wool skirt, which I thought must have made the walk a challenge. I could tell immediately that Ingy and Bente were awed by her style. She was sophisticated, with a colorful kerchief tied around her neck and flowing over a light purple cardigan sweater buttoned up the back. She was a cut above the young women we typically saw in Brooklyn, that was for certain.

I was trying to place her in the context of her family. I thought, let me get this straight: Tante Hedwig's sons and daughters are all my cousins. I had heard Tante Hedwig talk about "the boys and their families" on Long Island, but these cousins I didn't really know. But today, Dagmar, the oldest daughter and the most elegant, had graced us with her presence. She had an aura about her that was hard to define; she was mysterious.

With Maggy was her boyfriend, Axel, whom I didn't like one bit. Dagmar was seated next to them on the living room's overstuffed sofa, replete with pretty arm and head rest coverings that Tante Hedwig had crocheted. When Ingy commented on how skilled Tante Hedwig was at crocheting, Dagmar explained, "They are supposed to keep the furniture clean. Mother calls them 'madagascars.'" With that explanation she gave a little laugh.

Suddenly the screen started to look like snow. With that, Maggy said, "I can fix that," and came to the TV and moved the thin metal rods that sat atop the set. "'Rabbit ears,'" she explained, as the screen slowly resumed its images. I glanced at Axel, who was looking furtively at Dagmar while Maggy's back was to him. There was more than one show in progress.

In the kitchen, my parents were having coffee and smørbrod with Bestemor and my Brooklyn aunts and uncles. Mama's brother Sverre and sister Magda were there, too, but these two stood in the archway that led into the living room with Goody, the three as fixated on the TV as we were.

Bestemor, curious at the noise emanating from the living room, wandered to the archway and stopped, dumbstruck. She was astounded that sound and picture could come through a box on the floor. "Now I've seen everything!" she exclaimed. That made us giggle. She then made her retreat back to the kitchen and her daughters and their husbands—and, of course, the coffee and smørbrod.

Pretty soon, Goody went to the kitchen and came back with a plate of smørbrod for us too, and we picnicked on the floor in front of the set. Tor Asbjørn evidently knew a thing or two about TVs since many of his friends had them. He announced, "It's going on 7 o'clock. Let's put on CBS and watch *The Gene Autry Show.*"

"That's the 'singing cowboy,'" said Onkel Sverre. "Who do you like better, Gene Autry or Roy Rogers?" he asked us all. I, of course, knew about neither one.

Just then Papa popped into the room and announced, "No cowboys who carry guns. That's not what you want to see. Change the channel." That reconfirmed for me that Papa could be having an adult conversation in a different room while still being aware of everything we were doing. He didn't miss a thing.

Tor Asbjørn turned the channel to NBC, and we watched *Mr. Wizard*. It was pretty interesting, but the screen repeatedly got fuzzy, and Maggy kept authoritatively adjusting the rabbit ears for us, and each time she did, Axel took the opportunity to admire Dagmar.

Soon, alas, we had to go home because we had to get a good night's sleep to be fresh for church in the morning. In the Powerglide heading back to 80th Street, Ingy and I once more entreated our parents to get a TV. "No," said Papa. "We are not bringing the world into our Christian home." Okay, that's settled, then, I thought, and Ingy and I laughed a little at our grandmother's amazement at modern technology.

But it turned out she had a few more amazements coming. It was soon to be Hallowe'en, and we prepared with gusto. I would be a hobo carrying a stick with a sack, wearing one of Papa's old flannel shirts and loose pants gathered at the waist with a rope. This Hallowe'en we would go to Tante Clara's, and I would go trick or treating with Tor Asbjørn, Alice, and Sonya. Ingy and Bente had determined this event would be too childish for them, since they were teenagers.

We were in the living room, all set to leave the flat and venture outside. Alice was dressed as a princess, and Sonya as a nurse. Tor

Asbjørn had a Lone Ranger mask and a gun belt with a toy gun tucked in it. He informed us he was going trick or treating with his friend Eddie, not us. "Oh sure, because you can't be seen with three girls, can you?" smirked Alice.

Just then, Bestemor came from the kitchen with Mama and Tante Clara to see how we were dressed for this American custom. "You all look like the real thing," Mama commented encouragingly, then added "be careful and stay together, girls, so you'll be safe." Bestemor, however, was wide eyed. She just stopped still and blanched. "Now I've seen everything," she said.

Tante Clara explained what Hallowe'en was like in America to our grandmother. "You mean the children actually go begging?" she said, aghast.

"It's not really 'begging' but more like a tradition here," Mama interjected. "It's all in good fun."

It was just dusk, and we set out. What a trio we girls were as we marched up to front doors, rang bells, and waited for them to open. Most people gave us candy, some hand-wrapped in little waxed paper bundles tied with string. But some gave us pieces of fruit or nickels and pennies. What a bounty we collected. We hurried back to Tante Clara's and spread our loot on the kitchen table, making comparisons and exchanging treasures with each other. Whoever didn't like Tootsie Rolls got to exchange them for Life Savers. It was a satisfying ritual, and I could tell Ingy was sorry she hadn't gone with us.

"Where is Tor Asbjørn?" asked Tante Clara. "Did you see him when you were on the street?"

"Not at first," said Alice, "but a little later we saw him with Eddie. They were laughing pretty good."

No sooner had she said that than the doorbell rang. Clara went to answer, and we could hear an angry male voice. That spurred Onkel Olav to walk toward the door as well. Of course, we girls quietly moved into the hall to hear what was going on. In the doorway stood Mr. Jensen, a neighbor from the street, with Tor Asbjørn by the arm. "The doorbell rang. I came to the door, and no one was there," Mr. Jensen fumed, "but there was a paper bag on fire, all by itself, on the front steps. So, I stepped on it immediately to put the fire out. And the bag was full of dog shit! Look at my shoes!"

"Oh my goodness," said Tante Clara. "Tor Asbjørn, how could you do that to poor Mr. Jensen?" Tor Asbjørn looked sheepish, but I could tell he was readily enjoying every minute of the drama. Mr. Jensen was muttering under his breath and left in a huff. "Deal with that boy," he said as he strode off.

"Boys will be boys," said Onkel Olav, throwing his hands in the air behind his wife, but he didn't seem all that concerned. Once Mr. Jensen was out of earshot, Onkel Olav turned to Tor Asbjørn and asked, "What in the world made you think to do that?"

"Hey, the street is full of dog shit," he said. "And anyway, it was Eddie's idea, but it was sure funny," he added.

"It won't be so funny when you can't play outside for a week," said Onkel Olav. "Maybe then you'll think twice before you do something like that again."

"What in the world happened?" asked Bestemor, and Mama tried to explain. Well, then Bestemor started to laugh, and it was uncontrollable. Soon she was wiping tears from her eyes, and we started to laugh, too, simply because it was contagious.

Life progressed and after a while we were happy to learn that Mr. Jensen had calmed down some and even saw the humor in what Tor Asbjørn had done. As for me, I hoped I would remember the prank and carry it out next year.

Brooklyn gave us another opportunity to go begging. In school in November, we had made Pilgrim hats and bonnets, and on Thanksgiving Day, we would wear them, going door to door, ringing bells, and asking, "Anything for Thanksgiving?"

Sometimes people would simply say, "No." But other times they'd give us an apple or nickel.

The Thanksgiving after the burning bag incident was an especially good one, since it was the first uniquely American holiday that Bestemor would experience, and it would be at our house on 80th Street. In the weeks before, Mama had been busy, and she put us to work as well. I dusted the venetian blinds row by row, Ingy washed windows, and we polished the Norwegian silver cutlery till it shone. This year we would be many. Tante Hedwig, Onkel Werner, and Dagmar, Goody, and Maggy were to come, and probably that creepy boyfriend Axel, too. So were Tante Clara, Onkel Olav, Bente, Tor Asbjørn, Alice, and Sonya, and Onkel Sverre and Tante Magda, as well.

"What about Tante Ragna and Onkel Leif?" I asked. "Are they coming, too?" And what about Tante Signe and Tante Marit in New Jersey?

"We can't have everybody," Mama explained. "There's not enough room at the table. And Tante Signe and Tante Marit are not related to Bestemor. They are on Papa's side of the family. We're just having Bestemor's Brooklyn family this Thanksgiving." Man, it was hard to keep track of who was who.

We had a big turkey, the traditional fare with all the trimmings, eating earlier than usual for a Thursday—mid-afternoon and later than our Sunday middags. We children stood by the table and, in unison, said *I Jesu Navn,* and then Papa gave a little prayer of blessing for all of us. With that, Ingy and I along with Bente, Tor Asbjørn, Alice, and Sonya retreated to the kitchen table, because, as I said, it was a full house. We didn't have to watch our manners or the way we sat at the table because the adults were engrossed in conversation and couldn't see us. I noticed, though, that Bente was miffed. "Why do Dagmar, Goody, and Maggy get to sit in the dining room? They're cousins, too, just like us."

Ingy replied, "It's not fair, but they're older than we are, so that's probably why Mama put them at the grownups' table."

"Yeah, even Maggy's boyfriend, that Axel," added Bente disdainfully. And we continued to eat our meals quietly while Tor Asbjørn made a mashed potato volcano spewing gravy lava.

After dinner, we felt stuffed, and Ingy poked her head into the dining room and said, "May we be excused?" With affirmation, Ingy and Bente retired to Ingy's room to listen to the radio. The rest of us kids set out to ring a few doorbells while our mothers cleaned up and the fathers talked about the red menace and the spread of communism. And Papa and the his brothers-in-law clearly had solutions for the world's problems, if only the politicians would wise up and do the right thing.

When we got back to the house with our paltry "anything-for-Thanksgiving" pickings, we used the back door leading into the kitchen, and immediately heard the grownups and Goody and Maggy deep in discussion in the living room. So naturally we stood very still and listened, as was our habit. You never knew what you would hear, and this was quite a conversation, mostly in Norwegian, but with our cousins Dagmar, Goody, Maggy, and Tante Hedwig chiming in in English.

Mama was saying to her brother Sverre in earnest, "I know you love Gerd, but you have to stop thinking about marriage. It's not for you."

Hedwig chimed in with "Don't upset the apple tart. Things may still work out with Reidun." What? Who was Reidun anyway?

"Look," said Sverre, "I will probably never see Reidun again. Or my little girl. She is almost grown up now I imagine."

"I know you tried to find them," said Onkel Werner soothingly.

"Germany is a big country, and I surely tried after the war, but the way that country was bombed, it's a miracle there were any records at all." Sverre explained. "As soon as I could after the war I went to Norway to enquire about her. Someone told me Reidun and her

German officer had gone to Dresden to live, and that city was devastated even more than Berlin. So, yes, I tried to find my wife and child, the one who thinks that German soldier is her father."

At that Goody spoke up. "You have a daughter, then. Why did you leave them in Norway?"

Sverre, sounding exasperated, said, "I didn't leave them. The war stranded me in New York. I was with the Norwegian Merchant Marine when the Germans invaded, and we went to America to keep the Germans from taking the boats. All on board were stuck with no way to get back to Norway."

"Okay," said Goody, "That's how you somehow came to be in the U.S. Merchant Marine. I always wondered."

"Sverre," said Mama, "I know it's hard for you, but you can't marry Gerd if you're already married to someone else."

"You know," said Tante Hedwig, "It turned out to be a blessing in the skies after all. If you had been in Norway, you might have been kilt by the Germans. Many people died trying to free the land from the Nazis.

"Safe!" exclaimed Sverre, exasperated. "The ship I was on was torpedoed by the Germans off the coast of Georgia! What do you mean safe? It amazes me so few people know the Germans were in U.S. waters taking down ships carrying war supplies. Why in 1942 alone, when the *SS Byron D. Benson*, the ship I was on, went down, 10 of the 37 men on board died. I was one of the lucky ones. I was on watch on the deck that night."

Onkel Werner spoke up then and said, "The war caused great tragedies on all sides. I learned that along the east coast of America, 175 ships were lost, and in the Gulf of Mexico, 46 ships went down. Mostly what we hear about are the battles and mass murders in the camps but little about the countless lives lost supporting the war effort for the U.S."

"Yes, the war took a terrible toll. Don't think for a minute that I didn't experience the it," said Sverre. "And my tragedy was also that I lost my family. Don't you think I deserve a little happiness? Gerd and I are going to live together, then, if we can't get married."

"Oh my," said Mama. "You can't do that. What will people say? What will I say to people when they say my brother is living in sin?"

"People be damned," said Sverre. "I don't care." With that Mama gasped audibly. We all knew "damn" was a curse and thus a sin. Hedwig interjected with "Sverre, listen to reason..."

At that point Sonya sneezed loudly enough that the adults heard, and there was a heavy pause in the conversation. Then Papa said, "Ya, ya. Look, here are the kids."

That family dinner had left us awed to learn that our uncle might have been lost at sea, the victim of a German torpedo. And we were surely wondering about a cousin we evidently had, whom we didn't know, had never even heard of before, and was living in Germany. What was her name? What a conundrum. But we vowed somehow we'd find out more about her. We never did. We were smart enough, however, not to question the grownups, and we kept what we had heard to ourselves.

About a week after that big family Thanksgiving, Papa announced that he had a surprise for us, and that we would like what we saw when we got home from school. I had a hard time concentrating in class, and rushed home from school when we were dismissed. "My, did you fly?" asked Mama. "It's not even ten past three, and here you are already."

"Where's the surprise?" I demanded. I could hardly breathe and was having that anxiety thing again.

"Calm down," said Papa. "There's enough air for everyone to breathe. Go look in the living room."

I promptly did, and there it was: a television. It was nestled into a mahogany cabinet that stood as tall as my chest, and it had doors that could shut and hide the screen. It was a dandy Philco. Pretty cool, I thought. If anyone from church came, my parents could simply shut the door and pretend it was a storage chest.

"Is it ours? Are we going to keep it?" I asked eagerly.

"Yes," Papa said, "But we will be very careful about what we watch. I bought it because the evangelist Billy Graham's *Hour of Decision* is on each Sunday night. You can watch TV, but only the shows your Mama and I permit you to."

We now had a TV! I could invite my next-door neighbor Neil in to watch, and maybe my 79th Street friends Mary Anne and Gina would come, too. But truth be known, I didn't see them that much anymore. Besides, Mary Anne had told me that her parents had bought a house in Dix Hills on Long Island and would be moving soon. Still, sad as that was, I had a TV. It was progress. It wasn't too long after that the *Hour of Decision* was canceled, but we kept the TV anyway.

We became fans of *The Colgate Comedy Hour* and *Arthur Godfrey's Talent Scouts*. We had ABC, CBS, and NBC to choose from. CBS brought us *The Jackie Gleason Show* on Saturday nights and *Two for the Money*. These were "healthy" programs, my parents said. But sometimes I would have the TV to myself. That's when I got a glimpse of Uncle Fultie, as Bishop Fulton Sheen called himself on his show *Life is Worth Living.* I was fascinated. He was dressed in a black cape and literally floated across the stage where he preached to the TV audience. Then, of course, Papa came into the living room and shut the TV off. "You may not watch that Catholic!" Again with the Catholics! What was up with that?

But I soon learned Protestant evangelists were televising as well. These were the ones Papa liked to watch. They had just as much gumption as Uncle Fultie on the screen—calling, no, screaming for people to repent and "come to the Lord." And, I can't forget, "Drive the demons away," and "Heal her now!" I witnessed people who were wheelchair-bound rise and walk because their faith was strong enough. Truly it was miraculous. One day when I had fallen while roller skating and scraped my knee, I decided to put my faith to the test. I found that televangelist, the one Papa liked, spewing forth salvation and healing.

"You must have faith. If your faith is strong enough, you will be healed," he declared boisterously while the audience said things like "Yes, Lord," and "Bring on the power of the Lord."

I closed my eyes and called upon the Lord to heal my wounded knee. I put my hand on the TV and stood patiently by. I waited while the televangelist healed a crippled man using crutches, and the man threw them down and walked up and down on the platform. Then I looked at my bloody knee. Still bloody, it was, so I concluded I must not have enough faith.

My knee healed by itself, despite my lack of faith. Our family soon settled into a TV routine. *Father Knows Best* was a hit with us, as was *December Bride* and *I Love Lucy*, even though Lucille Ball was married to a Cuban who was most likely Catholic to boot. *Kukla, Fran, and Ollie, Rin Tin Tin*, and *Lassie* were acceptable, too. But best of all, according to my parents, was *I Remember Mama.* Of course, it was. Mama on that show was Norwegian!

Once word that we had a TV got out, there was talk. I remember being outside our church and hearing Mr. Christiansen, one of the church deacons, admonish Papa for having brought "the world into your home." Papa replied calmly, "Well, you know if you don't want to see what's on TV, you can just turn it off. It's not on all the time, you know."

Then Papa said something profound: "Television will revolutionize evangelism. Think of the people it will reach. It will change the way people hear the message. Think of what it must have been like before the printing press. Once the world had that, people could actually read scripture for themselves. Now they'll be able to hear and see the God's word being preached."

"I agree we are in an age where there will be repentance and commitment to God," replied Mr. Christiansen. "But people may come to think they can attend church at home by turning on a television. That will keep them from church, not in," he declared solemnly.

"What will bring them to church are revivals," said Papa.

"Ah," said Mr. Christiansen, "we are planning to have Jack Wyrtsen come here. We have been talking to his team."

Papa then said, "What about Billy Graham? I think he's the man of God who will truly bring more people to Christ."

"Him? He's 'Mr. Facing Two Ways,'" said Mr. Christiansen. "Graham has been criticized for his unscriptural direction by such great spiritual leaders as Oral Roberts. Why he even invites Catholics and Jews to his rallies. Disgraceful! He just doesn't have the right attitude. He is disobedient to the commands of the *Bible*. He's just a Fuller Brush man, but instead of selling brushes, he's selling religion."

"Well," Papa slowly responded, "he is a good salesman, and what better product to sell than salvation?"

"Humph," responded Mr. Christensen. "Graham is a fraud, an opportunist. There are real evangelists out there. Wyrsten and

Roberts are both true men of God. Why Wyrtsen even attended Oral Roberts University!" Then he added, almost as an after-thought: "Evangelicalism is not just about saving souls. Evangelicalism is anti-communism."

I stood there listening to this debate, really a lecture delivered to Papa, wondering if communism—the thing we had so often heard the grown-ups talking about with fear and loathing—was something that could take hold here in America. Papa simply said in response, "Ya, ya."

Then Mr. Christiansen added, "We will be announcing a revival meeting soon. All the churches here will. There's a tent meeting planned for next month right on 60th Street, between 8th and 9th Avenues."

That revival on 60th Street did occur in late spring, when it was warm enough to sit outdoors in the fresh air. Flyers handed out in Protestant churches throughout Brooklyn read, "Come hear the man of God Preach. This is the Voice of Healing."

Of course, our family went. Ingy and I didn't have to get dressed in our Sunday clothes, though, because the meeting was outside under a huge brown canvas tent, held high by wooden pillars and fastened down with ropes tied to stakes in the ground. The earth beneath our feet was carpeted with hay—not too deep but enough to keep your shoes from getting muddy.

There was an air of excitement, palpable almost. An upright piano had been brought in, and a woman pounded out *Leaning on the Everlasting Arms* as we took our seats, and many people sang along, even though there were no hymnals. This was a song we all pretty well knew, a favorite from Sunday School, and it was in English. In fact, the whole meeting was in English.

Pretty soon the preacher began to do his thing—with a big, black *Bible* in one hand, he shouted at us: "If you love the Lord, raise your hand." Of course, we all did. Ingy and our cousin Bente were sitting behind us, and I realized Ingy wanted to be close to Ole-Jakob Samuelsen. Whenever she saw him in church, she got a goofy look on her face. Here he was, and they were not in church. Maybe she was hopeful.

I was sitting next to the Samuelsen twins, Stein and Nils, who whispered to each other in that special language they had. Then some ushers passed a plate—"So we can continue to spread the Good News," the preacher said.

People dug in their pockets and complied. That's when Nils grabbed my arm and whispered to me, "Look. Some people are dropping coins into the hay. Try to remember where they sit. Because you know our parents will have stuff to talk about after this meeting, and we can find the money." And that's just what happened. I fished a few coins out of the hay and put them in my shoe.

When we climbed into the Chevy and started on our ride home, Ingy hissed, "I saw you take the collection money that fell into the hay."

"What?" exclaimed Papa in alarm. "That money is for God's work. Taking it is very sinful! What if someone saw you?" When we got home, I got it big time. I think Ingy might have felt sorry she had spoken up.

That was the same year Jack Wyrtsen came to our 66th Street church. It was packed, and I was sitting with my cousins Alice and Sonya. We had been allowed to sit by ourselves, after promising to behave. Okay, the rally was in English, in the Norwegian department, and we were upstairs in the balcony on the front right-hand side, looking down at the platform.

Mr. Wyrtsen spoke at length, or should I say, he droned on. We also got to sing. I always liked *The Old Rugged Cross* and knew all the verses by heart. The organist managed the hymns beautifully: *What a Friend We Have in Jesus, In the Garden,* and so many others that we knew so well. The music was good. Then Wrytsen called upon us to "Come forward and repent of your sins." So I did.

Chapter Seven

Gangs of New York

I had mostly gotten used to PS 201, and after I had been in the 3rd grade for almost a whole school year, Mama let me make the walk myself if, for one reason or another, Ingy wasn't going. Then Mama would accompany me to the corner to watch me cross 10th Avenue. Why Mama didn't worry about 11th Avenue was a puzzle to me, but perhaps she knew there would be other students, and we could cross together. The usual routine, however, was for me to follow Ingy, who would be finishing the 8th grade by the end of June. She no longer took my hand as we crossed the avenues, and she walked several feet ahead of me, as if I weren't there. Greeting our arrival at the big brick building was always a clamor of animated voices, and often some arguing or bickering. I got used to it, and it became familiar to me.

It was in Mrs. Resnick's class that I learned how students got extra attention. When we had work assignments which we were to complete individually, all a pupil had to do was gesture to Mrs. Resnick and say, "I don't understand." Then she would kneel down by such a student and kindly point out how to add numbers or spell certain words. We had a spelling book that showed the words we were supposed to memorize every week, and I knew all the words. Still, I wanted the attention Mrs. Resnick bestowed on select classmates. I held up my hand and said, "I need help."

Mrs. Resnick came to my side and asked, "What's giving you trouble?"

"Everything."

To this she replied, "I don't think you're having trouble. I think you're bored. I think you could do some more difficult work. Let's see what I can find for you." And she did.

I heard the boy behind me snicker, and he said under his breath, "See what asking for help gets you? That's why I never ask, even if I don't understand. I'm no dummy." Nevertheless, I was pleased because Mrs. Resnick had paid attention to me and, besides, the work was interesting. Mrs. Resnick told me it was 4th-grade level, and I felt good about it. I was eager to tell Mama and Papa.

When I got home that day, prepared to tell my parents about my 4th-grade work assignment, Mama and Papa were in deep conversation, talking about the story in *The Daily News* about gangs in Brooklyn. "What's a gang?" I asked as I put my books down on the kitchen table, forgetting about my classroom achievement.

"They are young men who have nothing better to do than scare ordinary folks. This story is about the Dragons and ViceRoys—they're Puerto Ricans, and they fight over territory—really city streets—and girls," said Papa.

To this Mama said, "They should be deported and told to never come back. You know they're not white, and they don't belong here in America. They should go back where they came from."

This was a lot to think about. Why would gangs want to scare people? Where's the good in that? Where did they come from, and how did they get to Brooklyn? And since they were here in our borough, why didn't they just stay on their own streets and away from the streets claimed by rival gangs? "Shouldn't we make sure our doors are always locked?" I asked.

"Of course, but the really bad gang trouble isn't taking place here," Papa said. I went to my room to change into my play clothes, then started downstairs for my afterschool snack. Midway on the stairs I heard Papa talking about the Egyptian Kings, who had attacked five members of the Jesters, a rival gang. I stopped moving and listened hard. Where did that happen, I wondered. Papa then said the Egyptian Kings had killed a 15-year-old boy named Michael Farmer.

"Awful," said Mama. "You'd never hear of such a thing in Bay Ridge."

"But we're really not in Bay Ridge, although everybody thinks we are. This house is in Dyker Heights, and you know there are a lot of Italians here," Papa said. "They're not really white either, especially the ones from Naples and Sicily." I wondered if my friend Neil would join a gang when he was older. After all, he was Italian.

Coming into the kitchen, I posed this question: "Why would anyone want to join a gang?"

Papa said, "Just like most boys, they want to feel important, and a gang gives them a kind of family that accepts them. Maybe they don't get enough attention—or Godliness—at home. Growing up in homes that don't know Jesus leads children into all sorts of trouble."

I had my snack, glad to know Jesus was on our side, and asked Mama if I could keep my school shoes on—my penny loafers were the best shoes for my roller skates. It was always risky to do something like that without Mama's permission because it could set her off, and you never knew what was coming. This time she said, "Okay, but be careful."

I went next door to find Neil, who was by our street standard the best skater on the block. "Hey," he said, as he came to the door, "They've just paved 81th Street. It's as smooth as silk. Let's go there."

I had some misgivings, because I knew that if Mama came to the door to look for me, she wouldn't see me. But if that happened, I'd have to think of something to say later. We went up to 10th Avenue, turned past St. Phillip's and onto the pitch-black, newly laid pavement and started to glide. I remember thinking that Neil was right; this was good street skating. Neil and I raced like the wind. As luck would have it, Ingy came walking down the block, having been at a friend's house to study. "Uh oh," I thought. "This could be trouble." When it started to get dark, I knew it would be time to go home for supper, and so I warily did.

But Mama and Papa were in the living room, watching TV, and Mama asked, "Did you have a good skate?"

"Yup," I replied. "I'm almost as good as Neil. We raced." Then I went to wash up for supper. I sat on my pink chenille bedspread and waited for Mama to call me for dinner, while pondering what I would say if Mama and Papa found out I had gone to 81st Street to skate.

At the table, after we had said *I Jesu Navn* and passed the food,

Ingy calmly announced, "Solveig was skating on 81st Street. I saw her."

Great, I thought. She waited to tell, so I would be on the spot. I looked down at my mashed potatoes. "Hmm," came from Papa, who glanced at Mama.

"You're not supposed to leave our street. You know that. What if I needed to find you?" And then in an exasperated tone she added, "You will go to your room without dessert, do your homework, and get in bed."

Well, that wasn't as bad as it could have been. On my way up the stairs, I heard Papa say, "Ingrid, you shouldn't be such a tattletale." I felt better. I did my homework, then brushed my teeth and got into bed, in my head calling Ingy a "snitch." It would be a long night, since I wasn't tired at all. But eventually I went to sleep, facing the door as I always did, just in case. That night danger wasn't coming at me through the door, the evil presence I remembered from the room I had shared with Ingy on 79th Street. No, that night the danger was in my dreams. I dreamt about the Egyptians and the Jesters uniting with each other to run after me. My legs wouldn't move; I was frozen in place. I tried to scream, but no sound came from my mouth.

In a sweat I woke up. It was early morning, and dawn was just beginning. I went to the window in my room; it overlooked the alleyway between our house and our neighbors', but I didn't see a gang or even a single gang member lurking in the shadows. I could hardly breathe.

I heard Mama in the kitchen, saying goodbye to Papa, who was leaving for work. "I need to go all the way to Bayonne to catch the boat," he said. Eager to hug him before he left, I hurried down the stairs in my nightgown. But he had gone, and Mama said to me, in the angry tone she often adopted when Papa left, "You are not going to school like that! Go upstairs and get dressed!"

"But," I started to say, "I just wanted to…"

"Just go get dressed," said Mama, her tone threatening, and I knew I'd get a good wallop if I tried to explain. Up the stairs I went and put on a school dress, the one I had worn two days ago, and came back down the stairs, my head held low. Ingy was at the table, and she glared at me. I ate my oatmeal quietly, got my books, and followed Ingy out the back door.

"Do you think the gangs will come here?" I asked.

"Don't be ridiculous," Ingy said. "You are such an idiot." We walked the rest of the way wordlessly and parted at the big metal double doors to the school where I joined my classmates who were lining up in the hallway, ready to march into our classroom.

"Hey," said Victor, the tall, dark boy who sat behind me in class and was standing behind me now, "I hear the Baldies are coming." That got the attention of some of the girls and boys around us, and we began chattering.

"What? Who are the Baldies?" I asked.

"They are a really bad gang, and they kill people. And they like to come to schoolyards," said Anne, the pretty redhead. "And they especially like to hurt girls."

Mrs. Resnick, who had been standing quietly at the front of our queue, piped up and said, "Let's get to our seats, and we'll talk about 'the Baldies.'"

We marched into our classroom, took our seats, and waited expectantly while she came to the front of her big oak desk and announced, "There are some places in New York where gangs do bad things to other gangs, but let's be clear here—this is Brooklyn, and where we live is residential. They won't be coming here."

Victor never a shy one, put up his hand, and Mrs. Resnick said, "Yes, Victor?"

"The Jokers are here in Brooklyn. They stomped a 40-year-old man to death because they didn't like his whistling as he walked home from work. My father and mother were talking about that last night."

"I did hear about that," replied Mrs. Resnick, "but that was in Park Slope, not here in Dyker Heights."

I had something to add, so I raised my hand. "Yes, Sue," said Mrs. Resnick.

"Yesterday, my parents were talking about two gangs called the Dragons and ViceRoys who fight with each other. They're Puerto Ricans, and my mother says they should be deported. Wouldn't that take care of some of the problems?"

"The fighting certainly isn't good, but if they're Puerto Rican, then they're Americans. Puerto Rico is a U.S. territory, an island in the Caribbean." I had nothing to say to this, inwardly aware that Mama had been dead wrong. As for me, I had had a geography lesson of note.

Our discussion was far from over, however. James raised his hand to share this: "There are the South Brooklyn Boys. My cousin said they hate the rival gangs, the Untouchable Bishops and the Mau Chaplains." By now the class was abuzz, and Mrs. Resnick brought her hand down hard on the desk.

"They are not coming here. Period."

"Yeah," piped up Dominic, "you know who lives here, don't you? They wouldn't dare!"

"Who is he talking about?" I whispered to Victor.

"Oh, it's Anastasia, the mob boss. Nobody messes around here. I guess then the Baldies won't be coming here either."

"Settle down," Mrs. Resnick said, and added again, "They are not coming here. Period."

We calmed down then and started our day with the *Pledge of Allegiance* followed by our lessons. Still, there was something a little titillating to think of imminent danger, a shivery feeling that was both scary and exciting.

When I got home, I told Mama what we had talked about in school. And she said, "I guess it's good that your teacher explained that you are safe. You are, you know. Parents do everything they can to keep their children safe, too." I felt reassured that we were safe. Later, though, I heard Mama and Papa talking about what the world was coming to, and it wasn't good.

They were talking about the music that Ingy and Bente seemed to like, the kind the girls called "rock and roll" and listened to whenever they were together. Papa said that new music "isn't music at all. That singer Elvis Presley ought to be put in jail. It's disgraceful how he moves when he sings. Ivar at church called him 'Elvis the pelvis.' It's obscene."

"I'm surprised Ivar would use that word," said Mama. And I thought, what's a pelvis?

"I heard there was a riot at an Elvis Presley concert in Florida," Papa said, adding, "That will tell you what that kind of music does to people."

"Well, it's just a phase," Mama said. "Rock and roll won't last, you'll see."

"It's illegal in England, I read," said Papa. "It should be like that here, too. We must make sure Ingrid does not listen to it."

That would be too bad, I thought, since I was beginning to like it also and listened to the radio with Ingy and Bente at Bente's house. Tante Clara didn't seem to mind the music at all, but then we couldn't see the singers on the radio. I had heard Bente telling Ingy that the pastor in the English department at church warned them about the evils of listening to rock and roll, and even advised them to break their records if they had any. I knew Ingy didn't have any, but I wondered if Bente had. One thing I knew for sure was this: Papa would never condone breaking anything on purpose if it had cost money. This contradiction posed a dilemma for me, and I vowed to give it more thought.

While Papa guarded money closely, he still wanted us to look good. Easter was coming up, and that signaled the time when we would get new clothes, everything from our socks and underwear to new dresses and accessories. I liked that, but I didn't like the actual shopping, which was boring.

We went to Mays one afternoon after school was out, riding the RR train to downtown Brooklyn. Mama found Ingy a blue suit, tailored and sophisticated. Ingy was starting to sprout breasts, and I was fascinated by the changes she had been undergoing. Ingy seemed pleased with the suit; it tapered at the waist and had seams under the arms to allow for body curvature. I had to admit, she looked good in it. The white blouse finished it off, with a pretty lace collar that peaked out over the suit.

For me, Mama found a pink dress, one with poufy sleeves and a ribbon belt. "You will be able to wear these clothes for Easter, and the missionary luncheon the following week," said Mama. I understood that it was important to Mama to have us look good when we went to church. I liked looking good, too.

Easter Sunday came soon enough, and I got out of bed earlier than usual, to take the bobby pins out of my hair and comb out my curls.

Ingy was luckier—no bobby pins for her, for her blond hair was naturally curly and thick. But I noticed she pulled scotch tape from both sides of her forehead to reveal little comma-like curls. "Spit curls," she told me. I wondered what Mama would say, but she said nothing.

Waiting on the server in the dining room were our Easter baskets, loaded with chocolates and marzipan, purchased from the confectionary run by two Norwegian ladies who attended our church. I looked forward to delving into them, but Mama said we must wait until after church. We said *I Jesu Navn* and ate our hard-boiled eggs and boller (a Norwegian version of hot cross buns) in our slips, as WOR radio's *Rambling with Gambling* gave way to *Easter Parade*, not the usual *Pack Up Your Troubles in Your Old Kit Bag*. I pictured myself "the grandest lady in the Easter parade" as I dressed for church.

The Powerglide took us to church, Papa at the wheel wearing a blue suit with a hat just purchased and carefully creased. My, he looked dapper. Mama looked beautiful too, in her spring coat sporting a corsage Papa had brought home the night before. Ingy wore her new blue suit, and I my pink taffeta dress with a light wool topper that came to my hips, allowing the skirt of my dress to swing as I moved. Everything was perfect.

Ingy and I sat pristine and still, and Ingy insisted the windows of the car remain closed so no wind would mess her hair—or, heaven forbid, disturb the spit curls. Once at church, we found our friends and cousins, preening like baby chicks in their new Easter finery as we waited for the services to begin. Finally, the powerful organ music drew us in, Ingy to the English department, me with my parents to the Norwegian service in the upstairs sanctuary.

I could hear the jubilant singing from downstairs, accompanied by the piano. It was audible but muted because the doors were closed. "He lives, He lives, salvation to impart. You ask me how I know he lives, He lives within my heart," the English congregation sang. How I longed to be downstairs while the Norwegians in the main sanctuary began to sing in unison, holding their Norwegian hymnals. If I had known then what a dirge was, I would have labeled it thus. I was acutely aware that the music was slow and ponderous, following the tempo set by the organist, and it didn't seem too happy, not like the music Ingy and Bente listened to outside of church. In my mind I was trying to remember the words to *Rock Around the Clock,* the one rock and roll song I liked best—happy and fast, and about dancing to boot. If Mama and Papa only knew.

About a week after that Easter, there was a luncheon for a missionary the church supported. She was home on furlough for a month, and our church would rejoice with her for the souls she had saved in darkest Africa. It was to be in the downstairs sanctuary, which had been set up with long tables and a buffet.

Ingy sat with Bente and other adolescents, including Ole-Jakob, who looked less like a boy and more like a movie star with his blond hair tumbling over his forehead. "It's Teddy style," Ingy had once remarked on how popular boys combed their hair. That's it, I thought: Teddy style. I saw Ingy glance at him with a dreamy look in her eyes, and so did Bente.

When the Norwegian pastor said welcome, the pianist started to play, and we sang *I Jesu Navn*, slowly in time to the beat from the piano. What a grace it was—we said it every day, but we could sing this prayer, too. *I Jesu Navn* was followed by people queueing up to fill their dinner plates. The food was good—boiled potatoes and ham cooked by the men of the church and lots of jello molds, quivering on their plates in multi-colors, having been lovingly prepared by the women of the church.

After we had eaten and the women had cleared the plates from the table, the missionary, a tall gaunt woman named Selma Olsen, spoke to us in English about her work in Kenya. I thought it must be good to be able to save so many souls and vowed to become a missionary when I grew up.

The adults talked for a while outside the church while Stein and Nils, Ole-Jakob's younger twin brothers, showed Alice, Sonya, and me their Brooklyn Dodgers baseball cards. For me, I couldn't have cared less about baseball, nor did I care who Tommy Lasorder, Roy Campaneller, PeeWee Reese, or Jackie Robinson were. But when I looked at the cards, I saw that Jackie Robinson was a black man. How could that be? I also learned that boys were pretty different from girls, and that they liked different things—not clothes or dolls, but uniforms and sports.

After a while, our parents herded us into their cars, and Papa said Stein and Nils would ride with us, and Ingy with the Samuelsens, for they were coming home with us for coffee and cake. What fun these boys were. Why, they were just like our real cousins.

While the parents talked in the living room, Stein and Nils and I sat at the kitchen table to read comic books I had brought from my room. *Little Lulu!* Stein exclaimed. "Don't you have any others?" I was happy that Mama now allowed me comic books other than just *Little Lulu,* but she always made sure that what I had in my room met with her approval.

"Here's an *Archie,*" I said. "But let me go to my room, and I'll see if I can find some more." With that pronouncement, I went upstairs, not straight to my room, but to the bathroom. I was glad I didn't have to announce that I needed to pee because I had said I was going to fetch comic books. The bathroom was next to Ingy's room at the back of the house. As I passed her room, I stopped, thunderstruck. Ole Jakob and Ingy were almost naked. He stood facing Ingy, holding onto her, touching her breasts. His backside was round and firm, and Ingy looked over his shoulder in horror at me.

Down the stairs I went, quickly to Mama's side and whispered. Mama bolted to her feet and said, "Come with me, Adolph!" Up the stairs went my parents, and I heard Ingy start to cry. The Samuelsens must have figured out what was going on, and they hustled their boys from the house, Ole Jakob looking sheepish, the twins confused. Me, I still had to pee, and my breathing was shallow as I struggled to inhale and my heart pounded. I wondered when I'd see the twins again.

The twins were not in Sunday School the following Sunday nor the next, nor the one after that. We soon learned that the Samuelsens would not be coming to our church anymore.

Chapter Eight

On the Move Again

The spring when I was nine was to be memorable. We had big plans and were happily anticipating summer. The school year would be over in June, and Papa had promised we would go to Rowlands in Pennsylvania. I had told Neil that Papa had reserved cabins for us—for us and the Hansens. That meant Tante Clara and Onkel Olav and our cousins would be going, too. Ingy and Bente wouldn't be with us the whole time, though, since they had successfully petitioned to go to Camp Witness for a week.

Camp Witness had real army tents and a lake with a dock where kids could swim. It was in Pennsylvania, so it couldn't be that far from Rowlands. I knew because I had heard Ingy and Bente talking about it and the boys who would be going too. I had heard Ingy mention Ole-Jakob specifically and wondered if he could still go to camp if he didn't go to 66th Street church. The camp seemed to promise some intrigue, and I was curious.

"Why can't I go to Camp Witness?" I pouted.

"You have to wait until you're older—at least 13," said Mama. That's the way it always was—Ingy got to do the fun things, and I was restrained. But, still, I loved going to Rowlands, and Tor Asbjørn, Alice, and Sonya would be there to play with me and swim in the river right where the aqueduct loomed high over us and the river pooled. I focused on how I would become a proficient swimmer, better than anyone else.

Fate intervened, however. One day in early June, Papa got a phone call from his uncle's neighbor in St. Albans. Papa was visibly shaken when he got off the phone and announced, "Onkel Torleif has died, apparently from a heart attack." Then he added, "Onkel was never the same after Borghild died. It was just the two of them, and all they had was each other." I knew that the old aunt and uncle hadn't had any children, but never knew why. They had been kind to us each time we visited, but visits were infrequent. Still, it was sad, and I couldn't comprehend it.

"We were his children in a way," said Papa. "He loved me and my sisters, and we will all miss him." Then he called Tante Marit and Tante Signe in New Jersey and gave them the news. The next day, Onkel Bendix and Tante Signe showed up at our house. They had driven all the way from West Orange, and now they were to go to St. Albans "to take care of things," Papa said.

About a week later, there was a funeral, but Ingy and I didn't go. We stayed at Tante Clara's until our parents returned. The death of Onkel Torleif was a fulcrum, evidently, because it wasn't too long after that that Papa got a new car, a Ford Fairlane, blue and white, and mighty impressive. I knew with a certainty that Papa would explain to the men at church what a good bargain he had made and what a superior car this Ford was. That's pretty much what happened.

More changes were coming our way. We did go to Rowlands in July, and Ingy and Bente went to Camp Witness, but August brought another doozy. "We are moving," Mama told us one day. "Papa and I have bought a new house, a one-family that's not semi-attached like this one."

"Where is it?" Ingy asked pointedly.

"It's on 92nd Street, between 3rd Avenue and Ridge Boulevard," Papa said.

"I'm not moving," I said matter-of-factly. After all, I had done this before, and the first move took me away from Mary Anne and Gina, and now they wanted me to leave Neil. I was having no part of it.

"Well, see, Solveig, you don't have a choice. We have buyers for this house, and we have to get out."

"What? Tell them they can't have it, that we've changed our minds."

"It doesn't work like that. But wait until you see the new house. You will love it," said Mama.

"But how will I get to PS 201? That's on 12th Avenue. How far is the house from school?"

"You will go to PS 104, The Fort Hamilton School," said Mama. This was dreadful news to me, and I said so.

"Doesn't matter to me," Ingy chimed in. "I just finished the 8th grade, so I have to change schools anyway." That was true, I knew. Ingy and Bente had discussed at length where Ingy should go to high school. They decided on Bay Ridge High, partly because that's where Bente already was, having just finished her freshman year. Besides, I knew Mama and Papa really liked the idea of Ingy going to an all-girls school.

I just didn't see the fairness in it. When we left PS 127, Ingy had just finished the 6th grade, and she needed to finish through the 8th grade before she could go to high school. I had to leave PS 127 and the kids I knew, then go to PS 201 and get to know new kids. Now they were making me change again. I was doomed; my chest constricted.

"You will like it," Mama reaffirmed. "I'm sure of it."

"What about Neil? He's my best friend," I said.

"You can always visit him," said Mama. Oh sure, I thought. That's not going to happen. I could see it coming. I took a deep breath, and then another, and then panicked, heading for the security of my room, which wouldn't be my room much longer. There it was again: the hard-to-breathe, not-enough-air sensation. I stood in my room, gasping.

The next weekend, having already given us the news about the impending move, Mama and Papa took us to see the house. We couldn't go in because the closing hadn't yet occurred, as Papa explained, but we parked the car and took a walk on the sidewalk, admiring all the smart, well-groomed homes. Then Papa said, "Here it is." We stood agape before the house that was to be ours. "It's not semi-attached like the house we're in now," he announced again, but that was clear to see. I looked up and saw not two, but three floors. "It's called a Victorian, and it has cutout wood trim, just like so many houses in Norway."

"Can I have that room with the window on top?"

"That's a small room," said Mama. "It's mostly storage space—an attic, really. The window makes it look like a nice place from out here, but it's just extra space. There are three very nice bedrooms on the second floor. You'll have one of those."

The front of the house had a nice garden, but not as nice as the neighbor's, which had a tree cut in a spiral. I had never seen a tree like it. "Did it grow like that?"

"I don't think so," said Papa, laughingly. "The homeowner must have worked very hard to trim it like that." I was clearly puzzled but decided not to ask any more questions. We walked up the driveway to the backyard and saw a garage, a garden, and a back door with a pretty overhang. I was beginning to ponder the idea of living here, even though I liked where we were living just fine.

After that visit, we took inventory and started to pack up. I decided I had outgrown some of my toys, and Mama announced her intent to take them to the Norwegian Children's home. "It's kind to think of others who can enjoy these toys as you did when you were younger," Mama said.

"What's the Norwegian Children's Home?" I asked.

"When children have no one to take care of them, they can live in the children's home. It's a nice place, and the children are Norwegian," Mama explained, then added, "mostly."

"Do they go to school? Who cooks for them? Who buys them

clothes and other things they need? Don't they have mothers and fathers?"

"My, so many questions," said Mama. "Sometimes families have a hard time, and the parents can't take care of the children. Or maybe a mother or father has died, and the remaining parent has to work and can't be home with the children. Sometimes there are no aunts and uncles or grandparents in this country to help out, so the children can't live with them. There are many reasons why children are at the home."

"Do the children grow up there?"

"Some do," said Mama. "But many stay there for a short while only, while the parents get their lives back in order. And you know in those cases, the parents visit often, so the children know their parents love them."

"What about the children who don't have parents?"

"Ah," said Mama, "the lucky ones get adopted into good homes and grow up there. But the children's home is a good place, and the children who live there have it good. In fact, so many of the Norwegian churches see the home as a special mission, so the children get lots of good attention."

Okay, I thought. Not everybody grows up with a mother and father, and surely not everyone has a room of one's own, like I already did. I went with Mama when she drove to the children's home to deliver the boxes packed with my old toys. I was curious but, once there, fascinated to find so many eyes looking at us, and I saw that the children in the main room were excited that there would be "new" toys on site. But they were probably wondering who we were.

"Hello," said a girl about my age.

"Hello," I said back, and then averted my eyes. I couldn't think of anything else to say. She looked at me, hard, then at her foot, lifted her heel, and moved it back and forth. Her movement held her in rapt attention. I looked at the floor, but not at her.

As we drove back to 80th Street, I sat in the front seat, perfectly still.

"You are so quiet, Solveig," said Mama. "What's wrong?"

"Nothing," I mumbled, looking out the window and not at Mama.

It was late August when we moved. Papa and Mama had closed on the house two weeks before the closing of the house on 80th Street. That gave us time to take carloads of things to the new house and for Papa and Onkel Olav to paint and hang wallpaper. It seemed Onkel Olav was always there to help. Not only did he help Papa, but he was always so interested in me and Ingy, asking about what we were doing, what we liked, and generally how we were getting along. He also praised the new house and reassured us how happy we would be to live there. "Such a lovely neighborhood," he said. "You are lucky girls." And to Papa he said, "In a year or so, you'll have to paint the outside, too. Lucky you."

Moving day was foggy, and there was a hint of salt in the air, wafting inward from the harbor, which was closer to this new house. I heard a low, mournful foghorn for the first time, and knew that sound belonged to this, our new neighborhood, so much closer to the bay. I'm going to like it here, I told myself, but that was more an effort to convince myself to like it. I tried hard not to be sad about leaving 80th Street and Neil. It wasn't working.

I was ready for 4th grade. Going to a new school would be daunting, and that was an underlying worry I also associated with the move. I had recurring bouts of anxiety, gasping for air, but Mama simply said, "Stop that. Just slow down and take a deep breath." I tried. I took a deep breath and let it out slowly. Then I gasped, sucking in air over and over again until my chest hurt. "Oh, Solveig," said Mama, clearly disappointed. "There's no need to carry on so." Even so, Mama must have sensed that I was anxious. One day a little later, she said, "I have a nice surprise for you."

"What?" I wanted to know.

"You'll be having lunch in school, just like at PS 201, but you don't have to carry that scratched pink lunch box with the princess on it. I bought you a new one, a special one." With that she reached into the bag on the table and brought out a brand new, red plaid lunch box. It was so pretty and didn't have little girl designs on it. The handle was black, and it had a snap closure. It was nice. I would be proud to carry it, and I understood that Mama knew it, too.

Mama had registered Ingy and me for our new schools, and after Labor Day, the school year began. My first day would be dreadful, I anticipated, and I felt very alone since Ingy wasn't there to walk with me. No, she had taken the 4th Avenue Subway, the RR, to Bay Ridge Avenue and from there walked to 67th Street, where Bay Ridge High, the yellow brick school, stood. There, of course, our cousin Bente, who was an old pro starting her sophomore year, would be waiting for Ingy outside. Once again, I knew Ingy had it easier.

Mama walked me to 4th Avenue where there were crossing guards. The school was just about where 4th Avenue and 5th Avenue converged, so I had to cross two avenues to get to PS 104. She stood and watched as I went across both avenues, guided by the crossing guard who held a stop sign for traffic. I had my lunch box in my hand, and I gripped it tightly. The closer I got to the school door, the tighter my hold on the lunch box became.

At the door, I was greeted by a teacher's aide who led me to a group of several other students, and we waited quietly until one more boy was brought to our group. Then the aide led us to our classroom. It was a nice room, airy and bright, and my teacher, Mrs. Ludwig, welcomed us warmly. It might be okay, I thought. I noticed when she took attendance in the morning and called out our names so we could reply "here," almost everyone had an American name, not a Norwegian name like mine. When she called me 'Saul wig,' I said softly, "Please call me Sue."

When I got home, I was excited to share my day's events, and I had school-issued books to cover. Ingy came home a bit later, and she had plenty of books, more than I. High school would be a challenge, she declared, because she would be learning Latin, doing geometry, and reading Jane Austin. With that she plunked her books on the kitchen table, ready to cover them.

I said little, which was unusual for me, but I knew with a certainty that my mathematics and social studies books couldn't compare to hers. I silently put them on the table. Mama had cut open some brown bags from the Grand Union supermarket, and we set about covering our schoolbooks, while Ingy told us about Bay Ridge High. It had been a school for both boys and girls, she said, but then New Utrecht High opened, and Bay Ridge became an all-girls' school. I had this feeling Ingy would have liked to have had some boys there.

"But now it's the girls' school that's the same as the Brooklyn Tech school for boys," she said importantly. What's Brooklyn Tech? I thought but didn't ask. One of the things she did say was that Bay Ridge High had its own song—and she had the words. "A Song for the Bay Ridge High," she sang, "Let us sing with right good cheer...." Wow, its own song. How long would it be before I could go there?

I counted out the years in my head. An eternity!

What she said next totally amazed me. "I am learning classical Latin, and it stopped being the language of the courts in the 5th century. Vulgar Latin developed from it, but it's really Italian. Italian is a vulgar language. It's spoken by vulgar people," she sneered.

"Now wait a minute. Neil is Italian. He's not vulgar. Neither is Gina," I replied indignantly.

Surprisingly, Mama said nothing. I was certain Ingy was dead wrong. I knew some of the kids in my class at PS 104 were Italian. I knew that the boys named Nunzio and Gino were Italian, and so were the girls Constanza, whom we called Connie, and Bella. They seemed pretty okay to me.

It wasn't long after we had started school that Mrs. Ludwig handed out notices for a clinic on 86th Street where families could get free polio shots. I wasn't keen on getting a shot, but Mama was enthusiastic. "Remember how we talked about families keeping their children safe? Well, this is one way to do that," she explained.

I thought about Arthur, who was in Sunday School with me. He walked with crutches that had bands that slipped over his arms, and he put his weight on the hand grips while he dragged one foot behind him. He had had polio, I had heard. Indeed, it was a terrible thing.

The next day after Ingy and I had come home from school, we walked to the clinic. The waiting room was packed with mothers and their children. As some of the children came out of the doctor's office, they were crying. Some boys put on brave faces, and others gave us knowing looks. Two of the mothers were talking loudly enough for us to hear: "It's a live virus, I understand. And there's a risk that some children will actually get polio from it."

"It's a very small risk," the other woman replied. "The benefit is that 99 percent of the kids getting shots will never have polio." I wondered if Mama had overheard that conversation too, but if she had, I couldn't tell. She just looked straight ahead at the door to the doctor's office. Then it was our turn, and we got our shots, which hurt pretty bad, but we were happy to have it over with and eager to go home. It was a long walk, and I was feeling achy and complained. Ingy glowered at me, but I persisted.

"Keep it up, and I'll give you something to complain about," said Mama. Accordingly, as I was wont to do, I shut up, and trudged alongside my sister and mother until we reached our house on 92nd Street.

When we got home, I wanted to watch TV, but Mama said I had to do my homework. "But I don't feel good," I said. "I need to rest. It's the shot."

"Well, you can rest in your room," she said. "I don't want to hear any more complaints. The shot was good for you and will keep you safe." I heard her but didn't believe her. I knew I would soon be walking with arm braces and dragging a leg. But as time progressed, I didn't get polio after all.

Our daily routines continued. School went on as usual, and for Social Studies, we were instructed to bring in articles from the newspaper, stories we would explain to our classmates. I diligently searched *The Daily News,* looking at the centerfold for pictures that told the story with little text. Sometimes I would clip articles from *The Brooklyn Eagle,* for that paper had real stories that applied to where we actually lived. But pretty soon, I had only *The Daily News,* because Mama said *The Brooklyn Eagle* had stopped its presses, and the paper would be no more. Instead, she bought *The National Enquirer*. "Much better news," she said.

I set about collecting news of interest from *The National Enquirer* and *The Daily News*, two papers that were now regulars in our home. Mrs. Ludwig didn't like it, however, when I brought in an article about a man who was walking along the street in Manhattan, minding his own business, only to have a metal pipe fall from the top of a building and impale him. Lots of blood and gore and sure to get my class interested, I thought. I was surprised, however, when Mrs. Ludwig said, "That's not news. It's not something we can learn from; it's sensationalism, and it sells newspapers, but it doesn't tell us much about society." A few classmates snickered at this pronouncement, but I maintained it was "human interest" and thus news of a sort. That argument didn't hold, and Mrs. Ludwig said rather sternly, "I don't agree." With this reprimand, I lowered my head and looked at my hands in my lap while several classmates giggled.

"Human interest stories should tell us something," our teacher continued. "Think about the red hawk that has taken up residence on a building ledge in Manhattan. What does that tell us?"

Joseph, the blond-haired, quiet boy in the back of the room, raised his hand. "That tells us," he said, "that nature adapts to its surroundings."

"Very good," said Mrs. Ludwig. "Now it's interesting." Me, I was wondering how Joseph, who was usually so shy and retiring, knew the word "adapts." I determined to look it up when I got home. I was not going to admit I didn't know the meaning.

Once home, I looked it up in the old dictionary we kept with the phone books in the telephone table in the dining room. "People need to adapt," I announced at dinner.

"What does that mean?" Papa asked.

"If things around us change, we have to change a little, too," I announced.

"I guess that's true," said Papa. "'Adapt' is a good word, and it applies to us." With that, he proceeded to tell us about a new change, one that would require us as a family to adapt. "We are looking for property in New Jersey, not a place to live all the time, but a place to go in the summer and some weekends, a place not as far away as Pennsylvania. Maybe by a lake. Now this is something for us to think through, and we have a long winter before we'll actually buy anything. But this is the plan."

A change I had in mind was simply that I would join the Girl Scouts. I was impressed with several of the girls in my class who wore uniforms or vests or sashes on the days that the scouts met at St. Patrick's, the big Catholic church on 4th Avenue. Some girls had brown uniforms, some green. "How come they are not the same?" I asked Lisa, who was in a brown uniform.

She replied, "Most of us are still Brownies. The two girls in green are a year older but in the same grade as us because their families travel so much, and they missed some school."

"Why did they?" I asked.

"Their fathers are in the Army, stationed at Fort Hamilton, which is pretty close to here. That's why they call this 'The Fort Hamilton School.'" Regardless of the color of their uniforms, however, they had this in common: they talked about which badge they were working on and when they thought they would get it.

"What are those badges? What do they mean?" I asked one day when Janie wore a green sash festooned with several colorful embroidered badges.

Janie replied, "You get a badge when you master a skill. This one is for camping," she said, pointing to it. "I'm working on some others. In fact, I have lots of badges, since I was a Daisy Scout, then a Brownie Scout, and now I'm a Junior Scout. Look," she added, "this is an official Girl Scout Membership Pin. And this one is the Girl Scout Junior Safety Award."

Susan, who was wearing a green vest and listening attentively to Janie, piped up with "I just got the Bronze Award." Hmm, I thought, digesting this information. Janie was proud of her achievements, as was Susan, and this was a way to let everyone know what they are. "How long did it take you to earn those?"

"You just keep going until you are proficient," said Susan. Me, I was wondering what "proficient" meant, and I was determined to find out but wouldn't risk letting either Susan or Janie know I didn't know.

When I got home, I asked Ingy what "proficient" meant. "It means you are good at something," Ingy explained. "Don't you know anything?"

I decided I was proficient at roller skating and swimming. But I didn't have any badges to show with pride. Thus, I announced to Mama that I would be joining the Girl Scouts of America.

"You won't be doing that," said Mama. "They let girls join who aren't Christians."

"But I heard Susan, this girl in my class, say 'God and country.' Why would she do that?"

"It's just something they say, not something they actually mean," responded Mama. "But I'll tell you what. You can become a Pioneer Girl in the spring."

"What's that?"

"Our church is starting a Pioneer Girls program. It's just like Girl Scouts, only better."

"Why is it better?"

"Because Pioneer Girls are Christians."

In the spring, I became a Pioneer Girl, meeting on Saturday mornings at 66th Street church, wearing a blue sash. And pretty soon I had mastered the kitchen badge. It was boring, and there was no way I would wear my blue sash to school where most girls hadn't heard about Pioneer Girls. I did learn the song *We are Pioneers for Jesus*, which began, "We are pioneers for Jesus. We're looking unto Him. We believe his word, and we trust in Him with a faith that will not dim." While I knew the words, I didn't actually believe them, but to keep the peace at home, I pretended I did.

When the days got warmer and longer that spring, Mama and Papa would put us in the car and head out to New Jersey to look for a house they could afford to buy. "A hytte," Mama declared.

"What's that?" Ingy asked.

"It's a small building in the country, just like they have at home," Mama replied. Here I knew "home" yet again meant Norway.

Off we would motor, heading on the Gowanus to the Brooklyn Battery Tunnel, the West Side Highway in Manhattan to the

Lincoln Tunnel, and into New Jersey. I tried not to look out the side windows because I still could get plenty carsick. I leaned over and asked Ingy, "Do you think we'll find a hytte?"

"Oh, you bet," whispered Ingy, leaning toward me. "It's important to them," meaning Mama and Papa. "It will tell everybody we know how rich we are." Really? Just then I had an epiphany: a sudden understanding of my parents as people distinct from me and Ingy, people motivated by the standards set by the community in which they lived. While this realization struck me like a thunderbolt, in the years that followed I would have more such experiences, insights beyond the obvious as life unfolded around me, but this was a first.

That spring just before I turned ten, we continued our forays into the country. I came to dread the endless driving, the examination of old wooden houses on plots of land overgrown with weeds. Mama and Papa finally decided Budd Lake was the place to be. "New Jersey's largest natural lake," a sign proclaimed. The lake didn't look that big to me, and Route 46 ran right alongside it. When I mentioned this to Papa, he said, that's what makes it so convenient when we come from Brooklyn. We can drive on the highways the whole way through New Jersey.

When Mama and Papa finally found a house they deemed suitable, I expressed my dismay. Papa said, "You have to look beyond how it is now. We can make it nice. We can paint the house inside and out. And the yard can be cleared. We'll plant grass and flowers, and it will be cozy. And there's the lake, right down the road, where you can swim."

It was true you could see the lake from the left side of the house where there were steps leading up to the entryway. The house was on a street called Lakeview, which slanted uphill from Lake Shore Drive, the road that wound its way along the lake's shore. The house itself was not pretty, but it had three bedrooms, so Ingy and I would each have our own space. It had a red brick fireplace, too, and I asked Mama if it burned real wood and if we could cook our dinners in it.

"Dinner, no," said Mama, "but the people we bought it from said they had a popcorn maker that they held over the fire until the corn popped. Can't you see us playing Old Maid and eating popcorn in the evening? We'll have fun here. We can spend the whole summer here."

Now wait a minute, I thought. Does this mean we won't go to Rowlands for a few weeks? Before, we had spent at least half of the summer in Brooklyn. And now that I had had my polio shot, I thought we could go to the pool in Bliss Park, a thing Mama never allowed before, since everybody knew that's how you got polio. I was primed to swim in Brooklyn, and now that wouldn't happen.

We wouldn't be taking the ferry to Staten Island either to play with our cousins in Clove Lake Park. It was looking pretty grim to me. "Will people at least come to see us?"

"Of course. Your aunts and uncles and cousins will come. We're going to get bunkbeds for each of your rooms, and the living room can be another bedroom if we need it. We'll have lots of room. I'm sure there will be other families coming here to the country during the summer. You'll meet other children."

The next Sunday at Sunday School, I announced proudly, "We have a house in the country!" Mama and Papa set about furnishing the place on weekends, and sometimes I would miss Pioneer Girls because we set out early on Saturday mornings. The store Two Guys from Harrison in Dover was a place to get furniture at a reasonable price, and Papa asked his two brothers-in-law, Bendix and Karl, to lend a hand since they lived in New Jersey and were carpenters who had trucks. These uncles brought our new furniture to the lake house, and they had paint and plaster, too. I had decided I wanted a green room—my favorite color. Ingy wanted pink, and Mama blue. And in no time at all, Papa and the uncles had painted the bedrooms.

They set up bunk beds in two bedrooms. In the third, Mama and Papa installed a double bed. A used table and chairs found their way into the kitchen, as did pots and pans and dishes from our house in Brooklyn. It looked better, at least on the inside. The outside needed something, though I didn't know what.

Papa had already figured out what it needed, however, and he enlisted both Uncle Bendix and Uncle Karl to help him build a porch on the side of the house, one where you could see the lake. They worked with fury, and pretty soon the porch took shape. While they did that, Ingy and I ventured afoot to see and possibly meet our neighbors, but the scant houses showed no life.

"Wait until we are up here when school is out," Mama said. "I'm sure there will be children."

And there were. Edel and Else Nelson were sisters from Staten Island. Their parents owned a house just off Lake Shore Drive. Raymond and Barbara Edelmann, who were from the Bronx, stayed the summer, too, because their parents rented a bungalow. "We come every year," announced Raymond, who was just about my age. We proceeded to become fast friends, meeting at the beach every day it didn't rain. Swimming was reserved for the afternoons, after lunch and the mandatory one hour wait. Because the lake was so shallow, it warmed early in the season, and we could wade out pretty far.

Sometimes Edel and Else's mother would join our mother and sit on the beach, watching us. That's how Mama found about the Lutheran Church on Hillside Avenue in Succasunna and accepted the mother's invitation to go with them when Papa was on the job because, of course, he took the car. That was hardly good news to me, because it meant we would have to go every Sunday, all summer long.

On those days when it rained, we were disappointed. Mama, however, was happy, because it meant the marigolds and red salvia she had planted would grow. Sometimes on a rainy day, Ingy and I would visit Raymond and Barbara, often joined by Edel and Else. Monopoly or Parcheesi awaited us, and we played with gusto. Raymond and Barbara's mother was always kind, offering us little snacks she called rugala with homemade lemonade. It was during one of these offerings, as we sat around the kitchen table, that I saw her arm had black numbers on it. As curious as we were, both Ingy and I declined to mention it, perhaps because of some ingrained sense of propriety.

When we got home, it was another thing. "Their mother has numbers on her arm," Ingy announced. Mama looked at Papa knowingly.

Papa took a deep breath and said simply, "It means the parents were in Europe during the war and put into camps to do work for the Germans. The numbers were how the Nazis kept track of the people in the work camps." Then he added, "But they are here now, and enjoying the freedom that is America. And so are their children." I had a sudden flashback to the *Life* magazine I had surreptitiously looked at when Tante Magda brought it to our house when Eisenhower was running for President; I remembered the stacks of naked bodies. Had they been "workers" too?

Looking back now, I reflect on the magnitude of what I learned that the first summer at Budd Lake. I remember the glorious mornings when the sun would rise behind our house, streaming light into the two back bedrooms, the sound of *Rambling with Gambling* on the radio, the smell of coffee that Mama brewed early each day, and the knowledge that, for us, life was good.

By August, however, things changed. It started to rain, and rain, and rain, with lots of thunder and lightning. It was scary, but at the same time an adventure. We would find our way to the Edelmann's, where there was a TV. Mrs. Edelmann explained to us that the rain was the result of Hurricane Diane, which had made landfall in North Carolina, and the storm brought torrential rains to the northeast United States. But it did stop, and when we ventured to the lake, we found it had overflowed its banks. The water on the road was waist deep—it was an adventure to lie down and float on the road, and for the first time, the water in the lake was really deep.

It took a week for the water to subside a bit. Cars could finally make their way along Route 46, and the normal traffic patterns resumed. For a long time after the storm, we continued to find dead small animals and a snake or two. These discoveries delighted Raymond, who would pick up a dead snake and wiggle it at us, while we five girls screamed bloody murder.

Chapter Nine

Rullepølse

Christmas was always a big deal. Our excitement was palpable—as soon as Thanksgiving was over, it was all about Christmas. This year would be different, though, because Bestemor wanted the whole family to spend Christmas Day together. She had so far spent Christmas in America with Tante Hedwig, Onkel Werner, and their children on Long Island, and that was the pattern we expected. But this year Bestemor wanted all her bestebarn (grandchildren) together.

The plan was that we would go to Staten Island to celebrate with Mama's brother Johann Torvald and his wife, Hulda, on Christmas Day. I hardly knew this pair, nor their two children, Sven and Vigdis, whom Mama told Ingy and me about. They were our cousins, older than we, and even Maggy and Goody. Mama said her brothers Jakob and Leif and their families would be there too. Onkel Jakob we didn't really know, but Mama told us his wife was

Bergitta, and they had three sons. Onkel Leif and Tante Ragna we did know well because we would visit them on Staten Island, and they would sometimes come to Brooklyn with their four children in tow.

Mama also explained that Tante Hedvig and Onkel Werner's sons, their spouses, and children from Long Island were going to make the long trip to join us. And, of course, Goody and Maggy would come as well, and maybe Dagmar. I knew Ingy and Bente would love it if she did, because she embodied what they aspired to be. I just hoped that creepy boyfriend of Maggy's wouldn't come. But all in all, it was exciting to think so many cousins would be together under one roof on Christmas Day.

In anticipation of this most special of Norwegian holidays, Mama started baking early in December, and Tante Clara and Tante Hedwig would come on some evenings to help. We knew there would be company before and after Christmas, even though we would go to Staten Island on Christmas Day. Tante Clara brought her sandkage forms, and Mama let Ingy and me help press the dough into them. The dough was cold because after Mama made it, she chilled it in the refrigerator. "So, you can press it into the forms, nice and thin," she explained.

We waited until the sandkage came out of the oven and Tante Clara turned them upside down on a kitchen towel and tapped the bottom of the forms. Gently she urged the cookies out, looking like little pie crusts. Every now and then one would break, and Ingy and I could share it. Baking was fun and the results delicious. We repeated this routine until all the dough was gone. We knew Mama would make tyttebær (lingonberries) whipped with cream to fill them, and we anticipated these future treats, happy to be making these delicate morsels.

We made other cookies, too. We needed to have at least seven different types, and Mama said in Norway it was usual to have fourteen. We made spritz, rosettes, and my favorite, berliner kranse, made from Tante Ragna's recipe, the one the whole family shared. We made Ingy's favorite, too, fattigmann, which my friend Neil had said tasted like stale donuts, and I had to agree.

Other times we would help roll up krumkage, the delicate cookies Mama made with a flat iron that opened, accepted dough, and closed like a bellows. We had wooden cone-shaped tools, and as soon as Mama lifted a cookie from the iron, we worked to roll it on the wooden form while it was hot and pliant. I remember when we made them, Ingy commented that her homeroom teacher had noted that there were many Norwegians in her class, and would they please ask their mothers to make "those cone cookies" if they were planning to give the teacher a Christmas gift.

"Some nerve, even to ask," said Mama. "She has no idea how much work krumkage are. Let her go to the bakery." So Ingy and I surmised that our teachers would not be getting Christmas gifts from us. Mama later surprised us, nevertheless, by telling us she would make Yulekage, a rich, sweet, cardamom-flavored bread with candied citron and raisins, and we each could give a loaf to our primary teacher on the last day of school before Christmas break.

I liked the delicious aromas emanating from the kitchen during those December days, especially when it was cold outside, and the house was warm and cozy. One day, I came home to find Mama and Tante Hedwig busy in the kitchen, but nothing was in the oven. Tante Hedwig said she had brought her buttery oatmeal cookies for me and Ingy to have as a snack. They were, she exclaimed, "expecally good for you."

"I love them. Thanks. But what are you doing?" I asked, perplexed by what I saw.

"We are making rullepølse to take to Staten Island for Christmas Day," said Tante Hedwig. Wow, I thought, they actually know how to make this delicacy. We had rullepølse on special occasions, but normally we bought it in the deli on 8th Avenue that carried Norske varer (Norwegian goods). Fascinated, I watched as they pounded a piece of lamb thin and flat and laid slices of pork on top. Then they sprinkled salt and pepper and perhaps some other seasonings on it, carefully rolled it up, and believe it or not, sewed it into a long roll with an upholstery needle and heavy thread.

"There," said Tante Hedwig to me, "This will be deliciousity itself." Then they immersed the whole thing in a tub of salted and sugared water.

Mama brought the tub to the basement—"a cool place," she said—and proceeded to put the heavy portable Singer sewing machine on top. "This will make sure there are no air pockets, and that it holds together when we cook it in a few days." What she didn't realize was that the machine displaced the water, and the top of some of the meat was no longer underwater. When it came time to remove the meat, it had a very strange smell, very off-putting. The next thing I knew, she had put the whole thing in the garbage. That precipitated her other plan for Christmas on Staten Island. It would soon unfold.

There was so much to do to prepare for Christmas, and it was important that the house be spotless for Julen (the Christmas). Ingy, Mama, and I washed windows, even though it was cold outside. We dusted, vacuumed, and polished the silver. We weren't the only family immersed in cleanliness. I heard Mama tell Papa one night that her brother Johann Torvald and his wife, Hulda, had had all the downstairs rooms freshly painted in anticipation of our big Christmas Day celebration at their house on Staten Island.

When I asked why our Onkel would actually paint parts of his house for Christmas, Papa said, "Your Onkel Johann is a big Staten

Island contractor. He builds houses and has lots of subcontractors who work with him. That's probably who did the painting." And then as an afterthought, muttered more to himself than me, "He can certainly afford it."

Christmas day would be exciting, I knew. But before then, celebrations abounded all around us. At the First Evangelical Free Church on 66th Street, the Sunday School practiced for the children's program, one of the big events for us. My class would join Alice and Sonya's classes in reading chapter two in the book of *Luke* in *The King James Bible.* Alice was proud to be one of the readers. "It came to pass," she practiced in different tones of voice—high, low, fast, slow. What would it be?

Those of us who wouldn't be reading would sing with gusto. *Away in a Manager* was my favorite, although I never could fathom why baby Jesus should "Sleep in heavenly peas." *Little Town of Bethlehem* was another of my favorites, but there was a puzzle there too: how could "hopes and fears" meet? I liked *We Three Kings* as well, but I had to wonder where "Orientar" was! I had, nevertheless, learned not to question such things and simply sing in unison with my classmates. We practiced until our Sunday School teachers were satisfied that we could perform without embarrassing them.

The Sunday School fest was on a Sunday afternoon in the main sanctuary, and it would be in English, not the droning Norwegian I was used to in that place. The sanctuary was magical. A big, fresh spruce tree graced each side of the platform where we would sing. No ornaments adorned these verdant beauties, just blue lights. I thought I had never seen anything so marvelous. We marched double file down the aisles and climbed the few steps to the platform, where we lined up by height, the taller girls in their Christmas dresses and boys in their white shirts and ties behind the mostly younger, shorter Sunday Schoolers in the front. Our parents watched us with pride, and we knew it. We also knew we would have cookies and cake afterwards in the downstairs sanctuary.

Yes, indeed, there was nothing like Christmas. We had saved all year to buy Christmas presents, and 5th Avenue and 86th Street stores awaited us. I had carefully saved my money—mostly gifts from our most generous Onkel Sverre—and I had twelve dollars to spend. That meant I could spend four dollars each for Papa, Mama, and Ingy. I was sure I would find the perfect gifts. We had walked by the storefronts on a Sunday afternoon, "window shopping" as we called it, because the stores were closed on the day of rest. We looked carefully and added up ideas for the perfect gifts.

And then, of course, we had to buy a tree. For that we needed Papa, so it had to be when he wasn't on the boat. We were bundled up when we went to the tree lot because it was blustery, and snow was starting to fall. We looked at many trees, finally settling on one, which Papa paid for and tied to the roof of the car, and we brought it home. Papa cut the bottom of the trunk and put the tree in the stand, tightening the four screws so it would stand upright. Then he poured water into the stand, "So it will stay fresh," he said. It stood like that, clean and green, until the next night.

The next evening, Tante Clara, Onkel Olav, and our four cousins joined us for lapskaus (stew), our standby dinner. Then Onkel Olav and Papa put the lights on the tree. Papa had gotten them all on when suddenly they went off. "Uff," said Papa and fiddled with the bulbs until the lights flickered and came on again.

"Be careful not to move the lights when you hang the ornaments," said Onkel Olav to us as he placed the angel on top. Then, while the adults had coffee, we six kids set about decorating the tree. We hung the ornaments with care, and piece by piece we draped the tinsel on the branches so that the tree glistened. The final touch was the strands of Norwegian flags which we draped like garlands around the tree. It was magnificent.

On the day before Christmas, Lille Jul Aften (little Christmas Eve), Mama took the Fairlane to 8th Avenue, and we went to the Norwegian deli. "I called to order rullepølse a few days ago," she said. Don't slice it. I want it whole, about this big," she gestured with her hands. Give me the end piece," she said. Then she bought lots of marzipan pigs. "For the children," she explained to the Norwegian deli man, "on Christmas."

Finally, Christmas Eve arrived. It was our tradition to open our gifts on this night, after supper. Ingy had rebelled this year, however, by announcing that the English department pastor had said that we ought to be in church on Christmas Eve, celebrating the birth of the Lord Jesus, if we were any kind of Christians. "Nonsense," said Mama. "What does he know about being Norwegian?"

I hadn't thought about the English department pastor much at all but asked, "Isn't he Norwegian?"

"He's not Norwegian, but he's a free church man," Mama explained. "I think he's maybe German, but I'm not sure. He came from Wisconsin to be the pastor here." I was learning something: you didn't have to be Norwegian to be part of the First Evangelical Free Church, even though almost everyone we knew in our church actually was Norwegian or married to one.

There was no question about how we would spend Christmas Eve. We did what most of the Norwegians who attended 66th Street church did: we celebrated at home. This year Tante Clara and Onkel Olav and our cousins joined us at our house—we would alternate from year to year. We had boiled cod and lefse with white potatoes. "The white food symbolizes purity," said Tante Clara. While we didn't care why the food was white, and we didn't like the boiled fish with white sauce, we ate it because we knew we would have cookies and exchange gifts afterwards.

When the table was cleared and the dishes washed, Papa read the Christmas story from the second chapter of Luke in English. I had gotten to know that chapter almost by heart, and I knew Alice surely did. Of course, I couldn't understand why "All the world should be taxed," and how was that even possible more than 1900 years ago? But we accepted the story as Papa read it, and Onkel Olav nodded and said, "Ya."

Mama had bought gifts for the cousins, and Tante Clara had done the same. We exchanged our presents gleefully, sitting on the floor as boxes and wrapping paper piled up around us. Then we looked at the TV for a bit—a Christmas show with beautiful holiday music—until Onkel Olav announced that it was time for them to go home. "Don't forget, we are going to Staten Island tomorrow. It's going to be a big crowd." That was something to look forward to, and I was happy to go to bed.

When we got up the next day, Mama tasked us with cleaning up the wrapping paper and boxes and taking our presents to our rooms to restore order to the living room. Then we got dressed, and after lunch piled into the car. When we got to 69th Street, Papa groaned, "Look at the lines for the ferry. We will have a long wait. Maybe we should park and board on foot."

"We can't," said Mama. "I have the rullepølse and marzipan pigs." So that settled it. We waited until the ferry had gone back and forth three times before we could drive on board. So many people were headed to the island that day. When we debarked, we drove to Todt Hill, where our Tante and Onkel lived. It was a magnificent house, and it made me think our house was small by comparison. This house had a big yard, and there were lights aglow in the bushes, even though it was daylight.

"I see Werner and Hedwig are already here," said Papa, "and there's Olav's car and Leif's car, too." I knew then that Onkel Werner and Onkel Olav had had the good sense to leave Brooklyn earlier than we had, and probably didn't have to wait too long for the ferry. Onkel Jakob and Onkel Leif, of course, lived on Staten Island, so transporting their families was an easy job. There were several other cars, and I didn't recognize them.

"Those cars must belong to Werner and Hedwig's boys, Werner and Wilhelm," surmised Papa as he appraised the vehicles. And then we rang the doorbell.

The door was opened by a tall, good-looking blond man. "Hello,

Sven," said Mama. "We're here. Give me a hand with the rullepølse." As soon as we were in the door and had taken our coats off, we heard Tor Asbjørn howling! "My goodness," said Mama. "What now?"

"He shot me; he shot me," wailed Tor Asbjørn pointing at Harold, who was looking sheepish and holding a BB gun.

"I told you the BB gun was not a good gift, but you insisted," said Tante Ragna to Onkel Leif, and she gave him a look over the top of her glasses, which were perched low on her nose.

"Now, now, calm down everybody," said Onkel Leif in quiet English. Come here, Tor Asbjørn. Let's have a look." Tor Asbjørn went with Onkel Leif into the dining room, and we could see him dropping his pants behind one of the double doors.

Ingy and Bente started to laugh. "Harold shot my brother in the ass," said Bente. Ingy covered her mouth with her hands, suppressing her laughter.

"Don't use such language," admonished Tante Clara, also in English. "Your brother is hurt, and you shouldn't laugh either." By now, lots of people were laughing, especially after Onkel Leif announced, "He's not hurt. It's just a BB pellet that hit him in the rear end. He's fine."

It was mostly pandemonium from then on. I noticed our elegant cousin Dagmar, the one who lived in the city, speaking with a woman I didn't recognize.

"Who's that woman?" I asked Bente in a low whisper.

"I think she's Werner's wife, who is Dagmar's sister-in-law Her name is Agatha. Werner is over there," Bente said, pointing discretely. "He's named after his father and grandfather.

"What about him?" I asked, pointing directly.

"Don't point," Ingy hissed, and added, "I'm not sure."

Maggy, who was standing nearby with her sister Goody, heard me, or perhaps she saw me pointing, and said, "He's my other brother Wilhelm, and his wife is Nina. She's the one in the dark blue dress over there, behind him." I was hoping there wouldn't be a test on who was who.

But while I had Maggy's attention, I thought about that creepy boyfriend of hers; I had scanned the room looking for him, but he didn't appear. "Maggy," I said, "do you still have that boyfriend, the one that used to come to our house when you babysat?"

"No," said Maggy, "We broke up. But I'll tell you, he loved to come to your house when I babysat. More than once, I found him coming out of your bedroom. He said he just loved watching the two of you sleep. You were so lovely." I was pretty sure Ingy hadn't been sleeping back then, and I surely had tried hard to pretend I was. And right then I experienced a feeling of dread, just like I used to back in our bedroom on 79th Street. I gasped and took a deep breath, trying to regulate my breathing.

"Are you okay?" asked Maggy. Her question told me then that she knew what he was about. The sudden insight had taken the breath out of me, but then, breathing calmly wasn't my thing.

"Yes," I mumbled and backed away, making my way to Alice and Sonya, who were telling Tante Hulda, the aunt I scarcely knew, what they had gotten for Christmas.

"Christmas is different now than when I grew up in Norway. And your uncle Johann Torvald was poor because there were so many children in that house in Jorstad," Tante Hulda told us in pretty clear English.

"I know there were ten altogether," Alice said.

"No, twelve," said Tante Hulda, as Bente and Ingy joined us.

Alice said she knew Onkel Arne and Tante Torhild lived in Oslo, and Tante Augusta and her family lived in Grimstad. Everyone else was here in America—and she counted on her fingers: Hedwig, Johann Torvald, Jakob, Magda, Leif, my mother, Clara, Cornella, and Sverre. "That's ten," she said authoratatively.

"Your grandmother," Tante Hulda said, pointing at Bestmor, who was engrossed in hearty laughter, "had two others. A baby named Anton who died a few weeks after he was born, and a daughter named Borghild who died when she was young of the Spanish flu that took hold in Norway in 1918."

We were getting a family history lesson, and I was trying to place the cousins with their parents as Tante Hulda recited who was who. Onkel Jakob and his wife Bergitta had three sons—Sigurd, Stanley, and Salve. That would be easy to remember—the S men, I thought to myself. Now to stir it up just a bit, Tante Hulda added, "Your grandmother has great grandchildren, too. Hedvig and Werner's two boys have children of their own." With that she pointed at Werner and Wilhelm, whom I already knew about from Bente and Maggy. But now I suddenly noticed they both bore a striking resemblance to Onkel Werner. They're handsome, I thought, and their wives are pretty.

Which kids belong to Wilhelm and which to Werner, I wondered, so I posed the question to Tante Hulda. "Wilhelm and Nina have two little girls, Margit and Karen; one is three, the other just nine months old. Werner and Agatha have two girls, Liv and June, and one boy, Johnny. My daughter, Vigdis—over there," she said, pointing, "is married and has a little boy, Karl Johann. That's him over there," she gestured. "He's four. Her husband isn't here today because he's on the harbor; he's a tugboat man. Karl Johann is my grandson, and your Bestemor's great grandson."

Oh my, this would take a while to grasp. Nevertheless, I hoped I would understand it all eventually. As I mulled over what Tante Hulda had just explained, she announced she needed to get into her kitchen and start putting food on the dining room table. "Can I help?" I asked.

"No, Solveig, your Tantes and your mother are all the help I need."

Curious about the goings-on in the kitchen, I went to the doorway anyway and watched the preparation. Tante Hedwig was cutting the rullepølse, nice and thin. Tante Hulda said to her, "That's the rullepølse you made, isn't it? It's beautiful, as fine as any you could buy."

Tante Hedwig looked perplexed, but she kept slicing and arranging the meat artfully on a red platter. Mama had a platter of potets kage in her hand, and she approached Tante Hedwig. "Shall I take this platter to the dining room table, too?"

Hedwig drew herself up and said, for a change, in Norwegian, "This rullepølse doesn't look like the one we made at your house. For one thing, the end is clean cut."

Mama said, "Don't be silly. Of course, it is. And it's delicious. The cut on the end is because I wanted to taste it just to make sure."

With that Hedwig replied, "Look at this. There are three types of meat in it. Lamb, pork, and I think veal. We only used lamb and pork." Mama simply turned on her heel and took the potets kage into the dining room, apparently not having heard Hedwig's speculation.

When all the food had been brought to the buffet table, Tante Hulda, standing in the archway to the living room, announced, "Vaer sa god." ("Help yourself," but literally "be so good.")

As people started to move toward the dining room, Papa said in a loud, clear voice, in English: "But wait, we must say grace." So, I thought it would be *I Jesu Navn* and was prepared to chime in. But Papa began to pray in English, for the benefit of the spouses and children who spoke no Norwegian, thanking God for the gift of his son, and the gift of our all being together on this Christmas Day. He asked for God's blessing on Bestemor for being the matriarch of this good family, and then addressed her in Norwegian, saying, "We are so blessed you are with us," and then, "amen." Of course, she understood not a word but his blessing to her, but she knew everything he had said was a prayer.

We feasted that Christmas Day in Onkel Johann and Tante Hulda's beautiful house, children perched on the stairs, grownups holding plates on their laps in the living room, a few sitting at the kitchen table. The smørgasbord was beautiful, replete with quivering jello salads laden with fruits and vegetables, cold cuts, potets kage, rullepølse, home-baked bread, and kringle. A beautiful centerpiece of fir, white carnations, and red roses graced the center of the table, and a huge punchbowl sat at the end, surrounded by pretty glass cups. In the sparkling crystal bowl was a strawberry punch, with sherbet making a sort of floating island. It was surely "mye god matt" (lots of good food). I knew Tante Hulda had really worked to get us all together, and it was all for Bestemor, who wanted the whole family together this Christmas.

Mama remarked that she wondered where her brother Sverre was. "Just like him," she said. "He'd choose the beerhall over us every time."

"Now, Cornella," said Tante Hedwig in her pointed English, "You know what the ferry traffic is like today. He probably just started out late and got stuck in the ferry or maybe he had a feather bender." And just as she said that, Onkel Sverre came through the door. We hadn't heard him enter, because the house was pretty noisy, animated with happy talk. On his arm was Gerd, his girlfriend, and she was pretty fat, anyone could see that.

Mama's eyes grew wide as she looked at her brother and Gerd. "No wonder she wants to get married," Mama muttered to Tante Clara.

Tante Clara didn't reply but simply rose from her seat and

approached Sverre and Gerd. "We are so glad you could come, and we are so glad there will be a new addition to our big family," she said, taking both of Gerd's hands in her own.

"Thank you," said Gerd gently. "Sverre and I decided to marry at the City Hall in Manhattan. We are very happy."

"Well, come and have some food. We have plenty," Tante Clara said. "And then I want to hear all about how you married and where you live."

After we had eaten, Tante Hulda brought out riskrem and rød saus—the Norwegian version of rice pudding with a warm red lingonberry sauce—and more than 10 varieties of cookies. "You've been busy," Mama commented, looking at the beautiful display of baked goods arranged on imalia (enameled) plates.

Sverre had helped himself to the punch and took a swig from a little flask he took from his pocket. I heard one of Onkel Jakob's sons, Stanley, I think, jokingly say, "At least he didn't pour it into the punch."

"Sure, that's why he's always so happy and red faced," his brother Sigurd joined in.

"He could use some more fresh air."

"Let's us get some fresh air," he said. They got their coats and hats and bundled up, for it had begun to snow lightly.

Mama commented, "They are going out to smoke. My mother hates that."

After a while, they returned, and Sigurd announced, "It's mighty cold out there. Almost as cold as the day we left Norway. Think about it, that was April, and it was colder back then than it is here now on December 25th."

"Remember that, do you?" said his mother, Tante Bergitta. "You were only ten when we boarded the ship to come to America."

"I do remember, very well," said Sigurd. "It was an adventure, so many of us cousins on the ship as it left Bergen. We will never forget it."

Tor Asbjørn piped up. "What? Why did you leave Norway, and how many cousins were there?"

"Let me tell it," said Tante Hedwig. "I have a good remembery. It was 1940, and the Germans were going to invade Norway. We had decided that we would leave when it was understood they were coming. Werner's father had predicted it, so we booked passage on the *Bergensfjord*, and got the boat in Bergen."

With that, Onkel Werner joined in, "My parents left Germany in 1939 for Switzerland, a neutral country. My father said he needed to keep my mother safe and that it would be bad in Germany, worse than during the first world war. He was able to go to Switzerland because he had business contacts there who arranged for him and my mother to come to Bern. My father strongly advised me to take my wife and children and get out of Norway, because the Nazis were doing awful things to Jews and anyone who opposed them, and it was certain they would take Norway."

"I wasn't worried," said Tante Hedwig, "because I didn't think the Germans were smart enough to think out that my mother-in-law, Werner's mother, who was English, was also Jewish."

By now, a hush had fallen on the room, and we were enrapt. Onkel Werner was Jewish! Who knew? I had heard many people at 66th Street church—and even my own parents—say things like "The Jews are awful people," "The Jews are money-mongers," "The Jews will take every dime you have, if they can," "Norwegian Jews are the worst." And if that wasn't bad enough, "The Jews killed Jesus." And now we learned that we had had a Jew in our very own family!

Tor Asbjørn asked Tante Hedwig to continue telling the story about the exit from Norway in 1940. "We planned to leave, Werner and me, with the boys and our little girls. Werner encouraged his two brothers-in-law to do the same. My brother Johann Torvald, Hulda, and their two, Sven and Vigdis, joined us. Also on board were Leif and Ragna, but their children weren't born until after they arrived in America."

"But how did you get to go?" asked Bente.

"We traveled forth and back to Kristiansand to get tickets on the *Bergensfjord* for all of us, and we did good. Then we all traveled to Bergen and got on the ship, which sailed on April 7, and it was cold, bitter really, with sleet coming down on us. Two days later the Nazis were in Norway. Werner's father had been right. I imagine there was so much contusion when the Germans took control, but no, they knew the ship had sailed."

Onkel Werner piped in. "It was a little frightening, because we knew the Nazis could easily find us. And instead of mass confusion, the Nazis radioed the ship and called it back to port."

"Ya," said Onkel Johann Torvald, also in English, "but the captain was brave. He ordered that all the running lights on the ship be turned off, and the cabins' windows blacked out. He knew the Norwegian Sea was full of U-boats, and the adults were afraid."

"But we also knew," said Onkel Werner, "that there were rumors that the Norwegian government had moved the crown jewels and silver out of the country when it looked like the Germans were on their way.

"So, the captain gambled that the Nazis wouldn't sink the ship, and it was a good gamble. But to be sure, with the ship blacked out, he didn't follow the usual cross-Atlantic sea route, the one the Germans expected the ship to take. He went way north into the Artic sea and brought the ship west to America from there. By the way, the Nazis also knew that the Norwegian-America Line could sail directly from Norway to New York. Many ships at that time had to stop in England or Ireland to refuel before crossing the Atlantic. But the Nazis were looking at the established route, the direct one. They didn't expect such a detour."

Onkel Werner's son Werner spoke up: "When we set sail from Bergen, Wilhelm and I were on deck standing by the railing in the front of the ship. So was Sven. The little girls were in the cabins with the parents."

"I was scared stiff, thinking you were in the brow of the boat," said Tante Hedwig, "but Werner calmed me down, saying you would be all right. There were crewmen on deck. You boys liked to go on deck and did so almost every day until we docked in New York on April 15th."

"That's an amazing story," said Tor Asbjørn. "We don't have adventures like that here. It must have been so exciting!"

Onkel Werner said, "Exciting for the children, maybe, because they didn't understand what might happen. But the ship docked in New York in the East River, Pier 8, where we were met by our relatives. We knew then that we were safe."

"What happened to the ship after that? asked Tor Asbjørn. "Did it go back to Norway?"

"No, how could it?" responded Onkel Werner. "It was requisitioned by the British Ministry of War a while after we arrived and converted to a troop ship in Liverpool, England. She carried Axis—that's what we called our enemies—prisoners of war, and Allied troops. The beautiful *Bergensfjord* served a big role in helping to defeat the Germans. I know for a fact that by the end of the war, she had carried over 150,000 troops and sailed some 300,000 miles for the war effort."

This was fascinating, especially to the boys. Tor Asbjørn commented confidently: "I am going to be a sailor when I grow up."

"Oh, sure," said Alice. "I thought you were going to be a bus driver."

"Ya, ya," said Papa interrupting that discussion, "That's all for the future. Right now it's time to go or we'll miss the ferry."

As we were heading to the door, I heard Tante Hedwig say to Tante Hulda, again in her unique English, "This was wonderful. You had so much food. You will have many overlefts."

"Ya," said Tante Hulda, "but Johann's mother is with us, so we will make good use of it."

Bestemor, who would be staying with Onkel Torvald and Tante Hulda for a few weeks thereafter, said in her Sørlandt's Norwegian, "I love you all so much. This has been the best Christmas." And we left with a good and satisfied feeling that we all belonged to each other.

Chapter Ten

Pending Nuptials

January was cold, I mean really cold, so we stayed in a lot, even though snow was on the ground, and I normally clamored to go out and play in it. But then, we were pretty new to the neighborhood, and I hadn't made any friends. Ingy was past playing in the snow—she was a bona fide teenager, replete with pimples and mood swings. She was really into rock and roll, and I would hear the radio emanating from her room. *Blue Suede Shoes* was popular, and she would sing along, liking the lyrics, and I liked hearing her slightly off-key voice. I liked *Blue Suede Shoes* too, maybe because I heard it so often, and would go around singing "Don't you step on my blue suede shoes." I was getting interested in rock and roll, just like Ingy and Bente. Even Tor Asbjørn, Alice, and Sonya seemed to like it. We pretty much liked what our big sisters did.

Winter dragged on, and one day while we were with the cousins on 67th Street and listening to the radio, we heard our fathers talking in the kitchen. "It's just a phase," said Onkel Olav. "It's not really music—it's the beat the kids like." Ingy and Bente looked at each other and smiled.

Tor Asbjørn said knowingly, "Oh sure." With that we all giggled. What would two old Norwegian men know, after all?

Papa continued by saying, "You know, at church the minister advises us to admonish our children not to listen to it, that it's from the Devil. I just don't know."

"Ya, ya," replied Onkel Olav. "I heard that too, but it seems a little extreme. Give the kids a few more months of this, and it will pass."

"I don't know," Papa said softly. "Look at that Elvis fellow—he swivels his hips. It's obscene. 'Elvis the Pelvis' a man in church called him. Did you know that rock and roll is another word for sex? That's what negroes call it. I think the whole thing is a disgrace. There will be an end to good music if this continues."

In the living room, Tor Asbjørn turned to us and said, "So do you think this is a phase? Elvis the Pelvis—hah! My friend Eddie calls him 'Enis the Penis.' We've heard our parents criticize Elvis before. They don't like him, but Elvis is hot stuff!"

"No way; it's no phase," said Bente. "I have a record collection—45s—and I'm going to build it."

“Hah,” said Ingy. "Our pastor in the English Department thinks we should have a record-smashing party, the way some of the other churches are doing. Bet you wouldn’t smash Elvis.”

“No way,” said Bente. “I’m going to own every record Elvis makes. I already have *Heartbreak Hotel, Blue Suede Shoes, My Baby Left Me,* and *Hound Dog.* You go smash your records, if you want."

“I don’t have any to smash. Papa says they’re a waste of money and sinful. The radio is good enough.”

While we were pondering the logistics of breaking records—like what would they do with the all the broken pieces—the conversation in the kitchen changed. Papa and Onkel Olav talked politics, as they always did when they were together. Sure, they couldn’t be in the same room before the talk turned to government.

"Eisenhower announced he would seek a second term. He will be a shoo-in. Look at what he’s accomplished. He balanced the budget; he authorized construction of CIA headquarters; and he raised the minimum wage from seventy-five cents to a dollar," said Papa. That was Papa—focused on money. "This country is so rich—we are blessed."

"Ike did a lot of good things in his first term. Don't forget he ended the Korean War," added Onkel Olav. "But he's going to be up against Stevenson again, and his Vice President, that Nixon fellow, isn't all that likable."

"Oh, you just don't hear that much from him. But he's a family man."

"Have you noticed how crooked his face is—one eyebrow is higher than the other," Onkel Olav said. "He looks sneaky; he's not a good backup, a man who could be President if something bad happens."

"If Eisenhower trusts him, then we have to, too. Ike's a progressive conservative and has a strong moral fiber. You know, he comes from a religious family—why his mother, a pacifist, objected to his going to West Point. She was opposed to war. I wonder what she would make of this son of hers who went on to lead the Allied Forces in World War Two and make them victorious. He probably single-handedly saved the West and democracy."

"Well," said Onkel Olav, "there were a lot of heroes, and it took the joint efforts of many to win the war."

"Ya, Ya," said Mama, changing the subject. "You can't do much about politics, and what will be will be. But I have some news. Hedwig called this morning and told me Dagmar is engaged to be married."

"Oh my. Why didn't she bring the boy to Johann's on Christmas?" Tante Clara quickly asked. "We would have liked to meet him."

"Well," said Mama, "Mama Andrea wanted just the family there. And to tell the truth, I think Hedwig was afraid it would cause some commotion."

"Why is that?" Onkel Olav asked.

"He's not Norwegian. He's Catholic, too," Mama replied.

"Oh no," said Papa under his breath.

You can bet that got our attention in the living room, and we fell silent to listen intently. "There are lots of perfectly fine Norwegian boys here in Brooklyn. She should stick to her own kind. Is this someone she met in the city?" Papa asked.

Mama responded with this: "According to Hedwig, he came into Gimbels men's department—that's where Dagmar works—and that's how they met. He evidently kept coming back looking for her, and then finally asked her to have coffee with him. He lives in Brooklyn, somewhere in Sunset Park."

"But he's Catholic. How can Hedwig and Werner allow that?" Papa asked. Now, this was interesting since we knew Hedwig had married Werner. The odd thing was this: no one much mentioned Onkel Werner's Jewishness. It was as though they couldn't acknowledge it, and it didn't exist. In fact, it was only recently that we had first heard the story of how the German-raised Werner, whose mother was Jewish, met Hedwig and then got married in Norway.

"The boy talked to Werner," Mama explained, "and Werner likes him."

"Will they get married in a Catholic church?" Clara asked.

"Hedwig said the family goes to the big church on 60th Street and 6th Avenue—OLPH which stands for 'Our Lady of Perfect Health,' I think she said."

"Well, well, this is certainly a bit of interesting news," Onkel Olav said, leaning back in his chair, arms crossed.

Meanwhile, Bente and Ingy began speculating about what the wedding would be like. I was sure we'd get to see it at least, if not attend the reception. We had seen several weddings in the 66th Street church. Mama would bring us, and we'd watch the ceremonies from the balcony.

"Dagmar will be a beautiful bride," Bente said. "I think she looks like Grace Kelly, the movie star."

"Yeah, maybe," opined Ingy. "She certainly is elegant." This turned the conversation to the movies. "Who is your favorite actor?" Ingy asked us all.

Bente was quick to respond with Ray Milland, explaining that the girls at Bay Ridge High went to the movies and talked about actors and actresses, so she knew.

"I like Frank Sinatra. He has those gorgeous blue eyes, and he can sing," Ingy said.

"Me, I like Marilyn Monroe. She's a bombshell," said Tor Asbjørn. "You girls don't look anything like her, that's a fact," he said, outlining a big an hourglass shape with his hands and smiling.

"Well, you know Marilyn Monroe isn't her real name. She calls herself that, but she was born Norma Jean Mortensen—a name that ends in 'sen' just like our names, Hansen and Torgersen," said Bente. Then we began to realize that Bente and Ingy were planning something big. They were conspiring. They were going to go to a movie, and not just any movie. They would go to Radio City Music Hall.

The plan was this: they would tell the parents they were going to stay after school for a study group, but in reality they would take the Sea Beach Express to Manhattan. I knew what they were planning to do was play hooky, but I was intrigued, and we decided their secret was safe with us.

On hooky-day, about four-thirty in the afternoon, Ingy arrived home exhilarated. "The study group was really helpful," she told Mama. "We were in the auditorium. They let us stay as long as we wanted."

Then she whispered that she had something important to tell me, but first she swore me to secrecy. "We went to Radio City Music Hall and saw the Rockettes dance on stage—and what a stage. It is just magnificent. Then we saw *Carousel* with Gordon MacRae and Shirley Jones. It was fantastic," she gushed. What can I say? I was envious. Ingy told me Bente would like to become a Rockette when she graduates from high school. And me, I was curious about the dancing Rockettes.

I was also more and more aware of how Ingy was growing up. She had dared to defy our parents, a scary act; she had lied, too, which was a sin. Moreover, at fifteen she still had those beautiful blond curls and blue eyes, but her body had taken on some curves. I had seen the boys at church looking at her, but she seemed painfully embarrassed by a blotchy teenage complexion. Her pimples were her nemesis.

Mama had taken her to a doctor, who prescribed a sun lamp. Overly zealous, Ingy sat in front of it until her face was lobster red—and the pimples were still there. The doctor had also recommended eliminating iodized salt and using a product called Acnomel, a kind of pancake makeup that was supposed to conceal the pimples and even help heal them. "It's pancake makeup," she said. "And Mama and Papa are letting me use it." Then she showed me her baby pink lipstick. "I put it on after I leave the house," she explained. Aha! I had to wonder how old I would have to be before I could use makeup, and if it truly were a sin, what would be the price?

One Saturday morning in early February while I was in my room, and Ingy in hers, listening to *Shake, Rattle, and Roll,* we heard the phone ring. "I'll get it," Mama said to Papa while they were sitting at the kitchen table having coffee. When she got off the phone, she said, "That was Clara. Gerd had the baby, a girl. She is going to the hospital to see Gerd, Sverre, and the new little one."

Having heard, "baby," I came hurtling down the stairs. "We have a new cousin, a new cousin. What's her name?"

"Aslaug," said Mama.

"Can we see her?"

"Not right away, maybe in a few weeks' time." Mama was being evasive, I knew, but I didn't know why. It was later at Tante Clara's that we finally got to meet the new arrival, a tiny bundle in pink. Clara had invited us to stop by one Sunday after church and have middags with the whole family. What Mama didn't know was that Tante Clara had also invited Onkel Sverre and Gerd—the woman we hadn't yet learned to call Tante—and little Aslaug. Mama was startled to see her brother and Gerd, and I could tell she still disapproved of their union. And I knew why. We had overheard the conversation some time ago: Sverre was still married to a woman who now lived in Germany. The brand-new Aslaug was his second daughter. We never said a word, never let on what we knew. Bente, Ingy, Alice, Sonya and I were delighted with the baby, Tor Asbjørn not so much so.

"She looks like me," exclaimed Sonya. And indeed she did.

Onkel Sverre was beaming, a grin from ear to ear on his handsome Nordic face. He said to Bente and Ingy, "You may be my babysitters pretty soon." I could tell they liked that idea; a little more income would give them money to sneak off to the movies, no doubt.

Two months after Aslaug appeared in the family, we again gathered at Tante Clara's for a big occasion: we would watch the wedding of Prince Rainier of Monaco and Grace Kelly on the Philco television set at Tante Clara and Onkel Olav's. The bride was an American movie star, a girl who hailed from Philadelphia. We were familiar with the story. They had met while the beautiful Kelly was at the Cannes Film Festival in France, a place mysterious to us, but evidently a location where the rich and famous went. It was there the two fell in love.

Ingy and Bente were mesmerized as reporters talked about the wedding. The couple had been married the day before in a civil ceremony, but this day's event was the religious one, the one the reporters were calling "The wedding of the century." The wedding dress was also a prime reporting topic. It had been designed by the award-winning Hollywood costume designer Helen Rose and paid for by MGM studios. Thirty-plus seamstresses worked together for six weeks to produce the end result, with antique Belgian lace, hundreds of tiny pearls, and a cascading train.

"They must really like that girl in Hollywood," said Onkel Olav when they heard that MGM studios had gifted the dress to the bride.

"Yeah," said Papa, "but she's under contract, and look at all the publicity they get for free. It's all about the money for that Hollywood racket."

A reporter was saying that Kelly, upon her marriage, would be known as "Her Serene Highness Princess Grace of Monaco."

"But she'll still be 'Mrs. Rainier,'" Sonya piped up.

With that, Bente smiled at her younger sister and said, "the family name is Grimaldi."

Then the cameras focused on St. Nicholas Cathedral, and we watched intently as guests filled the sanctuary. Over 600 would attend, according to the newscasters.

"There's Cary Grant," said Bente enthusiastically.

"And Ava Gardner," added Ingy.

"And how do you know who those people are?" Mama asked, an odd tone to her voice.

Startled, Ingy looked sideways, at nothing in particular, took a breath, and said, "The girls at school have magazines with movie stars in them. That's how we know."

"Ah, I see," said Mama dubiously.

Then we watched as the wedding party walked down the aisle. Six American friends were bridesmaids, Kelly's sister was the Matron of Honor, and there were four flower girls and two pages. "The brides' attendants are in pale yellow organdy dresses," the announcer said, "and the children are in white." To us, the bride's attendants looked to be all in white on the black and white Philco screen. The groomsmen looked to be in black or at best dark gray. The announcer continued with a description of the Prince's attire: "He designed it himself: a black tunic with a red and white sash representing the Order of St. Charles, an impressive array of medals on his chest, and light blue pants with a golden stripe on the outside of each pant leg."

When the priest declared them married, he said to the onlookers, "May I present His Serene Highness Prince Rainier Henri Maxence Grimaldi and Her Serene Highness Princess Grace Patricia Grimaldi."

"That was incredible," said Bente.

"It was stupid, that's what," said Tor Asbjørn and retreated to his room. Then we began to talk about our cousin's upcoming marriage. After what I had just seen, I was dubious that the 59th Street Lutheran Brethren Evangelical Free Church could measure up to St. Nicholas Cathedral, nor could the church called OLPH. But we would see.

Shortly thereafter, Mama and Papa were at the kitchen table for their mid-morning coffee ritual when the phone rang. "That was Hedwig. Dagmar has the day off and they are looking for wedding gowns."

"Can't she get that at Gimbels? She must get a discount because she works there," said Papa.

"They are going to Kleinfeld's on 5th Avenue and 82nd Street," Mama said. "After that they are going to stop in here for coffee."

"Okay," said Papa. "It will be good to hear more about this boy she's going to marry."

A few hours later, the doorbell rang, and there stood Tante Hedwig and her daughter. Ingy and I were awed by the beautiful Dagmar, today aglow with pleasure. We proceeded into the kitchen where coffee was brewing. "Tell us about the shopping. Did you find anything?" Mama asked in English.

"Oh," said Tante Hedwig. "We looked at so many dresses. Dagmar, while tall, is tin. She has such a model's figure, that most fit her well. Each gown was more beautiful than the next."

"Did you choose one?" asked Ingy.

"I think I know the one I want. Hedda Kleinfeld was such a big help—she's the owner—and she waited on us herself. She said three gowns looked really good on me, but that I should think about it, and then let her know. She says her seamstresses are excellent and whichever gown I choose will fit me perfectly." I was thinking, I bet she wouldn't have three dozen seamstresses working on whichever one she chose like Princess Grace had. "The one I like best had tiny little buttons all the way down the back, and it has a train. There's a hook in the skirt so I can pin it up. 'It's for when you have your first dance as husband and wife,' Hedda said." And I, startled, thought, dance! Mama and Papa remained stone-faced. "We also looked at bridesmaid dresses, but I think we can get those at Gimbels," Dagmar said. "I get an employee discount."

"When is the wedding going to be?" I asked. "And where? Who will be your bridesmaids?"

"The end of August," said Dagmar. "In 59th Street church. After all, that's where I was confirmed. My sister Goody will be my maid of honor and Maggy a bridesmaid, and we hope, also Richie's sister, Marie. My brothers, Werner and Wilhelm, will be groomsmen and Richie's brother, Sean, will be best man. If Marie can't be a bridesmaid, I'll ask my best friend, Lois. I wanted to ask, but didn't, if the younger cousins would be invited. There were so many of us. Then she said, "Sonya will be our flower girl." Now, if Sonya got to go, and we didn't, I would be so disappointed.

"What about your brothers Werner and Wilhelm's children? Won't they be in the wedding party?

"We thought about it, but they are too little. Sonya is just the right size," Dagmar explained, and we know her so well.

Then Tante Hedwig said "Her financee's sister is a pretty girl, and we're planning on her being in the wedding but there's a little bump in the path."

"That's fiancé, Mother," said Dagmar, rolling her eyes, "and it's a bump in the road, not the path. Yes, his sister, Marie, is afraid to commit. Her mother is furious at Richie, my fiancé, because I'm not Catholic. She wants him to get married at OLPH, Our Lady of Perpetual Help, but we can't unless I convert, and I don't want to."

"Does Richie go to church?" Mama asked. I was thinking maybe it was better to be Catholic and not go to church than to go there believing all the things they taught you. In a flashback, I remembered the cross in Gina's house back on 79th Street, and the image of the dead Jesus on it. Catholics didn't know, evidently, that He didn't stay dead.

"Well," Dagmar began cautiously, "Richie's mother asks him every Sunday if he's been to mass—that's the Catholic service—and he always says 'yes' even though he doesn't go. It keeps her happy, he says."

"Do you get along with his mother?" Ingy asked.

"Well, I thought I did. That is, until we got engaged. When we told her, she took my arm, leaned over to me, and said, "'Richard has never given me anything but trouble and now this!'"

"Wow," said Papa. "That must have hurt." Then he added, jokingly, "Or maybe we should just call you 'this,' from now on."

"Well, it did hurt—a lot. But it worked against her, because Richie saw how pained I was and said we would get married in my church and never mind his mother. Richie's father seems to like me, so he says he's coming to the wedding no matter where it is. Besides, he's Protestant."

"What?" exclaimed Mama. "She married a Protestant, but her son can't! What a hypocrite!"

"She says he converted," Dagmar explained. "But I never knew him to go to the big church."

"It will work itself inside out," said Tante Hedwig placatingly. "Richie is such a nice boy. And so good looking. They'll have beautiful babies."

"Are you going on a honeymoon?" I asked.

"My, so many questions," Tante Hedwig said. "They had big plans to go to KoonKan—that's on the Gulf of Mexico—but they've changed their minds."

"Mother, it's Cancun," Dagmar said. "That's what we thought right away we should do—it would mean flying to Mexico. But we talked it over and made a practical decision; Richie has bought a new car. We both have three weeks' vacation, so we're driving to Florida."

Then we asked about the reception. Still in my mind was the question of whether we would all be invited, but I didn't ask.

"Where will you have the reception?" asked Mama.

"We think it will be at the Danish Club on 65th Street—it's a nice place," said Dagmar.

Of course, we wanted to know more, but then the doorbell rang, and Dagmar's face lit up as she announced, "That's Richie." We stood up from the table and went in unison toward the front door. When Dagmar opened it, there stood a good-looking, or should I say beautiful, young man. His hair was almost black, but his eyes were a startling blue. And he was tall and slender. Better looking than Elvis, I thought to myself. Ingy just gaped at him.

"Hi, DeDe," he said as he gave Dagmar a hug. He called her DeDe.

"Is that your nickname?" Ingy asked.

"Yes, Richie always calls me DeDe, and after he showed up at Gimbels calling me that, people at work started to call me that, too. Dagmar is an unusual name here."

"Is that your car out there?" Papa asked, peering over Richie's shoulder at the street.

"Yes, just picked it up a few days ago."

"It's a Buick Special, isn't it?" Papa was showing his knowledge of cars.

"Yes, said Richie. "It's loaded—a 322 V8 2-speed automatic and Dynaflow transmission." I wasn't so interested in those details, but I noted the red and white exterior—shiny and clean—the red interior, and the wide white wall tires.

"What are those three holes on the side?" I asked.

Richie looked me straight in the eye, smiled, and said, "They're port holes. All Buicks have them." And with that direct look, I was enchanted.

Papa commented that a road trip in that beautiful car would be an adventure. "Yes," said Richie, "American vacations from now on will be road trips. Eisenhower is talking about the National Highway System and how states need to be connected by excellent roadways. Dede and I hope to make it all the way to Key West—that's the farthest south you can go on the east coast. Don't you think the car will look that much better with DeDe in the passenger seat?"

Papa chuckled and said, "For sure." It wasn't lost on me how he kept glancing at Dagmar.

"So, you must have a good job to afford a car like that," said Papa. I knew he was fishing—what did Richie do that he could buy such a car?

"Well, I have a secure job. I work at Bush Terminal for the Luckenbach Steamship Company."

"You're a union man, then," said Papa.

"Yes—a longshoreman."

Tante Hedwig piped in with "He's building senuority. It's a good, solid job."

"Seniority, Mother," interjected Dagmar.

"What's it like?" stuttered Ingy, afraid to make eye contact but wanting Richie's attention.

"Well, if you've seen the movie *On the Waterfront,* it's sort of like that. But I don't work with Marlon Brando," Richie said laughingly. There it was again—first, dancing a topic in the conversation, now movies. Again, Papa and Mama were stone-faced. Tante Hedwig smiled at Richie.

"How did you get your job?" Papa asked.

"Well, my father was a longshoreman, too. When I was a kid, he was really busy working the waterfront during the war. Evidently, he was well thought of, and people at Luckenbach liked him, so when I, right out of high school, went looking for a job, it was easy."

"Come into the kitchen," Mama interrupted. "We'll have coffee and cake. I wanted to serve it right away, but Hedwig said—looking at Richie—we had to wait for you." With that, Mama opened the green box with the brown cross hatching and pulled out the Brooklyn Blackout Cake from Ebinger's on 86th Street and sliced it up.

"Funny name for a cake, isn't it?" asked Richie, "But it's always been one of my favorites—so chocolaty it's almost black."

Papa said knowingly, "It's named for the blackouts imposed during World War II in England—they turned off all the lights in towns and cities as a defense against the German bombers."

"My mother's family is from Belfast in Northern Ireland, so we know about the blackouts. During the war, she was worried about her family back in Ireland because the Luftwaffe—the German Airforce—also bombed Belfast. In fact, while helping the country avoid the nightly bombings, the blackouts created their own problems. Everybody got blackout material to hang in their windows. Car lights were blacked out, too, and there were so many accidents in the dark—even though drivers were advised to drive at what in the U.S. we know as 20 miles per hour."

"Goodness," said Papa. "I guess there was no avoiding mishaps of war," he added, trailing off.

"Well," said Richie, "ever wonder why we have white lines in the roadways? In England they painted lines in the road to help drivers stay on their own sides and keep from hitting other cars."

"No kidding. Did your relatives in Ireland make it through the war?" asked Ingy.

"Yes, they were lucky, but others weren't so much," answered Richie.

"We were lucky, too," said Papa. "The Germans never attacked us on American soil, but we were ready. You know, Richie, I work on the waterfront, too. And I worked there, like your father, through the war. After Pearl Harbor, when the U.S. had entered the war, New York was the principal port for the war effort. The navy sent its ships to sea from the Brooklyn Navy Yard. I fueled those ships carrying troops and supplies, and sometimes bringing prisoners back. Why, in 1943 there were more than 500 ships anchored in the New York harbor. It's amazing to think that just a year after I came to America in 1938, there was an American Nazi rally in Madison Square Garden, and over 20,000 people attended. There was even a German American Bund Parade. Then two years later, we were at war with the Nazis. Suddenly, America hated the Germans; they were the enemy."

"Well, you know we didn't much like them, not after they invaded Norway. Norway had already felt how mean the Nazis could be," added Mama. "But they didn't really attack us here."

"Back up a little. People think the Nazis didn't attack us directly," said Richie, "but I remember my parents talking about a ship called Columbia or Coimbria or something like that being sunk off the coast of Sandy Hook in New Jersey. That's mighty close to New York Harbor. And there was another ship sunk off Long Island, a funny name, Normesh or Norness, I think."

With that, Ingy piped up with "Our uncle Sverre was torpedoed off the Georgia coast, so isn't that an attack?"

"I guess so," said Papa pensively. "Those ships were all in U.S. waters, inside the three-mile limit."

We had a lively visit. Richie knew a lot, and he engaged easily in conversation with all of us until Tante Hedwig announced they must be going. Tante Hedwig, Dagmar—whom we now knew as DeDe—and Richie got into the car for the drive to Tante Hedwig's house where our cousin would spend the night before heading into Manhattan and her little apartment the next day. As they drove away in the pretty car, Papa said to Mama, "He's a nice boy, even if he's Catholic. And he must be doing pretty good—that car cost a pretty penny."

Things quieted down a bit over the next few months. Tante Hedwig kept us apprised of the developing wedding plans. Talk of bridesmaid dresses, wedding cakes, and flowers kept us captivated. DeDe had said the reception was to be at the Danish Club on 65th Street. This would not be a church basement reception. Would there be dancing? Bente and Ingy talked a lot about the wedding—Ingy having been privy to the first information about the coming nuptials and thus the most well-informed. I knew they were also musing about whether or not we would be invited.

Me, I continued to trek to school every day and went to Pioneer Girls at church on Saturday mornings. The days turned into weeks, and the weeks into months. And then school finished up for the year. We rushed home on the last day, eager for summer vacation to begin. We had packed our clothes and games, and they were already in the car. We rushed to get out of our school clothes, and, in shorts, we climbed into the car for the ride to Budd Lake and our house on Fairview.

Papa was eager to beat rush-hour traffic, and we were through the Lincoln Tunnel before five o'clock. It wasn't until we had finished the stint on Route 3 and were well onto Route 46 in Dover that I announced I was going to puke. "Gross," said Ingy, as Papa pulled the car over next to a park, and Mama and I got out and everything in my stomach came up.

The house on Fairview was a little musty when we arrived late on that Friday and set about putting our clothes into the small dressers. Mama quickly unloaded the food she had brought from Brooklyn and plugged in the refrigerator, which she still called the "ice box," and it was soon humming nicely.

"We want to go out," Ingy announced after supper.

"Okay, but just for a little while," Mama said.

Off we skipped down the road to the house the Edelmanns rented each year, and sure enough, there were Raymond and Barbara sitting outside on the front steps—what we kids from Brooklyn called "the stoop." "Are Edel and Else here yet?" asked Ingy. "How funny it is that her name is 'Edel' and your last name is 'Edelmann.'"

Raymond said, "Sure. 'Edel' is a German name, and 'Edelmann' was a common last name in Germany. But to answer your question, they came up just before you did. So did we." We were happy to reunite with our lake friends.

Our days that summer were idyllic, crisp, and clear. We would ride our bikes along Sand Shore Road, lightheaded and free. Occasionally there was the pungent smell of pitch when Mt. Olive Township sprayed the graveled road, and our bike tires would pick up the black tar. Sometimes Tante Signe and Onkel Bendix would come to visit with Arvind and Odd in tow and eager to swim with us. Since we had no telephone in the cottage, it was always a surprise, albeit a welcome one. For my part, I was always wanting to let them know how well I knew Budd Lake, New Jersey's largest natural lake. "It's a very important lake," I said authoritatively, wading in and waiting for the water to reach my crotch. "It connects to a branch of the Raritan River."

"Know it all," said Ingy, glaring at me, then looking at Arvind for confirmation. But he didn't take the bait.

One time Tante Marit and Onkel Karl came with a welcome surprise: in the backseat of their car was not only Erick but our other grandmother—Bestemor Alma. She had just come from Norway and would be living with Tante Marit in the house they now owned in West Orange. All felt good and complete to me. Papa's eyes teared up just a bit when he hugged his mother, and it surprised me. But Mama held back, arms crossed on her chest, face impassive, until Tante Marit said, "And hello, Cornella." And then Mama smiled. Bestemor Alma did not. Tante Marit said, in Norwegian because our grandmother spoke no English, "You remember Solveig and Ingrid from when they were at Hundingsland. Look how they've grown—just like Arvind, Odd, and Erick." Then Bestemor Alma just responded with "I see that." She didn't crack a smile even then.

A few weeks later, we drove to Lake Hopatcong because all the West Orange relatives, including Bestemor Alma, were to meet us there, at Bertrand's Island, which our cousins had told us had good swimming and even an amusement park. "Let's go on the rides," said Ingy.

"Ingrid, you are here to visit with your cousins, not to go on rides," Papa said sternly. I knew he said that because he had paid an entry fee to get into the park. Swimming was to be our only entertainment. We had black inner tubes, and we took turns spinning each other around in the water. There was a lot of boat traffic, too, and we enjoyed the waves. Lake Hopatcong was huge—it made Budd Lake look like a pond, and Budd Lake was never the same to me after that.

Papa would come and go from Budd Lake according to his work schedule. When he was gone and it was Sunday, Mama made us go to Hillside Church in Succasunna with the Nelsens. I wasn't too fond of that, but at least the service was in English.

In the middle of July, Papa pulled into the driveway beside our little cottage and emerged smiling. In his hand was a stack of mail delivered to our house in Brooklyn, and he held up one envelope and asked, "What do you think this is? To me it looks like an invitation."

"Open it, open it," cried Ingy. Me, I had my fingers crossed. The envelope was addressed to Mr. and Mrs. Adolph Torgersen, and I felt a letdown. Sure enough, it was a wedding invitation, but inside was another envelope that said, "Mr. and Mrs. Adolph Torgersen and the Misses Ingrid and Solveig Torgersen."

We whooped with glee and joined hands and spun each other around. We would go to our first real wedding—the whole thing—not just to the church but to the reception as well. Mama took the invitation and read it through in English. "It's at 59th Street church at the end of August. They're not going to have the reception at the Danish Club after all. It says here, 'Reception to follow at Bush Terminal.'"

Papa then said he had met Onkel Werner in the Bay Ridge Savings Bank on 75th Street in Brooklyn, so he knew the details. "Your mother," he said, addressing Mama, "insisted that all the grandchildren attend, so Richie arranged to have the hall in Bush Terminal for the wedding. It can accommodate so many more. It's probably more reasonable for this many than the Danish Club," he added.

Then Mama said, "It has some funny letters on the invitation: RSVP. I wonder what that means."

The next day I mentioned the invitation and the odd letters to Mrs. Edelmann, and she smiled and said, "Respondez s'il vous plait. It's French, and it means you have to let them know if you are coming or not."

When I told Mama, she said, "Why would they put French on an invitation? How stupid!"

Why indeed? Dagmar was sophisticated. We knew that. That night, after Ingy and I had gone to bed, I heard Mama and Papa talking in the kitchen.

"She used French in the invitation. How ridiculous!" Mama said. But then she added, "When you get back to Brooklyn, call Hedwig and tell her we will attend."

Our days at the lake continued in sun and rain. One rainy day toward the end of July, we huddled around a Parcheesi game on the living room floor at the Edelmann's cottage, with the TV on behind us. Suddenly, from behind us, Mrs. Edelmann said, "Mein Gutt." It was so much like Norwegian and I understood, "My God."

"What?" asked Raymond.

"The *Andrea Doria* has gone down in the Atlantic. It's an Italian ship." We stopped to watch the newscast about this disaster at sea. While the ship was approaching Nantucket, an island off the coast of Massachusetts, it was apparently going too fast in the heavy fog caused by the Labrador current of cold water heading south meeting the Gulf Stream waters heading north. Just before noon it was struck broadside by a Swedish ship, the *SS Stockholm*, which was on the way to Gothenburg, Sweden, its one hundred and third routine crossing. Speculation was that it was apparently also going too fast. Once the hull of the Stockholm hit the *Andrea Doria,* she started to list severely to the right, and that caused half of its lifeboats to be unusable.

But there was a dramatic rescue at sea, and many boats responded to distress calls. What should have been a routine crossing from Genoa, Italy, to New York harbor ended badly for 1,660 passengers and crew who were transferred to other vessels; it was even worse for the 46 people who lost their lives. Thus we witnessed, via a small TV and subsequent stories in *The Newark Evening News* and *The Star Ledger* newspapers, the worst maritime disaster in United States waters since the *SS Eastland* went down in 1915. Which shipping line was at fault was never really determined, but what we knew was this: eleven hours after the collision, the *Andrea Doria* sank to the bottom of the sea.

Chapter Eleven

Fireworks

For the rest of the summer, we were excited about the wedding. Papa had dutifully called Tante Hedwig and Onkel Werner to let them know we would all be coming to the wedding at the end of August. When Papa was at the cabin with us, Mama would take us shopping to the supermarket on Route 206 in Flanders. One time she drove all the way to Chester so we could look for dresses that we could wear to the wedding. Mama said she had a nice dress she could wear, but Ingy and I had grown over the summer, so the clothes we wore for Easter would no longer fit. In Chester, we found a dress for me that was a tad big, but pretty nevertheless.

"The wedding is a month away, and you may grow some more," said Mama. "Besides, you can also wear it at Thanksgiving and Christmas." Okay, I thought. It was yellow taffeta with a bow in the back. It would do. Ingy's new dress was pale orange, and she looked good in it. Together we looked like sherbet, said Papa, "good enough to eat." This was the first time we actually looked forward to going back to Brooklyn.

That summer at the lake was satisfying nevertheless. We continued to swim with Raymond and Barbara, and we would gather at their house in the early evening to watch television. Despite our pleas to have a television at the cabin, Papa was adamant—"Absolutely not. You have fresh air and sunshine. That's all you need." Rainy days drew us to Raymond and Barbara's house, and we were cozy, playing Parcheesi and eating little delicacies that were different from anything our mother made.

That summer we left Budd Lake earlier than usual. Labor Day had been the official designated departure time for the return to the city since school always started the day after the holiday. But the wedding impelled us, and we set out for Brooklyn in late August for the wedding at the end of the month. When we got home, the air in the house was stale. Heat wafted through the house as we opened windows to let fresh air in.

The next thing Mama did after we had unpacked was to call Tante Clara on 67th Street and then Tante Ragna on Staten Island. Mama wanted to know if they had met Richie and what they thought of him. I overheard her say "Katolik" many times into the phone. When Tante Hedwig called us, however, Mama never mentioned the word. I caught the gist of that conversation, though. "Of course

I know that RSVP means we should reply. I can't believe so many don't. Where are their manners! I'm so sorry you had to call everyone who didn't respond. Are they all coming?"

Mama and Papa set out one day to buy a wedding present. "Something grand, something that will remind them of us," she said. Sometime later, they arrived at our house with a floor lamp lying across the back seat, the top part sticking out of the rear window on the passenger side, the lamp shade on the seat. Papa proudly brought it into the house and set the lamp in place. "It's a beauty," he said, placing the shade on top.

"It's not just a lamp," said Ingy. "It's a table, too. A table lamp." I marveled at the Formica table part which encircled the post. "It's pink," I said. "How do you know if it is Dagmar's taste?"

"Of course they will like it. It's modern, and all young people like modern," said Mama.

"It's a monstrosity," proclaimed Ingy under her breath, and we let it go at that.

On Saturday, Mama tied a bow to the lamp, and Mama, Papa, and I got in the car. I had to sit in the front seat between my parents, because the monstrosity took up the whole back seat. Ingy had declined to go, offering instead to dust the venetian blinds in the downstairs rooms, an offer that made Mama beam. I knew, however, that Ingy's offer was self-serving. She didn't want to witness the presentation of the wedding gift. Then off we went, the three of us, to Onkel Werner and Tante Hedwig's flat on 57th Street where Papa proudly carried the lamp in. I could see Onkel Werner was taken aback, but, gracious as always, he said, "What a practical and useful gift."

Onkel Werner and Papa sat in the living room talking politics. Mama in the kitchen asked Tante Hedwig about the wedding, and of course I, too, wanted to know the details. And then Tante Hedwig took us into the bedroom and showed us their gift for their daughter and soon-to-be son-in-law. While their two sons on Long Island had wives and children, Richie would be the first male admitted to the family as an in-law. On the floor sat a beautiful dusty blue chest—Rosemaling, Tante Hedwig said, explaining how she had meticulously painted it. Onkel Werner had crafted the chest from pine he had secured from the Bay Ridge Lumber Yard, and Tante Hedwig opened the lid to show two shining brass hinges. "As smooth as silk," she said. For me, I marveled at the intricate pattern—almost paisley-like in swirling deep reds, greens, and dark blues with whites intertwined. Now this was a gift!

“How could he build it here?” I asked.

“He’s the supper for the building, so he built it in the basement,” said Tante Hedwig proudly, looking at me. "Supper," I mused—but no one but Dagmar, aka DeDe, ever corrected her, and I wasn’t about to because I wasn't sure how to.

"It’s beautiful," said Mama. "You always were the talented one, and it’s clear Werner is, too."

I woke early the day of the wedding, and the heat was already intense. It had thundered and rained heavily in the morning, making it steamy. Ingy complained about her hair. “It will go flat,” she said, “from the steam.” But I knew her hair would be beautiful, as it always was.

As we started out toward the church on 59th Street in the late afternoon, we plowed through puddles, the vestiges of the morning’s storm. By McKinley Park there was a huge puddle, and cars had to go slow to make it through. "What a storm," said Papa. "Let’s hope it’s over for the day."

Mama then said, "It’s supposed to be good luck if it rains on your wedding day." I’ll bet DeDe wasn’t thinking that. We had to park on 7th Avenue between 59th and 58th Streets and walk to the church. Why didn’t Papa let us out in front and then go park the car? It seemed stupid; Ingy was worried about her hair, and Mama was wearing those ridiculous red high heels. People were standing on the sidewalk chatting, waiting to enter the sanctuary. I saw some people I didn't know and thought they must be Richie's family. So, they had come after all. Music wafted softly from inside as we approached the big oak doors.

An usher gave us each a program and took Mama's arm, and Papa and Ingy and I followed them to seats on the left side of the sanctuary, the bride's side, right behind Tante Clara, Onkel Olav, Bente, Tor Asbjørn, and Alice. The program identified what the organist was playing to be *Allegro Maestosa* by Handel. When the guests were all seated, an usher escorted Tante Hedwig to the front row. Two ushers moved to the front and took hold of the corners of a white runner and walked to the back of the church for a "pure" walkway for the bridal party. Tante Hedwig then arose from her seat and stepped up onto the platform where she lighted one candle and used it to light the three others in a stand on the left side; then she did the same with the candles in the stand on the right and returned to her seat. Richie and the ushers stood on the right side of the altar, and the minister took his position.

Then the organ became more powerful. The program identified the music as *Jesu, Joy of Man's Desiring* by J. S. Bach. From the pew in front of us, Bente leaned over and whispered to Ingy: "This music is fantastic." Sure it was, and Bente would know because she often talked about the music appreciation class she was taking at Bay Ridge High. It was nothing like I had heard in church before, not at any of the weddings we had gone to see as spectators at 66th Street church, at least as far as I could remember.

The music was a signal for us to stand up, and we did, looking to the double doors of the church. Sonya, the first member of the bridal party, stood there, looking lovely in a long lavender dress and holding a basket of rose petals. I knew she was proud to be there—she had bragged to me that the Bride and Broom had chosen her among all the girls in the family. But now she seemed nervous, and I saw a dark-haired beauty behind her lean over and whisper in her ear. Sonya started down the aisle slowly, serious and unsmiling, looking down and strewing petals along the white runner.

Then the dark-haired beauty in a lavender gown followed. She carried a bouquet of white roses. Marie, Richie's sister, I thought. Then came Maggy, also in lavender and holding white roses. She was followed by Goody, the maid of honor, attired in a slightly darker shade of lavender, holding white roses with sprigs of purple intermixed.

The female attendants took their places on the left side of the platform, looking to the altar. That's when the organ burst forth with "Here Comes the Bride," but that's not what the program said. It read *Bridal Chorus* by Wagner. Suddenly, in the doorway, was Onkel Werner with DeDe on his arm. She was wearing an elegant white satin gown with embroidered white roses on the bodice; at the waist more roses wrapped around to her back and cascaded down her long train. A veil attached to a tiara of roses covered her face. Father and daughter started down the aisle, moving slowly, until they were facing the minister.

The minister asked in a baritone voice, "Who gives this woman into holy matrimony?"

Onkel Werner answered, "I do." And with that he lifted DeDe's veil, gave her an embrace, and sat down next to Tante Hedwig.

The wedding had to include a sermon—of course! What did the minister have to say? "Welcome all the children the Lord gives you." I saw the back of DeDe's neck redden a bit. But then the minister admonished the couple "to live within your means." Huh? It was going to be pretty hard if they had a baby every year. But we would see. Once DeDe had promised to "love, honor, and obey" Richie, the minister pronounced them "man and wife." Not "man and woman" or "husband and wife." Did that mean Richie now owned our DeDe? I just couldn't see it, but I knew how much Richie idolized our beautiful cousin, and I didn't really think those words would have any lasting effect.

After Richie kissed DeDe right in front of the whole congregation, the organist played the recessional—the *Wedding March* by F.

Mendelssohn, according to the program. It was a happy, fast paced piece, and once the bridal party had exited the church, we did too, in an orderly fashion, starting with the first rows on each side spilling out into the center and side aisles, followed by the subsequent rows, until the last pews were unoccupied, and guests and uninvited wedding spectators were on the sidewalk.

It was steamy. We were overdressed for the weather, and the humidity enveloped us instantly. Just as we had descended the steps, we heard a woman shriek. It was Tante Hedwig's good friend Beate. At her feet lay her husband, Magnus. People rushed to kneel by his side. One woman, a widow, got down on her knees and said loudly over Magnus, "If you see Søren in heaven, tell him hello from his wife."

With the commotion over him, poor Magnus opened his eyes and looked at the face a good two feet from his own and said, "I'm not dead."

"He just fainted from the heat. He had to work this morning laying carpet, so he's exhausted," explained his distraught wife. She might have been distressed, but we weren't. As several men helped Magnus to his feet and walked him and Beate into the sanctuary to sit down, we started to giggle. Soon it was full blown laughter; even many adults saw the humor in what had just happened. While all this was going on, Richie and DeDe had quietly gotten into the red and white Buick Special and departed. No fair! We hadn't thrown very much rice. But with the bride and groom gone, we made our way to the reception at Bush Terminal.

Bush Terminal was not a pretty place, but there were signs that said Wolff-Leaky wedding, and we followed them until we were in a big hall, decorated in purple, lavender, and white. The adults had seats at round tables; we younger cousins had two rectangular tables off to the back, where we could watch the goings-on. And such goings-on they were. We watched Onkel Sverre go to the punch bowl and drink from the ladle, laughing as he did so.

Tor Asbjørn tried to do the same, but Onkel Olav quickly rose to stop him. "That is not for children! You have your own punch on the table in the back." Onkel Olav's admonishment must have meant there was alcohol in the punch bowl. There was dancing, too. A small group of musicians had been playing softly in the background, and Richie and DeDe had their first dance to *You Are My Sunshine,* with Richie holding his bride close and her train neatly buttoned up at her hip. After that, it was rock and roll, but of course we cousins couldn't dance, not with our parents watching.

Two things I remember from that night in the Terminal: Onkel Sverre fell down, and Gerd (still not Tante to us) came to Papa and Onkel Olav and asked them to get Sverre up. They did so and steered him to a seat in the back of the room near us. We overheard Gerd say, "He does this a lot."

The other thing I remember is Papa going to Richie and giving him the receipt for the lamp. "If you don't like it, you can return it. As you can see it cost a pretty penny." Ingy was mortified, and then she and Bente were betting it would be the first thing Richie and DeDe did.

When the wedding party was over, Richie and DeDe made their way to the parking lot, and most of us followed. There was the Buick Special with a dozen empty tin cans attached to the rear bumper and "Just Married" written in white soap on the rear window. Richie put his hand over his mouth when he saw it, and I wondered if he was angry. But he started laughing and pointed at his friends and brother, Sean. Then he escorted his bride to the car, and they both got in, and he drove away, with a cacophony of sound. "Like fireworks," Bente observed.

We didn't hear from Tante Hedwig for a while after the event. She had declared herself exhausted. When we did, it was with news of the honeymoon. Richie had gotten the car cleaned up by the next morning, and they set off on their road trip. It took them almost four days to make the drive to Key West. Dede had called from a phone booth to tell them of their safe arrival. The Blue Marlin Motel was where they stayed, a place with a huge fish on its sign—

a blue marlin, no doubt. They spent a bit more than a week watching the pleasure craft and fishermen bringing their catches for market. Ernest Hemingway lives there, too. He's a famous writer, and he has lots of cats, Tante Hedwig added authoritatively.

Summer turned to fall pretty quickly, and we settled into familiar routines in our pocket of Brooklyn. Ingy and Bente learned at Bay Ridge High that Elvis would be appearing on television for the first time. Elvis had a fan club at that school, and no doubt at every other school teenage girls attended. On the designated night, we gathered at Tante Clara and Onkel Olav's to watch *The Ed Sullivan Show*—all of us—on the television Clara and Olav had acquired shortly after we got ours. Ed Sullivan said, "We have a really big shoe tonight." That's how he said "show."

When Elvis came on and started to sing, Papa was again incensed: "He swivels his hips like a madman. It's disgusting." Elvis the Pelvis he surely was. Ingy and Bente were mesmerized, however, and I could only imagine what they were thinking about this singer with the teddy haircut. My own thought was that he was gorgeous.

This would be the first year I was allowed to go to the English department and enjoy listening to the language I now spoke more proficiently than Norwegian. The Sunday after the memorable Ed Sullivan show, the pastor commented on Elvis "being of the world" and admonished us to avoid being tempted by evil, which Elvis clearly embodied. This was, after all, the same pastor who recommended smashing rock and roll records.

I had been excited about attending the English department, but after a few Sundays, I decided I disliked it just as much as the Norwegian services. I was stuck, nevertheless, and had to go. I carried my *King James Bible*, the one I had received in Sunday School when I was seven. One Sunday I told my parents I was bringing a pencil and paper to take notes, but I enjoyed doodling and tuned out every word of the sermon. Sometimes I passed notes to my Sunday School classmates, making fun of the pastor and the congregation. Growing older had given me freedom to defy the rules of proper and pious behavior, and I ignored the disapproving glances of the women who attended the English service.

At PS 104 as well, my interests were expanding. The boys in my class were agog about baseball and the excitement was contagious The Brooklyn Dodgers had won the pennant the year before, and boys were certain they would do it again at Ebbets Field, the stadium at the intersection of Bedford Avenue and Sullivan Place. Enthusiasm was high in the classroom and at home as well. Onkel Olav liked baseball, and he spoke fondly of the Dodgers as "dem bums." "They'll do it again, those boys. They are hard-working lads, and they know how to win," he explained to us in his accented English.

Alas, that was not to be. The Brooklyn Dodgers lost that year to the New York Yankees. Our pride in our home team didn't diminish, however. "Wait 'till next year" was our motto. Onkel Olav was less enthusiastic. "They may not be at Ebbets Field much longer. O'Malley, the Dodgers' manager, is threatening to move the team out of Brooklyn if the City Planning Commissioner, Robert Moses, won't allocate land for a new stadium." That would be terrible, but surely that couldn't really happen. No way could Brooklyn lose the Dodgers!

While the Dodgers didn't make us proud that year, we had a breakthrough that made us glad. Papa announced that we would be going to the movies. Really? Evidently the Norwegian minister at 66th Street church had advised the congregation to see *The Ten Commandments,* that it was biblically based and of value. It would show us the tribulation of the chosen people and how they were freed from Egyptian bondage. Thus, it was with great excitement that, in October, we went to our first movie as a family—and I didn't mention that Ingy had been to the movies quite a few times before with our cousin Bente.

Charlton Heston was Moses, and Yul Brynner was the Pharoah. Moses lived in the palace, and one day a slave grabbed him by the sleeve and said something like "You must stop the progression of the stones, pushed forward on great logs. A woman is caught and will be crushed if you don't."

Moses replied, "She's a slave. What does it matter?"

With that the messenger said, "She's your mother. She set you adrift in a basket when you were a baby, and the Pharoah's daughter found you and raised you in the palace." This was a moment of epiphany: Moses realized who his people really were and put the effort at exodus in motion, demanding "Let my people go."

Personally, I didn't know why he'd want to leave the palace because it was a pretty nice place, but that's what he did, leading the Hebrews to the sea, and with the hand of God, he parted the waters to allow the people to cross. Meanwhile, the Pharoah had second thoughts and sent his soldiers after the people—mind you, Egypt was losing all its cheap labor! The state wanted them back. But God had other plans, and the soldiers followed the Israelites across the bottom of the sea. Just as the last of Moses's people reached the opposite shore, the water flooded over the soldiers, their chariots, and their horses. Why had God killed those animals? How merciful was that? That was my takeaway from the movie.

The Ten Commandments was to be the only movie we ever saw as a family. "I don't like it," declared Papa. "It's all Hollywood, and they're all Jews making the movies. We won't go anymore, and neither will you," he said, looking directly at Ingy and me. Hah, I thought. If he only knew.

Late one Monday in early November, just as it was getting dark, the doorbell rang. "Who can that be?" said Mama. "Go and see, Solveig."

I went to the window first and saw the Buick Special parked by the curb, so I knew. I opened the door to let Richie and our cousin in, happy to see them. Mama heard us talking and came from the kitchen, wiping her hands on her apron as she walked. "How nice to see you," she said, as she gave DeDe a quick embrace and nodded at Richie. "What brings you to this part of Brooklyn?"

"We are looking for an apartment, and we like your neighborhood," explained DeDe. "My little place in Manhattan is too small for the two of us, and Richie has to travel to Brooklyn every day to get to work. Plus, he has to leave the car by his parents' place. It's inconvenient."

"Yes, and you can get a better deal here in the other boroughs than in The City," Richie added. It was still confusing to me, since I had learned in school that "The City" was more than Manhattan; it was also Brooklyn, Staten Island, Queens, and the Bronx, five separate boroughs that made up one New York City, which itself was in New York state, so there it was: New York, New York. Yet the whole family to call Manhattan simply The City.

"Where have you been looking?" asked Mama.

"Why, right around here. There's an apartment available on 93rd Street, just down from 4th Avenue, and there's an RR stop on the corner. We can both get to work by subway pretty easily. The only downside is that it's a four-floor walkup, so it will be challenging bringing in groceries and stuff."

"Yup," said Richie. "But the good news is that there's a Grand Union just a few blocks from there, so it's really convenient."

"It sounds ideal," said Ingy, who came into the parlor to hear the last part of the conversation. "I would love it if you lived close to us. Now tell us about your honeymoon. Your mother said it was nice, but we want to know more about Key West."

"Well," said Richie, "Key West is a beautiful place, a place where men's men go to fish. Its most famous sportsman is Ernest Hemmingway, who is also a famous writer."

"What did he write? Have you read any of his books?" I queried.

"Oh, Richie is a great reader, aren't you?" DeDe said, smiling at him.

"I have always liked to read, and I've read *The Sun Also Rises* and *A Farewell to Arms.* Hemmingway actually finished writing the book in Key West, so it was great to see the house where he did that. While we were there, I picked up *The Old Man and The Sea*, a book that was awarded the Pulitzer Prize. I think Hemmingway is our greatest American author. He has even been awarded the Nobel Prize in Literature. He was also brave. During World War I—which was called 'the great war' until World War II happened, and history decided it needed a number—he was a volunteer in the Italian army ambulance unit. Later, he was awarded the Italian Silver Medal of Bravery.

"Those experiences fueled the two books I read, but he wrote about the actual action he saw as a correspondent. Here's a little irony: his newspaper boss told him to give up writing, that he'd never be any good at it." With that, Richie laughed at the stupidity of the newspaper guy. "Knowing about Hemmingway was probably one reason we decided to go to Key West in the first place. People call him 'Papa Hemmingway'; it's a sign of respect and admiration."

I was making mental notes to see if the school library had any Hemmingway books. If Richie had read them, they must be good. Another mental note was to look up "irony." What always struck me about Richie was that he knew so much about so many things, and it was a treat when he visited.

It turned out that they did manage to get the apartment, and soon they settled in. It was three rooms in the back of a smallish apartment building on 93rd Street with a 336 address and on the fourth floor. But it was nice, and DeDe made us tea one Sunday afternoon. We asked how it was to commute from 93rd Street to Gimbels on 34th Street in Manhattan. "Oh, it's fine," DeDe said. "There are usually seats, since we're so far out, and I can read as the train goes. For Richie, it's even shorter, and sometimes he actually walks to the terminal."

'Wow," Ingy said. "That's a hike."

"Yes," said DeDe, "but Richie is fit, and he says it's good exercise. And he looks forward to going to work; he likes his job."

With that, I remembered how he had told Papa about his job as a longshoreman. It was with pride and intimated a "good old boy network" of which he was a part, as was his father. I was sure, too, that he was so fit because he worked outdoors, loading and unloading heavy materials daily.

The air those days was heavy with political talk. Eisenhower's first term as president would expire in January. Would he be reelected? When we exited the English department in the downstairs portion of 66th Street on those fall Sundays, we would connect with our parents and wait while they chit-chatted. Conversations were animated and centered on Ike and Stevenson, who was challenging the president, intent on besting him for the position of leader of the free world. Stevenson's dream was not realized, however, and in November, Ike won a second term as America's commander-in-chief.

Thanksgiving came and went, and many of us noticed how quiet Bestemor was these days. "She doesn't feel well," Mama said, "but it will pass."

"What's wrong with her?" Ingy asked.

"I'm sure it's not anything to worry about. She has had these spells before, and she always gets better," said Mama.

That's a relief, I thought. I had grown really fond of my grandmother, who always told me I was her favorite. One day while we were at Tante Clara's, I mentioned that Bestemor wasn't feeling so well, but Mama said she would get better. "She always tells me I'm her favorite," I announced importantly.

"What?" said Sonya. "She tells me the same thing!" So, after that we began to ask the cousins what Bestemor told them. You guessed it. We were all her favorites. Yet we instinctively knew that she loved us, probably each of us in a different way, making us feel secure and protected.

At school one day, the teacher announced that Arlene Bentzen would be absent for a few days. Her grandmother had "passed away" and the family would travel to Minnesota for the funeral. I didn't know Arlene all that well, but she was popular with the kids in class and always dressed so nicely. She seemed to me nearly perfect. How could it be, then, that such a tragedy happened to her and her family? It was a mystery. I was relieved that Mama had said my own grandmother always recovered from her "spells." It was hard to comprehend what it meant to die, and here Arlene got to know about it firsthand.

Death would visit Brooklyn soon, however. On December 3, after I had stayed to help the teacher wash the blackboard, I was on my way home from school a bit later than usual when there was a tremendous roar, and the ground shook, windows rattled and some broke, spewing glass onto the sidewalk. People in the street looked at each other, stunned. One woman carrying a sack of groceries let go of it, and canned goods rolled away in several directions. I quickly scrambled to help her, setting my belongings on the sidewalk, before chasing the runaway cans. She regained her composure and calmly repacked her sack from the Grand Union. "My," she said, "what in the world was that?"

The folks standing still on 4th Avenue turned to face the direction from which the sound had come. I stood with them, agape as flames and a mushroom-shaped cloud arose and lifted into the sky. "It's an attack," said one man.

"It's the Soviets," said another. Me, I hurried home as quickly as I could.

Mama had heard the sound and was convinced we were under attack. "Would there be radiation as there had been when the U.S. dropped the bombs on Nagasaki and Hiroshima?" she asked herself quietly. "Would this be a retribution for what America did to those people in Japan?"

Papa was home that day and simply said, "We don't know yet what the cause is." What we learned later from the news was that there had been an explosion at the pier at 35th Street, almost 60 blocks away. The cause was an accident. A worker was using an oxyacetylene torch and the flame touched a steel column on the pier, setting off sparks in several directions. Some sparks connected with 26,365 pounds of ground foam scrap in burlap sacks. The burlap quickly ignited, and then the entire pile was engulfed. That was bad enough, but there were over 35,000 pounds of an explosive called Cordeau Detonant Fuse lying nearby. Within half hour, it exploded, killing ten people and injuring 247. One of the dead had been a good 1,000 feet away from the explosion. Another was decapitated by flying metal. Horrible news.

It was the Luckenbach Steamship Co. pier, the longest in all of New York Harbor, with a 1,760-foot length and walls of corrugated iron and a tar and gravel roof, and it went flying that December afternoon. One piece of steel framing landed in Erie Basin, a half a mile away, starting a fire there. Manhattan fire companies determined it was a four-alarm fire, and one lane of the Brooklyn-Battery Tunnel was shut down to let fire trucks speed their way to the site. It wasn't until almost 7 p.m. that the Fire Chief told the city the fire was under control, but it would take another day to put it out completely.

"Isn't the Luckenbach Steamship Co. where Richie works?" I asked, with a kind of sickening feeling.

I knew the answer before Papa answered, "Yes."

Mama was quick to get to the phone to call Tante Hedwig. "It's still busy," she said after several tries. Next she called Tante Clara and asked if they had any damage and if she knew anything about their sister's son-in-law.

From Tante Clara she learned that 67th Street had some broken windows, but nothing serious. More important news was that Richie was not among the dead. "He's in Long Island College Hospital downtown, in intensive care. It's touch and go. He may not live."

Richie remained in the hospital through Christmas, with DeDe at his side. Gimbels had given her some time off, but as she said, she would be useless at work, waiting on customers less than cheerfully. As for us, we all prayed that Richie would make it through. In fact, prayer was more frequent than usual, and DeDe's handsome husband was the prime subject. We were convinced God would answer our fervent prayers, and he would recover. Slowly he did, and when in January he came home to the apartment on 93rd Street, we went to visit.

"We prayed so hard," Ingy said, "and God answered our prayers."

"Yes," said DeDe. "I hope he will recover completely." Richie was using a cane to walk, for a big piece of shrapnel had imbedded itself in his left thigh, and another had gashed his left check, which had been stitched and was now scarlet with newly-forming skin. "In time, that scar will be white," said DeDe. "But I wonder about the trauma; can you heal from that?"

"Was it awful?" I asked.

Richie smiled at me, a sign that he was still the Richie we knew and loved. "I was driving a forklift with some pallets when the explosion occurred. I saw a man, my friend Warren, get decapitated. I will never forget. The people on the pier weren't the only ones who died. One of the guys died in the hospital from smoke inhalation, and my friend Johnny, who was a checker, doesn't remember a thing. Maybe he's lucky."

Chapter Twelve

Comings and Goings

Our prayers for Richie were working. He continued to improve daily, and by February he was back at Luckenbach, limping on the job and helping restore the shipyard to its former productive state. One Sunday afternoon in the apartment on 93rd Street, where I had tagged along with Ingy and Bente to visit DeDe and Richie, he told us, with pride, what a great company Luckenbach was and how, as a union guy, he would retire from there; a great future was coming, based on a great past.

"I was talking to some of the guys on the job," he said, "and I learned a lot more about Luckenbach. You know New York was a huge port for transporting troops and equipment during the war. Edgar Luckenbach himself was proud that his ships shuttled more military personnel between the United States and Europe than any other shipping line. Talk about contributing to the war effort!"

"Did any of the Luckenbach ships get sunk?" I asked. "I mean, that must have been dangerous bringing soldiers and supplies to fight Hitler."

"Well, there was one mishap," Richie said. "I just learned about it the other day. During the war, in 1943 or '44, Luckenbach sent a 60-ship convoy on route to Europe. The ships had 11,500 tons of military equipment on board, and the Germans knew it. The lead ship, the *Tucurinca*, was torpedoed by a German U-boat—that's a submarine—and the ship sank in 10 minutes. Crew members reported having seen a periscope—the thing submarines send up to look at the surface—going down right after the hit."

"So, the crew members weren't military, then," Bente concluded.

"The crew were like many people supporting the war effort by working on the harbor and ships. When the first ship was hit, the captain ordered 'abandon ship,' and people jumped overboard, knowing there were 59 other company ships coming up behind them."

"So, they all got rescued?" queried Ingy.

"All but 10 people," Richie explained. "There was a gun crew on board—the company's ships had gun stations back then, just in case something like this might happen. Nine gunners took a direct hit and died immediately. The tenth person to die was a hero, an officer who couldn't swim, yet gave his life jacket to a crew member."

"How come we never hear about this stuff in school?" I asked.

"I'm sure there are lots of stories like this," Richie said. "Probably too many to learn about in school. But I know for certain, my company contributed to the Allied victory. Why, its ships were even in the South Pacific, transporting troops and supplies. Yep, it's a great company to work for, and it's going places. Just last week, the foreman told a bunch of us that there were going to be some big changes—the big bosses were talking about reorganization and going more international with more intercoastal trade."

"Richie's lucky to have such a great job, and the company was really good to him while he was recovering. It's good to have security like this," DeDe added. Just then, the doorbell rang, and DeDe got up and rang the buzzer to let someone into the lobby of the building. "We're expecting Richie's sister, Marie. You remember her from the wedding, don't you?"

I surely did. She was almost exotic looking, with her big deep blue eyes and shimmering dark hair, and in a few minutes, she mounted the four flights of stairs and walked into the apartment.

“Hey,” she said, “It’s great to see you again. I come most Sundays to have supper with DeDe and Richie and watch *The Ed Sullivan Show* on TV.”

“You were so beautiful at the wedding,” I stammered, unable to think of anything else to say.

“Oh yeah, the wedding,” said Marie, more to Richie than to me. “I think Mom has finally settled down. It took her months to get over it, you marrying a Protestant, and in a Protestant church! She says people at OLPH ‘pity’ her.”

“Yes, that’s my mother,” said Richie, drily. “It’s all about her and what other people think.” Then he added sarcastically, "Poor her."

Now that was food for thought. After we left the apartment, we walked to the subway on the corner of 93rd and 4th Avenue, where Bente got the RR train. Ingy and I then walked home in silence until I blurted out, “The Catholics are just like the Evangelicals. It’s all about what other people think!”

Ingy didn’t say anything to that, but I could tell she was thinking hard.

When winter was ebbing and we had the first hint of spring in the air, with crocuses popping their heads through the remnants of dirty, crusty snow, Mama got a phone call—and we knew it was for us, because this house didn't have a party line. I heard her gasp and then say, "It's not so." She was visibly pale when she got off the phone, and I asked her what was wrong.

"It's my mother. It's my mother. She's sick, and when Clara took her to the doctor, he said 'It's best not to do anything.'" Now, that made no sense; doctors were supposed to fix things.

"We will pray," I said. "God will heal her, just like he did DeDe's Richie."

"We will see," said Mama, who wiped a tear from her eye with the apron she always wore in the house. It was pretty dramatic to see Mama close to a full-out crying spell. But I was reassured when a few days later we went to Tante Clara's and saw Bestemor. She looked just fine to me, and she gave me a hug and called me "Gulle" (goldie). Our big cousin Ole was there that day, and he held her hand and spoke softly to her in that southern dialect they all spoke when together. I thought to myself, when he was my age, he lived in Norway and got to see Bestemor regularly, something denied to us American-born kids until Bestemor came here.

"My sister is coming to America," Ole said to Bestemor, who started at his words.

"Annalise," our grandmother said softly. "It will be good to see her. I know it hasn't been easy for her."

"Greta will be with her. She's fourteen now, a beautiful young lady, my niece. I can't wait to see them both." I noticed Mama looking at her lap, saying nothing, but Bestemor was smiling.

"This is good," said Bestemor.

"Who is Annalise?" Sonya, Alice, and I asked almost simultaneously. "And who is Greta?"

"Annalise is my sister," said Ole, switching to English, "and Greta is her daughter. They are your cousins. I haven't seen them since I left Norway for America. They are flying here. They will have a layover in Newfoundland, and then it's on to New York. I'm picking them up at Idlewild on Thursday after Easter."

"Where will they stay? Can they stay with us?" asked Sonya.

Ole held out his hands palms down, and said, "Enough questions. It's all settled. They will stay in Onkel Johann's house on Staten Island. I spoke with Onkel and Tante Hulda, and they said they will be happy to have her, and besides, they have the biggest house of any of us. Sven and Vigdis remember my sister well from Norway before the war. Annalise is only two years older than Sven, so they were often playmates. Sigurd, Stanley, and Salve, Onkel Jakob's boys, live on Staten Island, too. They also remember Annalise from before the war. You guys she'll meet after she gets here." I digested these details and said to myself, we have two more cousins that I didn't even know about. How come Mama didn't tell us?

Soon after, Easter morning dawned bright and sunny, and we first checked the buffet in the dining room for our Easter baskets, as Mama said, "Look, but don't eat that candy yet. I have toast and butter here for your breakfast." That was okay with me, because Mama let me put sugar on the butter, which melted on the toast. When we had quickly downed the bread, we scurried upstairs to put on our new clothes. I had a suit this year, tan with a straight skirt and three-button jacket. I felt pretty grown up in my first real suit, and Mama had bought me a little purse to match. Ingy, though, had a car coat that had a Martin's label inside behind the collar. Now, I knew where she had bought it, and it wasn't Martin's. I wondered which of Mama's coats she had pilfered the label from.

Papa took us to church for Sunday School, and excitement hung heavy in the air. We girls assessed what we were wearing while the boys, most in suit jackets and ties, looked decidedly unhappy. After Sunday School the basement was set up for the English service, and Rolf, our English department musician, began to play the piano as we found our seats. The pastor welcomed us, and then we rose to sing.

> "He lives, he lives, salvation to impart. You ask me how I know he lives, he lives within my heart."

The Easter songs were joyous, and we were happy to be there. When the service was over, we met Mama and Papa outside the church, where they chatted with other folks. Mama had on a big-brimmed hat and those red high heels she liked so well. I was proud to see how pretty she looked, even though she was plump.

When we got home, we sat down to eat middags. After we said our ritual *I Jesu Navn*, we feasted on roast chicken, put in the oven before Mama and Papa came to church, and mashed potatoes and mixed vegetables, prepared as soon as we got home. "Today is such a beautiful day," said Papa. "Let's go to the botanic garden. The plants will be starting to bloom." That's what we did. We piled into the car and drove to the Brooklyn Botanic Gardens and strolled along the pathways. We were still in our Sunday go-to-meeting clothes, and I carried my little plastic purse, which came in handy when I saw coins in the bottom of a fountain near the Japanese Pagoda. I took off my jacket to free my arms to dunk in the water. I had collected quite a little stash before Papa told me to stop when he saw some Sunday strollers stopping to stare at us. Ironically, he did not command me to toss the coins back into the fountain, so I kept them.

Papa went to work the following day, and Mama announced that she was taking her mother hat shopping while we were in school, and after that to Tante Clara's. When I came home from PS 104, Mama was on the phone, presumably with one of her sisters, saying, "She is impossible. I kept trying to describe the type of hat she likes in English to the clerk, and our mother kept interrupting in Norwegian, gesturing with her hands, saying 'like this.' Embarrassing," added Mama. Then she became silent, listening hard, and gasped a bit.

When Ingy came home, Mama sat us down and said Bestemor was feeling sicker. No problem, I thought to myself. Hat shopping could probably do that to you. We surely needed to pray more. I knew it was also a good thing Ole was soon picking up Annalise and Greta at the airport. That will make Bestemor rally. The next weekend we went to Tante Clara's to meet these cousins whom Ole had chauffeured from Staten Island. Bestemor was sitting in an easy chair, a blanket tucked around her legs, and she was smiling at her granddaughter and great granddaughter. Annalise was tall and blond with sparkling blue eyes, her daughter much like her. Then Annalise sat down next to Bestmor and the two were soon deep in animated conversation. Does she have a husband? I thought. If so, why isn't he with her?

I said something to Greta in English, but she clearly didn't understand, so I switched to Norwegian. She smiled shyly, and I thought to myself, she's nice. After a while the doorbell rang, signaling more visitors. Tante Hedwig, Onkel Werner, Goody and Maggy came in, with a young man right behind Maggy. After we had greeted each other, Tante Hedwig said of the young man, "This is Paul, Maggy's friend boy." Then she leaned over Annalise, gave her a big hug, and said in Norwegian so she would understand, "So this is your little girl. She's so beautiful, just like you."

"She looks a lot like her father," Ole said quietly.

With that, Tor Asbjørn blurted out, "Who is her father, and why isn't he here?"

Ole said, "He was killed in the war. He was German."

Mama said, in English, so that Annalise and Greta couldn't understand. "Greta is a Lebonsborn child. She's lucky my sister Augusta, Annalise's mother, let her keep her when she was born."

"What?" asked Bente.

At this, Onkel Werner spoke up. "The Germans did some bad things. The Lebensborn program was one of them. German men were encouraged to get Norwegian girls pregnant. In return, the girls got more food rations and supplies."

Ole jumped in at this and said, "I knew this German officer. His name was Nils. Unlike many of the men participating in the Lebensborn program, he was unmarried, and he seemed to really like Annalise and she him. Right after Greta was born—that's what we call her, but the name on the birth certificate says Gretl—he was transferred to Russia where he died. But before he shipped out, he promised Annalise he would come back and marry her. She was heartbroken when she heard what had happened to him.

"The neighbors were disgraceful, saying Greta had 'tainted blood' since she was half German. My mother, though, knew her daughter, and once she saw Greta, her heart melted, and from then on they lived under the same roof. After the war, though, a bunch of men grabbed Annalise as she was coming out of a store and shaved her head, calling her 'a German whore.' She was also advised to put Greta in an asylum, where many Lebensborn children went because they were half-German, but my mother and father, my brother, Arnt, Annalise, and I determined that this toddler, Lebensborn child 5029, would carry the Saudeland name, the same as the rest of us.

"Once she started school, Greta had a hard time with kids calling her a 'Nazi brat' or 'German bastard,' terms they must have learned at home. It was pretty tough for my sister and niece, but fortunately she had the support of her family. Other Lebensborn women did not fare so well. They were paraded through the streets and spat at."

I learned many years later when I researched these cousins' history that Lebensborn means "fountain of life" and that Heinrich Himmler encouraged women of "pure blood" to bear blond, blue-eyed children. It was a program to establish a pure race. The program included the forced sterilization of people with hereditary diseases, and it didn't begin with the war; its history dated back to 1935, with the goal of halting the high rate of abortion and the declining birth rate brought on by the depression in Europe. In Norway the program included a registry and Christening services that were SS rituals. Mothers with three or more children got extra benefits such as not having to wait in line while shopping, discounts on rent, and cheap state loans.

For mothers who decided not to keep their children, Lebensborn ran an adoption service. In Norway, Lebensborn was more widespread than in Germany itself or Holland, with around 12,000 births. After the war, thousands of young women were arrested and many of the children were institutionalized. Of boys it was especially feared that they would bear the taint of German masculinity. I have to ask now: Was the Norwegian government in agreement with Lebensborn? Probably, since there was a provisional government, headed by Vidkun Quisling, a German collaborator.

Living in Brooklyn in the '50s, however, we could not fathom such a thing, and of course the adults in our lives spared us the details, if they even knew them themselves. We soon got to know Greta and loved to visit with her, although she lived on Staten Island with Onkel Johann Torvald and Tante Hulda. That seemed appropriate, since Sven and Vigdis had known her mother the longest. Ole was good to them, clearly proud to have his sister and niece in New York. Sometimes he would bring them to Brooklyn to visit.

One day, Tante Hedwig called to say she had Ole, Annalise, and Greta with her, and they would come to our house. They had spent the better part of the day in Manhattan and arrived looking tired and disheveled. "We sightseed," Tante Hedwig announced. "Greta loved it when we went into the Entire State Building and took the elevator to the top, and she could look at the city. It's so good to have them here, isn't it?"

"What do you think of New York?" Papa asked Annalise.

"It's very big. You hear about New York in Norway, but we never imagined it was so huge," Annalise said in what seemed like flawless Norwegian, much more refined than the dialect we all spoke. Nevertheless, I understood her—her speech was not like that of the pastors in the Norwegian department at church.

"It's big," Greta volunteered. Wow, I thought, she's picking up English quickly.

Then Tante Hedwig gave us some news: "Maggy's boyfriend Paul, the one who was with us at Tante Clara's when Annalise and Greta were first here, propositioned Maggy, and she accepted. She has a beautiful diamond ring now, and Werner and I will have another wedding to plan. Maggy said it was okay to tell the family. She is so excited."

I, for one, was happy to learn she hadn't reunited with that creepy boyfriend Axel and hoped Maggy would behave herself. I wondered if we'd be invited to that wedding.

"Is he Catholic, too?" Mama asked.

"Oh no, he's Lutheran. The family name is Bensen, and they go to the Lutheran Brethren Church on 4th Avenue, but they'll get married at 59th and very soon, so that Maggy's grandmother can see her get married."

That was good news—good that Maggy was getting married—and bad news at the same time: why the urgency to get married for Bestemor's sake? What were they afraid of? We soon found out. Our grandmother's health was declining rapidly. Our response was to pray more fervently. She died anyway.

There would be a wedding, but there was no rush now, because first there would be a funeral. This was not the order in which the events had been planned. The family became morose; bringing their mother to the United States had been a huge undertaking, and after just a few years, she was gone again, this time not to be buried in Norwegian soil next to her husband, as was her wish. It was true that many of the 66th Street church people shipped bodies back to Norway for burial, but not this family. Papa assessed the cost of doing so, and Mama and Papa talked to the family. The logic was that they would eventually die, and they could be buried beside her. So it was that Greenwood Cemetery would be her final resting place. But first there would be a service celebrating her life, and it was held at 59th Street church.

Her daughters worked hard to make the service meaningful; the pastor would talk about her life in Norway, the children she spawned, and her legacy here in America and Norway. When the big day came, we assembled in the church, a bit teary but, in truth, fascinated to be at an actual funeral. For me it was a first-time experience. I looked around and saw all the cousins and aunts and uncles from Staten Island, and Hedwig and Werner's boys from Long Island with their wives and children, as well as DeDe and Richie, Gudrun, and Maggy and her fiancé, Paul. We were sad that Bestemor had not lived to see Maggy married.

We settled into a pew beside Tanta Clara, Onkel Olav, Bente, Tor Asbjørn, Alice, and Sonya. I looked around me; way in the back was Onkel Sverre and Gerd with baby Aslaug on her lap; beside them was Tante Magda, whom we saw infrequently. I espied Leif and Tante Ragna with my four cousins from Staten Island. There on the left side of the church sat Johann Torvald with his wife Hulda, Sven, Annalise, and Greta—but no Vigdis. Right behind them were Onkel Jakob, Tante Bergitta, one of their sons and a woman I didn't know. It takes a funeral, I realized, to bring such a large family together.

The flowers, a lot of gladioli, were beautiful. The service began with dirge-like organ music. Then the pastor, the one from the Norwegian department, somberly talked about Andrea Gabrealsen and her progeny—and we were mostly all there, except for Onkel Arne and Tante Augusta and their families, still in Norway. The pastor's Norwegian was that of the capital city, and difficult for us to understand, yet he looked at us all directly as he spoke.

So overcome was he by the size of this family that he proclaimed that the grandchildren and great-grandchildren should mount the platform and hold hands in tribute to the Norwegian matriarch. Mama and Tante Clara gave us a nudge and whispered for us to go to the platform. "Say a prayer for your grandmother and great-grandmother, and say it in Norwegian, the only language she herself knew," the pastor said to us in English. Now that was quite a commandment and one no one had expected. The older cousins didn't begin because they were clearly befuddled by this turn of events. But Bente, Tor Asbjørn, Alice, Sonya, Ingy and I knew what to do. We nodded to Karl, Johann, Harold, and Liv, and we began:

> "I Jesu navn gar vi til bords,
> A spise og drikke pa dit ord."

We got as far as "Deg Gud til aere, oss til gavn," when the congregation began to giggle, and the pastor said, "excuse me," and exited the platform, his hand over his mouth. We were perplexed, and Tor Asbjørn was clearly miffed as he realized our gaffe. But then it was the only prayer any of us knew in Norwegian and probably the kids from Long Island, whose mothers were maybe not Norwegian, had no idea. The pastor reappeared after what was for us a humiliatingly long time, and the congregation, many of whom were laughing outright, calmed down.

"Let's all hold hands again, and I will pray for your grandmother," the pastor said to us. And that's what happened. When we had taken our seats, I looked at my lap and failed to appreciate the rest of the service. I was sure my face was red. When the service was over, a hearse took our grandmother's casket, and we followed to Greenwood Cemetery on 25th Street in Brooklyn on what was a beautiful May day.

As they lowered the casket into the ground, Tante Clara said to her kids and us: "Your grandmother would have loved what you did and maybe she was laughing in her casket." We felt better. Nevertheless, we cried, and I thought it was so sad that she would lie alone in grave 775 with our grandfather buried in Norway.

Papa said to us on the sad ride home that our grandmother had gone to be with the Lord. "She's in heaven now, and that's good for her—no more suffering, no more struggle with the things of earth. She was a good Christian, devout, God-fearing, and *Bible* reading. It's really a beautiful ending for a great lady. We should all be happy and praise the Lord for that." Mama, sitting beside Papa in the front seat, dabbed at her eyes, and Ingy was stone-faced in the backseat next to me. I didn't much feel like praising the Lord.

We would be praising the Lord very shortly however. In church the following Sunday, the pastor in the English department had an important announcement, and surely the pastor in the Norwegian department upstairs made a similar one: "*The Billy Graham Crusade* will begin on May 15th. Try to go; it opens in Madison Square Garden and is an enormous step for Christianity. Graham has declared that New York is truly a metropolis in need of healing, and he has been called by God to minister to the sinners in this city. It promises to be magnificent. I understand the planning has been going on for months, and that there's a 1500-voice choir to sing about the glory of God. Masses will come and be saved. Pray that the spirit of the Lord touches the souls of those who attend." With that he bowed his head and prayed that God would deliver as many souls as possible from the "grips of sin."

Okay, but we are already Christians, I thought to myself. Why should we go? When we got home, I asked Papa about attending the crusade, and he said, "No need for us to go, since we are already saved." Nevertheless, Onkel Olav and Tante Clara took our cousins to one of the meetings and came home to speak of the glorious healing that Graham was achieving, and the music! Oh, the music! The choir was incredible: 1500 voices, and George Beverly Shea with his deep baritone sang *How Great Thou Art.* I could tell Bente was impressed; she, after all, knew about music. About two weeks into the campaign, ABC began to air live coverage of the Saturday evening services, and we watched each meeting while we were still in Brooklyn. For the first time, we were actively encouraged to watch TV.

There would another memorable experience the month before we left the city for our summer in the country. The *Nordiske Tidende* announced that the *Christian Radich*, the beautiful Norwegian windjammer training ship, would be coming to New York harbor and on board would be 42 young seamen in training. More importantly, we learned that Onkel Sverre would be the pilot to bring it into the harbor. Onkel Sverre had himself gone to sea when he was just 14 on the *Sørlandet,* an older and equally beautiful Norwegian tall ship, and now he would pilot a sister ship in U.S. waters. We clamored to visit the ship, and this time Papa gave in. Ingy explained, "He is proud of his brother-in-law, and he sees himself as a seaman, so of course he'll go."

We planned to visit when the ship was open to visitors at the 59th Street Pier on the west side of Manhattan. Papa, Mama, Ingy and I met Onkel Sverre, Tante Gerd, and their little Aslaug on the pier, and Onkel described how he knew the shifting shoals in the harbor, and that's why New York, like many seaports around the world, wouldn't let ship captains bring their own vessels to dock. A pilot was necessary, and now Onkel had a fledgling company—the Sandy Hook Pilots Association—and he bid for the job and probably got it hands down from his history with Norway's school ships. He told us how he took control in Gravesend Bay from the Captain, Ingvar Kjelstrom, because he had related how well he knew this sort of ship and had done so in Norwegian!

How proud Onkel Sverre was as he went on board, this time as a tourist, with the six of us behind him. When Onkel spotted Captain Kjelstrom, he called out to him in Norwegian, and in response the master of this beautiful ship approached us, clearly happy to be recognized and be in the port of the city of New York. Onkel Sverre shook his hand and introduced us collectively as "my family."

Papa quickly spoke up and said, "I am a seaman, too."

The captain politely inquired as to what work he did, and Papa said, "I work on the harbor and fuel ships, but never one like this."

Then the captain politely said, "They say the sea is in the soul of every Norwegian." With that he bid us good day, and sauntered around the deck, greeting other visitors.

Then Onkel Sverre told us how he had gone to sea at 14 on the *Sørlandet,* a square rigger without auxiliary power, at the mercy of the sea and wind. It was one of three school ships; the others were the newer *Christian Radich* on whose deck we stood and the *Statsraad Lehmkuhl,* the oldest. He explained how these ships would train young sailors, and that's how he himself had come to love the sea and make a career of it, first in the Norwegian Merchant Marine and then in the U.S.

He pointed to the masts and related how he had climbed similar ones, working in unison with other boys to hoist the sails or unfurl them, "just like those boys over there have done the whole way over the Atlantic. For them, it must have been quite the adventure—bad weather at first, then the warm air of Madiera, and then across the sea, following the path that Columbus had taken. But the ship I was on—that one made history. It was the first of the Norwegian tall ships to cross the ocean to the United States."

We looked where he gestured and focused on the young seamen on board, all older than I but not Ingy. She was speechless and held her head high, eyes half-veiled, but I knew she was looking at those Norwegian boys. They were indeed good looking, fair-haired, blue-eyed boys in uniform with flat hats jauntily cocked on their heads as they answered, in English, questions visitors posed to them.

"They speak English!" Ingy exclaimed.

Onkel Sverre turned to Ingy and said in English, "Well, you know the first thing is this: the captain met hundreds of applicants, and after careful scrutiny, he chose 42, from 14 to 21 years of age. You know that only the brightest and best are chosen to sail, and here they are. They are all smart. And when they sailed, the king even came to see them off." Then he added that when he was piloting the tall ship into the Hudson River, he himself had remarked how well so many spoke English. When he had been a teenager on the training ship, hardly anyone spoke anything but Norwegian.

Onkel continued, "These remarkable boys found an old storage room no longer in use and asked to have it as sort of a club room. Here it was 'English only' and they labored at learning from books they had brought on board. And do you know what? If anyone spoke Norwegian, they had to put 25 ore (Norwegian coin) in the can. Now that was some incentive!"

Just then, several of the young seamen appeared with bass guitar and accordion and began to sing of the girl back home in Norway,

Kari Waits for Me. Then they launched into *The Village of New York* with lyrics that told of "the land of liberty...all the way from Norway to the village of New York...and girls dressed in pants who swing their ponytails." I am one of those girls, I thought and swelled with pride. I didn't want to leave, but when the seamen finished singing, Papa said it was time to go. As we walked across the gangplank, Papa and Onkel Sverre were deep in conversation. "I imagine they'll eventually put an engine in her," said Onkel.

"Why is that?" asked Papa.

"It would be a safeguard. If there's no wind, she's at the mercy of the sea. If a storm were brewing, she'd be able to get to safe harbor more quickly. I think that German ship, the *Pamir,* was a wakeup call for the Norwegian Navy."

"Why, what happened to the *Pamir*?"

"She went down, with almost all on board lost. Like the *Christian Radich*, she was a school ship, but a four-masted bark, a black beauty on the sea. She got caught in a hurricane and foundered. Pity—all those young boys", Onkel Sverre added softly.

In the car going back to Brooklyn, I asked Papa what would happen to the boys on the *Christian Radich*. Papa said they'll have had an adventure, and then go back to their lives in Norway, whether they go into the Merchant Marine or not. I was happy to hear it.

When school was out that year, we headed for the lake in New Jersey, and as always, I was happy to go. Papa said, a little wistfully, that it would mean missing a lot of the Billy Graham programs, and that was a shame. I said we could watch at the Edelmann's, but Papa said it was highly unlikely that they would be interested, since they were not Christians. But we soon learned, from newspapers, magazines, and just plain people talk at the Hillside Church that the crusade was dynamic.

What Graham started had taken on a life of its own. The July issue of *Life* magazine featured a cover story on the crusade. Vice President Richard Nixon was a guest speaker at a service at Yankee Stadium, and Martin Luther King Jr. said opening prayers at a meeting in mid-July. The press continued to cover the events, reporting on the masses who came forward to receive the Lord. By the end of the summer, when the Crusade ended, 2,397,400 souls had been won for the Lord. It was pretty impressive overall.

Mostly, however, we filled our days biking, swimming, and playing games with Raymond and Barbara and Edel and Else. When Papa was off the boat, he would come driving up our little road from Sand Shore Drive, usually bearing bread and pastries from Lunde's or Leske's bakery, the *Nordiske Tidende*, and mail that had arrived at our house in Brooklyn. The next day Mama was having her coffee on the porch and reading the *Nordiske Tidende* when she gasped. "My," she said mostly to herself. "I suspected."

When I asked her what she suspected, she simply said, "There's a small announcement. Maggy married Paul at City Hall sometime in late June." I wondered first why we hadn't heard about the marriage while we were still in Brooklyn, but most of all I wondered what it was Mama had suspected. The fact that there hadn't been a church marriage, but rather a legal civil ceremony, was curious to us, but then so many things about Maggy were curious.

The summer continued and we were brown as berries by the time we were ready to return to Brooklyn. Mama had slathered us with baby oil to keep us from peeling, but we felt slighted because Edel and Else's mother added iodine to the oil, to make them "brown faster." The funny thing was this: Mrs. Edelmann didn't put anything on the backs and shoulders of Raymond and Barbara. I commented on this one day, and Mama said, simply, "Those two are of different blood; they're already browner naturally, so they won't burn." It was true, I had to admit. Barbara, especially, had golden skin and big brown doe eyes, not like us Norwegians, pale and blue-eyed. Still, we would go back to school with our tans that bespoke vacation time.

School started up on schedule, and it was satisfying to reenter a familiar routine, but the world around us was in flux we soon learned. In early October my social studies teacher announced we were witnessing the dawn of a space age. This is just the beginning, she said. Mankind will begin to understand new technologies and scientific discoveries and see the terrain of the whole earth and all because the Russians had launched a small satellite, no bigger than a basketball, and they called it *Sputnik*. It took just 98 minutes for this little dynamo to orbit the entire earth! The boys immediately wanted to know how heavy it was. “About 185 pounds, I think,” said the teacher.

“Why doesn’t it fall down, then? My father weighs 185 pounds, and he can’t fly,” said Steven, who sat behind me. With this, several of the boys began to giggle.

“Listen up," said our teacher, "there’s a long history here. The concept for a satellite began five years ago with scientists forming the International Council of Scientific Unions. These scientists understood the cycles of solar activity and decided that if a satellite could be successfully launched, it should happen between July 1957 and December 1958. The launch happened early in this period because the atmosphere was right for it. The U.S. was working hard to get a satellite into space, but the Russians beat us to it. But we’ll do it too, and it will be better, you’ll see."

At home that night the TV carried news of *Sputnik I*. "It means 'companion' or 'pal,'" one newscaster reported. Also discussed were fears that, if the Russians were this far ahead of us, what was to keep them from launching ballistic missiles that could bring nuclear weapons from Russia to the U.S? This was, after all, the cold war. Would the Russians heat it up?

Meanwhile, on the home front in Brooklyn, another fear developed, one that Onkel Olav knew all about. An enthusiastic Dodgers fan, he was alarmed that O'Malley, the Dodgers' owner, could not come to terms with Robert Moses, the City Planning Commissioner, to build a new stadium for the Dodgers. Ebbets Field had too little parking for the people who wanted to see the game in person, even though WOR had been airing the home games. Attendance was dwindling, Ebbets Field was in a sad state of repair, and O'Malley's plan was not well received.

His plan was to construct a new stadium along the Atlantic Railroad yards in downtown Brooklyn, at the intersection of Flatbush and Atlantic Avenues; Moses vetoed it because it didn't fit under the Title I Housing Act of 1949. "What is wrong with that man?" Onkel Olav asked. "Politicians are known to bend the rules, and he could if he wanted to. I wonder what his real motive is. O'Malley wants to keep the Dodgers in Brooklyn, and that's where they should stay. Look, this team has won more games than any others in the League, and only the Yankees have won more—but they are both New York Teams. They need to stay in this city."

Tor Asbjørn, who shared his father's love of the team, proudly added information: "The players are Brooklyn boys active in the community. Then he recited their names from memory: Sandy Koufax and Don Drysdale are the younger players; PeeWee Reese, Roy Campanella, Carl Furillo, Sal Maglie, Gil Hodges, Duke Snider, Carl Erskine, and Don Newcombe are all in their thirties. Johnny Padres was in the Navy; a few players were minor leaguers; one was in college; one hadn't finished high school. What a mixed group they are, just like the rest of us who live in Brooklyn."

Alas, such enthusiasm, no doubt shared by thousands of New Yorkers who loved the Dodgers, could not prevent what happened next. O'Malley announced that Los Angeles had made an offer too good to pass up. On September 24, the Dodgers played their last game at Ebbets Field, winning over the Pittsburgh Pirates. *The Brooklyn Eagle* and later the *New York Journal-American* vilified O'Malley, reporting that people said of O'Malley, "He's worse than Hitler."

But Onkel Olav, ever the voice of reason, said the one person who the fans should hate was Moses, because he was the reason O'Malley chose what he did. Plus, the Dodgers would have the third-largest city in the United States all to themselves in terms of major league baseball. "And you know," he said, "when a city wants a team, they make pretty good offers in terms of money and facilities, so I'm not surprised."

"Yes," chimed in Onkel Werner, "but Moses's motive in letting this happen may be related to something even bigger. The city has confirmed that a bridge connecting Brooklyn to Staten Island will be built."

"Where could they possibly do that? The harbor is too big," said Papa.

"It's going to be from the Fort Hamilton area in Brooklyn to the Ford Wadsworth area on Staten Island, the two military bases that guard the mouth to the harbor, and there will be an expressway across Staten Island connecting to the bridge going to New Jersey, and in Brooklyn starting at the Brooklyn Battery Tunnel. It's going to mean big changes for Bay Ridge."

"Never happen," said Papa.

Chapter Thirteen

Never Happen?

Maggy was getting fat, I noticed one day when Mama and I were visiting Tante Hedwig, and Maggy stopped in, surprised to see us there. She had quietly married Paul, and married life must be agreeing with her I thought. Mama evidently had quite a different thought and said under her breath: "I see what's what."

"Tante Cornella," Maggy said, rising to the bait. "I'm pregnant. I got pregnant right after we were married. I'm just showing early."

"Uh huh," said Mama, but offered nothing else. Maggy's happiness was readily apparent, as was Tante Hedwig's, despite Mama's scowl.

Right after Thanksgiving, Maggy had a baby. Tante Hedwig called to share the news. Mama got off the phone and promptly announced to Papa, "Maggy had a boy. Hedwig said he came early, but he's big for an early baby. They're calling him Lars after Paul's father. Hedwig says he comes from good stock and that they're all big in that family. Why Paul himself is six foot five—a strapping man." Then I heard her tell Papa that she always knew how Maggy was. Whatever did she mean?

"Never mind," Papa responded. "They are married now, and they seem to like each other. They'll give that boy a good Norwegian home. I hear they have an apartment on 7th Avenue, right across from McKinley Park. It's a nice place; they'll have the park for the baby."

At supper that night, after we said *I Jesu Navn,* I asked about Paul. He was tall and blond and blue-eyed. "What does Paul do?"

"Werner told me he's a fireman," said Papa, clearly and in English, since he had used it on the job for years, and more often now lapsed into it at home. "He's with the firehouse on 3rd Avenue. You know, working for the city has its benefits, so he'll be set for life. He'll get early retirement and still be young enough to do something else. Good for him."

I determined that I would visit and see the new little cousin soon. I wondered if they would come to the 66th Street church since it was closer, or if they'd go to the Lutheran Brethren Church on 4th Avenue or maybe the Lutheran Evangelical Church on 59th Street. Would they christen the baby or baptize him, and while I had these thoughts it occurred to me that at 59th Street they baptized babies; at 66th they christened them; what did they do at Lutheran Brethren? And what's the difference?

"Don't we need to get a baby present?" I asked Mama. "I really want to see the baby." Mama called Tante Clara, and we agreed to meet in McKinley Park and go together. When we got to Maggy's apartment, we were pleased to find Goody also visiting. She was always a solo act, so self-sufficient and composed. We had not told Maggy we were coming, so both she and her sister were surprised to see us, but pleasantly so. Maggy's apartment was nice—on the second floor of a two-family house—really a flat, but it was sparsely furnished. In their bedroom was a pretty bassinet, which Maggy proudly told us her father had made. Paul was at the firehouse, Goody explained, and she was staying with Maggy for a few days to help out. Help she did; she immediately took over and set coffee on to perk. Tante Clara had brought some Vienna brød, and that's what we had.

"Can I hold him?" Bente asked.

"Oh, let me," said Ingy.

"You can each hold him a little bit, since he's awake now," said Maggy, as she directed Bente to sit in an easy chair and placed little Lars in her arms. "I don't want him to get used to being held all the time," she explained. "It will spoil him. Sometimes I let him cry himself to sleep," she added.

Ingy took her turn holding the blue-swaddled bundle, but when Sonya, Alice, and I wanted to, Maggy said no. "Maybe when he's a little bigger."

"So, Maggy," said Tante Clara, "Do you miss working?"

"Well," said Maggy, "I hadn't been working for long. You know I was with Beverly Shops on 5th Avenue. You know, where Goody works. She's the assistant manager there. That's how I got the job. If I go back to work it will have to be something that lets me be home more. Maybe I can work weekends or days when Paul is home. We'll see."

As we were leaving, Maggy said, "You have to come back when Paul is here. I know he wants to get to know you all." I really did want to know more about this man who was Maggy's husband.

We walked with Tante Clara and her girls from McKinley Park on our way to 69th Street where we would get the bus and then transfer to the 5th Avenue line, which would take us to where 4th and 5th Avenues converged, our last stop. From there we would walk home. But as we walked behind our mothers on the way to the bus stop, we heard Tante Clara say to Mama, "I don't think Paul was eager to get married, but Olav told me that Werner had told him he had talked to the boy. And he talked to the Bensens, Paul's parents. Together they persuaded Paul to marry Maggy. It's a rocky start, but I hope they'll make it. The baby is beautiful, though, isn't he?"

That conversation was much on my mind, and I brought it up the next time we were visiting our cousins on 67th Street. "Figure it out, dummy," said Ingy. "It takes nine months to grow a baby, and Maggy and Paul have been married just about five months."

As an afterthought, Bente said, "Maggy is lucky. A girl named Mary in my school had to quit—when the school saw she was pregnant, she couldn't stay any longer. Her sister Ellen, who's in my grade, told me her parents were so ashamed. A teacher even said to Ellen that she hoped she wouldn't follow her sister's dirty ways, and this she said so nastily that Ellen burst into tears. I saw Ellen right after that happened as we were getting our books from our lockers.

"Ellen, through tears, told me her sister Mary was a good girl. She had been dating Donny for two years, and she was crazy about him. I asked why they didn't just get married, and Ellen said her parents wanted them to. They even did what Onkel Werner had apparently done: they talked to the boy and to his parents. Both families go to OLPH, so they knew each other, and they certainly knew both kids pretty well since they had been dating for so long, even visiting each other's families and having dinner and some celebrations with them.

"Do you know what Donny's father said? 'How do you know it's Donny's baby? Donny swears he's not the only one who had had sex with Mary.'

"Ellen's father became so furious at that, that he yelled 'My daughter is no slut!'

"'She just might be,' said Donny's father. Later that same week, Donny's father came to visit Ellen and Mary's parents, and they had Donny and two of his friends with them. 'Tell her parents what you told me,' he demanded of Donny.

"'Sure, I had sex with Mary. It was easy. But I wasn't the only one. Joseph and Luke here did too, and we know for certain there were others.' With an air of being wrongfully accused, they left. Ellen told me that her parents were so horrified by that conversation, that they yelled at her sister incessantly, calling her a whore and a low-life. What would people think of them as a family if their daughter couldn't keep her knees together? They told Mary they were disowning her, and that she could go have her little bastard by herself."

"What happened to Mary?" Alice asked.

"She went to live at the Angel Guardian Home and had her baby. "

"Where's that?" I chimed in.

"It's on 12th Avenue and 64th Street. It's not that far from here."

"Do you know what happened to Mary after that?" Ingy asked.

"Ellen told me she had her baby, a girl, and that the nuns arranged to have it adopted. Babies are always better off with two married parents, you see. Ellen also said after a couple adopted the baby, she would visit her sister, unbeknownst to their parents, and that Mary was depressed. She had wanted to keep the baby, but couldn't see how, and her parents didn't want it. She had no choice. Mary went to live with an aunt in Queens after the birth, a place where no one knew what had happened to her. Her parents didn't want to see her anymore."

"I think that's a really awful story," said Ingy. "And the boy got off scot free."

"Sure, Ellen told me he even bragged about how easy it was for him to get sex when he wanted it. Ellen hates him, but she thinks Mary may still love him. So sad."

Ingy and I talked about it afterwards, and we agreed that there were worse things than getting married because you were pregnant. What happened to poor Mary was far more dire. And again, Onkel Werner was lifted in our esteem because he had negotiated a good outcome for Maggy. Even better, both Tante Hedwig and Onkel Werner loved little Lars. Once Mama asked them sympathetically, "Aren't you worried about what people will think?"

To that, Tante Hedwig replied sagely, "We can't live our lives wondering what other persons think. We all make mistakes, and if we can, we make the best of things."

Christmas came and went, and the January weather was bleak. I guessed Maggy wouldn't be taking little Lars to the park too often, especially when there was snow on the ground. As January progressed, however, days grew longer with the sun setting later in the day, a harbinger of things to come.

A month into the new year, the United States launched a satellite, Explorer I, and so began the Explorer program. "It's because of those Russian Sputniks," explained Onkel Olav one day. "It's a space race with the Russians, but we will win it."

"It will make the world smaller," said Papa. "The Russians probably know everything we're doing, and they're ahead of us here. Humans were never meant to leave solid ground. If they were, God would have given us all wings."

"I think the Russians recognize the future of mankind," said Onkel Olav gravely. "Maybe they have had a head start, but America is smarter and richer. You'll see, we'll put those Russians to shame."

"It's the future," piped up Tor Asbjørn. "See how everyone who comes from Norway flies? They don't take the boat anymore."

"Yes, and do you know what I'm going to be when I get out of Bay Ridge High? I'm going to fly," said Bente.

"You gonna grow wings?" Tor Asbjørn quipped. Bente gave him a look that stopped him cold, but clearly, he was amused with himself.

"Bente will be graduating in June," offered Tante Clara, "and she is planning for her future."

"I am going to be a stewardess," Bente said proudly. "I am going to Kansas City in April to interview with TWA during spring break—that's Trans World Airlines—I've already applied and been accepted." And shortly thereafter, off she went for an initiation and came back elated. As soon as she graduated from Bay Ridge High, she would be part of the crew.

When Bente was back in Brooklyn after her initial training, the three sisters and their families were at Sunday dinner at Tante Clara and Onkel Olav's, Hedvig couldn't help herself and blurted out: "Why that's pitch red, that lipstick." It didn't seem like a criticism, though. It was more like admiration. Tante Hedwig's three daughters and two daughters-in-law all wore makeup, and Mama often had something to say about that. But makeup enhanced Bente's good looks. She looked grown up and sophisticated, I realized. And then I had a thought: pitch is black, not red. In my mind I pictured Bente with black lips and began to giggle.

"What's so funny?" asked Tor Asbjørn, and I whispered to him.

With that he whispered back, "Mama doesn't like the lipstick, but our father said it was okay. After all, she's almost an adult." I was surprised then when Ingy asked Bente if she dared to wear lipstick to church.

"Oh, I do, and you wouldn't believe what it brings out in people. Just this morning, before church, I was in the ladies' room, and that old maid Gertrude said I would go straight to hell for what I had done to myself."

"Were you shocked?" asked Ingy.

"Just a little, but I told her in no uncertain terms, that it's less important what you put on your lips than what comes through them."

"Hah, you told her," said Tor Asbjørn. "I wish I had been there. That's rich."

It wasn't long after that exchange that Ingy came downstairs, ready for school, wearing pink lipstick. I had to admit she looked pretty, but then she was always good looking, kind of like the actress Tuesday Weld. The makeup just accentuated her lovely features. To our mutual surprise, Mama stood still, dish towel in hand, and stared at Ingy, but said nothing.

By the time Bente graduated from high school, Ingy wearing lipstick was the norm. I was acutely aware, however, of the snide glances many of the older women in our church threw her way. And when Bente showed up at church wearing earrings, it caused quite a stir. One Sunday morning, Pastor Muhlsen, who was new to our church, having left a congregation in Minnesota to minister in Brooklyn, had this to say: "It is sinful to adorn your bodies, to alter the way God made you. I inwardly plead with God to forgive those women who have adopted worldly ways and paint their faces and wear earrings that glitter like demons." Wow, that was something! When we got home that Sunday, I wanted to know what the pastor meant.

My mother and my aunts all wore wedding and engagement rings, and mama had a few lovely brooches, one particularly nice one with a deep blue sapphire that she affixed to the lapel of her spring topper. "How come it's a sin to wear earrings, but not rings and pins?"

"It's the message the earrings send to everyone who sees them," explained Papa. "It's that in the world people think they can improve upon what God has made; that's why it's sinful. Understand, too, that earrings just make you look cheap. It's disrespectful to think you can alter God's work."

That's when I vowed to myself that I would someday own lots of earrings, but I wasn't sharing that thought just yet. I had only this one question under my breath: "Why does Mama get permanents then? She changes how God made her."

With that, Mama, who had overheard, sputtered, "My sister had curly hair!" Okay, I got it, and so did Ingy, who simply rolled her eyes.

At church there were more pressing issues than how we looked that bore discussion. Construction of the bridge connecting Brooklyn to Staten Island had been approved. As a result, many church families had been forced by the city to leave their homes, and the destruction of Bay Ridge began, despite the protests of the congregation and its leaders. The English and Norwegian department ministers had petitioned city hall to reconsider. It was a last-ditch effort that yielded nothing. Our stately church would remain functional to the last, but its demise was certain.

Our cousin Maggy and her husband and baby were among those who had to find a new place to live, but otherwise our extended family hadn't been directly affected. Tante Hedwig told us that Maggy and Paul were taking little Lars and moving to New Jersey.

"To live permanently?" Ingy asked.

"They can't do that," exclaimed Papa when he heard. "He's a city worker and has to live in the city. It's the rule."

"Yes, they can," explained Onkel Werner. "It may be the rule, but it's not one that's enforced. Why at Paul's firehouse there are men who live in New City and Long Island, and another in New Jersey. When you think about it, it's a stupid rule, when you consider they sleep in the firehouse when they're on duty."

"Where in New Jersey? Will they be near Budd Lake so we can see them in the summer?" I asked.

"Looks like Clifton is where they'll be. It's close to the tunnel, and Paul will be able to drive to Brooklyn, no problems," added Tante Hedwig. And straightaway after that, Maggy and Paul took their baby and moved.

Our summer was the usual: idyllic lazy days on the banks of the lake. Time flew by, and not much altered from day to day. When we came back from Budd Lake, however, we saw that change had been quick and dramatic. The destruction was startling: buildings were coming down through the center of Bay Ridge. This ruthless clearing ultimately resulted in 800 buildings demolished and 7000 people displaced. We awaited the inevitable demolition of our church, which held on while brick and mortar came tumbling down around it. A swath was being systematically cut through our community, starting at the Gowanus expressway arching up to 7th Avenue and extending to the route of the projected expressway, and it would decimate all the residential habitations and mom-and-pop stores between 6th and 7th Avenues in its path.

Newspapers regularly printed photos of the broken bricks and boards that were once parts of solid buildings. Several exposés pointed out the futility of such demolition actions long before the bridge construction itself had even started. Why didn't they build the bridge first and then clear the way for the roadbed? The interstate to come would cut across Staten Island from the new bridge all the way to the Goethals Bridge connected to New Jersey, and on the Brooklyn side the roadway from the bridge would link to the Gowanus Expressway which connected with the Brooklyn Battery Tunnel and the Brooklyn/Queens Expressway. It wasn't long before the newspapers pointed out the health hazards of razed buildings lying in fields which sprouted weeds and provided a playground for rats and mice. It wasn't pretty.

While Brooklyn seemed to be falling apart, I was in transition from childhood to becoming a teenager, a pre-teen to be precise, as was my cousin Alice. This was the year I had started the eighth grade at PS 104, and Ingy her senior year at Bay Ridge High. It was also the year I started attending confirmation class, along with my cousin Alice and 20 others, all of whose families attended our church. Classes were every Friday at five p.m., led by Pastor Muhlsen, followed by the church Youth Group, also a first for me and Alice.

We were instructed to read the entire *Bible* and memorize the names of the books, Old Testament and New. Those of us who had older siblings knew the routine since we had witnessed their transformation as they achieved this milestone. What is confirmation, exactly, Karl, an outspoken boy, queried. "It's the receiving of the gifts of the holy spirit," said Pastor Muhlsen, "and recognition of Christ as the head of the church, just like a husband is the head of the wife and family. What is necessary is to adhere to the teaching of the *Bible*, which is inerrant, and shun the things of the world. In other words, be Godly."

Muhlsen, whom we soon privately called the Mule, was firm in his assertions: we would shun all things worldly. That meant for girls no significant jewelry and no makeup; for all, no movies, no dancing, no pool halls, no bowling alleys, and most important, no skipping church services. What the Mule taught us was that it pretty much wasn't fun to be a Christian, especially when he produced notes for us to bring to school that said we could not participate in dancing in the gym, even if it was with 50 other girls.

"Why not dance?" asked Torhild, the lanky, dark-haired girl who was a year older than the rest of us and already a freshman at Fort Hamilton High. "My mother and father go to the Sons of Norway dances, and they say they're great fun." Torhild, whom we soon called Tory, was new to our church and we all sensed that her life experiences had been quite different from ours, as homegrown free church kids. We liked her and were intrigued by her stories about the Sons of Norway, an organization our parents didn't belong to. My thoughts flew to Onkel Sverre and Tante Magda, who were members, but then, they were drinkers, so that figured. They danced, too, I knew.

"Hey, we parade around the Christmas tree downstairs after the Jule Fests (Christmas celebrations). That's kind of like dancing," piped in Karl, a son of solid Norwegian free church members. "It's fun. We sing Christmas carols in Norwegian, too!"

Exasperated, the Mule threw up his hands and proclaimed, "When you're older you'll understand. It's not dancing itself, but what it encourages. When a boy and girl get close, it could lead to something that could ruin your life, especially if you're a girl. So, say no to dancing! You'll take these notes from me to your teachers."

It wasn't long after that that Pastor Muhlsen and his petite wife, Liselle, adopted a baby whom they named Bernard after his father. "I know why they had to adopt," Tory told us one Friday night between confirmation class and Youth Group. "They've only been dancing. Can't get a baby that way."

Confirmation class continued, and although the pastor gave us lots of points of instruction, we had many more questions. When we talked about confirmation and receiving the gifts of the Holy Spirit, Tory offered openly that her mother had told her confirmation was actually confirmation of her baptism as a Christian. She had, she explained, been baptized as a Lutheran long before moving to Brooklyn. Her parents chose this church because her uncle attended. Well, gee, we free church kids mostly hadn't been baptized, so how could that be?

The knowledge gave rise to a question: we're not Lutheran, but Norwegian free church people, so what exactly are we free from? Pastor explained that we were free to govern ourselves as a church. At home, however, the same question posed to Papa brought this explanation: "In Norway the 'Free Church' is free from government control. The government oversees the state church, which is Lutheran. The government appoints ministers, and there's no guarantee that they are actually spiritual and ministering to the people and not simply holding down a job."

"When the Norwegians came to Brooklyn, then, they brought their 'free' church with them, is that right?"

My father's father, my Bestefar, whom I had never known and had died when my father was a teenager in Norway, had been an Evangelist. This I knew from shared family history. "Was he a free church man, too?" I asked.

"No, actually he worked for the state church as a travelling evangelist," my father explained, in slow and deliberate English. "But when he was in Brooklyn, when he was young, he was caught up in the evangelical movement that had its roots in Denmark originally, and then spread to Norway. But when he went back to Norway—and brought us all with him—the best job for him, with his experience as an evangelist in America, was with the church. You don't understand, though, that those were tough times in Norway. It was the depression, just like in America, and the state church gave my father steady work."

Now I had learned that the free church was "free" from government control, but that was what all religions in America were, and we had learned in school about separation of church and state. Here it didn't seem like we were 'free' from very much with all the arbitrary rules we were held to. Confirmation class continued to elicit questions but few satisfactory, concrete answers. I wanted to know where in the *Bible* it talks about confirmation. Muhlsen said that the book of *Romans* alludes to confirmation: "The Spirit himself testifies with our spirit that we are God's children." With that he was off and running: "Think about confirming that the Holy Spirit lives within you. The *Bible* tells us to examine yourself to see if you are faithful, so it's like a test. That's confirmation of your faith and your knowledge that we are saved by the shed blood of Christ."

Tory had naturally become our most vocal class member, and she had no qualms about challenging our pastor. Sometimes I sensed that The Mule was irritated by her relentless questioning, but he did his best to hide it. Still, we could tell.

The confirmation process, those weekly drills, homework, and occasional quizzes, provided the comradery that results from regular social interaction for 22 young people on the cusp of the hormone-charged teenage years. We looked forward to attending the Youth Group meetings which followed our class, especially since there were lots of high school kids in the group, and it wasn't lost on me that some of those boys looked pretty good. Nobody talked about being, as we had in confirmation class, "Soldiers of Christ," but it was clear that there was a mutual understanding of faith throughout, and that felt like a good thing.

The Youth Group was dynamic. Sometimes there would be guest speakers, like a policeman or a missionary. Usually there were group games which we played in teams. There was always laughter and comradery. Once a month, on a Saturday night, there was a Splash Party held at the Young Men's Christian Association, or simply the YMCA, on 9th Street. A number of the Norwegian churches participated, so there were usually lots of young people. Volunteers would carpool us from the church to the YMCA, and once there we gleefully changed into our bathing suits in separate areas and united in the pool, boys and girls. I was aware of my changing body and noticed some of the boys looking at me. It felt odd. The boys my own age were mostly much shorter, and we eighth-grade girls towered over them.

My sister rarely came to the splash parties that year, since she was now a high school senior, and the Youth Group was beneath her dignity. Bente had moved on to be a TWA employee, so I felt pretty light and free with no one to carry home criticisms of what Alice or I had said or done. Other girls Ingy's age more or less posed poolside by the chlorine-haloed lights for the attention of the teenage boys. When the supervisor from our church or one of the other churches blew her whistle, we climbed out of the pool, and headed for the showers. There was a flower shop nearby, however, and once we were clean, dried, and tidied, our chaperones waited while we girls bought large chrysanthemum corsages which we would wear to church the following morning.

As confirmation neared, we took the RR local train to downtown Brooklyn and Abraham and Straus, or A&S, to buy a white confirmation dress. Why Mama didn't make me wear the same one Ingy had four years ago was a mystery, but I was now as tall as Ingy, so probably four years ago she had been more petite. "You need your own pure white dress, a new one," Mama explained. We found a pretty one, white lace with a short-sleeved bolero type jacket. I felt beautiful when I put it on. Mama then took me to Thom McGann for white shoes, and lo and behold, she let me get white leather pumps with little heels.

Confirmation day dawned bright and sunny, and excitement hung in the air at church. Ours would be the last confirmation class at our church on 66th Street, so it was therefore extra special, and a topic of Pastor Muhlsen's introduction of the confirmands to the congregation, which included almost all of my aunts, uncles, and cousins. In unison, we recited the books of the *Bible,* from *Genesis* to *Revelation*. Then he quizzed us all on various Biblical topics. We were exceptional. Then he explained that we had all written essays about what it means to be confirmed and he had selected the best one to be read from the pulpit. Now, we had all read our essays in our last confirmation class after Muhlsen had graded them. I thought Tory's was the best with my cousin Alice's running a close second, but it was Karl who read his that day. After all, Karl's father was a deacon in our church. It figured.

After the ceremony, we went to the Seaman's Church in downtown Brooklyn for a turkey dinner to which Mama and Papa and Tante Clara and Onkel Olav had invited all the relatives. What a crowd we were. It was really a multiple celebration: my and Alice's confirmation and our cousin Ole's 30th birthday, which happened to fall on the same Sunday. Onkel Olav said grace, and then our parents said how proud they were of me and Alice. When we got home, there was a present: a brand new, 3-speed black English racer, just like Ingy had gotten for her confirmation.

From that day forward, I rode every day I could, covering lots of ground in Brooklyn. I could make it to Tante Clara's in record time to visit with Alice and Sonya, and I rode all along Ridge Boulevard, Colonial Road, and Shore Road, often passing Fort Hamilton High School, the edifice I would attend in the fall.

Graduation from P.S. 104 was a milestone for me. Grammar school was done, and it was off to the big league. By the middle of my 8th year at 104, I had said I wanted to go to Fort Hamilton, a coed school, and Mama and Papa said it was okay. Yet four years ago,

Ingy had started as a freshman at Bay Ridge High, an all-girls' high school, and I remembered how adamant our parents had been that she go there. So much was curious to me.

Ingy, though, knew she was destined for a new experience. By the middle of her senior year at Bay Ridge High, she had declared she wanted to go to college. Mama and Papa had pretty much ignored her assertions. "Girls don't need to go to college," Papa said. "What good would it do? Girls get married and tend house and have babies. What a waste of money!" Ingy persevered, however, and pretty soon Papa was listening more intently. His argument soon became one of piety. "Colleges teach worldly ideas, liberal ideas, even communistic mindsets. College can ruin you!"

Mama piped up with this: "If you want to go to more school, you can get a hospital diploma of nursing at the Lutheran Medical Center. Several of the girls in your Sunday School class are planning to do just that."

"It's not college," Ingy retorted, "I think I want to teach."

"The nursing diploma is the best thing for you," Mama continued. "Why, the Medical Center has a grand history. Its founder was Elizabeth Fedde and she was from Flekkefjord, not far from Lyngdal and Spangareid. This place knows its Norwegian history. And think of how you'll be able to help others. Isn't that what you want to do?" Ingy had probably expected this, because she was prepared. She announced that she had spoken with Pastor Muhlsen's wife, Liselle, about going to college and gained some support there. "There are Christian colleges," she said, "and she has some recommendations."

Well, if the pastor's wife was endorsing the education of Ingy, Papa would have to relent, and so he did. Plus, I knew, there would be the status in telling people he had a daughter in college. In consideration was Wagner College on Staten Island and Kings College in New York State because both had religious affiliations. The one they finally chose, however, was Upsala College in New Jersey because it had Scandinavian roots. So, it was to there that Ingy applied and was accepted.

Upsala must have felt a comfortable option, since it was Scandinavian—albeit Swedish, not Norwegian. But still, it had a long illustrious history, having been founded in Brooklyn in 1893 and affiliated with the Swedish-American Augustine Synod of the Lutheran Church. The student body was mostly from traditional Lutheran backgrounds, and by the time Ingy was set to go, the campus was in East Orange, having moved from Brooklyn, to Kenilworth, New Jersey, and finally to its present locale. There it sprawled over a 400-plus acre campus off Prospect Street.

As soon has Ingy had been accepted, Papa and Mama and I went to see it, and Papa went directly to the Admissions office while Mama, Ingy, and I strolled about the campus, discovering that the Student Center was called Viking Hall. That felt familiar and reassuring, and I knew I would look forward to visiting my sister, who was assigned to the West Campus dormitories.

On our ride home to Brooklyn, Papa asked Ingy if she would prefer a part-time job working in the bookstore or the Kenbrook Cafeteria. With this Ingy started. "Work? I'll be studying!" Papa calmly explained that the Office of Admissions had offered a choice of two positions in exchange for a reduced tuition rate, and he had agreed.

"Bookstore," mumbled Ingy, close to tears. And that's all we heard about it.

Now that was something for the whole family to digest. She would be the first of our family, including our many cousins, to go beyond high school. I could tell Papa had weighed this decision carefully and was torn between what it would cost and the pride he would feel being the father of a college student, and pride had won out.

Chapter Fourteen

Change Is the Constant

We were sitting in the Edelmann's cottage at Budd Lake early in July because the weather was horrific—rain, thunder, lightning, and hail. But we were glad to be there, Edel and Else and I with Raymond and Barbara, because this family had a television and good board games, and it was the best place to be when we had to be indoors. As always, Mrs. Edelmann talked to us, and I liked it because she spoke to us as though we were adults.

"So, where is Ingrid?" Mrs. Edelmann asked.

"Oh," I replied, "She applied for and got a job at the Budd Lake Diner on Route 46. She works part time, and because she's going to college in the fall, she wants to have some extra money. She's working 15 hours a week as a waitress. She can take her bike, or even walk. It's a pretty good deal for her."

"Where's she going?" Mrs. Edelmann asked, meaning college.

I responded: "To Upsala, that's in East Orange, near where my aunts and uncles live in the next town."

"I can't say I've heard of that college, but as long as it's accredited, it's a good thing. I was never sure your parents would encourage higher education."

That comment caught me by surprise. I can't say I ever thought too much about what they would encourage or not, but I did know they didn't think girls needed to go to college. Still, it was noteworthy that they had consented to Ingy's going.

Then Mrs. Edelmann asked me and Edel and Else an odd question. "Have you been following what's going on in our government? What happens now will shape your future. We have a really interesting election coming up. President Eisenhower's term is almost up, and Vice President Nixon's the Republican candidate. The primaries for the Democratic party have been revealing. The young senator John Kennedy from Massachusetts seems to be gathering momentum. That he's not a Protestant is even more interesting." Why, I wondered, would that ever matter to her?

Raymond said, "I really like Kennedy. He's a war hero; he served in World War II in the Pacific and was a PT boat commander." I was only half listening. A bit older than I, Raymond was becoming buff, and I appreciated his maleness, not that I would ever want him to know that.

I nodded sagely and said, "I agree," not knowing a thing about this Kennedy fellow, but wanting Raymond's approval.

"We can't forget, though, that Eisenhower liberated so much oppression in Europe, and that's where we're from," said Mrs. Edelmann. "Nixon shared Eisenhower's politics."

"Well, Kennedy is sure good looking," said Edel. "And his wife seems so elegant. They have a family, too."

Mrs. Edelmann then interjected with this: "He's really young, only forty-three, but maybe he's young enough not to make the political blunders of the past, but old enough to know how to move America forward. We'll see."

A week or so later, we learned that, on July 15, John Fitzgerald Kennedy accepted the nomination during the Democratic Convention at the Los Angeles Memorial Coliseum in front of 80,000 people. Ingy was ecstatic. He was good looking; he was forward thinking; he had a wife whom she aspired to be like. I was hooked. My parents were less enthusiastic.

When Papa's sisters arrived from West Orange with their husbands a few days later, talk soon turned to politics. "They'll never elect a Catholic in this country," declared Papa. "The American people won't have it. You'll see."

Onkel Bendix agreed. "If a Catholic were to be in office, he would have to answer to the Pope in Rome. We'd have the Pope running this country. So, no doubt you are correct. He's unelectable."

"He'll have to choose a Vice Presidential candidate. That might change how the American voters feel about Kennedy," said Onkel Karl. "Newsmen are talking about a few candidates: Lyndon Johnson, Adlai Stevenson, Stuart Symington, and our own governor, Robert Meyner."

"Stevenson's a real liberal, a spender, and I haven't seen anything good come to this state from Meyner. At any rate, it's stupid to speculate, since Kennedy can't win."

Time would prove our elders wrong. For us, in the meantime, life at the lake continued in bucolic sameness, except this year it rained more than usual, and we were more often than not housebound. How many games of Parcheesi could we play? A nice diversion was the summer Olympics taking place in Rome, Italy, which we watched on TV at the Edelmann's. The depiction enforced our belief that any young people from anywhere in the world could win the gold if they just worked hard enough. All seemed right with the world as 5000 amateur athletes from 83 countries took part in 150 events, with the United States, Italy, and the Soviet Union taking most of the medals.

Yet, all was not right with the world, apparently, because that summer we also learned that the Russians had sentenced United States Pilot Francis Gary Powers to years imprisonment and hard labor for spying in the Soviet Union. We had learned back in the spring that Powers had been shot down by surface-to-air missiles after flying from Pakistan into Soviet territory. When he survived the crash, Powers was taken into custody. The adults in our lives had been adamant that the U.S. wouldn't be conducting espionage, and Powers himself explained he had simply strayed off course. Yet the Soviet Union had calmly produced the remains of the aircraft along with photos of military bases in Russia. Powers's hard sentence dispelled the warm feelings of unity between nations the Olympics had given us, and it would trigger an acceleration in spy satellites for reconnaissance by the U.S. and the Soviets going forward.

As summer drew to a close, we learned that Hurricane Donna was forecast to make landfall in Florida and travel up the east coast. Before we left the lake for Brooklyn, Papa calmly boarded up our bungalow with plywood over the windows and brought what little outdoor furniture we had into the living room. Progress had made our ride back to the city considerably less time-consuming. A new roadway was under construction: I-80, an interstate that would ultimately link the George Washington Bridge and New York City to the Bay Bridge and San Francisco, but for us, in the waning days of summer, it was simply a leg in that project that we called the

Dover-bypass, Dover being a city on Route 46 that had always slowed us down with traffic lights and vehicle congestion. The new six-lane extension let us make better time, and with less stop and go, I experienced less carsickness.

We were eager to see what changes had occurred in Brooklyn during the two months we had spent at the lake. We soon learned our church on 66th Street was slated to meet a wrecking ball and the property on which it stood would soon feature a roadway, a link between the Gowanus Expressway and the approach to the planned Verrazano Bridge. Church families had received instructions that English church services would take place at the private Poly Prep School on 7th Avenue across from the Dyker Beach Golf Course and close to the Veterans Hospital and the Fort Hamilton military base. For us it meant we could walk to services from our house on 92nd Street, but our parents would drive to the Second Evangelical Free Church on 52nd Street and 8th Avenue for Sunday morning meetings.

For Youth Group, we had been invited to join the young people at the 52nd Street church. This was an imposing brick building that sat squarely on the avenue we called Lapskaus Boulevard, in the heart of Norwegian Brooklyn. It was a trek to travel there for me, and I began by taking three busses, 5th Avenue to 69th Street, 69th Street to 8th Avenue, and 8th Avenue to the church. I had done that but once or twice when I learned to take the 5th Avenue route and walk from 5th Avenue to 8th Avenue. As luck would have it,

Hurricane Donna struck New York, mainly ravaging Long Island, but bringing pelting rain to Brooklyn. I traveled to Youth Group solo in this storm, arriving soaking wet with an umbrella blown inside out and my hair plastered to my forehead. I was alone in my sodden misery, since Ingy wasn't attending Youth Group anymore. There was no sense in it, she said, since she was a high school graduate who would be leaving for college in another week.

Alice and I and our co-confirmands from 66th Street readily joined the 52nd Street Youth Group, and we already knew many of them from the monthly Splash Parties at the 9th Street YMCA hosted by multiple Norwegian churches. The routine was so similar to what we had experienced at 66th Street, and we soon felt very comfortable and simpatico with our expanded circle of friends. The best experience, however, was at Doddenhoff's, an ice cream parlor on 8th Avenue between 59th and 60th Streets, and when Youth Group was over, that's where we headed.

Dodie's—that's what we all called the place— brought us together with other teens we also knew from the Splash Parties: those from the 59th Street Lutheran Brethren Church. This shop would soon become our teenage hangout, and it was the place where the Norwegian kids from the three Norwegian churches congregated. We were many in number, and older siblings frequented it as well. Situated directly across from the Sons of Norway, it drew

Norwegian revelers as often as did Duffy's and the Match Box, the bars on the same block as Dodie's. In this milieu, Norwegians dominated, but we interacted with folks from different cultures often. Irish and Italian young people intermingled with us, and over time, strong friendships formed.

New as well to me and my cousin Alice was Fort Hamilton High School, which we had started attending right after Labor Day. I could easily walk to this big stately brick building that looked solemnly out over a park and Gravesend Bay from Shore Road. Alice, however, took the Fort Hamilton Parkway bus, using a pass that allowed students to ride for a nickel all the way to 86th Street and Shore Road. We all were assigned lockers, this so we wouldn't have to tote all of our textbooks to every class. Getting used to leaving a room when a bell rang was daunting, but we stumbled into the hallways and made our way to our next scheduled classes. I had signed up for an art class, as a balance to the academics an advisor suggested, and from the art classroom window I could see the beginnings of what would become the Verrazano Narrows Bridge.

While I was getting oriented to my new school, Ingy was preparing to go to New Jersey and begin her higher education as a Freshman at Upsala. College classes started in late September, and I realized a little sadly that Ingy would live away from us.

Nevertheless, these changes were exciting, and we welcomed them but not without some trepidation. Still, Ingy told me that she could come home pretty easily, since a bus ran from East Orange to the Port Authority in Manhattan, and from there she could get the 4th Avenue RR train. But, as it happened, she would spend many a Saturday working in the college bookstore.

Right after Ingy had settled in at Upsala as September was waning, Mama, Papa, and I joined Tante Clara, Onkel Olav, Tor Asbjørn, Alice, and Sonya to witness another first time happening: the first televised presidential political debate between Senator Jack Kennedy and Vice President Richard Nixon. This debate would be followed by three more.

"I never liked Nixon, you know," said Onkel Olav. "He still has that angry, intense look on his crooked face."

With that, Tor Asbjørn announced "I wouldn't buy a used car from that guy!" That made the grownups chortle. My cousin had become obsessed with cars, and at 17 with a learner's permit, he was saving to buy one, researching makes and models and becoming increasingly authoritative about automobiles.

We focused on the TV as handsome Senator John Fitzgerald Kennedy took a seat on the podium as did Vice President Richard Milhaus Nixon. The difference in appearance was startling:

Kennedy exuded strength, vitality, and charm while Nixon looked haggard, weary, and in need of a shave. Seventy million voters watched this debate, and as many more listened in over the radio.

Kennedy, who was a Harvard graduate from a privileged background, waxed eloquent about America's potential for economic growth and prosperity, calling the last year a witness to the lowest rate of economic growth of any major industrial society on the globe. Nixon was quick to refute this claim, citing the gross national product as one of the highest in the world today. The bottom line for both candidates was that they looked for economic growth and prosperity and the defeat of communism.

Nixon was quick to point out that President Eisenhower had endorsed him, and, if elected, he would continue Eisenhower's forward momentum as a Christian candidate. After all, he had spent eight years as part of a popular administration led by the man who had liberated Europe in World War II.

When asked how his religion might influence his decision making if elected, Kennedy replied, "I'm not the Catholic candidate for President. I am the Democratic Party's candidate who happens to be a Catholic. I do not speak for my church and the church does not speak for me."

We learned later that people listening to the radio thought Nixon had won, but those of us who had witnessed the televised debate knew better. "Still," Papa would repeat, "he's a Catholic, and Americans will never elect him, no matter how charming and good looking he is."

What we also came to realize was this: Kennedy had good advisors and the backing of the wealthy Kennedy family. The media posted photos of Kennedy and his brothers Ted and Bobby, their wives, and children, and of course Kennedy's own beautiful wife Jackie and their two small children, Caroline and John Jr. The media covered Nixon as well, showing him with President Eisenhower performing duties of the office. Both candidates were strongly anti-communist and that seemed a good thing to us.

Kennedy was evidently very cognizant that being Catholic could be a detriment since, if elected, he would be the first Catholic in office. Further, he would be the youngest President, the first to have been born in the 20th century. But he proved himself capable. He spoke to the Greater Houston Ministerial Conference and stressed separation of church and state; indeed, this was something with which we were all familiar since we ourselves attended a "free" church. Kennedy also gained the endorsement of Martin Luther King Jr. after King was arrested for leading civil rights protests in Alabama. Kennedy had subsequently called Coretta King, the wife, and offered to help secure a safe release, which he did.

Nixon proved himself an opportunist and cited his endorsement of the Civil Rights Act of 1960, which Eisenhower had signed into law, and in fact the administration, in which Nixon had played a key role, had initially signed the Civil Rights Act of 1957. The new Act closed a few loopholes in voter registration, but more importantly, extended the life of the Civil Rights Commission, which was set to expire. So, yes, both candidates endorsed civil rights. It was a close campaign, but on November 8, Kennedy emerged the winner, albeit by a very small margin.

At Fort Hamilton High School, my civics teacher asked my class to form an argument about a case the United States Supreme Court had decided in December, Boynton v. Virginia. What did we think? Bruce Boynton was an African American law student who had been arrested for entering a "whites only" restaurant in a bus terminal and trying to order food. The court had ruled in a 7-2 decision that racial segregation in public transportation was unconstitutional and a violation of the Interstate Commerce Act. Our class had a lively discussion, and those few students who defended segregation were slowly won over to see the civic "wrongness" of it. Mr. Mann, our teacher, was so clearly logical that it was hard not to agree with him.

For me, living in New York, the idea that some Americans by virtue of the color of their skin could not participate in society equally with white people was shocking. Segregation was a concept I simply couldn't fathom. When Mama asked at the dinner table how school had gone that day, I broached the subject of segregation, explaining the class exercise. I was further shocked when Papa explained slowly in English, that the colored in this country were brought here as slaves, so they are a servant class, and thus not equal to white people.

"That doesn't seem right," I said. "How do you know they are not equal?"

"A few things let us know this. The *Bible* very early talks about what is known as the 'curse of Ham.' Ham was a son of Noah, and the father of the Canaanites. Ham looked upon his father when he was naked, and Noah cursed him, saying he and his lineage would be servants. We believe Ham was colored."

Mama uttered this: "The *Bible* tells servants to be obedient to their masters. That means negro people are to be obedient." Then she added more affirmatively, "If they don't like it here, they should go back where they came from."

Papa sat there mute as I answered. "If they were slaves in America, they wouldn't know where they came from. So why don't you go back where you came from? You know where that is, and you have family there!"

"This is a white Christian country. We have a right to be here. They don't."

"Where would they go?" I parried.

"If they can't go back where they came from, the government should give them their own state."

"Great, Mama. How about if we give them New York? Then where would we go?" The conversation stopped there as Mama slammed her hand on the kitchen table. Papa continued to remain mute as I cleared the table and started the dishes.

I was having a hard time digesting my parents' viewpoints in the days that followed, but I was thinking hard. The next Friday at Youth Group I asked the group Leader, Harold Abrahamsen, whom we all fondly called Hal, about colored people in the United States, explaining that I had learned from my civics class that negro people, especially in the South, can't use the same toilets, drink from the same water fountains, or eat in the same restaurants as white people.

Hal, a young man in his early twenties, explained that many people shared the same viewpoint as my parents, and that they believed it kept order in the country. But he added, "We are making strides. Eisenhower in his second term ordered desegregation of schools. While it was progress, there were huge social ramifications, and the administration called for the National Guard to maintain order."

"What do you yourself think now?" I asked.

"Oh, that's a whole different ball of wax. I'm starting to study for seminary, and what I believe is that I can help change how people think. There's a verse in the New Testament that definitively says humans are equal." With that comment he grabbed a *Bible* and looked up the verse he identified as *Galatians* 3:28. Here's what he read: "There is neither Jew nor Greek, there is neither slave nor free man, there is neither male nor female; for you are all one in Jesus Christ."

"Hah," said Tory, still the vocal one from our Confirmation class, "I like the 'neither male nor female.' Does this also say men and women are equal?"

To this Hal responded, "It would seem so, but our world is also burdened with social mores that dictate more about how we behave. In fact, social mores ingrained for generations are probably the root cause of the civil rights agenda in this country today. And sexual inequality, too," he added as an afterthought.

I liked Hal, and I liked how he talked to us progressively about ideas that were for many of us ingrained purely by virtue of our upbringing. I could see that he would influence how people thought over time. Certainly, he was opening our eyes.

Thus, because of Youth Group and high school, my perspectives were changing; my concept of what was going on around us was broadening, and I was becoming amenable to viewpoints diverse from those most of my family embraced.

I liked, too, how in the lunchroom at Fort Hamilton we could sit with our friends—mostly those who frequented Dodie's on Friday nights, freshmen like us and upperclassmen as well. We would discuss our teachers and the assignments they meted out. We got advice about what teachers to request the following year, but most importantly we bonded in those hallowed halls of learning. We also talked about the upcoming Christmas vacation and planned on ice skating on Wolf Pond on Staten Island. Hannah suggested we plan a trip to The City and skate at the Wollman Skating Rink if Wolf Pond didn't freeze. We were looking forward to Christmas and the week between it and New Year's Eve.

A little more than a week before Christmas, a tragedy occurred: it was the deadliest aviation crash in history, and it startled Brooklyn out of its glittering holiday spirit. It was December 16, when a Transworld Airlines Super Constellation collided with a United DC8 over Staten Island, sending both aircraft to the ground. The TWA plane fell to Miller Field on the south shore of Staten Island, and the United plane glided powerless into the heart of Park Slope in Brooklyn.

On Staten Island the bodies of 44 people who had thought they would land at LaGuardia airport in New York were brought to Seaview Hospital. Likewise, the 84 people on board the United flight had anticipated setting down at Idlewild. Instead, their bodies wound up at Brooklyn hospitals. The trajectory of the United plane caused it to devastate 7th Avenue and Sterling Place, setting an entire block of buildings ablaze with spilled excess fuel and destroying ten buildings. Six unfortunate bystanders also lost their lives.

The crash was big news on the TV and radio, and for a day there was one glimmer of hope: an 11-year-old boy, Stephen Lambert Baltz, who was traveling alone, was thrown from the plane on impact into a snowbank and miraculously survived. Taken to Brooklyn's Methodist Hospital, a doctor asked him how New York looked from the air, and the boy responded that it was beautiful. He succumbed the next day.

At Fort Hamilton, it was pretty much our topic of conversation. I usually sat with Hannah and Josefina—whom everyone called Joey—my friends from 59th Street church who had the same lunch period as I. "I just can't believe that boy died," said Hannah, referring to the 11-year-old who had been thrown from the plane alive.

"I know," I said. "I really thought he was going to be our Christmas miracle. You have to wonder why God lets things like this happen to innocents."

"My mother says it's all in God's plan," interjected Joey, "but we can't ever really understand the mystery of God. We just have to trust that it's part of the divine pattern."

"Still, it's so senseless—all those people dead, and probably because one of those pilots made a stupid mistake," I stated. "No one else will die anytime soon. Here we are, ready to celebrate the birth of Jesus. It's bittersweet after the deaths of those people this week."

My words did not forecast what was to come very well. One of my classmates came to school four days later with a copy of *The New York Times* which told of a horrific fire that had erupted on December 19 at the Brooklyn Navy Yard, barely two miles from the twisted wreckage of the United airliner lying in Park Slope. Here's what happened: a worker operating a lift truck struck and damaged a 500-gallon fuel tank, spraying its contents afield. The fuel came in contact with a lighted torch in use by a welder, causing a fire that quickly fed on wooden scaffolding and other materials in the immediate vicinity.

This conflagration took over 12 hours to get under control.

Severely damaged was the *USS Constitution,* an aircraft carrier under construction at the Navy Yard. In this accident, 50 workers died, and 330 were injured. Yet this incident received very little media coverage, and we knew about it only from *The New York Times* article. So it was that the events of December that year put a somber face on the festivities of the season.

Young as we were, we were resilient nevertheless and celebrated Christmas Eve with our families. Ingy arrived at our house the weekend before in the front seat of our cousin Arvind's 1956 Chevy convertible. My, Arvind was handsome, and my first thought when I saw him was this: I bet the girls at Dodie's would be crazy about him, if they could just get a glimpse. Ingy was looking good too, but a little heavier than when she had begun her first semester at Upsala. Papa was delighted to see his nephew, and he certainly admired the car our cousin drove. He exclaimed over and over how nice it was of Arvind to have driven Ingy home.

"The snow was really bad, and the busses to Port Authority were running irregularly, so my father said I should call Ingrid and tell her I would drive her home. The snowplows had cleared most of the main roads, so it was no problem, really," Arvind explained. "Besides, Ingrid looks tired, and my mother said she shouldn't travel all the way to Brooklyn alone."

For my sister, it was a tense holiday since she would return to

Upsala after New Year's to take her final exams. She whispered to me that her math class was giving her problems, but under no circumstances was I to tell Mama or Papa. Ingy spent most of the week visiting her friends from 66th Street and our cousins, causing Mama to comment, "She's supposed to be home for the holidays, but she is not!" Bente had vacation time and had come home for the holidays from Kansas City, where she now lived. She probably wasn't at home on 67th Street any more than Ingy was at our house.

We met the New Year with optimism. Now that we had Dodie's as a place to congregate, we did so as often as we could, meeting by pre-arranged plan or simply randomly. There was almost always someone we knew from one of the three Norwegian churches and our high school, and my cousin Alice and I frequented the place as regulars, looking for our girlfriends and sizing up the boys. Friday nights after Youth Group and almost every Sunday afternoon were reserved for Dodie's. The place centered us, and we gravitated to it like flies to honey. In these teens I formed friendships that replaced the ones severed from my life every time we moved.

January, I remember, was bitterly cold, and when I arrived at school my legs were numb, and by second period they were tingly. Alice, Hannah and Joey fared better. They took the bus, even though for them it meant walking to 83rd Street on Shore Road from the terminus of the bus on 86th Street. We didn't mind the cold, however, when we had heavy snow and the schools were closed for the day. When that happened, we put on woolen pants, hats, scarves, gloves, and winter jackets and went outside. Sometimes I would travel to Alice's, and we'd walk in the snow. As often as not, we made our way to Dodie's where we met our "crowd" and had hot chocolate or cherry Cokes.

By mid-January the days had started to grow longer, and the occasional warmer day held a hint that winter would eventually come to an end. The third Friday of that month dawned bright and cold, with a fresh layer of snow blanketing our nation's capital. It was the day that John Fitzgerald Kennedy became our 35th President. This event we had awaited eagerly, totally absorbed in the activities of this nearly royal family, and once he was officially the leader of the free world, we were jubilant, watching clips of the inauguration on the evening news.

"Look at him. He's not even wearing a hat, and it is bitter cold," said Papa.

"But look at that head of hair. It is enough to keep that head warm." Mama said looking pointedly at my father's bald spot, very visible through his thinning hair.

"I learned in my civics class that one president, a long time ago, Willliam Henry Harrison, didn't wear a hat or a coat, and a month after his inauguration, he died of pneumonia," I offered in support of Papa, who I knew hadn't missed the comparison between himself and the young President.

"You see, he's very foolish already," Papa commented, and I knew for a fact that he thought Nixon would have been the better man.

Me, I had no such feelings. I, like most teenagers I knew, loved everything Kennedy. The morning of the inauguration, Kennedy had attended Holy Trinity Catholic Church in Georgetown, then joined Eisenhower to travel to the Capitol, where he was sworn in by Supreme Court Justice Earl Warren on an inaugural platform that extended from the White House. On site also was Poet Laureate Robert Frost, who read one of his poems to the crowd gathered around the platform.

Kennedy's speech was formidable and uplifting—calling for unity and a quest for peace. I was moved by his words when he said "...let us begin anew—remembering on both sides that civility is not a sign of weakness, and sincerity is always subject to proof. Let us never negotiate out of fear. But let us never fear to negotiate."

"I think he's great," I opined.

Papa just said, "We'll see."

Then Kennedy continued by saying we need to heed in all corners of the earth the command of Isaiah to "undo the heavy burdens...and to let the oppressed go free."

"See, he knows the *Bible*," I offered hopefully.

"Or his speech writers do," rebutted Papa.

When Kennedy concluded his address, he said this: "Ask not what America will do for you, but what together we can do for the freedom of man." Then he called upon the Lord: "let us go forth to lead the land we love, asking His blessing and His help, but knowing that here on earth God's work must truly be our own."

I loved this guy, truly. I was equally enamored of his beautiful wife, Jacqueline, and the two adorable children, Caroline and John John. It wasn't long after this family was in the White House that the press started calling it Camelot.

The Eisenhower era was over, and we were primed for new leadership. Eisenhower and his wife, Mamie, made a quiet exit from the limelight. First and foremost a military man, our former president requested that he be called hereafter General Eisenhower, rather than President Eisenhower.

Chapter Fifteen
A Foot in Each Culture

We were sitting in Fort Hamilton's lunchroom in early February, as usual complaining about what we thought to be excessive homework. Hannah and Joey both had the same lunch period as Alice and I, and we shared some classes, although Alice and Joey were taking Spanish, while Hannah and I were taking French. The Spanish teacher was tough, said Joey, but Alice thought she was more or less okay.

"Why don't they offer Norwegian?" Alice said. "That would be so easy!"

"Yeah, but the dialect we speak is different from that of the capital city, Oslo. I can remember being in the Norwegian department at 66th Street and not understanding a word. And then when we had a guest speaker from Sørlandet, I understood everything," I said. "So even if they offered Norwegian, which they don't, it would probably be just like learning another language."

"You'll be glad when you can speak another language," Hannah said. "You'll be tri-lingual when you master one of these Romance languages. They're really beautiful, not like Norwegian, which is harsh, sort of like German."

I had learned in French class about categories of languages, and knew that Norwegian, like the other Scandinavian languages and English, Dutch, Afrikaans, and German itself, belonged to the Germanic group. The really beautiful languages, I thought, were from the Romance group: French, Spanish, Portuguese, Italian, and of all things, Romanian, spoken in a country that was behind the Iron Curtain. That made it sound exotic, and I vowed I would at least master French.

"My sister Bente is studying Spanish, too," interjected Alice. "She's a stewardess for TWA and flies to South America a lot, and she's learning the language so she can enjoy her layovers in Chile and Peru."

"Wow," said Hannah. "That must be such a fabulous job, going to different countries and learning about different cultures. I think I'll become a stewardess, too," she opined.

Our musings were interrupted when Henning and Otto stopped at our table to chat, and we grew shy. Alice had confessed to me that she thought Henning was good looking and so nice. This she would often whisper to me as we left the 52nd Street church Youth Group, which both boys attended.

"Hey," Henning said, looking at Alice and me directly, "why don't you come to basketball on Tuesday nights? Fifty-ninth Street church plays on Tuesdays, and we're all invited to join them. Otto and I went last Tuesday, and it was fun."

"I know," Joey said. "I was there, but I don't go every week, only if I finish my homework before."

Hannah looked at us, with her chin resting in her hand, and said, "I'll go next Tuesday. Meet us at Dodie's first at 5:30, and we can walk to the school together. It starts at six."

"Where's the school?" I asked.

"It's on 61st or 62nd Street, near Fort Hamilton Parkway, PS 310. The school lets the church use the gym every Tuesday night. It's fun."

I decided I would join them, but it would be a hard sell, since we lived all the way out in the 90s, and it would mean traveling in the dark on the way home.

"I'll get my brother to drive us. He's 18 and has a driver's license," said Alice. "And, Sue, you know he's been saving for a car, and now he has one, a 1953 blue and white Ford. This is his last year of school, and my parents won't let him drive to Fort Hamilton. They say it would be too much of a temptation for getting into trouble. I'm sure he'll want to drive us, and my parents will let him because it's for a church sort of thing."

I had study hall for a period on Tuesday and managed to get most of my homework done; the rest I finished as soon as I got home from school. At 5:00 Tor Asbjørn rang the doorbell.

"Welcome, welcome," Papa said, and then, "Let me see your car." With that, Papa and my cousin went to the curb where the car was parked, leaving our house door ajar, and I heard Papa say, "Looks like a bit of rust here."

"I'm going to work at Frank's Auto Body shop on 60th Street," Tor Asbjørn announced. "I'm all set. I've been helping Mario—he's the owner—on weekends now, and he says I can have a full-time job as soon as I graduate in June. It's great—right between 9th Avenue and Fort Hamilton Parkway."

"Good for you," Papa said. "What do you say we take a little ride, just you and me?" I wasn't fooled. Papa wanted to see what sort of driver his nephew was before he'd let me ride with my cousin.

They couldn't have gone more than a few blocks before they returned, and Papa said to me, "You need to be home by 10 o'clock at the latest. It's a school night."

I got in the passenger side, and Tor Asbjørn started the engine, and off we went. We picked up Alice at Tor Asbjørn's house on 67th Street, as Tante Clara beamed at us. It was as though she were realizing her boy was reaching manhood. Personally, I felt pretty good as Alice slid in next to me in the front seat, and in a few minutes, we were at Dodie's, with Hannah, Joey, Tory, Henning, and Otto waiting for us. "I'll pick you two up here at 9:45," my cousin said to me and his sister, "so you'll get home by 10."

We lingered a bit, just talking, before we decided to walk to the school. It was brisk as we crossed 8th Avenue and headed toward 62nd Street. Now this was a street I'd never walked on before; it ran right along the railroad tracks for the Sea Beach Express, the train that terminated at Coney Island. I startled in the dusk as I saw several large figures standing by the track, lined up like mummies, shrouds flapping in the wind. "What are they?" I asked, clearly shaken. My companions burst out laughing.

"Fig trees," said Otto. “The Italians who live across the street planted them, and the city doesn't seem to mind that they're on railroad property. It keeps the ground looking better than it would if it went to weeds."

"They don't look like trees," I said hesitatingly.

"They're wrapped in burlap—for the winter. They can't take the cold climate here. This isn't Italy, you know."

We trudged on and arrived at the school a bit early and were greeted by Hal, our Youth Group leader. I was surprised to see him, but he volunteered that this was his first time, and adults from the three churches would be taking turns overseeing the basketball play. A smattering of other Youth Group members filtered in, and we girls went to change into gym shorts and sneakers in the girls' locker room. Otto and Henning and the rest of the boys did the same in the boys' locker room, and they emerged ready to play. Otto grabbed a basketball and began some fancy dribbling and shot a clean basket as more Youth Group members arrived. Bringing up the end was a person I was shocked to see: Maggy's old boyfriend, that creep, Axel.

Hal divided us into teams, explaining that he wanted to balance our collective heights for more equitable play. Then he explained the rules to my team and showed us how to hold the ball and send it into the air. Axel was doing the same with our opposing team. We took our positions, and Axel blew a whistle, signaling us to begin play. I was pleased when I made a basket, not so much so when at half time we changed sides, and I shot a basket for our opposing team. "Really, Sue?" said Alice. I felt myself going red and decided passing the ball to a teammate was a better option than trying to shoot a basket. At 7:30, we ceased play and chatted a bit before heading for the locker rooms.

As we approached the door, we heard Tory shrieking, "How dare you! Get your filthy hands off me!"

"Hey, I didn't mean anything here. You looked like you would enjoy a little handling," came a voice I recognized as Axel's, and sure enough, the door opened, and Maggy's old boyfriend sidled out. We weren't sure if Hal had heard the exchange, for he was on the other side of the gym collecting equipment.

Tory joined us as we began our trek back to 8th Avenue and Dodie's, where most of the other players were also headed. "That creep," said Tory. "He tried to help me take my shorts off, and I told him in no uncertain terms to lay off. What nerve he had to be in the girls' locker room even!"

"He used to date my cousin," I said, "and I never liked him. I'm really glad our cousin married Paul instead. But you, you need to tell Hal what happened."

I guess she must have done so, because Axel stopped coming to our ball games, and Tory came to our Youth Group less and less frequently, but we continued to see her at Dodie's, and of course at Fort Hamilton. As the days grew warmer that spring, we would exit the school at lunch time and head to the park along Shore Road. Someone, probably Reidar, suggested we play buck buck. We thought this a grand idea and encouraged Alice to be the "pillow." She leaned her back against a tree, and Henning leaned over and put his head on her tummy and wrapped his arms around her and the tree.

"All right," said Otto, standing ten feet away, and then he loped toward the two, leaping onto Henning's back. With that Mia leapt onto Otto, and I leapt onto Mia. That's when we began to topple and fell to the ground laughing. We were still laughing when the bell rang, and we scurried to our classrooms. Settling into our seats, we heard the static on the PA system and the booming voice of our principal, Arthur Thornsby, whom we called Thorny, utter these words: "There will be no playing Johnny on the Pony in the park. We will be watching lunch hours, and anyone who violates this mandate will get detention."

Martin, who sat next to me, whispered, "You'll have to get out of range, so they can't see you," and then he giggled. True to form, playing buck buck—aka Johnny on the Pony—and eluding Thorny and the teachers on lunch duty became a game, soon joined by more students. Our buck buck numbers grew, and we were heady with the power of defying school authorities. It didn't last too long, though, and I soon had to explain to Mama and Papa why I had a week's detention.

Our lunchtime park shenanigans came to a close for a while, but then two of the upperclassmen introduced themselves as Frank and Louis to Hannah, Joey, and me. I, for one, was flattered. They were good-looking lads, indeed. They had a suggestion: we should skip school in the afternoon and take a ride instead. Frank had a car parked in the alley behind the school. "They only take attendance in the morning. Your afternoon teachers won't know whether you were in school or not for the whole day."

So it was that day in early May that we climbed into a 1955 Chevy with Frank at the wheel, Hannah beside him and three of us in the back seat. Frank deftly drove the car onto the Belt Parkway, turning the wheel with his right hand, his left elbow jutting out the open window. In a short while, he brought us to Nellie Bly's, a go-cart park on 25th Avenue and Bay 41th Street. "Wow," I said as soon as we arrived. "I never knew this place was here! Can we ride the go-carts?"

"Sure, you can," said Louis. "Frank and I, we've come here so many times, so we'll just grab a hot dog and wait while you girls ride. Our treat." We got into the carts. Joey had to hike her really tight skirt up to her thighs, but she thought nothing of it, and off she went. Hannah followed; then I did, maneuvering around the oval track with ease. I noticed Mike and Tony standing by the fence, grinning, as Joey made a turn right in front of where they were standing, her legs spread, feet working the pedals.

Our go-cart experience finished, we piled into the car once again, and Frank drove us home, me first, since my house was closest to Fort Hamilton. "Let me out on the corner," I said. "I'll walk to my house, so my mother will think I'm coming from school." What I learned that day was how easy it was to skip school. No one would suspect I would do such a thing, especially since I was in several honors classes.

The next Sunday was the 17th of May, or Norwegian Independence Day, and there would be the annual parade on 8th Avenue. Immediately after church services at Poly Prep, I set out for Dodie's, where Joey and Hannah and I had agreed to meet to watch the parade. It was sunny and clear with a cloudless sky as we stood on the sidewalk across from the Sons of Norway and listened for the music that announced the parade was making its way toward us. The sidewalks were packed with people holding American and Norwegian flags, some quite boisterous. A good number were holding beer cans in front of the Sons of Norway or the bars, Duffy's and the Matchbox.

I looked around to see whom I knew and spied Tor Asbjørn and his friend Mike, who worked with him at Frank's. Then I saw Reidar and the twins, Erica and Elise Brestland. "Here come the four breasts," said Otto to Henning, and they both had a good chuckle.

"That's not nice," said Hannah. "Those poor girls, don't you think they'd feel bad if they heard you? What a name to be saddled with!"

"I feel bad for them," I added. "I wish you wouldn't say things like that."

Just then I felt a tap on my shoulder and turned around. There stood my cousins from Staten Island, Karl and Johann Gabrealsen. "How did you get here?" I blurted out.

"Ferry, of course," said Karl. "I have a new car, and we wanted to take her for a spin."

"She's a beaut," added Johann. "A Ford Galaxie, all white with pale blue interior."

"Who's your friend?" Karl asked me quietly, motioning with his eyes toward Hannah.

"That's Hannah," I said. "We hang together a lot," I explained.

"Mmm, very nice," said Karl, with a lilt in his voice.

"I'll say," added Johann. And with that we grew quiet as the parade marched by us. So many of the women and girls wore beautiful bunads, the traditional costumes of different provinces in Norway. Many men wore the traditional garb as well.

"I love the Hardanger one the best," said Joey. "And look at those soljes" she said pointing to the elaborate silver pins affixed to the outfits. "Do you have a bunad?" she asked me.

"No, my father says they're really a waste of money, since you only wear them a few times a year, and besides, I'm still growing, I think."

Each group in the parade announced its presence with an identifying banner. We watched as a police precinct came by with some officers on horses, followed by a fire station marching band. Multiple Sons of Norway groups, from Brooklyn of course, but some from as far away as Rockaway, New Jersey, and Valley Stream, Long Island, had prominent places in the procession. One Sons of Norway had a Viking ship on wheels, with helmeted "Vikings" on board. And then there were the churches, and we waved eagerly to people we knew from our Sunday services. There were also officials from the city, followed by that year's beautiful Miss Norway in a cocktail dress draped with a banner announcing her status. She was seated on the trunk of a red and white convertible Chevy Bel Air, between the two runners-up, all six feet on the back seat. The girls waved gleefully to the crowd. We watched until the entire parade had passed on its way to Leif Erickson Park, where some city official was giving a speech. Usually that's where we wound up after the annual parade, but this year we lingered in Dodie's because that's where the boys were and thus where we wanted to be. It was cherry cokes all around, and we talked about our respective youth groups and school. Hannah and Joey had not been given the no-dancing dictate as had we teens from 66th Street. "It's ridiculous," pronounced Hannah. "You'd be dancing during gym class with other girls. Fifty-ninth knows that. Besides, dancing is great exercise."

I realized then the mistake we had made: my cousin Alice and I had given the Mule's note to the gym class teacher. I vowed I was going to learn to dance, not that I didn't already know something about the popular dances. At PS 104, someone had had a portable radio playing *At the Hop*, so one of the girls showed me the basic steps for the lindy, and I caught on quickly. Then there was *American Bandstand*, a program I could only watch if I had the good luck to be in another student's home after school. Yes, then, I could dance a bit, but never anywhere the adults from our church could see me, especially Mama and Papa.

At lunch recess in the park, we girls took to dancing, sometimes to music if any of us had a transistor radio. It was during one of these learn-to-dance episodes that I realized Otto had been watching me. "Would you like to go out with me?" he asked tentatively.

"I guess so," I said, because I had been watching him as well. He was taller and broader than Henning and most of the other boys, and he had blue eyes darker than any I'd seen before. "Where would we go?"

"We'll take a walk in Bliss Park, and then take a ferry ride to Staten Island and back," he said.

When I told Mama I had a date, she laughed and said, "That's nice. Who is the boy?"

"Otto, from 52nd Street. I know him from playing basketball."

"He'll come here first. So I can meet him," Mama said her voice rising after the word "first."

"I'll tell him," I promised.

On Saturday, he came to the house, and then we did as he had suggested. By the end of the day, I was sure I was in love. It hadn't been lost on me how other young girls eyed his handsome good looks as we passed them on the street or the deck of the ferry. From then on, we were an item, sitting with each other at Dodie's, hanging out at school, and exploring Brooklyn's parks. When he brought me to his apartment on 56th Street, I met his mother, and I liked her. After a few visits, I realized there was no mention or evidence of Otto's father, no senior Steinberg. At some point I asked, "What does your father do? Does he work on the boats, or is he a carpenter or carpet layer?"

"My father died in Norway," said Otto. "That's why my mother and I came here when I was four. Her sister lives here in Brooklyn, and my mother thought it would be a better life for us, so we immigrated." Poor Otto, I thought. I admired Otto for his scholarship at Fort Hamilton, though, and for his acceptance that his was a one-parent home.

Towards the end of June, Mama answered the phone and said, "Johann, what a surprise!" Then she said to me, "He wants to talk to you."

"Listen, Solveig," he began. "When Karl and I were in Brooklyn at the parade, I, like my brother, really noticed your friend Hannah. I'd love to go out with her. Do you think she'd go if I asked?"

"I think so," I said and gave him Hannah's phone number, the one I knew by heart. Of course, I mentioned this to Hannah at school the next day, reminding her of our meeting with Karl and Johann at the parade. It seemed she had noticed my cousins that day as well, and she said yes when Johann called. Then he called me and offered to get me a date.

"No need," I said. "I have a boyfriend, and I'll get him to go."

The next Saturday, Johann came to my house late afternoon and picked me up in his brother's Ford Galaxie. "It's really noisy," I said.

"Yup, Karl put straight pipes on it. They're so cool."

Then we drove to Lapskaus Boulevard—aka 8th Avenue—and picked up first Hannah and then Otto. Off to Coney Island we went, Hannah and I on a double date, with my handsome cousin and even more handsome boyfriend. The boardwalk was alive with activity and noise, with hawkers shouting for passersby to come and play, to come and win a teddy for the girlfriend or wife. For me, it was the first time I had walked on the very wide boardwalk once it was dusk. I knew Coney Island well from our trips to the beach, but the amusement park with its glittering multi-colored lights in the growing darkness was a whole new adventure.

"Let's ride the roller coaster," Johann said.

"Which one?" queried Hannah. "There are three—the Tornado,

the Thunderbolt, and the Cyclone."

"The Cyclone," said Otto. "It's the biggest one."

I had never ridden the Cyclone before, so I had some trepidation. The boys got tickets, and we climbed aboard, Johann and Hannah in the very first car, Otto and I behind them. We buckled up and the rollercoaster made its slow ascent up the first incline. When we got to the top, Otto yelled, "Here we go!" And go we did. I was terrified. I was frozen in place with a death grip on the handle in front of me and failed to realize that Hannah loved it, screaming gleefully with every hair-raising plunge and rickety turn.

"That was great," Hannah announced once we were on solid ground. "Where to next?"

Otto said, "We have to do the Wonder Wheel. You'll get a great view of the ocean and the entire boardwalk." We marched ourselves to the giant Ferris wheel and climbed aboard. Otto suggested we ride in separate cars so we could look out at the sea and sky rather than in at the mechanics of the ride. When our car crested the top, it began to slide forward, and I was sure our car was disconnecting from the wheel and we'd be flying through the air. I screamed, and that's when Otto grabbed me, laughing, and said, "It's part of the ride. Some of the cars slide." I felt a fool. And then he kissed me.

Our dinner out was hotdogs and cokes from Nathan's, and they were delicious. Before we headed home, we took another stroll on the boardwalk, and Otto and Johann pitched some beanbags at angled boards, trying to sink them into little holes. That's how I came home with a pink elephant, a cute thing that would sit on my bed for years. For the first time, I was actually sad when the school year ended and didn't relish going to Budd Lake. I simply didn't want to leave Otto. I had no choice, however. "See you in September, when the summer's through," Otto sang—and I promised that would be so.

Ingy would not be at the lake for much of the summer. Through her connections at Upsala, she had taken a job at the Fort Lee Children's home in New Jersey and would spend her days supervising children. It would be good experience, she said, since she was planning to become a teacher. I, on the other hand, had connected with our summer friends and had to say Raymond had become even more buff. I couldn't hide it: in my mind I said goodbye to Otto and went all out for Raymond's attention. Pretty soon, we would be walking the sandy roads at night, waiting for curfew at 9:30, and Raymond, after a few nights of the same routine, impulsively reached over and grabbed me, kissing me on my lips—not my first kiss, but the first one that made me tingle. I liked it.

When Tante Signe and Onkel Bendix stopped by one sunny

August afternoon, we were delighted to see them. Mama served iced tea and smørbrod, and we sat on the deck, commenting on how beautiful the lake looked, as a warm breeze ruffled the surface, and the sun made it glisten.

"What are Arvind and Odd doing this summer?" I asked, disappointed that they hadn't come with their parents.

"Oh, Arvind has a job. He's painting houses. He needs money for college, and Odd, well, Odd, he's girl crazy. He's with his girlfriend, Lillian, today." That proved to be a perfect segue for what followed.

So," said Onkel Bendix, addressing me, "do you have a boyfriend?"

Aghast at the question, I quickly thought of Raymond, but Mama piped up with "Oh, sure. He's a nice boy in Brooklyn. His name is Otto. He's good looking and polite."

"What's his last name?" asked Tante Signe.

"Steinberg," I said quietly, not wanting this conversation to go any further, and I excused myself, retreating to my bedroom to read.

I couldn't help but overhear, however, the direction the conversation took. "You know, I knew an Otto Steinberg in Norway. He was a traitor, and when the Nazis left, he was shot."

"What?" exclaimed Mama. "There must be more than one Steinberg in Norway!"

"Otto Steinberg had a wife and a little boy. They lived just outside Austad, not far from us. The wife and boy left Norway for America soon after Steinberg was shot. I think the boy's name was Otto, too."

"Well, even if that was so, the boy was innocent. And if he is the young boy Solveig sees, he's a fine young man," Papa responded. "But tell us how it was, then, after the war."

"Well, you know there was a Nasjonal Samling—they were the people who supported the Nazis, and most probably did so because they thought the Germans would be victorious. Of course, we know now they weren't. But there was so much confusion during the war itself. Did the Norwegian law remain in effect? Was the occupying power in charge? Reichskommissar Josef Terboven headed up the German force, with Vidkun Quisling assuming leadership of Norway.

"After the war, the Norwegian parliament and the Supreme Court concurred that the Norwegian government had given up its struggle to save the homeland, this to avoid harsh measures by the Germans. Meanwhile, the government in exile, in England, took the position that anything or anyone that helped or encouraged the Germans during the occupation was essentially traitorous. Right before the war ended, the government in exile assembled the paramilitary

Milorg, which was Norway's resistance movement, and paired it with Norwegian police who had been trained in Sweden, so they were ready to take over as soon as the Germans left."

"But why kill people, when they probably thought they were doing what was best for Norway?" queried Mama.

"Oh," said Onkel Bendix, "many people thought executions were barbaric, but Norway's main newspaper, *Dagbladet*, insisted severe penalties needed to be meted out to prevent anything like this from happening again."

"But they were occupied!" said Mama. "What choice did they have, really?

"Well, that was the great debate. After the war ended, almost 30,000 people were rounded up and questioned. Most of those were released, but more than 5,000 were detained. Still, 25 people were executed by firing squad in five or six prisons throughout Norway. The weird thing was many who actually joined the German SS and fought on the eastern front alongside German soldiers were never tried for war crimes, just charged with treason. Yes, it was very unfair for the most part."

"So, it could be that Steinberg wasn't guilty of much at all, then.

Couldn't that be the case?" Papa asked.

"Yes, that's certainly possible, given the hysteria of the times," concluded Onkel Bendix.

"Ya, ya," said Mama. "Who wants more iced tea?" And with that, the subject changed. I had heard every word and thought about Otto. Poor Otto. Not only was his father dead, but he had been declared a traitor to his own country. Otto wouldn't even be in America if that hadn't happened.

That night in bed I had a stark realization: I hadn't wanted to leave Brooklyn because of Otto. Now for sure, I didn't want to leave Budd Lake because of Raymond. I dreaded our return trip to the city, but I had a mission: to be extra nice to Otto.

Chapter Sixteen

Escapades

In my art class my sophomore year, Miss Gunther explained perspective to us—how things closer to us look bigger and those farther away looked much smaller. She gave an example of railroad tracks that of course are parallel but seem to move toward each other in the distance. Then she told us to come and stand by the window which looked out over Shore Road Park and the harbor. It was a blustery winter day, and you could see remnants of dirty snow in the park, white caps slapping over the harbor, and an angry gray sky overhead.

She pointed to a protrusion of concrete in the water, a solid mass seemingly anchored on a plot of land, but a fair distance from the shore. "That concrete is called a caisson and it extends below sea level," she explained. "There's another one across the harbor on the Staten Island side, but we can't see it from here. If we could, it would appear to be much smaller, but it has the same surface size as the one we're looking at. On these massive bases the towers to support the bridge will rise. One tower will rest close to Brooklyn on the concrete you're looking at; the other will go up nearly a mile away off the Staten Island coast and Fort Wadsworth."

"What are the caissons sitting on?" asked Roger.

"Good question. We are witnessing history unfolding. There was an island military establishment right there; it was called Fort Lafayette. The city bought it as soon as the bridge project was approved, and that's the little bit of land you can just make out. The caisson across the harbor sits on an island called Hendrick's reef—commonly known as Battery Weed. It also had a fort, but it has been demolished too."

Then she had us close our eyes and imagine the bridge completed. What would the bridge look like from where we were standing? Our task was to draw what we thought the new bridge would turn out to be. That was a difficult task since there had been no start to the actual construction of the bridge itself, no hint, just footings, the foundations for what was to come. Sure, the newspapers had published drawings of what the bridge would look like, but those were views from the water broadside, looking out to the Atlantic Ocean. From where we stood, it was a whole different perspective, and that was the purpose of our exercise. "Think of railroad tracks," Miss Gunther reiterated. "Once the roadbed and cables are up, the illusion will be that they become nearer to each other in the distance. Try to capture that."

It was a fascinating assignment, albeit somewhat incomprehensible, even if our teacher had revealed the details she seemed to know so well. Yet we imagined what might span our harbor and draw we did. Stanley was first to complete a sketch, and he ambled over to the window and gazed out. Once the rest of the class was done, we posted our sketches on the bulletin board, no names of course, and our class critiqued them. Simon, usually quiet, had this comment when he saw a specific sketch: "These spans are straight. How in the world would a big ship pass under it?"

"Good point," said Miss Gunther. "When you create something graphically, you need to consider practical applications. This sort of art is different than a pretty picture that makes you feel good. This type of art is an inspiration, a visual idea of what can possibly be and how it can impact how we live. It can be a beautiful work of art if it's done right." What was going on around us right now, however, was not art; it was decimation. It would become structural art eventually, but for us, then, we didn't know it.

The preparation for building the massive bridge continued with bustling activity, and we often walked from home to view the progress. On the Brooklyn side was a huge concrete anchorage that would support the roadbed. The main entrance to the bridge would be from 92nd Street, so close to where we lived. I had learned in school that the anchorages were 229 feet by 129 feet and contained 780,000 tons of concrete. A concrete workers' strike in midyear had halted construction for a while, and the Staten Island anchorage took longer to finish. Miss Gunther sure knew a lot about the bridge, and when asked how she knew what she knew, she simply said her uncle was a foreman, and he reported directly to the Engineer of Construction.

The newspapers also continued to report bridge progress, and since I lived so close to the action, I mentally catalogued what was happening as well, sometimes walking to Alice and Sonja's house along 6th Avenue, which had chain link fencing to keep the curious out and the workers free to work on the projected roadway to the bridge. On the other side of the construction was another road, a stretch of 7th Avenue. The one I walked would become a one-way service road to the bridge approach; the other was to be a companion service road with traffic moving in the opposite direction.

The demolished remains of buildings lay in the path of the future roadway and were heavy with construction equipment. Backhoes picked up debris, pieces of molding, broken windows, wallpapered sheet rock, and other remnants of what had once been habitats, small shops, and even our church and dropped them into Gull company dump trucks which hauled them away.

There was dust seemingly everywhere, and at home Mama complained about it constantly. And there was noise, the low thunder of heavy equipment at work. Repeatedly, Papa would grouse about the stupidity of building the roadways first, then the bridge itself. I knew, however, from my art class, that construction of the bridge had also begun but results were not yet all that visible.

After Youth Group at 52nd Street one Friday night, we sauntered to Dodie's. We were standing just outside, and I was pleased to see Tory since she didn't frequent Youth Group much anymore. She asked me if I was still dating Otto, and I said, "more or less." And that's when he came walking briskly toward us.

"Guess what?" he said. "I've been accepted to Cooper Union, and I'm going there in the fall. It's great—my mother won't have to pay tuition. The school is free, provided you meet the acceptance criteria."

"Shouldn't be a problem for you," I said. I knew he was plenty smart.

"Hey, it's Martin," he said, glancing toward Johnson's, the newspaper shop on the corner of 59th and 8th.

"Hey, yourself, Otto," said Martin. "Hi, Sue and Tory. Good to be out, but man it's cold. I just got a pack of smokes. Want one?" he said to the three of us.

Otto said, "Nah, I don't smoke. My mother says it's a filthy habit."

Tory said, "I smoke sometimes, Marlboros."

With that Martin and Tory lit up, and we were standing near the door to Dodie's, the two of them puffing away as we were engrossed in conversation. It was beginning to snow lightly, so we never saw the man walk up to us. "Oh shit," Martin muttered under his breath, then, "Hi Dad."

"Martin! What are you doing?" Martin's father barked, the "what" hanging in the air like a bomb about to detonate.

Martin looked down at his hand still holding the lighted Marlboro and said, "Dad, it's not what you think!" And with that he dropped the butt to the street, then stepped on it.

"We'll talk about this when you get home. Don't be late." With that he strode off, heading to 55th Street where Martin and his family had a flat in a four-family house.

"Shit, shit, shit," said Martin. "I'm in for it." That said, he pulled another cigarette from the pack and lit up again. We laughed in unison.

"How long have you been smoking?" I asked. I was intrigued and thought smoking did two things: it made you look sophisticated and older, two things we aspired to be. We went inside and found a booth, and our talk turned to the First Lady, the beautiful Jackie Kennedy, just as Hannah and Joey came in.

"Hey," said Joey. "What's up?"

"We were just talking about Jackie Kennedy. She's so beautiful," said Tory.

"Yeah, I love how she dresses. So elegant," said Joey.

Tory piped up, adding, "She has lots of help with that. Oleg Cassini, the designer, does a lot of her clothes."

"Still," I said, "she herself has a lot of class. Look how she carries herself."

"That helps. So does money," said Otto.

"Look," said Tory, "money doesn't necessarily give you bearing, and she certainly has that."

Joey jumped in with "Look at the fashion statements she makes. Do you remember the photos of her in Paris back in May? She wore that gorgeous pink Cassini strapless gown."

"She has a figure like a boy, though," said Martin.

"That's what gives her that tall, elegant posture. Even her husband gets it. When they were in Paris, he said, 'I'm that man who accompanied Jacqueline Kennedy to Paris.' The Parisians loved her," said Tory. "I wish I could look like her."

"Oleg Cassini seems to be her principal designer," said Hannah. "But it's more than the clothes, with her. It's the whole package. She surprised the Parisians by speaking French, and I heard she speaks Spanish and maybe Italian, too. And look at her hair—it's perfect. And she wears those little pillbox hats so nicely. Mostly her clothes are tailored, but beautiful."

"But I tell you what, I'd love to design clothes like the ones she wears," said Tory. "There's a school in Manhattan that teaches you how—it's the Fashion Institute of Technology on 27th Street, and you can get a two-year degree in fashion design. I'm going to apply, since I'll be a senior at Fort Hamilton next year."

"Well, we'll get a chance to see her on TV soon. She's redecorating the White House and she's giving a tour on Valentine's Day. We should watch it together."

The boys hadn't said very much since their interest in fashion was nil, but at the mention of the White House, Martin chimed in. "My father says it's a disgrace that she's spending taxpayer money like it grows on trees. How many administrations have lived there? Isn't it good enough for her? She called the house 'the dreary maison blanche.' I think she's a snob. And he's a jerk—look what he did when the Cuban exiles wanted to overthrow that dictator Castro. We trained 'em, and Kennedy promised air support, but at the last minute decided not to give it, probably on the advice of some political puppet. Lots of those guys died because of him. Not only that, my father says that he's sent military advisors to some rinky-dink Asian country—Vietnam I think it is. He doesn't mind sending American boys to die."

"That's awful," said Joey. "But those stupid decisions had nothing to do with Jackie." Joey then pointed out how she always seemed to be a good mother to her children, little Caroline and John John when they appeared in public. We affirmed then and there that we were Jackie fans and would watch the televised tour together. On the 14th of February we gathered in front of the TV in Tory's apartment to watch. While we were settling down, Tory's mother was making popcorn. Me? I was having a good look around. Tory and her sister, younger by four years, shared one of the two bedrooms in the four-room flat. Why, they're poor, I realized.

I said not a word, though, and pretty soon the CBS televised tour came on. "Welcome," said Charles Collingwood, the host. "We are about to begin the first televised tour of a presidential home. And here is our First Lady, Jacqueline Kennedy." We took in every detail of what she was wearing: a two-piece simple outfit, a three-strand pearl necklace, and low heels. We wondered what color her outfit was since the television was black and white.

"Welcome to my home," she said to him. We were stunned to hear her voice.

"She's squeaky," blurted out Joey. "I would never have thought she'd have a voice like that!" These were our sentiments as well, and we were disappointed. But soon they moved through the house as Jackie explained the renovations. Under President Truman there had been structural damage and repair, and to save money they furnished the place with department store furniture. Our First Lady explained how a committee formed early the previous year had set about finding authentic period pieces to replace the commercially purchased furniture in order to reflect the history of the White House and its occupants.

The beautiful Reception Area revealed an entrance of Tiffany Glass installed when Chester Arthur was in office. Moving on, the Great Hall, she explained, was red, white, blue, and gold and hung with paintings on loan. And in the State Dining Room they hosted dinners for over 100 people, and last year there had been two a month. She picked up a dinner plate, explaining that the Truman and Eisenhower families had left enough to use, but the glasses were Kennedy contributions. In this stately room were pictures on loan from the Boston Museum of Fine Art, and over the mantle on the fireplace was an inscription by John Adams: "The best of blessings on this house." Further along she pointed out Grant's table, Lincoln's bed, and Monroe's gold set, saying, "All these make the history of this house more alive to us."

"Agreed," said Collingwood. "It's a stronger panorama of our great story."

Tory's mother, who had been standing in the doorway between the kitchen and living room, spoke up then. "What do you think this all cost?"

As if on cue, Collingwood asked Jackie Kennedy the same question. "We were careful about expenditures, but what you see here is the result of a two-million-dollar restoration, all made possible by individual donors."

Tory's mother then said, "I think it's important that the leaders of a country live in a place that reflects the country's history. The Palace in Oslo is like that," she added wistfully, her voice tapering off. Tory rolled her eyes at that but said nothing.

At school, soon after the televised White House tour, my history teacher, Mr. Svensen, asked the class if we had seen it. About half the class raised their hands. "What did you think of it?" he asked.

Bernadette was the first to reply: "It's Camelot. It's like America has royalty." That summed it up for me.

"Yes," agreed Mr. Svensen, "it is indeed. You as a generation will see a lot of firsts—and you are lucky, because you are witnessing history in the making. A generation ago, people didn't have television; people crossed the oceans in ships, not planes; very few had automobiles; and many lived through the horror of war. Why, just look outside. There is a bridge in the making. It will be the longest suspension bridge in the world, and it will replace the 69th Street ferry pretty soon. That's progress, and that's history unfolding." Sure enough, we had begun to see the towers rise from their supports, harbingers of the bridge to be.

At home, though, Papa remained a critic of change. "I don't understand why things that are perfectly good can't remain the way they are now. Look what's happened to Bay Ridge. Will the bridge make it any better? It has split our community right down the middle, and our church will have to be rebuilt. Will it be an improvement? Just tell me how!"

"Well, at least we have Budd Lake. The country doesn't change all that much," I volunteered. But I knew it actually was changing even as I spoke these words. Ingy wouldn't be coming to the lake for very long when summer was here, and I was wondering if I could get working papers in New Jersey. I knew from last summer that Raymond wouldn't be there either. He was working in a Bronx hospital in July and August. Ingy would stay only for the first week, then go off to the Children's Home in Fort Lee, New Jersey, for her summer job.

By the time we actually set out for the lake months later, it was hot and muggy in Brooklyn, and I could tell Mama and Papa were excited to be going to the "hytte" as they called our cabin—of course, "hytte" just meant cabin in Norwegian, but that's what it was—our hytte.

I didn't find a summer job, and it was just as well. Edel, Else, Barbara, and I whiled away our days swimming and cycling and playing board games when it rained. We had visitors from West Orange, our two aunts and uncles, usually accompanied by Odd, who wasn't old enough to drive by himself. But we were especially happy when Arvind and Erick showed up in Arvind's Ford. Since we had no telephone, visitors were always an unannounced surprise. One Saturday in August a familiar green Studebaker came sailing along, right up to our cabin, and out stepped Otto. "Hey, I really wanted to see you, Sue," he said. "I need to talk with you."

"How did you find me?" I asked.

"Well, you said it was Budd Lake, and that was easy. Then I asked some girls at the beach if they knew which cabin was yours." Hmm, I thought. That must have been Edel and Else. I bet they were floored when Otto stopped to talk to them, and even more when they found out where he wanted to go. I went inside and told Mama that Otto was here. She came outside with me and greeted Otto cordially, as I climbed into the Studebaker. Man, I hoped Edel and Else or maybe Barbara were still at the beach so they could see me heading out with Otto. I felt good.

I didn't feel good when Otto brought me back, however. "I've been seeing Kari all summer, and I didn't want you to come back to Brooklyn and find out the hard way," he had said after we had gone a few miles.

"Take me home now," I said, close to tears.

Mama saw immediately that I was upset. "Where's Otto?" she asked.

"Gone," I said. "He broke up with me."

"What? Well, you would say you were 'more or less' boyfriend and girlfriend. I guess it's time for an end to it."

"Yeah," I said, "but I should have been the one to do it, not him." I was wounded.

But by the time we returned to Brooklyn, I had decided I was over him. It wasn't but a week into September when Sven slid into a booth at Dodie's beside me.

"Hey," he said. "I see Otto's hooked up with Kari. How about going to a movie with me?"

"Sure," I said, and so began a fledgling courtship. We would meet at Dodie's every Friday night after Youth Group at 52nd Street. Sven, I soon found out, was a carpenter, four years my senior. I liked it fine that he had an income and was my first not-in-school boyfriend to have a real job.

"I'm in the union, and get union benefits," he told me. Brooklyn was rife with unions. The Carpenters' Union also included carpet layers under the same umbrella. And sure, Papa was a member of the Tugboat Union. I came to understand the strength of unions when Papa and I were at the Bay Ridge Savings Bank on the corner of 75th Street and 5th Avenue, and his friend Harold spotted us and came to chat as we queued up waiting for a teller.

"The *Queen Mary's* coming into Gravesend Bay on Sunday," Harold announced. "And she'll be stuck there, unable to berth in Manhattan on Monday, since we're on strike." Harold was a tugboat man, and he spoke with authority. "We've got them good, now. There's nothing they can do; they'll have to fold, and we'll get our raise."

"I hope so," responded Papa. "The strike can't go on forever. It's hurting so much business."

"Sure," said Harold. "We've even halted construction on the bridge. Tugs can't bring equipment and materials for the work to continue. Yes, they'll have to give in."

At home, Papa related his meeting with Harold to Mama. "They'll fold for sure," he said of the union. "They are between a rock and a hard place."

"Sverre won't be able to bring her in either," Mama replied, speaking of her brother, the harbor pilot, with pride. "The pilots take control from the captain and bring the ship to the pier where tugs push ships to dock."

"The Queen Mary is loaded with passengers from Europe, and they won't stand for being stranded on board. They'll want to make land."

"How come the ship is in the bay on a Sunday?" I asked.

"It's pretty common practice," said Papa, switching to English. "Monday's a regular weekday, so the fees are always cheaper than on the weekends."

Well, I thought, that's that. So, when I came home from Fort

Hamilton on Tuesday afternoon, Papa and Mama were talking about a newspaper article. "Can you beat that? The captain, Watts, they say his name is, just took that ship to Pier 90 and docked her himself. No tugs. No tugboat crews." This he said in a voice tinged with admiration. What a sailor, I thought. And then, what drama!

Drama would haunt that fall of my junior year but not in a good way. On October 22, President Kennedy addressed the nation on television and revealed that a U-2 plane on a "routine" mission had confirmed nuclear ballistic missiles and light bomber planes on the island of Cuba, just 90 miles off the coast of Florida. Cuba under Fidel Castro's dictatorship was heavily aligned with the Soviet Union, our adversary in the cold war, and now it was escalating.

This discovery, Kennedy explained, had prompted a naval blockade in the seas around the island and sent the message that America would use military force if necessary to ensure our national security. Thus began a political and military stand-off between the U.S. and the Soviet Union, the country that had provided the missiles. Scary stuff!

In our history class, we asked Mr. Svensen about what was going on with Cuba. He assured us the U.S. would keep us safe and not to worry. Worry we did, however, and followed the news carefully. *The Daily News* was a paper we got regularly at our house. Our cousins, the Hansens, on 67th Street, bought *The Herald Tribune* or *The New York Times*. All the papers reported the same developments of what became known as the Cuban Missile Crisis. We were at real risk of war if the U.S. were to invade the island and take control of the missiles. Castro seemed to want war between The Soviet Union and the U.S. If the U.S. were to invade, that was a real possibility. News got worse when on October 27, a U-2 plane was shot down over Cuba.

"They've fired the first shot," the U.S. Secretary of Defense said. "It's new ball game." The U.S. had positioned ships along the Atlantic side of the Caribbean Island to prevent supplies from The Soviet Union from reaching land. Yet the newspapers reported Russian submarines in the area. It was as though our whole country was holding its breath. Then, after 13 days of tension, we learned that Russian President Nikita Khrushchev had agreed to withdraw the missiles if the U.S. would promise not to invade Cuba. This agreement vindicated Kennedy after his failed Bay of Pigs invasion a year earlier. He was still our hero, and we still had Camelot!

Even Papa had to admit that the U.S. had avoided war, and for that he was personally grateful. "We have a lot to be thankful for this year," he declared. And we were. We gathered at Tante Ragna and Onkel Leif's house on for Thanksgiving a few weeks later, having taken the big green ferry from the 69th Street pier and driven up

Victory Boulevard, a familiar route. Cousins Karl and Johann were home from college, and I hardly recognized them. They had taken on an air of sophistication that was foreign to me. Ingy was with us as well, home for a long weekend from Upsala, her college in New Jersey. She was delighted to hang with Karl and Johann, and I with Harold and Liv who were in high school as I was. We were in Liv's room, out of earshot of our parents.

Harold soon had us laughing, saying he knew just how many days of school he could skip before he risked not graduating come June. "Thirty-four," he said. "I'll get there."

His sister had a quick retort: "Keep it up, and you just might not graduate." Harold gave his sister a look that could stop a clock.

"Look," I said, "I play hooky, too. A bunch of us know what days the garbage is collected in the alley behind Fort Hamilton. When it's not garbage day, we stuff our books into a trash can and head out. If you're carrying books, it's a sure sign for the truant officer to haul you back to school and detention. I have a boyfriend who's a carpenter, and if he's not working, he'll pick me up in the alley and we'll go someplace, maybe the movies. But sometimes our Dodie's crowd goes to Nellie Bly's, and we ride the go-carts. We always make it back to the alley to pick up our books before we head home."

"Don't you have to bring an excuse the next day from home?"

asked Liv.

"Sure, but I'm really good at forging my father's signature. He actually has nice handwriting. I'm sure the school thinks I'm pretty sickly since I miss so much school, but since I'm in several honors classes, nobody much questions my absences."

"Hah," Liv said to Harold, "you're no honors student. You'll get a commercial degree if anything."

"What do you do when you skip school? I mean, where is there to go on Staten Island?"

"We go to Al Deppe's a lot. That's a drive-in restaurant on Arthur Kill Road. It's great. We play skee ball and feed the chicken," explained Harold.

"Feed the chicken? Are you kidding me? Is that a game?"

"No, no game. There's a live chicken in a wire cage, and if you put a nickel in a slot, feed pours into the cage and the chicken eats it. And then a ball pops out with a question tucked inside, and if you answer it correctly, they give you free ice cream. There's also miniature golf. That's fun, too," he added.

Soon Tante Ragna told us to wash our hands and come to the

table. Our hunger had been piqued by the aroma of roasting turkey wafting through the house. The table in the dining room was beautifully set, and the food graced it abundantly. Tante Ragna told us where to sit. Onkel Leif stood at the head of the table, and said grace for us, not *I Jesu Navn*, as we did at home, but an ad-libbed prayer in which he thanked God for so many blessings: the great country we lived in, the wise government that had spared us from nuclear annihilation just a month ago, for letting Ragna live, for our families, and finally for the food given through His bounty. When he was done, Papa added another "amen." Letting Tante Ragna live? Did he really say that? No one but Ingy and I seemed very surprised.

Ingy looked at our Onkel Leif and asked him what he meant. "What's wrong with Tante Ragna? Is she sick? Is it serious?" I looked at our cousins, shocked by what I was hearing, but they were stifling laughter and looking at each other. Mama and Papa were mute.

"I have new teeth," Tante Ragna interjected. "A full set." And with that she grinned broadly, showing us her new white dentures.

"I was sure the dentist had killed her," said Onkel Leif. "When it became clear that she needed a full set of dentures, not just the bridge, the dentist scheduled her to have the last of her teeth taken out. He also explained that he would give her nitrous oxide so she wouldn't feel a thing."

"That's laughing gas," said Johann. "It can make you laugh uncontrollably."

"Well, nobody was laughing that day, I can tell you. I went with her because, you know, unlike Cornella, she doesn't drive."

"Was it very bad?" I asked.

"I was scared stiff," said Onkel Leif. "And so was Ragna. I was in the waiting room for a long time, praying that all would go well. After a while, I heard the dentist yelling to his assistant, 'Call the doctor! Call the doctor!' I thought he had killed her."

"Oh, my goodness," said Ingy, clearly alarmed. I looked at Johann, Karl, Harold, and Liv—they were really having trouble suppressing their laughter, and finally Harold hit the table with his palm and guffawed.

Tante Ragna herself was smiling when she said, "I was so embarrassed."

Onkel Leif explained further. "He hadn't taken all of her back teeth out when she bit into his hand, and bit him hard. His index finger was sliced through to the bone, and he was bleeding badly. He was the one who needed the doctor."

"Of course, we had to reschedule to come back and have the last of the teeth removed and me fitted for the dentures. But I tell you, facing the dentist again wasn't easy for me," added Tante Ragna.

Their four offspring were by now laughing uncontrollably. "Still, they look really nice," I said. "And you couldn't help it; you were out cold."

Chapter Seventeen

Good and Bad

I met Tory in the hall between classes at school one Monday, and she was visibly upset. "What's wrong?" I asked.

"I took the SATs—the Scholastic Aptitude Test—in the fall and got a good grade. I was all set to apply to the Fashion Institute of Technology in Manhattan, and then my mother and father sat me down and said we are moving back to Norway in July."

"What? You don't have to go. You'll be 18 before that. They can't make you go."

"You don't understand," Tory said. "I was born there, so I'm not a U.S. citizen. I can't stay. My sister Karen is the only one of us born here. My mother was pregnant with her when we immigrated. I was almost four."

"We'll figure something out," I said, backing away from her as the bell rang, and I realized I was late for English class. I rushed to the classroom, sliding into my seat as Mrs. Wilson watched. "Sue, you're late. Ten minutes is plenty of time to move between classes. You've held us all up." My classmates were all looking at me, some of them smiling because I was on the spot. I felt myself blush.

"Let's get started," Mrs. Wilson said, and I was glad she wasn't going to write me up. "Writing is a process, and as we write our very act of writing triggers new ideas. Today we're going to do some collaborative writing. You'll all team up with a partner next to you and create a story," she explained as she passed out several pieces of lined paper to students in groups of two. Then she said, "Here's a first sentence: 'The air was crisp, and the snow was beginning to fall,'" and she wrote it on the chalkboard. "The person on the left will write a paragraph, and then pass it to the partner on the right, who will read it and add another paragraph, going back and forth until a story forms. Let's begin." Since I was the person to the left of Adam, I began tentatively.

> The air was crisp, and the snow was beginning to fall. Susan clutched the collar of her coat with her gloved hands, as she looked up at Peter and shivered, not really from the cold, but because she knew then that she loved him. The realization hit her like a thunderbolt, and she knew he had

> to feel the same way. "You know I love you," she whispered.

That's a good start, I thought, as I passed the first sheet to Adam. Here's what he wrote:

> What's with this girl? She's really weird making eyes at me like that thought Peter. I'm glad I'm joining the French Foreign Legion. I'm all packed and ready to go. I've got my duffle, my passport, and cash to tide me over until I get to Algeria. "I'm leaving for Idlewild in the morning to catch a plane," he said.

I wasn't liking the way this was going, so I penned another paragraph.

> Susan gasped at his matter-of-fact words. Then she realized he was kidding. He was a great jokester. After all, they had been dating for months and had even talked about a future together. "I know you're kidding, Peter," Susan said. "We could get an apartment together, maybe in The City." She put a hand on his chest, right over his heart, showing him her affection.

Evidently, Adam didn't like this twist, so he wrote another paragraph.

"Your the one who's joking. My whole family knows my plans. I've been reading up on warfare tactics. I'm going to make a difference for France. After all, that's where my family is from and they are very proud of the legion. I am going to be a part of something bigger than my life here," Peter said.

Oh yeah, I thought, as I scribbled another paragraph.

Susan was having a hard time understanding Peter. She thought he had lost his mind. Maybe he had. Did he have some strange mental condition that made him fantasize about faraway adventure? Maybe she should just tell him what she thought. "You know I really love you, but your thinking is very muddy. Maybe you should get psychiatric help."

Adam grabbed the paper, read it, and wrote furiously.

"Your the one who's nuts," said Peter. "I think you should have your head examined. I want nothing to do with love. But if I did, it wouldn't be with a jerk like you. I'm going to the dessert in Algeria for France," Peter said. Then he turned away from Susan and walked away confidently. He whistled while he walked, happy that he had put this matter to rest.

I had been looking at what Adam was putting down on paper as he wrote. "Give me that paper," I said, and I grabbed it and wrote rapidly.

> "I hope you drop dead in the desert or maybe I should say you should die in your dessert, since you obviously don't know the difference between the two. And by the way, 'your' and 'you're' are not interchangeable, asshole.'"

When I passed the paper back to Adam, he read the paragraph and slammed his pen on his desk, making a sound that startled the rest of the class. Mrs. Wilson looked up from the book she was reading at her desk, then stood and slowly walked over to stand between our desks.

"Adam," she asked, "is something wrong?"

"I can't work with Sue," he said sullenly.

Mrs. Wilson simply said, "Give me what you've written so far, and sit still and wait for the bell." And then, "Sue, come here, I have something to say to you." I approached her desk, unhappy with the way this exercise had gone. "You stopped writing a story and switched your focus to Adam. Can't you tell the difference between your co-author and your protagonist?"

"He just made me so mad!" I said.

"Okay, but this is a way to learn to cooperate. We'll try this exercise again, but maybe you need a different partner."

Once the class emptied into the hall, I said to Adam, "Look, I'm a little upset. I just heard some bad news before class. I didn't mean to criticize you directly."

"Forget it," he said, and stomped away. I was feeling bad about the way our English assignment had gone, and even more so because I knew I had frustrated Adam, a boy I sort of liked but knew didn't much like me. Now it was a given: he disliked me.

But the bottom line was this: I was disheartened about Tory's news. It can't be, I thought. Why in the world would anyone want to go back to Norway? My family, although Norwegian to the core, was here because America was the land offering more opportunity than Norway ever had, and my parents knew it. So here we were, all of us American citizens. We are American, I thought to myself, but at the same time I was so proud of being Norwegian. What a conundrum!

At Dodie's shortly thereafter, a bunch of us were talking about Tory's dilemma. We were in the back booth, nursing cherry cokes, when I noticed two guys in sailor uniforms sitting in another booth. "Who are they?" I was intrigued for sure. They were so handsome, and they looked so alike.

"Oh, they're my cousins, Al and Al," said Joey.

"No, really. Be serious. Al and Al?"

"Yup," she said. "Come, I'll introduce you."

So, we walked to the booth where the sailors were seated, and Joey introduced me to them—gorgeous boys in uniform, I thought.

"Hi, how can it be that you are both named Al?"

"Common question. We get it all the time. One of us is Albert, the other Alfred. We both go by Al."

With this, Joey interjected, "They're twins, but they have a younger brother, and his name is Alvin."

"Gee whiz. Three Als in one family, " I blurted out. What were their Norwegian parents thinking when they gave them these American names?

"Our brother Alvin goes by the name Vinny. Mom tells him it's an Italian name, but that's what he tells people his name is, and that's what everybody calls him," said one of the Als.

"Oh," I said. Still, I was intrigued by these two handsome servicemen. I had a sense that one of them was attracted to me, and while I knew him by his face, I had a complete lapse in memory of which Al he was.

"So," I ventured, "where are you stationed?"

"Brooklyn Navy Yard for now," Al, I think Alfred, responded. "We're on a sub that's undergoing some repairs."

"Really? What's it like?"

"Pretty crowded," the other Al offered. "And we sleep in hammocks in shifts."

"I'd love to see it someday," I opined, hoping to open the door for further interaction with Al, either one. There was no response other than how nice it was to meet me, in a rather dismissive way. It was just as well because my mind was still on Tory's dilemma, and we rejoined her in the booth as Henning and Reidar sauntered in.

"Hey, what's up?" asked Reidar. Tory gave them the news in a nutshell. Her lip was quivering as she spoke, and Henning told her the same thing I had at school when I first heard. And she responded the same: she was not a U.S. citizen.

"Why do you think they want to go back there?" I asked. "Is it because you're so poor? You're four people living in a small apartment."

"What! We're not poor. My parents have lots of money in the bank. They just never wanted to own much of anything in America. They spent as little as they needed to and saved every cent they had to return to Norway. I think they want me and my sister, Karen, to live in Norway with them. She doesn't want to go either," Tory added.

"I'll tell you what," Hannah said. "Let's go to the country on Saturday. My family has a bungalow in New Jersey, near Andover and Lake Iliff. If we put our heads together, we'll come up with a solution. Bring your ice skates. The lake will be frozen." She spread the word.

So off we went on a cold and blustery day in late February, thirteen Norwegian kids in three cars, Hannah directing us as we approached the cabin. "I know where the key is," she said. "I always do." But when she fumbled along the edge of the molding, it wasn't there.

"Shit," said Hannah.

Reidar said, "No problem," and took his jacket off, put it around his arm, and with his elbow shattered one of the nine panes of glass in the top half of the door. "Easy," he said as he reached inside and unlatched the lock. We had a nice day, skating on Lake Iliff, and then inside the cabin afterward drinking beer and eating sandwiches we had brought with us, while still dressed in our winter coats since there was no heat and the cabin was cold.

Our discussion, however, itself was heated, and Tory was on the verge of tears, as she so often was about her forced return to Norway.

"You could run away," said Hannah.

"But where would I go?"

Joey jumped into the mix by saying she would ask her parents if Tory could stay with them. After all, Tory would be out of high school and could get a job. "It's worth asking."

"My parents won't go for it," said Tory.

Reidar, who had just turned 19, suggested he and Tory get married. "I'll probably be getting drafted pretty soon, and they won't take me if I'm married," he explained. "That will solve both issues."

"Let me think about it," Tory responded. "I like you just fine, but I'm not sure I want to be married to you. Besides, Anders is my boyfriend." So that's where we left the issue.

As the day started to darken, Hannah asked, "What about the broken window?"

"Oh yeah, let's measure the space and go get some glass and putty. I can fix it," offered Reidar. So off went Reidar and Henning, with directions from Hannah, to the hardware store in Andover, returning shortly thereafter to replace the broken pane.

"Problem," announced Henning. Maybe they knew how to fix it, but they sure didn't know how to measure. The glass fit widthwise but was too short by at least an inch and a half.

"Put it in anyway," said Hannah. "When my family comes here in the spring, I'll just comment on how cold it must have been, because the glass shrank." With that, we packed up all the beer cans and headed back to ever-changing Brooklyn. The modifications to our surroundings were leading to some kind of resolution for the most part.

On Palm Sunday in April that year, we witnessed a significant milestone: our new church was finished, and we went to the dedication. I, for one, wasn't too keen on attending, but what choice did I have? At least I wouldn't have to attend church at that Poly Prep school, and Mama and Papa wouldn't have to go to the 52nd Street church anymore either.

We had driven by the construction from time to time as the church was going up, from the foundation to the steeple, and finally the roof. It had been a long work in progress, but it looked pretty impressive at the end. I knew for a fact that many of the carpenters who were church members had sanded down the dark brown chairs from the main sanctuary at the old church and made them like new, lighter and brighter. The original plan had been to install pews, as they did in the English sanctuary. But perhaps keeping the old seats was comforting, pieces of the old building, and of course it would cost less. I guessed Papa had had a hand in that decision.

Now that we were actually here to witness the official opening of our new house of worship, we marveled at what we saw. There were two sanctuaries, the one on the left for English services, the one on the right for those in Norwegian, and connecting the two was an administration area, which sat under an impressive steeple. The dedication was moving, and I liked that the Youth Group would resume here, even though I was now much older than the new members, those in confirmation class.

It wasn't long after that dedication that Tory showed up in Dodie's wearing a ring—a gold band with a small diamond. Was it from Anders, her Norwegian carpet layer boyfriend, or from Reidar?

"When I asked Anders if he'd marry me, he said no," she told me. "And so I told my parents I was going to marry Reidar. They're pretty upset, but they said at least he's a Norwegian boy." Tory and Reidar were thus the first of our gang to get engaged, and Tory wore an engagement ring, making her a sensation among the senior girls at school.

As my third year of high school was drawing to an end, we would spend our lunch hours in the park across from Fort Hamilton. It was still fascinating to watch the Verrazano bridge taking shape. I marveled at the workers who walked the cables as they were spun between the two tall towers, evidently unafraid of the height. What if one of them falls off, I wondered. When I posed the question to Johnny Jorgensen, my friend who had been in a few of my classes each year, he simply said,

"They don't fall. They're Mohawk Indians, and they are sure-footed. In fact, they are ironworkers on lots of construction projects. Construction companies value them for exactly what we're seeing here. There are Newfies up there, too."

"What's are Newfies?" I asked.

"They're people who have come here from Newfoundland—that's in Canada. Everybody makes fun of them up there. Here, too," he added. "They don't call them 'Goofy Newfies' for nothing!"

"I've never heard of Newfies before," I said. I was learning something every day, and not just in the classroom. Johnny's explanation made me think about Mr. Svenson's prediction that we would witness lots of history unfolding before us. Indeed, we were, but back then I didn't fully appreciate it.

I finished my junior year easily enough, and Tory graduated from Fort Hamilton with a commercial diploma. She and Reidar married at City Hall in downtown Manhattan the next day, which was fortuitous, since he got a draft notice the very next week. Her parents had calmed down and accepted the fact that Tory would stay in America when they returned to their homeland, and they had a little reception for the newlyweds at the Atlantic restaurant on 8th Avenue. This was an important event for our gang. A friend, not a relative, had married, the first of our group to do so.

I began thinking of whom I would eventually marry and took a good look around at the boys in our crowd. Nothing appealing caught my fancy. Of course, there was my boyfriend, Sven, but I couldn't see our relationship going anywhere. Would I want to be a carpenter's wife? Nope, I told myself. But in the meantime, he was making money, had a car, and took me places like the movies and bowling alleys, those forbidden places that no good Christian girl should go. Sven was good for now.

Trips to Budd Lake that summer were mostly for long weekends, since I had a part-time job at Robert Hall on 86th Street, happy to have some of my own income. Papa didn't quibble about my working, but he stopped giving me cash since I had my own, so my plans to save my meager earnings were thwarted. Still, it felt okay, but I wondered if I was moving forward in any way.

That summer had two memorable occurrences. Our beautiful pregnant First Lady went into labor early, and a baby boy was the result, but he was five and half weeks premature. The television news quoted *The Boston Globe*, "He's a Kennedy. He'll make it." He didn't. This had been the fifth pregnancy for Jackie Kennedy. The first, the news media reported, ended in a miscarriage in 1955. A second, a baby girl they named Arabella, was still-born. Then came Caroline and John John, and finally Patrick who succumbed shortly after his birth. We watched on TV as the President held hands with his wife as they left the hospital, clearly grieving. How terribly sad it all was. But it was still Camelot, taking the bad with the good.

Then, at the very end of August, Martin Luther King Jr., a southern Baptist minister, led a march on Washington. The decision to do so came after a series of violent attacks on civil rights demonstrators in Birmingham, Alabama. George Wallace, when he was sworn in as the Democratic governor earlier in the year, had been adamant about black/white segregation, saying in his inaugural speech, "segregation now, segregation tomorrow, and segregation forever."

The non-whites in the south had had enough, it seemed. How could segregation possibly be democratic? Shortly before the march, President Kennedy had met with civil rights leaders and voiced fears that there would be violence, adding that the country would need the support of Congress if we as a nation were to successfully achieve equal rights for all citizens. A big show at the capital probably wouldn't accomplish much, Kennedy said. The march went ahead in late August anyway with some 250,000 demonstrators at the Lincoln Memorial. Well-known actors were in attendance, and Marian Anderson, Bob Dylan, and Joan Baez performed musically. There were a series of speeches, and last to orate was Martin Luther King, who delivered his impassioned speech. It was a gospel singer, Mahalia Jackson, who implored King to "tell them about the dream."

And then he did, reiterating a familiar theme from earlier speeches: "I have a dream." We were enrapt. How in the world could so many people be denied equal rights under the law? It was so wrong, and it was a topic that would surface as school resumed in my senior year.

More thought provoking was learning that the U.S. had 16,000 troops in Vietnam, and 82 of them had died. The boys in our gang who had graduated already were either enlisting in the Navy or

National Guard and were apprehensive about draft notices. Reidar and Tory had gotten married, a ploy to save both of them. Vietnam was a war zone, and it was scary as hell. Kennedy, however, declared he would begin to pull our troops out. America has 13 percent of the world's population. It shouldn't be policing the world, he explained. Again, we just loved this guy, and Camelot continued to entrance us from afar.

Things were percolating locally in Brooklyn as well. Sven and I were standing outside Dodie's one day in early September when a gray Chevy convertible pulled up. "Look at them idiots," Sven commented. "That's not a convertible, really. Sean McMurphy owns it. He and his Irish friends just sawed the roof off the car."

"Holy cow. How crazy is that? What will they do when it rains?"

"It'll be a lesson about how stupid they are," Sven replied. As we stood there watching the driver park the car across the street in front of the Sons of Norway, we heard a loud rumbling, and eight motorcycles pulled up and parked in front of the Matchbox, the bar three doors down from Dodie's.

"Who are those guys?"

"Some of them are Norwegians, but they're a mixed bag—a few Italians and some Irish guys, and maybe a Newfie," he explained. "What they have in common is the bikes."

"Which one is the Newfie?" I asked. I really wondered if there were anything to my classmate Johnny's explanation that Newfies were goofy.

"Not sure," said Sven. "But I know there are several families from Newfoundland living around here."

I was taking this in as I watched the motorcycles park. "Are they a gang?"

"Nah, they're just a bunch of guys on bikes. There are a few more, I think."

Who is that really good-looking, dark-haired guy? I thought to myself. He carried himself with such authority as he took off his helmet and hung it on the handlebars of his bike. I was determined to find out and hoped these bikers would continue to frequent the avenue where we hung out.

I kept my part-time job at Robert Hall since the manager had allowed me to change my hours around my school schedule. I was laughing inwardly when families came in to buy clothing for their children and asked me to "see if it fits right." I had no idea, but I knelt and felt the shoulders of a child in a Robert Hall coat and pronounced "a beautiful fit."

A perk of working at Robert Hall was a discount on clothing, and with some of my earnings, I bought myself a black Chesterfield coat, a fashion statement I felt sure. Clothes had become a focus for the girls in our crowd, and I often wondered if Tory still yearned to attend the Fashion Institute of Technology in New York. I guessed she could if they could afford it, and if she didn't become pregnant. It wasn't long after I had that thought, however, that Tory and Reidar announced in Dodie's that she was in fact pregnant, having become so on their honeymoon in the Poconos. That won't be me, I vowed to myself.

The same day that Tory announced her pregnancy, Henning sauntered in and announced he had gotten a selective service letter, and pulled it out of his pocket, where it was neatly folded. I unfolded it and read out loud: "You have been drafted by the Selective Services and the President of the United States of America for duty and you are hereby ordered to Fort Benning, Georgia, for basic training for the Armed Services."

"Wow," we said in unison.

"Why you, and not Freddy or Martin?" I asked.

"It's by lottery. You get assigned a number, and if that number comes up, you get drafted," explained Henning. "My number came up. I just hope the war in Vietnam is over before I finish basic training."

"You're screwed, man," said Reidar. "It's 'Go to the army or go to jail,'" he said, quoting the popular saying of the times.

"There's another option. You can go into the Peace Corps," Henning replied. "I wish I had known about that."

"What's that?" I queried.

"It's the program Kennedy put in place as soon as he took office. You can apply and do some good in the world. They send you to countries where people are really poor, what we call 'third world countries.' If you're accepted, you are exempt from military service. I didn't know about it early enough. Plus, there's no guarantee you'll be allowed into the program. I think there are more than 5000 peace core volunteers right now. Wish I were one of them." And not long after that conversation, Henning went to Georgia. I knew my cousin Alice wouldn't be happy about that, because after years of having a crush on him, she and he had finally begun dating. Poor Alice. Poor Henning.

At Fort Hamilton, I took the Scholastic Aptitude Test, which would determine my eligibility for certain colleges. I would go to college just as my sister Ingy had, that was certain. The thing was, I didn't know where I wanted to go or what I wanted to study. I liked

English, and I liked chemistry, so those were the programs I would have a look at.

"It will sort itself out," said Mama. "You'll figure it out. You are laying the foundation for your future."

"There are many good schools in New York City. Why don't you think about going to one of them and living at home?" Papa added. Yup, that was Papa, always figuring the money angle. At least he hadn't argued against my going to college, though.

"We'll see," I muttered.

At school my cousin Alice and I, both seniors, and Sonya, now a sophomore, had the same lunch period, and often we would talk about what we would do after graduating from high school. "Me, I'm going to become a nurse," offered Alice. "Maybe I'll join the army, like Henning."

"Hey," I said. "Henning didn't join; he had no choice."

"I want to be a stewardess like Bente," Sonya said.

"And I have no clue," I volunteered. "My mother says I'm laying the foundation for my future."

"She's right," said Alice. "You are on the pathway to where you will end up. We all are."

Everything around us augured change. In my three-plus years at Fort Hamilton, we had watched as the very face of Bay Ridge transformed, and we were fascinated at the way the bridge was taking shape. My trigonometry class was on the third floor facing out on Shore Road, and from the window I could watch the progress of the build, which intrigued me far more than math, which I found boring. Now, tell me really, would I ever do a logarithm after I left high school? Here instead I was witnessing, as my homeroom teacher told us, 40-ton slabs of concrete being laid in place, one after the other, preparing the roadway for the traffic that was to come. The bridge was slated to open in the fall of 1964, and on the day it would, ferry service from the 69th Street pier would cease.

By October, we were becoming aware of another awesome development. The British rock band the Beatles was hitting the airwaves, and we were all listening. *Please Please Me*, *From Me to You*, and *She Loves You* played regularly on our radios, and we loved these songs because they spoke to us. Pretty soon the press coined the term "Beatlemania" to describe the furor the band incited as they toured Europe. The press covered this phenomenon well, showing photos of four mop-haired young men

in close fitting black jackets. Why, they're gorgeous, I thought, and we girls at school and at Dodie's would talk about which one we liked best. A few weeks later, the *Huntley-Brinkley Report* officially covered the group in a news report and fueled Beatlemania.
"It's Ringo," Joey said. "He plays the drums with such skill."

"Oh, come on," Hannah interjected. "It's John who I'd want to be with."

"He's married," I said. "But you can't beat Paul for good looks."

The boys didn't have much to say about the boys in the band. They just looked sullen as we talked about these handsome performers. Nevertheless, we knew they liked the music, too, and the Beatles tunes, originating in a nation that had once banned rock and roll, continued to captivate us. We knew they defined who we all were.

I was doing well in school, and pretty much content, singing the words to *She Loves You* as I walked home from school one day in late November. All was good, and I was happy. I arrived home from school at 3:30 to hear from Mama, "The president has been shot."

"Which president? President of what?"

"Of our country," was the horrific answer. Our president, John

Kennedy, had been riding in a motorcade in Dealey Plaza in Dallas, Texas, in a convertible with his wife, Jackie, sitting beside him when there were shots, and Kennedy slumped over, wounded, Mama explained.

"He'll recover," I said to Mama. I knew then and there he couldn't die.

"No," she replied. "He's dead. The shooting was about 12:30, in broad daylight, and it wasn't long after that that the hospital they took him to announce the news."

For the rest of the day, television programming was preempted by coverage of what had happened. I sat on the floor in front of the TV and learned that Texas Governor John Connally and his wife, Nellie, were in the motorcade as well, and he had also been shot. I watched in horror as footage showed Jackie Kennedy crawling onto the trunk of the Cadillac convertible trying to get out of the vehicle. A secret service guy rushed to get her back in the seat beside her fallen husband. The motorcade rushed to Parkland Memorial Hospital. And then the awful news came.

I was in shock. How could this be? As the afternoon progressed, Mama and I learned that former Marine Lee Harvey Oswald was the shooter and had been arrested a little more than an hour after the shooting. "I'm just a patsy," he claimed. Whatever did he mean? Evidently, he had also shot and killed a policeman just after the assassination. Could it be that there was more than one sniper? Could Oswald have fired the three shots that took out the president and the cop and wounded Connally? We would never find out.

Vice President Johnson was sworn in as our new president aboard *Air Force One*, with Jackie Kennedy and Ladybird, Johnson's wife, standing with him as he placed his hand on the *Bible* and became our new leader. Jackie's tailored pink suit was spattered with blood, yet she remained calm, still regal. "She's in shock," said Mama.

Two days later, the evening news showed clips taken by a TV cameraman earlier in the day. We watched in horror as the police escorted Oswald through the Dallas police station and a heavy- set man stepped out of the shadows and shot Oswald, who died a short time after. This shooter was Jack Ruby, a nightclub owner, who wanted to avenge "my president's death."

Was Oswald the sole shooter or was there a conspiracy? Speculation was rampant. The news media also reported that the records of the assassination would be sealed for 25 years and then released to the public. Yet after that many years, we were never really sure what had happened that fateful day in November of 1963.

Chapter Eighteen

Deception

Joey's parents were going to a New Year's Eve party on Staten Island and staying overnight at her mother's brother's house since the ferry wouldn't run after midnight. Once she knew that, she and her brother would be home alone, it was party time. I told Mama and Papa I was invited to a pajama party at Hannah's. Hannah in turn told her parents the pajama party was at my house.

Joey had done a good job planning this New Year's celebration. Some of the older guys had brought Southern Comfort and Coca Cola, and we mixed them and downed the concoction. Unfortunately for most of us, especially me, we had had no experience with alcohol, but we were titillated by the forbidden and the sinful, and it went down easily. To be honest, I have little recall of most of the evening. I do remember Joey's younger brother, Alf, leading me to a bedroom where I lay down on a single bed only to find the room spinning. I told him that I couldn't stop the spinning, and he calmly said, "Put a foot on the floor. That stops it." So I did, and it did. I woke up the next morning, face down in Joey's brother's bed, with him beside me. I was still fully dressed, and I had at least one shoe on. One of my hoop earrings, the ones I had put on clandestinely after I left my house, had come undone, and I was lying on it, my forehead pressed into it.

I realized I had thrown up as well, probably several times, and there was dried vomit in my hair. Oh my gosh, I thought, as I staggered into the bathroom and stared at myself in the vanity mirror, horribly ashamed. There it was: an imprint of a circle in my forehead. How would I explain that, I wondered, as I ran the water and washed my hair in the sink while my head pounded all the more since I was leaning into the bowl. I'm never going to drink alcohol again, I swore. Actually, over the years, that didn't prove to be true, but to this day, I still can't stand the smell of Southern Comfort. I had had an early lesson learned.

I staggered into Joey's kitchen, and there many of the other partiers, some in as bad shape as I. "How old are you, Alf?" I asked. "Why did you think it was okay for you to get into bed with me?"

"Well, for one thing, it was my bed. And I'm fifteen, by the way, and I know stuff, so I slept with you," he said.

"I never took my clothes off," I said. "So you're lying."

"No, I meant we slept in the same bed," he said. "And you can call me Alfie. That's what everyone calls me."

"Okay, Alfie," I said, "You can't go telling boys that we slept together. They'll all think something else!"

"Yup, I expect they will."

Oh geez, this can't be going anywhere good, I thought, as I made my way home. I arrived about three in the afternoon to my parents, my sister, and Tante Hedwig and Onkel Werner having coffee and fryste kage, an almond pastry I normally liked. That New Year's Day, however, all I had to do was look at it and feel the urge to vomit again. Tante Hedwig said how nice it was to see me, and then added, "It's so good that you have such close friends, almost like sisters. But what is that red circle on your farhead from?"

"I'm not sure," I replied. "There was some fancy metal work on the bed I slept in. Probably from that," I quipped. Then I said I was going to my room to change and would be downstairs shortly. I enjoyed my aunt and uncle so much and wanted to catch up. Upstairs, I drank glass after glass of water and downed some aspirin, hoping to quell the headache and nausea I still felt. I put on a brave face and calmly walked downstairs.

Mama said, "Tante Hedwig has some exciting news to share. But I'll let her tell you."

"It's Gudrun," Tante Hedwig said. "She is going to marry a lawyer. His name is William Johnson, and he works with the District Attorney's office in Manhattan. In the city," she added.

"He's nice," offered Onkel Werner. "We all like him."

"What kind of attorney is he?" I asked.

"He's a persecuting lawyer. He helps put bad people behind bars," Tante offered, pride punctuating her words.

Wow, I thought, Goody, the last unmarried offspring of my aunt and uncle would soon have a spouse. Mama had often opined that Gudrun would be an old maid. I guessed that wouldn't happen now. And I wondered inwardly if Ingy and I would be invited to the wedding but didn't dare voice the question. Instead, I asked about William Johnson, the groom-to-be.

"Well, he's a little older than Gudrun," began Tante Hedwig tentatively.

Then Mama interrupted with, "How old? Has he ever been married?"

Taken aback, Tante Hedwig, said, "He's 36, and I think he was married before, but there were no children, so it doesn't count."

"Hymph," was Mama's response.

I was savvy enough to change the subject, so I asked about Maggy and Paul and their little Lars, living in Clifton, New Jersey.

"Oh, gee," said Tante. "They don't like it as much as they thought they would. Magnhild and Paul are expecting another baby, and I think they would like to be closer to us and his family. Besides, they haven't made many friends in that community. The people there, from what she tells me, are more seclustionist. As a result, they miss Brooklyn, so we are hoping they'll come back."

"What about our cousins on Staten Island," Ingy asked. "What are they doing these days?"

"Well, you know as well as we do how Leif and Ragna's kids are doing. You are in touch."

Sure, I thought, Karl and Johann, my two handsome older cousins, and Harold, one year my senior, and of course Liv, their sister. These cousins we knew well, simply because we were together often, and like Tante Clara's kids here in Brooklyn, they were more like siblings than cousins. But these were not the ones Ingy was inquiring about.

"It's the other ones," Ingy said. "Why don't we know much about them? We've seen them from time to time, but not with any regularity. I remember them best from the Christmas we had at Onkel Johann Torvald's house when Bestemor was still alive."

"Uff. I don't want to say." She hesitated, then wavered and said, "But Vigdis, your Uncle Johann Torvalds's second born, is getting a divorce. Just think! The first divorce in the family! It's too hard to think on. I was talking to Hulda, you know, your aunt and Vigdis' mother, and she let it slip."

"Divorce is such a sin," interjected Mama. "What a disgrace for our brother, Johann Torvald. What will people say?" Now wait a minute, didn't we just hear that Goody's husband-to-be was divorced? Maybe that didn't count because he wasn't one of us. Or maybe we could overlook it since he was a lawyer and not a laborer. But evidently Vigdis was another matter altogether.

I was quiet. I had only once seen this cousin, Vigdis, who seemed old enough to be my aunt, at the same Christmas day party Ingy had mentioned. She had been there with her little boy, Karl Johann. Tante Hulda had pointed her out, but I never spoke to this older cousin. Never mind -- we had been a really big crowd. I had cousins I knew of but really didn't know. Perhaps I would when I was older.

Nevertheless, now I was intrigued enough to ask, "Did you ever meet her husband?" If anyone would know the family structure, it would be Tante Hedwig.

"I never met him," Tante Hedwig said slowly. "All I know is what my brother told me. He said, 'My son-on-law is a tugboat man.'"

"So," Ingy speculated. "Maybe he does or doesn't exist, since no one's ever seen him. Maybe they're just saying she's getting a divorce because she has a real boyfriend now, and all along they've been pretending she's married because she has a little boy."

"Aw gee," piped in Mama, "that would be even worse. That would make Vigdis an unmarried mother and the boy a bastard."

I had nothing to add to that. But I deliberated with myself, thinking about cousin Vigdis. How hard things must be for her. She's either married and getting a divorce, or she's never been married, and the family has just pretended that she was. With this realization, I blurted out, "What's her son's last name?"

Onkel Werner, who had been silent throughout this conversation, joined in with "They all go by Gabrealsen, the family name. "Why, we don't even know the first name of little Karl Johann's father."

"Ya, ya," said Mama, flustered by the turn the conversation was taking. "Let's talk about something else." And so the conversation shifted, and time wore on. As my aunt and uncle were preparing to leave, putting on coats and gloves, Tante Hedwig pulled Mama aside and whispered something to her. Left with Onkel Werner by the front door, I made small talk, telling him about my progress in my senior year at Fort Hamilton.

"What subjects do you like best?" he asked.

"I like chemistry and English best, I think." Then I ventured, "Your English is so good. I like that you have an English accent when you speak, from your mother. But does it ever bother you that Tante's English isn't as perfect as yours?" I and my cousins had reflected on this reality for a long time, and now I finally voiced my thoughts.

"You know, Solveig," Onkel Werner said, taking me gently by my arm, "your aunt has so many delightful things about her, and her little language twists, while amusing, are part of who she is, part of her charm. Why would something like that bother me? I rather like it." That's when I understood how love worked.

Later that night, I pondered the conversation that had taken place earlier that day with my family and my aunt and uncle. My aunts and uncles all seemed to have solid marriages. Of course, there was Onkel Sverre whose wife in Norway had run off with a German officer during the war, but surely divorce was not something Sverre would have initiated. Even if he had wanted to, how could you divorce someone you couldn't find? So then, was his marriage to Gerd even legal? Were they, as I had often heard Mama say, "living in sin"? Never mind, it was our cousin Vigdis who would bring open scandal to the family.

Was Vigdis a free spirit? Did she and her son's father have a great love affair? Or was the father a jerk who had dumped her when she got pregnant? Then I wondered if he was Norwegian, as so many of the tugboat men were. The little boy had a Norwegian first name and last name, the same as his grandfather's. From there, I questioned if women in this family needed to be with Norwegian men. It was a conundrum.

Tante Hedwig's family was mixed: Onkel Werner was English and German. And DeDe had married Richie, the Irish Catholic. The sons on Long Island, Werner and Wilhelm, were married. I guessed Agatha, Werner's wife, was at least part Norwegian -- if you weren't would you name a daughter Liv? But the other two offspring had good, solid American names: June and Johnny. And Wilhelm's wife might be Norwegian, at least in part, since their girls' names were Margit and Karen. What I remembered was that Tante Hedwig's daughters-in-law didn't speak Norwegian. Never mind. They were probably partly Norwegian, not purebreds like we and our cousins all were.

That line of thought brought a logical question. What about Goody's husband-to-be? He could be Norwegian. It would depend on the spelling -- and "o" or an "e" in the last syllable. Was it Johnson or Johnsen? With an "o" it could be British or Swedish. With an "e" it could be Norwegian or Danish. I guessed we would soon learn.

All I knew was that it was very important to Mama and Papa that Ingy and I date Norwegian boys from "good" families. They frequently stressed that to us. Nevertheless, around us were so many boys of different backgrounds. I wondered about the boys my sister must know at Upsala. Did she date at all? I knew she saw my cousin Arvind from West Orange quite a bit and seemed to like him. But they were cousins. Where could that possibly go?

Whenever Ingrid came home to Brooklyn from college, Papa pointed out to me and her that there were many Italian families with lots of offspring. "Those Italian boys, they would love to get a Norwegian girl. So, look out and be sensible. Best to stay away. You know people from the south in Europe are not all white, and you never want a mixed blood baby," Papa pontificated. He surely knew about Italians. "Why, when I go to the Bay Ridge Savings Bank on Fifth Avenue, I sometimes have to walk past those pizza places. The very smell from them makes me sick. What kind of people eat that kind of food?" It was a recurring lecture.

When Papa continued to preach at us about whom we might date, Ingy, on another weekend home from Upsala and listening to more diatribe, pointed out that those Italian boys' mothers probably wouldn't like it much if their sons hooked up with Norwegian girls. To this, Papa responded, "Of course they would like it. They all want Norwegian girls."

"I don't know about that," Ingy responded. "Look at the trouble DeDe had with her Irish mother-in-law. Probably still does. And DeDe's so pretty, too. Still, she's not good enough for her mother-in-law."

Despite my parents' strictly enforced dating mandate, here I was, thinking quite a bit about the dark-haired guy with the motorcycle. I had asked around and found out his name was Tony. How could I get to know him better? I decided to make that my mission, and at Fort Hamilton I told Alice, Hannah, and Joey about my quest. "We'll have to make it happen," declared Hannah. "It shouldn't be hard. Hey, on Sunday afternoon there's going to be a country and western show at the Sons of Norway. Let's go. Maybe Tony will show up at the Matchbox, and you can 'bump' into him." So we planned it. I didn't dare tell Mama and Papa I was going to the Sons of Norway. That would have been foolhardy. Instead, I told them I was going to Joey's for the afternoon and maybe Dodie's later.

On Sunday afternoon I experienced my first live music show in what had formerly been the Berkshire Theater and was now the Sons of Norway. The club's president, a big, burly Norwegian, came on stage and welcomed us warmly, telling us about The Grand Ol' Opry in Nashville, Tennessee, the home of country and western music, so similar to the type of folk music generated in Norway. First on stage was Minnie Pearl, who strutted out boldly. "Howdee," she said, the "dee" raised a few octaves. "I'm jest so proud to be here, and so excited I've forgotten to take the 98-cent price tag off ma hat." And then she lapsed into *Jealous Hearted Me,* belting out "jealous hearted me, I'm just just as jealous as I can be." Oh my, I liked it.

Whisperin' Bill Anderson followed with some mournful music. *That's What It's Like to Be Lonesome,* he sang, and then lapsed into *Po' Folks,* followed by *Mama Sang a Song.* Following him was Johnnie Cash, with Maybelle Carter and her daughter June. As the three sang together, Hannah leaned over and whispered, "They're going to be big!" They were followed by a pretty young girl, Skeeter Davis, who introduced herself as the little girl from Dry Ridge, Kentucky. She had started singing, she said, as part of the Davis Sisters, but had gone solo in the 50s. She launched into *The*

End of the World, a song I knew from the radio. That day I didn't know that I was witnessing live, on-stage, up-and-coming music greats. All I knew then was that the music rocked.

We spilled into Dodie's afterward, and as Hannah was standing by the counter talking to Joey, in strolled Skeeter Davis, who walked right up to Hannah, held out her hand, and said, "Hi, I'm Skeeter Davis!" I noticed, of course, and was duly impressed, but I was already in a booth, and my attention was more fixed on the doorway. Tony stood there with his buddy, and I felt my heart race. They looked around, walked in, and plopped themselves down in the booth right across from the one I was sitting in. There was no doubt about it: he was handsome, and the black leather jacket with the turned-up collar accentuated his dark hair and intense brown eyes. I was hooked.

Before long, he turned to me and said, simply, "Hi, I'm Tony Grasso. This is Jimmy Basso. Just call us Basso and Grasso. Who are you?"

"I'm Solveig, Solveig Torgersen," I said, immediately sorry I hadn't said Sue.

"That's a pretty name. What does it mean?"

"Well, 'sol' means sun in Norwegian, so I guess that's what it means, like 'way of the sun' or something like that. To tell you the truth, I've never much thought about it, and people mostly call me 'Sue.'"

"So, Sue, are you waiting for someone? Or can we join you?"

"My friends," I said. "Here they come. There's room for you, too."

Hannah and Joey gave me knowing smiles as they approached the booth, greeted us, and slid in beside me, leaving the other side to Tony and Jimmy. Talk turned to the Sons of Norway performances, and country and western or -- as the boys in our crowd called it -- hillbilly music. "My cousin Al is in a band called The Brooklyn Duelers. They do country, a lot of Hank Williams," said Hannah. "They're pretty good, but the guys in this show were really, really good."

"In Naples—that's where my family's from -- they make pretty great music, too, Tony said. But there's great music coming from England, too."

"We know. The Beatles are going to be storming the U.S," announced Joey. "February. Can't wait."

"They're going to be on *The Ed Sullivan Show*. We've got to watch it," said Hannah.

"You could go to Kennedy and watch them land," offered Jimmy. "It will be a mob scene." (John F. Kennedy was what the Idlewild airport had been renamed after the president's assassination.)

"Oh my God," I said. "My parents would kill me if I did that."

"Really?" Tony said. "They don't want you to have a normal teenage life?" I said nothing to that comment.

Then as we were exiting Dodie's, Tony touched my arm lightly and said, "Hey, see you around." Wow, I thought he wants to see me. I was psyched. Tony and Jimmy headed on down to the Matchbox, while Hannah, Joey, and I stood chatting in the cold on the sidewalk, planning on where we would watch *The Ed Sullivan Show*. Maybe Hannah's, we decided. I didn't think Mama and Papa would welcome us to watch at my house. As Hannah and Joey said goodbye, and I was heading for the corner to turn down 60th Street and begin my hike to 5th Avenue, where I would catch the bus to take me to the 90s and home. I had barely taken a few steps when Joey's brother and two of his friends were exiting the luncheonette that was wedged between the two bars, Duffy's and the Matchbox. Alf, or should I just say Alfie, called out.

"Hey, Sue. Wait up."

"Ah, Alfie, how are you?"

"You over your hangover yet? You were pretty plastered on New

Year's Eve."

"Look," I said, "that was pretty stupid, and I don't think I'll ever do it again."

"Well, I know a lot about you. I spent the night with you in bed, so I know you pretty well."

"Don't be ridiculous. I woke up fully dressed. And how old are you anyway? Fifteen?"

"I know something else about you," he added.

"What are you talking about?"

"It's human biology, I know," he stammered. "I know all about it."

"About what?" I asked, perplexed, trying to be civil, but a little annoyed that he thought he and I should even be having a conversation.

"About your period," he said. "I know you have it."

"What?" I couldn't believe it. "That's pretty personal, and it's none of your business."

"But I know," he insisted. "You have your period right now."

"Crazy," I said. "I don't. Now I have to go," I said turning away.

"Oh yeah, you do," he said.

"Look," I said, becoming angry. "It's none of your damn business, and I have no idea why you would be so rude as to actually say something like that!"

"Oh, stop denying it. I know."

"And how would you?" I asked, my voice rising as I turned away from him, calling over my shoulder, "You really are a stupid jerk. Do you work at it, or does it come naturally?"

"Hey, don't get mad. You just need to know that some of us guys know how women's bodies work. And the reason I know is because my sister got her period this morning, and all women get theirs at the same time every month," he called after me. "Joey calls it her 'friend.'"

With that I turned and faced him again. "Are you serious? Do you think females are machines? You're an idiot," I said and pivoted on my heel, turning to see Tony and Jimmy standing outside the Matchbox taking it all in. Blood rushed to my face as I realized they had overheard.

"Hey, get lost," Tony said as he strode up to Alfie. "You're a stupid ass." With that Alfie startled and scurried up to Dodie's and stepped inside, evidently fearing the two Italian bikers. Good, I thought.

Tony turned to me and said, "Please don't be embarrassed by that little twerp." Then he asked, "Where are you headed?"

"I'm going home. I live in the nineties. I take the 5th Avenue bus," I stammered, looking at the sidewalk, still embarrassed by the assault by Joey's younger brother.

"I'll give you a ride," he said. "It's the winter thaw. I've got my bike. Never mind the bus. I'll take you home." And it was indeed the winter thaw; temperatures had climbed to 60 degrees Fahrenheit during the day. It was still pretty balmy now, at least by our Brooklyn standards. Fortunately, I was wearing slacks, and I hopped on after Tony kicked the bike into action. I held onto his midriff, as we sped through the streets of Brooklyn according to my directions to Ridge Boulevard.

I said, "You'll have to let me off by the corner, so my parents will think I'm coming from the bus on 5th and walking." Tony pulled over and shut the bike off, and we stood by the curb talking.

"What grade are you in?" he asked. I replied that I was graduating in June and would be 18 just before.

"Then what?"

"I'm going to go to Brooklyn College," I said. "But I was accepted to Hunter as well. What about you? Are you in school?"

"Nah," he said. "I graduated a few years ago, and now I work as a longshoreman. Plus, I'm in the National Guard. I figured I better sign up before I got drafted. There's a war on in Asia, and I hear Lyndon Johnson is going to up the number of American GIs over there. The National Guard is a good deal. I'm assigned to an Infantry Division here in Brooklyn, Company C. That's a combat aviation brigade, part of the 42nd infantry division."

"How did you train for that?"

"Ah, we have a monthly drill at the armory in Brooklyn, and every year we go to Fort Drum upstate, near the Canadian border, for two weeks of training. It's pretty cool, but man, they work you hard." I was duly impressed by now and realized Tony was in good shape -- firm and muscular. I said goodbye and headed home, happy that Tony had said we'd go riding together as soon as the weather warmed up. I had a lot to report to my cousin Alice,

Hannah, and Joey at school the next day. It looked like, and I certainly hoped, Tony and I could be an item.

Two weeks later The Beatles touched down on United States soil, at John F. Kennedy, or JFK, the recently renamed Idlewild Airport. From there they were whisked through screaming fans to the Plaza Hotel in Manhattan. Two days later found Joey, Hannah, and me in front of the television at Hannah's, ready for *The Ed Sullivan Show*, "We have a really big shoe tonight," Sullivan said, again saying "shoe" instead of "show." Now this was a variety show and typically featured multiple acts, so we had to wait while our anticipation increased. We could tell that the audience was both animated and agitated, and Sullivan repeatedly gestured palms down to the audience, saying "Quiet down."

Finally, after what seemed like a much-too-long Anacin pain reliever commercial, the Beatles were on stage. We said not a word as they sang "All My Loving." Then Paul sang "Til There Was You." When the band lapsed into "She Loves You," we stood up and swayed to the music in Hannah's living room. God, how we loved these mop-haired lads from England! Walter Cronkite, the eminent newsman on CBS, a week or so later reported that *The Ed Sullivan Show* had had a record-breaking 73 million viewers. We've had a "British invasion of America." Indeed. The Beatles then began a tour that took them to Washington D.C., Carnegie Hall, and another Sullivan show on TV.

"You've become a teeny-bopper," Ingy said to me as I sang "She loves you, yeah, yeah, yeah in my off-key voice. "I don't like them," said she of the fab-four. Was she serious? Or did she just make it a point to dislike anything I liked? I'll say this for my sister: she was consistent.

Over the next few months, I found more and more time to be with Tony, but I had never dared bring him home, nor had he expressed any desire to have me meet his family. It became our pattern to meet in front of Dodie's, and take off, either in his car or on his bike, weather permitting. Tony had bought me a helmet, which he kept in his car, an old stick-shift blue Dodge. I didn't dare risk having Mama or Papa finding out I was a frequent passenger on a motorcycle or that I was dating an Italian boy.

As the weather started to warm up a bit, the bike was the vehicle of choice. Our rides opened new perspectives for me: Brooklyn's Prospect Park at night zipping along the park's internal roadways exiting by the Grand Army Plaza archway; the stately Brooklyn Bridge taking us into Manhattan and Greenwich Village, Times Square, or Central Park. "Hey," Tony explained," this is the theater district where my parents catch Broadway shows."

Columbus Circle was another first for me, and Tony acted like a tour guide, pointing out the impressive marble monument to Christopher Columbus, the Italian explorer, that graced the traffic roundabout. He said it was representative of the Nina, Pinta, and

Santa Maria, the ships that had made their way to the new world from Spain, the country that had funded the Italian's journey of discovery. Tony awed me with his knowledge of our city, comfortably and casually sharing information with me, information I knew I would never garner at home. I felt liberated, and was sure I loved Tony, especially when he kissed me.

We dated fairly regularly, but I didn't tell my parents about Tony, letting them think I still saw Sven from time to time. And I did see Sven occasionally, but there was no love interest there. We had become tentative friends, and I wondered what it was that I had ever actually seen in him. One day I was standing outside Dodie's when Sven sauntered up. "Hey, you," he said. "What's doing?"

"I'm about to graduate from High School, and in September, I'll be going to Brooklyn College."

"Why don't you go away to school, like your sister did?"

"I like my friends here," I said. My cousin Alice will be going into the nursing program at The Lutheran Medical Center, and Joey and Hannah are staying in the city, too. Besides, I have a boyfriend."

"Oh, yeah, I had heard that. He's a greaser isn't he?"

"Sven! What a thing to say! He's just dark haired and wears it slicked back."

"Brylcreem—a little dab 'll do you," Sven sang mockingly. "What do your parents think about this boyfriend?"

"They don't know."

But they soon would. It happened that Mama was shopping on 8th Avenue one day in early May, when she bumped into Sven. From that chance encounter, she learned that I was no longer dating Sven, and that I had a new boyfriend. She lost no time in confronting me the minute I came home from Fort Hamilton. "Solveig, I met Sven when I was at Olsen's bakery today, and he opened my eyes. He told me you have been dating another boy. Why haven't we met him? Why doesn't he come here to pick you up? What's his name?"

"Oh, Mama, we've had a few almost-dates, but really he's not a boyfriend, so that's why he's not interested in coming here."

"I asked you what his name is," she demanded, her voice rising.

"It's Anthony," I volunteered, adding quickly, "It's what Americans call the name Anton."

"Does he have a last name?"

"He told me once, but I don't remember."

Chapter Nineteen

Resolution

"Commencement," the valedictorian for the graduating class at Upsala explained, means "beginning." He addressed his classmates with encouragement, saying they now had the foundation, the beginning, they needed to make a positive impact in American society. It was a beautiful message on a beautiful day in late May, and the ceremony was outside, flanked by azalea bushes in radiant bloom. When Ingy walked down the grassy center aisle between rows of chairs on which sat friends and family of the graduates, she accepted her bachelor's degree in Early Childhood Education, and the college president shook her hand and wished her well. I saw that my parents were visibly moved, Mama to the point of tears, which she wiped carefully from her eyes with her hand-embroidered handkerchief.

My aunts and uncles from West Orange, of course, had been invited to the commencement since they lived in the city adjacent to East Orange, where Ingy's college stood. Ingy knew them better than I ever would because of four years of regular interaction. She had evidently embraced them as her immediate family, and they her. After the ceremony, the school served us lemonade and small cakes, and Papa, proud as could be, embraced his sisters and their husbands. "She is the first girl of our family to graduate from college."

As it happened, she may have been the first in age and gender, but Tante Marit quietly reminded Papa that Erick, his nephew, would be graduating from Stevens Tech in Hoboken, New Jersey, in two more days with a degree in engineering. That took the wind out of Papa's sails. Mama and Papa went to Erick's commencement, only to learn that he was the salutatorian when he was introduced as such and gave an address to the graduating class. Then they learned that he had been offered a scholarship for a Master's Degree at the Massachusetts Institute of Technology or, as it was commonly called, MIT. Erick had evidently invented some mechanism of note, and that had fueled a large industrial research company to tender the scholarship. Not only that, Erick would receive a salary as he pursued his degree. That stipend would enable him to travel from the university in Cambridge to his home in West Orange as frequently as he was able to.

As I moved into my final month as a high school senior at Fort Hamilton, Ingy surprised us with some news of note. She had interviewed, of all things, at PS 127, the grammar school she had attended as a child, and had been offered a job, starting in September. She would be teaching 4th grade. Mama and Papa were again so proud. Just imagine: a teacher in the family! I heard Papa telling Ingy it was "time to give back" and that she should also teach Sunday School at 66th Street. She agreed to that, too, in our beautiful new church.

All around me, family members were accomplishing amazing things. High school was simply ordinary, and by the time I graduated I would be 18, legally an adult. I could continue working part time at Robert Hall on 86th Street in the summer and go to the lake with my parents when they made the drive, now much easier with an expanding stretch of interstate highway. Papa also pointed out that when the bridge from Brooklyn to Staten Island was finished, we'd be able to get to New Jersey from the Staten Island expressway, which would link the bridge to the other end of the Island and the Goethals Bridge which terminated at Routes 1 and 9 in the town of Elizabeth. There would soon be an alternate route to our house at Budd Lake. So, it turned out that the project Papa had so vehemently opposed might just yield some benefits. Time would tell.

Tony and I had gotten in the habit of communicating through Hannah, who would relay messages in school or call me at my house. That's how I learned that Tony was going to Fort Drum in upstate New York for the mandatory National Guard training. I met him and his buddy Jimmy on 8th Avenue on a Saturday to wish him well. "You'll miss my birthday," I wailed as I kissed him. "But you'll be home for my graduation."

To which he responded, "I'll make it all up to you when I get back." Both he and Jimmy looked so handsome in their army fatigues with duffle bags slung over their shoulders. "Be back in two weeks. We've got to get moving now. We're checking in on Sunday." And off they went.

Graduation from high school came undramatically, and Alice, Hannah, Joey, and I received our diplomas. Mama and Ingy were there, but no Papa, who was on the boats. Tante Clara and Onkel Olav were enthusiastic spectators, as were the parents of Hannah and Joey.

In West Orange, my cousin Odd also graduated from high school, and his brother, Arvind, let him drive the Ford to and from the ceremony. Odd had been driving since he turned 17, the legal age in New Jersey. In New York, it was 18, and I vowed I would learn to drive. When I broached the topic to Papa, however, he said, "What will you drive? I'm not paying for more insurance just so you can have my car. Ingrid doesn't drive," he reasoned. "Why should you? Maybe if you were a boy," he said. "But you're not," he added redundantly. Well, I reasoned to myself, maybe Tony would teach me to drive his car. He had already taught me quite a bit in that old blue Dodge.

Driving could be problematic, I soon learned. It seemed that Arvind, our cousin in West Orange, had racked up quite a few speeding tickets and was in danger of losing his license, and the cops were on the lookout for him. The solution to this dilemma was for him to book passage on a tanker, car and all, to Norway. As soon as he got there, he joined the Norwegian Air Force. I rued his going, and it would be years before I'd see him again. It wasn't long after that that Tante Signe and Onkel Bendix followed, leaving Odd, who adamantly didn't want to go, to live with Tante Marit and Onkel Karl. It must be that girlfriend Lillian, I surmised. How soon would it be before Odd changed his mind and followed? I didn't like what was happening!

More change was afoot. Onkel Sverre, Mama's younger brother and the favorite of all the sisters, announced that Gerd had filed for divorce. For weeks that summer, Mama, Papa, and the rest of the family speculated on the reason. "Gerd says she can't take the drinking," Tante Hedwig said. "He's alcoholic."

"Well, if he's an alcoholic, he's the funniest one I've ever seen," said Onkel Olav. "He's a harbor pilot with two partners in a successful business that requires a lot of clear thinking and skill. And they do their jobs well."

Papa cleared his throat at this comment and said, "I work on the boats. I hear things more than you do in the Carpenters Union.

There's a lot of speculation that his partners cover for him. Remember the time no one could find him? He was in a cheap hotel on Staten Island for days," added Papa. "Why, Gerd was frantic with worry, then furious when he came home three days later, still drunk."

"Uff," said Mama. "That Gerd is nothing but a whore. Good riddance to her. If he drinks, she's the reason why."

I recalled, then, a conversation I had heard clandestinely between Mama and Tante Ragna that Onkel Sverre had asked Tante Ragna to open a bank account with him, to hide money from Gerd. Evidently, they had socked away a considerable sum, unbeknownst to Gerd. I had to wonder if Gerd had found out, and if that knowledge had helped confirm her decision to leave my uncle.

Difficult decisions were made outside the family as well, one of which would affect our entire country, and not in a good way. After an uneventful July, in early August our President, Lyndon Baines Johnson, issued a congressional decree to send more troops to Vietnam. The trigger, the government said, had been a North Vietnamese bombing of a United States ship in the Bay of Tonkin. As a result, President Johnson had authorized increased military force to defend South Vietnam.

At Dodie's, and yes, we still hung out there, we talked about Johnson and Vietnam.

"Johnson is a big oaf from Texas. You ever see how he holds his beagles? By their ears! What does he know about Southeast Asia? That's where this country is, isn't it Southeast Asia?"

"I think so," said Hannah.

"Yeah, it is," said Martin who sauntered in and sat down by us. "I heard they're going to send in thousands of combat units. Scary stuff. Me, I'm going to see if I can sign up with the National Guard. My parents are really urging me to do it."

"Good plan. Stay in this country. That's what my boyfriend, Tony, and his buddy Jimmy did. Doesn't anyone remember what Kennedy said? America should not police the world," I interjected. "Kennedy was planning to pull out the advisors in Vietnam, not add ground troops."

"Do you think that's why they killed him?" asked Joey.

"I guess we'll never really know."

"Nah, we'll know. They said they'd release the facts after 25 years," said Tony. "We'll just have to wait."

"Maybe sooner," I opined. "Robert Kennedy, JFK's brother, is still the Attorney General of the United States. I think he's a good guy, and he has some power. Why, he could even run for president when Johnson's term is up."

"He'd have to be campaigning by now if that is a possibility, and he isn't," Hannah reasoned logically.

"Well, maybe in another four years. We'll see. You have to admit, he'd make a great president. I'd like to see Johnson go back to Texas and stay there!"

"Yeah," Karl said. "Kennedy's running for the senate. From New York," he added. "My parents really like him. And for the record, he is opposed to the Vietnam war. And he's opposed to corruption and is taking on Jimmy Hoffa, the Teamsters Union president. Dad says that union is very corrupt. Kennedy is tough on crime."

As it turned out, the November elections didn't put Johnson's opponent Barry Goldwater, the senator from Arizona, in office. He was my parents' choice, and he was pretty conservative. Johnson won that election by a landslide with his "great society" and "war on poverty" campaign promises. The good news from that election for us was this: Robert Kennedy was elected senator from New York.

It wasn't long after that discussion that Hannah announced that her cousin, the youngest of the three Als, the one who called himself Vinny, had received a draft notice and would be heading to basic training. We all hoped that Vietnam wouldn't be part of his service. And what of Henning? He had finished basic training at Fort Benning in Georgia. Where was he off to?

"I heard Freddy got a draft notice, too," said Karl.

"Man, I'm glad they don't draft girls. If you're a girl and want to go into the Army, you have to enlist. Guys have to go whether they want to or not," said Joey.

I said to Alice, "Hey, you're going to be a nurse. You start training at the Lutheran Medical Center pretty soon, and I start Brooklyn College in September. It really is a commencement, a new beginning."

Ingy started teaching at PS 127 right after Labor Day. I began classes at Brooklyn College three weeks later. The campus was park-like, 35 acres just off Flatbush Avenue and East 32nd Street. It was a trek to get there. I had to factor in at least 45 minutes to travel by bus, but I could read and study while I rode. I had to take freshman composition, a course that required an essay each week. I was also taking introduction to chemistry, a history survey course, French, and calculus, for a total of 17 credits. It wasn't long before I started to hate the four-credit calculus course, and I debated dropping it and taking something more fun, like music theory. It was my chemistry professor who advised me that calculus would prove helpful if I were to have a career in science, so I stuck it out.

The workload was such that I had less time with Tony, and spent more time in my room at home, pounding the books. I loved it, however, when Tony was able to pick me up after my last class at Brooklyn College, always in the blue Dodge because I carried a lot of books. "Hey, babe," he'd say as he pulled up to the college gate, where I stood waiting for him. "Let's go to Jahn's for splits. If you're really hungry, we could have a kitchen sink," he said jokingly.

Now I had been to Jahn's just once before with Joey and Hannah and some of the boys, and I knew that the kitchen sink was a huge pile of mixed ice cream scoops and toppings, enough for ten people to eat. It hadn't appealed to me. I found all those spoons in the same dish gross. I cautiously said, "Jahn's is pretty far from here, isn't it?"

"Well, a bit, but we'll just take Nostrand Avenue, which is close to here, and follow it to Avenue Z; that's where it is. And when we're done, we'll just hop on the Belt Parkway to get home." I agreed readily, and that's what we did. "Hey," said Tony, "in another week, the bridge will open to traffic. Want to be one of the first to go across?"

"I bet it will be mobbed, and there will government people in motorcades making the first crossing. Still, it's exciting to think about. We'll be able to drive to Staten Island. No more ferry."

The bright, sunny, almost balmy day the Verrazano opened officially, there was a grand ceremony. Over 5,000 people attended, including more than 1,500 official guests. On the scene were the mayor, the governor, and the borough presidents of Staten Island and Brooklyn, who officially cut the gold ribbon. Then the motorcades began. There was a 50-cent toll for every vehicle, and the promise was that the toll would, in time, repay the $320 million the bridge cost to build. After that, there would be no toll.

Concurrent to the opening ceremonies was a boycott by the 12,000 workers who had labored to construct the span. The next day the newspapers reported that they hadn't been invited to the grand opening. Instead, many attended a church service in memory of the three workers who had died during the build. That day too, the papers told us, ferry service from the 69th Street pier ceased forever.

But on the day of the official opening, I was waiting with Tony and his motorcycle on the Brooklyn side for the officials to pass, and then we put our helmets on and mounted the bike. We had passed over many bridges on our bike rides, but never had we been so high. "It's grand," I said into Tony's neck and hugged him hard. As we neared the toll booth, Tony dug in his pocket and took out two quarters to pay. I looked around and saw many animated photographers snapping away.

Tony and I wanted to continue our clandestine romance, but fate intervened. It so happened that one of the pictures that made *The Daily News* centerfold was of Tony and me on his bike. My glasses and the helmet obscured my identity, but Tony's mother recognized him at once. Tony told me his mother was fiercely Catholic, and she wanted to meet the girl who crossed the bridge with him on his bike. Reluctantly, I agreed to dinner the following Sunday at his parents' apartment, where he still lived.

Of course, I knew he was Catholic, since all the Italian kids I knew from school were of that faith. How would she react to a Protestant, and one who had been raised as a fundamentalist?

The thing was, that actually even during my year in confirmation class, I had discerned that fundamentalism, the kind I had been raised with, wasn't what embodied true Christianity. Could I share my beliefs with my parents? Of course not. The odd thing was this: I never lost my faith, but boy, my understanding had developed a different face altogether.

At that time, when my grasp of my faith was fledgling, all I knew with certainty was that were I to tell my parents whom I was dating, they would object. Would they rail that he was Catholic or that he was Italian? I didn't want to find out.

Evidently Tony had a similar dilemma. He knew fully well why he had never met my family and now confirmed a similar mindset with his folks. "Sue, my mother is going to hate that you're Protestant, so when you meet her, don't tell her. And if you tell her you're Norwegian, she'll know right away, so try to be evasive."

Sunday came more quickly than I liked, and I told my parents I was going out with friends for sodas and sandwiches. "Doddenhoff's, I suppose," said Papa. "Just be home early, since you have an early class tomorrow."

I met Tony at 3 p.m. at the corner of 92nd and 3rd, where he picked me up in the Dodge. I could tell he was a little nervous, too. When we arrived at his apartment, his mother opened the door, saying, "Come in, come in. We've all been looking forward to meeting you." The "all" was Tony's father, also Tony but to me Mr. Grasso, his twelve-year-old sister, Francesca, his sixteen-year-old brother, Vincent, an aunt and uncle, Rosie and Alfredo, and two female cousins, about Tony's age, Roseangela and Laura. "And I'm

Regina," his mother added.

"Pleased to meet you all," I said, wondering how in the world I would ever remember the names. In the living room was a long table, a folding one, Tony explained, that opened when the family had lots of people for dinner. We made small talk, and Tony's cousins wanted to know where I was in school and what my plans were. The uncle remarked how fair and pretty I was. And Tony's brother, whose name I managed to remember was Vincent, stammered when he asked if I had ever eaten a "real Italian meal" before.

"He's just shy," Tony whispered to me. "He knows you're pretty."

I felt like I was holding my own as we had anti-pasta, followed by ziti in red sauce—"gravy" Regina said that she made every Sunday. In my mind I reminisced that I knew about gravy: my friend from 79th street when I was a young girl had shown me what Italian gravy was. That was followed by chicken. My God, I thought, do they eat like this every week?

"This is wonderful food," I ventured. "And there's so much of it." Regina looked pleased. Ah, I thought, maybe she could actually like me.

Tony answered the actual question with, "Every Sunday, whoever can make it comes here or goes to my aunt's house."

"That's so nice," I said quietly. "I have a big family, too. Lots of cousins and aunts and uncles." Uh oh, I realized I had probably opened a can of worms.

"So, tell us, Susan, a little more about yourself," Tony's father said to me, his eyes smiling as he did so.

"Well, sir," I began, not correcting the "Susan," "I'm an American girl, born here in Brooklyn, and I'm studying chemistry and English. I haven't decided which major I'll choose. I'm a freshman at Brooklyn College."

Epilogue

Family and Friends:

Of my family, most went on to become productive working Americans, some professional, some blue collar. My uncle Johann Torvald became one of the biggest contractors on Staten Island and employed his brother Jakob's three sons, Sigurd, Stanley, and Salve, as well as his own, Sven. His daughter, Vigdis, married a shop keeper who adopted her son.

Cousin Gudrun, or Goody as we called her, married her lawyer boyfriend, and they lived in a big east side apartment in Manhattan, but the whole family mostly lost touch with her. DeDe knew her sister well and told us Goody thought we were beneath her. DeDe and Richie remained enrapt with each other and had two boys. When the Luckenbach company closed its doors in 1971, DeDe's brothers, Werner and Wilhelm, offered Richie a job as manager of an auto supply store in Huntington, Long Island, that they had bought and which subsequently made them rich. Maggy and Paul moved back to Brooklyn, and they had a second child, a girl they called Anna.

My cousin Alice became a nurse, and shortly thereafter married a doctor. Sonya, however, fell in love with a Norwegian carpenter, married him in City Hall, and moved to Norway a year or so after. Their sister, Bente, married a TWA pilot and they stayed in Kansas City. Their only brother, Tor Asbjørn, became a partner in Frank's Autobody and remained single; he became an expert at auto restoration.

My cousin Ole initially worked for Uncle Johann Torvald but after a while decided to branch off on his own. He started Saudeland Construction and all went well until he had structural problems with some houses he had built. New owners promptly sued him, but another contractor, Luigi Petrocello, offered to help him financially, provided Ole meet his daughter, Fernanda. That's what he did, and after a while, he married her. Ole's sister Annalise and her daughter Greta managed Ole's books, and Annalise after a few years married one of Petrocello's employees. Greta went to college and eventually became a translator at the United Nations.

My Aunt Magda moved in with Uncle Sverre after his divorce, and the two were often seen at the local gin mills. No one in the family much saw Gerd or her daughter, Aslaug, after the divorce.

Uncle Leif and Aunt Ragna's two oldest boys graduated from

college, and one became an engineer, the second a lawyer. Harold, it seemed, had a different bent. He took up with his buddy, Fraser, and they became a couple who did interior design. Their sister, my cousin Liv, got pregnant in her senior year of high school and married the baby's father as soon as she graduated.

In Norway, my cousin Arvind finished his tour of duty with the air force and married a Lyngdal girl. His brother, Odd, who had remained in the U.S., married his girlfriend, Lillian, and they stayed in New Jersey, eventually buying a house in Livingston, a neighboring town of West Orange.

Papa's brother-in-law Karl had a heart attack and died shortly after Erick graduated from MIT. Aunt Marit followed her son, Erick, to Norway after he married a Norwegian au pair who insisted on returning to her homeland. My grandmother Alma moved back to the old country with her. And when she died, she was laid to rest next to her husband Gustav.

My sister Ingrid prospered as a grade schoolteacher. She married her childhood sweetheart, Ole-Jakob, with whom she had reunited after graduating from Upsala, and they rented an apartment on Shore Road. To us, it had always been high end real estate.

Though I truly loved him, I broke up with Tony when I was a sophomore at Brooklyn College. While Tony had opened my eyes to what was available in our beautiful city, college opened my eyes in other ways. I knew what was possible, and Tony's future was determined while mine was wide open. After I graduated, I went to graduate school and earned a Ph.D. in Chemistry, taking a job as a scientist with Merck in New Jersey.

I remained close with Joey and Hannah who both went to Wagner College on Staten Island, majoring in education. My friend Tory surprised us all and remained married to Reidar. It had been, after all, a good match.

The Turbulent Times:

As soon as he was elected in November of 1964, President Johnson began to escalate the war in Vietnam, and by the time it ended, under the Nixon administration, a total of 2,450,000 people had died: American soldiers, including Joey's cousin Vinny and two boys I knew from high school; North and South Vietnamese soldiers and civilians; and armed forces and civilians in Cambodia and Laos.

Our great hope for another Kennedy in the White House was

dashed when Robert Kennedy was assassinated in California on his presidential campaign trail. Another assassination shocked us all: Martin Luther King Jr., an ardent advocate of civil rights and non-violent protest for racial equality, was gunned down in Memphis, Tennessee.

The face of Bay Ridge, irreparably altered by the bridge and the interstate leading to it, was to change dramatically again as well. In 1965, our president, Lyndon Baines Johnson, signed the Immigration and Nationality Act which altered the American immigration system by ending national origin quotas. Before then, quotas had favored northern Europeans. With the new act, Bay Ridge no longer saw the constant arrival of Norwegians, thus changing the ethnic makeup of the community. Lap Skaus Boulevard, our 8th Avenue, would soon see an influx of Asians, mostly Chinese, and it soon became a thriving China town.

To correct an historical error, 18 years after the bridge opened, the city officially changed its name. The name Verrazano had been on the blueprints for the build and from there sprang the original misspelling. The namesake was Giovanni da Verrazzano, an explorer of North America under France, and the first European to explore the Atlantic coast.

After the build, the original toll fee of 50 cents was not abolished as had been promised, and the cost continued to rise over the years. The bridge, at first the longest suspension bridge in the world until some 30-plus years later Japan erected a longer one. The Verrazzano, still the longest suspension bridge in the United States became the most expensive bridge in the country, in time nearing $20 per crossing.

The bridge early on brought an influx of people to Staten Island, and within five years after the bridge opened, the population on that borough had tripled. The Metropolitan Transit Authority added a new bus route from the Island into Brooklyn. All the city's boroughs were now linked by roadways. Such was the way the Brooklyn we knew was transformed.

About the Author

Jan Carol Simonsen grew up in Brooklyn, New York, the daughter of Norwegian immigrants. She has taught English at university undergraduate and graduate levels and has been an international trainer in medical and technical, English as a second language, and document management. In addition, she has authored and co-authored 15 non-fiction pharmaceutical, medical device, and bio-tech trade books and multiple journal articles under her married name. She now lives in Tallahassee, Florida, with her husband This is her first novel.

Made in United States
North Haven, CT
02 February 2024